A TIME FOR LOVE

"Today let us pretend we're married . . . that we'll always be together," Zander said.

Beth's brows arched. "I assume you do not mean to find a bedroom in the country house toward which we travel and take that pretense to its logical conclusion?"

"I certainly would if you would, but I know you will not. No, merely a stolen kiss, or, perhaps, I might be allowed to feel you in my arms again? My hands allowed to touch you as they've done before?"

Beth had smiled seductively as she thought of the two of them in some private spot, enjoying the sun, his hands free to roam; hers as well . . .

Books by Jeanne Savery

THE WIDOW AND THE RAKE

A REFORMED RAKE

A CHRISTMAS TREASURE

A LADY'S DECEPTION

CUPID'S CHALLENGE

LADY STEPHANIE

A TIMELESS LOVE

Published by Zebra Books

A
TIMELESS
LOVE

Jeanne Savery

Zebra Books
Kensington Publishing Corp.
http://www.zebrabooks.com

ZEBRA BOOKS are published by

Kensington Publishing Corp.
850 Third Avenue
New York, NY 10022

First Printing: February, 1997
10 9 8 7 6 5 4 3 2 1

Printed in the United States of America

One

Alexander Knightly sat on the edge of the captain's bunk, the sheet pooled in his lap. To most of the world the well built young man was Viscount Hawksbeck, the son and heir of the Earl of Fairmont, but to his friends he was simply Zander.

Zander yawned, scratched lazily at the dark swirls of hair patterning his chest and yawned again before looking, not without satisfaction, around what had been the captain's cabin. Zander, on the King's business, had commandeered the vessel in Lisbon to sail to the Port of London.

Very likely, mused Zander, he'd not have argued with the easily unlikable Captain Smithson if the man hadn't been so outrageously arrogant, so tastelessly condescending. Condescension! Who did the foxy devil think he was that he could act in that manner toward a Knightly! The man simply asked for a set down.

The argument had ended by ousting the captain from his quarters. *Well, by God, he'd been put in his place! Or perhaps, one should say he'd been put* out *of it?* Zander grinned at the thought and a dimple slid into his left cheek.

Polished paneled walls and a silky Oriental carpet with a golden circle woven into the middle, salt-sparkly leaded panes in windows which looked out from under the stern, a long window seat padded with a multitude of tasseled cushions—all gave the cabin a rich appearance. It was not what one expected of a free merchant picking up goods here and selling them there. For an instant Zander wondered about pirates and pirate gold, but the thought drifted away as the nonsense it was. Pirates didn't sail impudently into legitimate ports such as Lisbon's.

Zander closed his eyes and stretched, luxuriating in the feel of muscles gradually losing nighttime laxness. Now that his eyes were shut against visual distractions, he felt an odd, albeit faint, vibration under the soles of his bare feet. Another oddity caught his attention, a whining sound like nothing he'd ever imagined. Perhaps one of the pesky mosquitoes he'd met in Portugal, one of gigantic proportions, might reach such a pitch, but insect noise wouldn't go on and on, growing more and more intense until it rang inside one's head.

Zander grabbed at his ears and opened his eyes—only to squeeze them tightly shut.

He was insane! There was no other explanation. Or ghosts? Did such beings actually exist? No. Zander didn't believe in ghosts so it followed that, sometime between the appearance of the evening star when they'd sailed on the outgoing tide and awakening to sun-lit waves, he'd gone mad.

He cracked open one eye. The other eyelid snapped open as well. Frozen, unable to move so much as an eyelash, Zander stared at the apparition gaining substance in the golden circle in the center of the captain's carpet. Pale hair swirled out from the creature's head in a golden aureole, coiling up to a point. Sparks flickered over faintly golden skin. A softly flowing gold colored material, silk perhaps, wrapped an obviously but not grossly feminine form—and it too glowed and glittered, the hem dancing around trim ankles and bare feet. Surrounding all, enclosing the being and the circle in which she stood, was a cone of golden light that had, inexplicably, appeared in the middle of the captain's cabin.

The vibration increased, the whine unbearably shrill. *Mad*

as a hatter, thought Zander with the small part of his mind not awe-struck into intense stillness.

The final strand of power connecting Beth Ralston to the twenty-first century snapped. She could move a little. Soon she'd discover where in the year 1813 Art Rescue Teams, Inc. had landed her. Beth rubbed her elbows to relieve the tingle time-travel induced. She'd first experienced the sensation at fifteen when an ART team, working at fantastic speed to save what they could from a gallery, the roof of which was about to collapse, had abandoned priceless art in order to save a panicked teen.

That first experience in TransPort, her earliest remaining memory, had jerked Beth from terror to quiet sobs. In that memory a giant bear of a man—or so he'd seemed to her disbelieving eyes—held her close. Suu-Van, her rescuer, spoke softly, telling it was quite all right to cry, seeing she'd just escaped a horrid death.

Her life before the rescue was lost in the murky depths of her unconscious but, occasionally, Beth wondered what and, more important than what, *when* that life had been.

But that had happened ten years ago. Ever since the fire and her TransPort to the ART's headquarters, she'd been trained for moments such as this one, purportedly her first solo operation . . .

Enough of that. Beth pushed aside unanswerable questions concerning her past and simply enjoyed the marvelously addictive sensation TransPort induced. One felt so wonderfully bubbly, both inside and out. But it was fading. It always faded too quickly. She'd soon meet Captain Smithson, the Resident Anchor in this particular historical period and would be told all she must know to accomplish what he'd been told was her assignment.

And then she'd begin her *real* mission.

Beth turned slightly—and met the wide, incredibly dark blue eyes of a naked man seated on the bunk. "Hello."

He didn't respond. In fact, his skin actually lost color, which was a weird reaction.

"What's the matter?" she asked. "Just wake up from a bad dream?"

"That's it," he muttered. "A dream."

His slightly raspy baritone slid up Beth's spine, leaving behind more bubbles—quite a different sort of effervescence than TransPort induced. Embarrassed by the sensation, Beth chuckled. "They didn't tell me you were a flirt." He frowned. "You weren't flirting?" she asked.

"Definitely not."

She studied the bemused man. "Then it wasn't a compliment, your calling me a dream?"

"Of course not." Zander shook his head, rubbed his eyes, and muttered, "Damn. Why am I talking to an apparition? Worse, why is it talking to me? What the devil is happening to me?"

Beth's eyes narrowed. "You aren't Captain Smithson."

"Lord help me, now my apparition insults me. Do I look like that arrogant prig?"

The description startled half a laugh from Beth even as she realized something was very wrong. *I've blown my cover!* she thought. *Suu-Van will have my hide—or Smithson's!* "So," she asked, "where is the arrogant prig? Why isn't he here?"

"I need a vessel and I need decent sleeping quarters—and why in Hades am I explaining anything to something which can't possibly exist outside my imagination?"

"I exist."

"Impossible. I watched you appear right there in the middle of the floor. There was nothing there. Then there was. You." The man shook his head, his face a picture of bewilderment, an almost comical expression which tickled Beth's ready sense of humor.

"I don't suppose you believe in witches," she suggested, tongue-in-cheek.

Zander straightened. "I didn't," he said slowly, "but maybe I will. A belief in witches is a far better solution than thinking I've lost my mind, or . . . I've a better idea." He quirked his head, looking her up and down. "All that gold. An angel perhaps?" His mouth firmed. "Except, that would mean I've died and would angels have anything to do with *me?* Doubtful. Therefore you must be from the devil and a succubus or, as you say, a witch or"—he shook his head as if trying to rid it of a ringing in his ears—"as I first thought and far more likely, I'm truly as mad as the King."

"You're sane enough, but what we're to do with you— Ah," she said, as the door crashed back against the wall. "This must be the arrogant prig."

Beth wished she'd thought before opening her mouth. Suu-Van said it was a major failing and would one day get her into trouble. Baaad trouble. Seeing the vicious look on the captain's face, Beth began to believe it.

"I am Captain Smithson and you are the poorly disciplined novice with whom headquarters stuck me. I warned them, but would they listen? No, You are here less than five minutes and already you've made a mess of things."

"I didn't hand my cabin over to a non-ART. *I* wasn't somewhere else when the alarms went off. *I*—"

"Miss Ralston, I am your superior. I need make no explanations, but the first lesson you should have learned when still in school is that, when in Time, you adopt local standards. In this particular age, a sea captain doesn't argue with an earl-in-training."

"Except," said the narrow-eyed Viscount Hawksbeck and future earl, "that's exactly what you *did* do . . . argue with me," he added when the captain turned a supercilious but questioning stare his way. "But this particular age? And when-in-time? What the devil does that mean? In the name of Old Harry, who are you?"

"At least," said Beth with calculated impertinence, "I made the suggestion I might be a witch. You, Smithson, just put your foot in it clear up to the knee."

Beth adopted a smug look, since riling Smithson might actually help the secret part of her mission.

Smithson's mouth snapped tight and he breathed long slow breaths through narrowed nostrils. White rimmed his lips and red blotched his neck above his tight uniform collar, a reaction Beth watched with interest.

"Miss Ralston," he finally managed. "You will hold your tongue and come with me."

He strode from the cabin, leaving the door open to the sun drenched deck. Beth, staring after him, tipped her head, her hands on her hips. "I was told he was difficult, but no one went so far as to say he'd be impossible. He *is* exceedingly competent, you know, or he'd never have been given such a responsible position."

Zander didn't appear to understand at all.

Beth sighed. "Unfortunately I must work under his direction so I'd better go." She winked. "Believe me, I'd much rather talk to you. See you." She smiled and gently closed the door.

Zander watched her leave. He was alone. The ship was quiet, the disturbing sensation warming his feet and the still more disturbing ear-hurting whine were no more. Had he imagined the whole of it?

No! No, he had not. Definitely not.

Zander threw back the sheet. He rose too quickly and sat down in a hurry. He'd forgotten, again, that the ceilings aboard ship were not designed with men approaching six feet in mind! Ruefully rubbing his head, he stood more cautiously. A sailor had emptied his portmanteau into a chest hidden under the long window seat. Which one?

Two would not open. Nor could Zander see a latch or a key hole or even nails, but he put that new mystery aside when the third seat lifted. He chose a clean shirt and fresh inexpressibles and washed at a washstand hidden behind a wall panel after making use of another essential facility concealed by yet another panel. He dressed quickly, considering it far more important he track down the captain and that fascinating female creature than that he appear prepared for a stroll down Piccadilly.

In shirt and trousers and still bare of foot, Zander went on the prowl.

". . . You have impressed our colleagues, but not me. Women don't impress me, especially one who doesn't know her place. Women are the invention of the devil," ranted Smithson, "not of God. She is necessary, but must be controlled and suppressed. And mustn't think for herself. Because," Smithson continued when Beth would have interrupted with an angry spate of intemperate words, "women make life impossible if put in a position where they make decisions. *Obey me you will,* Miss Ralston. You will do as you're told and will speak only when asked. You will *not* open your mouth, Miss Ralston, or you'll find yourself in irons—which, as captain of this vessel, I have the right to do."

"But you'll not enforce that right," said Zander softly from just behind the captain. "Miss Ralston, you may depend on me to defend you from this lunatic. I'd not allow him to behave in so vicious a fashion toward anyone, but particularly not toward someone so lovely as you." Zander beckoned. "Come to me. I'll see you safe."

Smithson snarled. "For this passage, I must put up with you, but no one, in the discipline of my subordinates, interferes." He grasped Beth's wrist and yanked her toward him.

Beth, only just managing to retain her footing, grinned over Smithson's shoulder to show Zander she wasn't worried. The grin faded fast. Before she could speak Zander's hands landed heavily on Smithson's shoulders. The smaller man was yanked back and one brawny English arm slid around his throat. Zander's other hand reached to squeeze Smithson's wrist

"Let her go or I'll snap your neck like I'd snap a rat's." Beth was suddenly free. "I'm taking Miss Ralston to my cabin. As long as you mean to behave like an escaped lunatic you'll stay out. I've no particular desire to see your ugly face again, but I'll put up with you *if* you can act with a modicum of civility."

This time Beth's abused wrist was grasped firmly, although far more gently, by Zander who pulled her along the deck and into the cabin. He slammed the door behind them and turned to survey his prize.

She looked at him with a sad look, slowly shaking her head. "You've really done it now, haven't you, big boy?"

Big *boy?* he thought. "I've rescued you from God knows what horrible fate and you *object?"*

"He'd not have dared harm me and you've only postponed whatever petty revenge he plans. Smithson is obviously the sort of man who can't stand"—she modified the phrase to one she thought more in keeping with the era—*"cannot abide* looking the fool. He'll find it necessary to punish someone when made to do so. Since he can't punish *you,* he'll take it out of my hide. I do wish you'd not interfered," she finished on a woeful note.

Zander's bewilderment at the morning's odd events faded in welcome outrage. "Of all the ungrateful wenches I've ever met you are far and away outside of enough."

"What do you expect? Kisses and hugs and—"

Heat reddened Zander's throat.

"—perhaps more." She cast him a look of loathing.

Noting her expression, Zander's volatile temper faded. He grinned, a smile which revealed white teeth and the elusive dimple. "I wouldn't object. Anything to avoid the tedium of the next few days, you know."

Beth blushed rosily. "I was joking."

"Joking?"

"Teasing, making a joke."

"Ah! You mean bamming or jesting."

"I do?" She sighed. "If that's what I mean. My language training wasn't nearly thorough enough. Bamming." She nodded, once. "Thank you. I'll remember."

Zander sobered. The exhilaration of besting the foxy captain wore off as he recalled how this female had appeared from thin air. Once again fear tiptoed up his spine but he shrugged it away. She'd done nothing to indicate she was a danger to him. Except to suggest she was a witch.

"Are you a witch?" he blurted. "Do such truly exist?"

Beth groaned. If he were willing to accept the notion, she should, by all the rules, encourage him to do so. "And if I were a witch?" she asked, needing time. She eyed him, thinking furiously, wondering how her assignment could have gone so wrong so quickly.

"Then that makes that monster Smithson a warlock." Zander pursed his lips. "No. I'll not believe it." The captain's ranting came back to him. "Training for when one is in time, he said. Time—*time* not *place.*"

Zander stared at her, shuddered. Horror grew. *"Time,"* he repeated in a whisper. "Time. Not *where* but *when.*" The words were a mere thread of sound. "He meant . . . the *future?* He . . . you . . ."

Zander straightened to his full five feet eleven and a half inches. He ignored the pain when his head once again came into firm contact with the ceiling, not taking his eyes from Beth's. Those eyes glittered.

"You . . . !" He pointed a long, well-shaped, finger directly at her heart, a finger which trembled only very slightly. *"You are from the future!"*

Two

"My God!" Awe softened Zander's voice to a near whisper. "The *future*."

Beth stared, stunned. To her knowledge, no one had ever before guessed the truth. *Well!* she thought, *Your mother didn't raise a stupid son!*

"You don't deny it." He blinked, his breathing deeper, more obvious. "It's the truth then. You've come from the future." The glitter in his eyes became more pronounced. "We've learned so much, but how much more there is to know! To discover how to travel in time, travel to the future! What one could learn. It is almost inconceivable, but someone, sometime, *has* learned the trick of it. Oh, what a wonder, to live where so much is known . . ." Zander's eyes were glowing sapphires.

Botheration, thought Beth. *Now what?* She turned away from both the formidable intellect and equally distracting physique which, she thought, might as well still be as naked as when she arrived. Form fitting buckskins. A shirt made of an exceptionally fine material, unfastened at the throat. They did nothing to hide the muscle and sinew of an active healthy male.

"Please put on more clothes," she said. "By Perry Como's last drink! On top of everything else I don't need, I don't need a half-naked man turning me on."

" 'Turning you on?' What does that mean?" Zander watched her rigid back, noted the hands she ran down her thighs before clenching them into fists. His left eyebrow arched. Could the chit be nervous? She was, after all, a woman, even if born in some inconceivable future. Perhaps women were not so different in her time? Perhaps she needed . . . comforting?

Zander crossed to Beth. He fit his hands to her waist and tugged gently. "Don't resist, Miss Ralston. Come," he soothed. "Let me soothe you, ease your fear. You've seen violence, undergone a great fright and . . ."

Beth chuckled, half from humor and half from incipient hysteria. How had she gotten into such a mess? She pried at his hands. "I obviously don't know nearly enough about this era, but it's my guess your women don't experience life in the raw. I assure you, that scene with my foxy-faced boss doesn't qualify as violence. And, so far, my only fear is that I might allow you to charm your way through my defenses." Her fingers tunneled under his.

When his hands fell away, Beth was a trifle surprised and *more* than a trifle disappointed. *Perhaps,* the cynical thought crossed her mind, *it isn't that I fear he'll seduce me—but fear he won't?*

"Please finish dressing," she said. "Then we'll talk. Too much has happened too quickly. Inconceivable as it seems, you've guessed the truth. Smithson must inform those who guide us. Besides," she shrugged and stepped closer to the window to escape from Zander's warmth, "I've a mission to accomplish. I don't need complications. You, whoever you are, are a complication."

"Alexander Knightly, Viscount Hawksbeck," he said softly.

"Hmm?" Beth turned and wished she hadn't.

"It's who I am. My friends call me Zander. Perhaps you'll be my friend?"

Friend? By the voice of the inimitable Ella, what wouldn't I give to be his friend! she thought, and knew such thoughts must be suppressed. *Keep it light . . .* she told herself.

"What do I do now? Curtsy? I'd look foolish, dressed like this!"

Zander's bow was anything but foolish-looking and, as he straightened, the dimple reappeared at the sight of her reddening skin. "I do like that blush. It puts roses under that odd, but very lovely golden skin. I want to touch it, want to see if it's as soft as it looks, to taste it, discover if it's different from other women's skin." She glared at him. Zander tipped his head. "I've made you angry. How? Why?"

"I wish you'd finish dressing." She also wished that hadn't sounded quite so waspish. On the other hand, maybe waspish was better than plaintive?

He frowned, considering. "I don't understand. You've been in my quarters alone with me for most of an hour—and part of that time I was naked as a babe. You've neither screamed nor swooned nor turned into a watering pot. Nor, I think, do you find me offensive. How can I assume anything but that you are experienced of a man's attentions? Why do you wish me to dress when it's my earnest desire that, very soon, I'll *undress* us both."

"Zander, if I'm free to use that name when I've no intention of being the sort of *friend* you appear to want . . . ?"

He nodded permission.

"You've guessed we come from your future. You might also guess things are different then. Relationships between men and women are freer, more open, more equal and lack the barriers of more artificial cultures, but that does *not* imply we indulge freely in . . . in . . ." Beth searched for words that were neither crude nor clinical.

"The game of love?"

Pleased by the euphemism, she nodded. "Precisely."

"And you have never so indulged?" he asked, curious.

Beth's fine skin glowed with embarrassment. That she hadn't wasn't the fault of the life into which she'd been drawn, but simply that she didn't find the men of that century to her taste—and vice versa, of course. Or maybe there was something, something forgotten, which wouldn't allow her to experiment with sex as most of her friends had done?

She glanced at Zander and found he awaited an answer. "That's a very personal question. In my time, it is one no one would ask!"

"But we are not in your time," said Zander reasonably.

Time. Zander wondered at how calmly he accepted the notion this golden woman had come to him from the future. He studied her and the more he watched the more he wanted to hold her, to touch her, make love to her . . . But what had she just said? Ah, that he shouldn't ask.

"Besides, it isn't true. I *must* question you, must I not? How may I understand your place in my life if I do not understand you?"

Exasperated, Beth closed her eyes. Exasperation was, however, tempered by a looming regret welling up from somewhere deep within. The emotion shocked her and she forced it away. "Zander," she said, "you are an intelligent man. I shouldn't have to explain that I've no place in your life. *None*. It's impossible. My existence in 1813 is, of necessity, of limited duration." She adopted a deliberately soulful look. "You understand?"

"You don't believe that nonsense any more than I do." He turned to lift down the coat hanging on a hook near the bunk. As he shrugged into it he crossed to pull a chain which rang a bell, calling for service. "Breakfast," he said, explaining his action and then looked around for his boots. "I've no notion what time of day you left my future to come here, but I need breakfast. You'll drink coffee at least? Does one still drink coffee in your time . . . ?"

Bemused, Beth nodded.

"And," he continued while pulling on the first boot, "when we've finished we'll call in that blackguard, the captain. Until then, we'll put him from our minds and talk. Tell me," he said, while searching under his bunk for the second boot, "do all women dress like that where you come from? It isn't a gown, is it? What do you call it?"

Bewildered by his acceptance of the situation and still more by his sudden change of topic, Beth laughed. "You're a most surprising man, Zander."

"Is that good?"

She ignored that. "Of all the questions you must wish to ask, you ask that one? Doesn't the revelation that I've come from the future make you wonder about far more important things than my sarong?"

"I wonder best when my stomach's full. As to surprise, why? What is, is. You are. I had my hands on you and you felt real and very right against my palms. That I watched you appear from nothing . . ." He shrugged. "If you tell me that *nothing* from which you came is a place in the future, why should I disbelieve you? Especially," he said and grinned that attractive grin again, "when I much prefer that explanation to the one I feared."

She smiled, remembering their odd introduction and his muttering. "You thought you'd gone mad."

"Besides, why *should* it be so difficult? We live with so many marvels. Amazing new inventions appear every day. Since it's already unbelievable, what man has discovered in just the last half century, why cavil at one more marvel, even something so marvelous as this?"

"What do you call a marvel?" asked Beth. "In your own time, I mean."

Remembered excitement colored Zander's voice. "Many years ago my father took me to ride behind a steam-driven engine that ran on rails. The speed of the thing! Some thought it might damage a man's insides to go so fast but I think they merely feared change. It is my belief that, some-day, such engines will become important, pulling many wag-ons along their rails. That engine, the Catch-Me-Who-Can, is gone from London, but you must view a balloon ascension one day. It amazes one, watching a man climb into the skies in nothing more than a frail basket hanging beneath a gas filled balloon . . . Beautiful in a far different way are the hellish foundries in the Midlands." He sobered, his expressive eyes deep blue and steady. "Those are truly awesome."

It took Beth a moment to realize Zander meant that literally. "In what way do they induce awe?"

"I once approached a city of foundries by night." He shuddered. "The incredible fires actually turn the chimneys a glowing red and the sparks, the smoke and ash! For the first time, I understood the fear which drove one of my tutors. He believed all men are sinners, you see, and that all will suffer damnation and eternal hellfire. How Satan in his Hell must envy that area of England which is a veritable hell on earth!"

Zander drew in a deep breath. "The foundries make iron day and night and that is wonderful, but I think it more interesting to see bales of raw wool go in one end of a factory and whole cloth come out the other." A smile faded in other memories. Sober, he added, "Then one learns how the workers live, particularly the children, so thin, never laughing, forced to long hours of work." His throat convulsed as he swallowed hard and his eyes glistened.

Beth remembered this was a more emotional age, one in which men had not concluded tears were unmanly. She lay a hand on his arm, offering comfort. "Human suffering," she said softly. "during the transition to an industrial world was bad, but things did—I mean," she amended, "things *will* improve. There will be second period of much suffering during another such transition some decades into the twenty-first century. Manufacturing will no longer require a great deal of human interference. The products will be produced by machines directed mostly by other machines. In that century the work ethic, which says man must *earn* his bread, changes for the simple reason there *is* no work, not in the sense of everyone earning his daily bread."

Zander's eyes glowed. "I would see such marvels," he said.

"Elvis's Pelvis!" Thoroughly disgusted with herself she added, "I should have told you none of that. If you don't wish to see me pushed overboard by our foxy captain don't tell him I've done the unforgivable." His brow quirked. "I've told you things you shouldn't know," she explained.

"You of the future are not to tell of that future?"

If he weren't so obviously a mature man, thought Beth, *I'd describe that expression as something very close to a pout.* She held back a smile. What had he asked? Oh. "I mustn't tell," she said apologetically, "I could dislocate the flow of history if you were to act on something I said."

"Then"—he tossed a sideways teasing look her way—"it's no use asking if the French hold San Sebastián over the present siege?"

She grinned. "No use at all."

He looked at his nails. "I could threaten to tell the Fox you've already said more than you should."

"You are, I hope, teasing—bamming, I mean. If not"—Beth turned to look through the window—"then you must tell him, because I've said more than I should already."

"You can only hang a man once. I thought it worth a try!"

So, he wasn't above "trying it on," as a friend recruited from the late twentieth century sometimes said. "You are involved in the war?" she asked, trying to forget how much she liked this teasing side of Zander.

"Only on the periphery."

Beth heard regret.

"I do what I can, but my father asked that I not buy a commission and chance my life. You see," said Zander, his ready grin returning, "although I've three elder sisters, all married, to say nothing of the one pert minx still in the schoolroom, I'm my father's only son. If the heir-presumptive were a man Father admired, he'd not care, but"—Zander's voice roughened—"he'll be damned, he says, if he'll leave his coronet, his lands, and most particularly his responsibilities to a namby pamby man-milliner with niffy-naffy ways and no more sense than a babe."

Beth chuckled at the unfamiliar but expressive words. "I can hear him say it though I've never met him. That art of mimicry is a gift, Zander."

Two seamen entered and transformed the cabin into a dining room complete with exotic flowers. When the sailors exited Zander peered at the blooms. "More of your infernal magic from the future?" He fingered a fleshy petal which immediately turned brown. He looked at his fingers, at the flower, and then put his hands behind his back like a little boy caught in mischief.

"One might call it infernal magic, I suppose," said Beth, frowning. "I'd call it a rather extravagant use of power. But we're allowed a certain amount for private transport and if Smithson wishes to use his for flowers, that's his business."

"They are from another time, hmm?"

"Either that or he has a growth room fitted up on board—which is, now I think of it, the more likely explanation."

"Growth room? A place for plants? A conservatory, you mean?"

"Sort of," she said evasively, unable to discuss gene manipulation and growth enhancement. "Now, what have we here?" she asked, lifting the lid to one of the platters.

For a moment she thought she'd not get away with changing the subject, but Zander, she was learning, was sensitive to hints. He realized this was something else she wasn't supposed to tell him and, although he gave her a look she interpreted as meaning he saw through her efforts, he allowed the change.

He poked at the food with a serving fork. "You must tell me what we have."

"Well, that's couscous, I think, from a North African cuisine. Those bits are vegetables and I can't identify anything which looks like meat so perhaps Smithson is a vegetarian? Shall we discover if it appeals to our taste buds?"

"Taste buds? More words from your future?"

Beth's lips compressed. "I see why we're lectured over and over that we must have no more than formal conversations with such as you. Again and again we're ordered to become intimate with no one! One cannot always know what is unknown, you see. Taste buds, for instance." She sighed. "I refer to nerve endings in the tongue which allow us to taste our food."

"I know the word nerve. In the future, a woman can become a physician, that you know such things?"

"Much is learned in nearly three centuries, Zander. Education becomes more highly valued, once needing a job of work becomes a thing of the past. Not just the wealthy, but *everyone* knows a great deal of trivia about a great many things most of which they'll never put to any practical use."

A muscle jerked in Zander's jaw as he turned to his food. His unfocused eyes had a look to them which made Beth wonder if, this time, Zander wasn't quite so excited by thoughts of visiting the future. He was, she decided, a bit chagrined by the notion that if he were to travel in time, as obviously he hoped to do, anyone, even a servant, would know more than he did.

Beth bit back a chuckle: It hadn't yet occurred to Zander there were no servants in that future he hankered to see! However that might be, Zander was jealous. And all because she'd done it again. Perhaps Zander could be tested, taught, and made one of them. That thought lightened Beth's heart of a burden she'd not realized she carried. Perhaps she and Zander might . . . well . . . After all, Zander was the first man ever to appeal strongly to her senses in *that* way. So if he were to become an ART Inc. agent, then perhaps, maybe . . . ? And maybe not. She sighed.

Nearly all Beth's friends had been born in the late twenty-first century. She'd long ago come to the conclusion she was not. Often she'd found herself amazed at something or shocked by something which, although she could not recall her past, *must* be different from the age in which she'd been born.

When that might be!

Because why else would she find it difficult, impossible really, to be truly intimate with anyone? Among things which had changed must have been notions of what was and was not attractive to the opposite sex, because whatever had passed between the year of her birth and the future which was her lifetime, insured that, not only was she *not* looked at the way Zander looked at her, but she didn't much care if the men she knew did or did not!

Beth reviewed what she knew of the early 1800s. Too much war, the roots of industrialization sprouting, pressure toward much needed government reform, an escalation in the work of socially active fundamentalist religions—all had resulted in social change. Then too, an incredible burst of invention led to a population explosion and to a dislocated populace. People left the land and moved into cities which were, for far too many, unpleasant places.

Something about all that, terrible as much of it was, felt comfortable, familiar. Was *that* why she felt a rapport with Zander? Why he had such a strong attraction for her? Was she, too, from this sort of historical era— perhaps the late twentieth century which had suffered similar problems as the Information Age began? Were he and she two of a kind in a way she and Smithson, for instance, could never be?

In fact, was it possible the early 1800s *was* her real life-time? *Out of all possible times?* Very doubtful. She sighed. Blast Suu-Van for refusing to tell her her history, for insisting she remember on her own or never know!

As she and Zander finished eating, the door burst open and Smithson strutted into the cabin. He scowled from one to the other as he pulled a chair into position before the table. He sat down, but he neither relaxed nor did the scowl lighten.

"You've talked to our superiors?" asked Beth quietly.

"I have."

"And?"

The scowl deepened. "They won't agree to the solution which solves all problems."

"Solution . . ." Beth's eyes narrowed. She reviewed what she knew of Smithson. Her gaze snapped to meet his. "You suggested killing Zander!"

She placed a hand on Zander's wrist as he half rose to his feet. He settled back, but she felt his muscles tighten when Smithson nodded complacently.

"Of course. Actually, to delete the both of you solves everything." He said it so calmly it was difficult to accept he discussed the possibility of their death. "They don't agree," he reiterated with obvious regret.

However, to "accidentally" do them in is just the sort of thing this sly devil of a captain might arrange—if he thinks he can get away with it! thought Beth. Zander must have had a similar thought, she decided, when his hand covered hers, a comfort and a promise of protection.

"So," she said with pretended calm, "what *did* they recommend?"

"We are to trust the future earl. We will use him. He will help."

"Help?"

"He can travel easily throughout England." Smithson shrugged. "You will be a distant cousin. He will bear-lead you."

Beth's eyes widened painfully. To relieve the tension she blinked. *"Bare* lead? I didn't think nakedness was proper in this era . . .*"

Zander smiled and then explained. "He uses an expression from this age. It means to guide and teach and protect someone for whom one is responsible, to have charge of them, as an itinerate entertainer trains and leads a dancing bear." He patted Beth's hand absent-mindedly and then lifted it from his arm. "You suggest I become mentor to Miss Ralston?" he asked, his tone curt.

"You understand." Smithson nodded, as if with approval for a difficult student.

"I've responsibilities. I carry dispatches which must reach the Horse Guards as soon as maybe, which was why I commandeered your ship. I'll be given new orders. I won't be free to help."

"You'll ask for personal leave."

"I might if I felt it important, but, frankly"—Zander cast Beth an apologetic look—"stopping Napoleon takes precedence over everything else."

"The army soon goes into winter cantonments," lied Smithson, who knew as well as Beth did that during this particular winter the fighting would continue right up to Napoleon's abdication, which would not be for several months and well into 1814. "The fighting for another year will over be," soothed Smithson, still lying. "There will be no orders."

"You're very certain of that."

"I am certain."

Beth made a mental note that Smithson could lie like a Trojan. For a moment her willful mind wandered off at a tangent, wondering if Trojans really had been liars, or if this was another expression which came down through the centuries with little basis in fact. Perhaps someday she could go back to really ancient times and find out for herself. What a wonderful mission that would be . . .

"In that case, Miss Ralston," said Zander, "I'll be free to help with *your* mission." Zander relaxed back into the window seat, his smile growing as he realized Beth was not attending. "Well, Miss Ralston? What do you say?"

Beth heard the faintest touch of laughter in his voice and realized she'd missed something. She raised her eyes to look into his. His were warm in that way which raised her temperature. She felt a blush come up under her skin and told herself she must *not* allow such feelings to interfere.

"Miss Ralston?" he asked again.

She looked from Zander to Smithson whose face was twisted into a sneer. So she'd been off in a mental-flip, her thoughts exploring a notion unrelated to the present and she'd missed something. So what? Did that make her a fluff-brain and worthy of such scorn as Smithson projected? Reluctantly she admitted that perhaps it did. By Lennon and Ono's great love! She *must* discipline her mind so it didn't race off after curious bits and pieces. She turned back to Zander and raised a querying eyebrow.

"I said," he repeated, "it appears that, after all, I am to aid you to accomplish your goal. Perhaps it would help if I understood what it is and *why* you travel in time."

"Ah. I'm not sure you want to get me started on that subject! I tend to go on and on and on."

"You will tell him about your mission only," said Smithson sternly.

Zander's eyes narrowed. "That will do for going on with."

Beth shrugged. "I'm to rescue two paintings from a manor in Sussex which will burn in February of next year."

Zander's brow's snapped together. "Why do you not simply tell the owner so he may prevent the fire?"

Beth sighed, her unhappiness clear in her expression. "You explain, Smithson. I'll end up crying. I always do, however much I understand that time must not be altered."

"It's the paradox, you understand," Smithson said with a touch of mockery. "If you change some vital thing so it doesn't happen, then you may change everything by which it's affected."

Zander's normally sensuous lips firmed and his gaze settled on some point across the room. Finally he nodded. "Yes. I see that. Perhaps someone does not die. Perhaps they have children. Perhaps those children do something which did not otherwise happen. Yes, it would change history. But it must nevertheless be a great temptation when you are actually there."

"Bah." Smithson was once again his sneering self. "Why would one be tempted? It's the past. It's done."

Smithson glared at Beth whose rescue by Suu-Van was known to all, a not uncommon bit of "interference" since people, who would otherwise die, were often recruited to work for ART Inc. It was a practice Smithson should not look down on, since he himself had been recruited in that fashion, although not from a very distant past . . . Perhaps, then, his glare was because she was a mere female and he a misogynist?

Smithson turned back to the viscount, explaining his philosophy quite patiently. For him. "When one is in the past, it isn't real. It has already happened, even if one now watches. You for instance. *You* are dead. One merely remembers that."

Zander swallowed shock. "And, remembering that, then you watch people die who might be saved if you acted?" Smithson shrugged. Beth shuddered and almost imperceptibly moved closer to Zander's warmth. "I don't approve."

"You would have us, perhaps, commit suicide?" asked Smithson politely, but a hint of the never ending smirk contradicted the seeming courtesy.

"Do what?"

Beth tried. "For example, Zander, if you change something in the past, even something as important as preventing someone's death, you may change the future so that you yourself will never be born. I'm not certain what would happen in such a case. Would the ART agent cease to exist? But if he did, then how did he make the change which brought about his disappearance? Or perhaps he still exists, but time no longer goes on as it did? Or . . ." She stared at Zander. "Can you see the problems?"

"Have there been instances?" he asked

Beth turned to her superior, a questioning look in her eye. "Smithson?"

"If so there be, then how would anyone in the future know of it?" Smithson shrugged. "They too would be changed and would only know the new form history takes—or so *I* think."

A gleam of sly humor lit Smithson's eyes, an unsettling, out-of-character note which unsettled Zander. The man was too serious to find humor in the *words* so Zander wondered what lay *behind* the words. Just what was Smithson up to of which ART, as the organization called itself, knew nothing. That the captain was up to *something* was as clear to Zander as if the fox had admitted it in so many words. Zander toyed with a piece of flat bread and, when Beth offered, held out his cup for more of the rich black coffee.

Zander watched the dark stream fill his cup and thanked God for his diplomatic training which helped him control his features. The arrogant captain must see no clue that suspicion had fallen on him. Zander suspected the unfeeling man would give short shrift to anyone who got in his way, which meant Miss Ralston must not be told. She was too clear-eyed, too innocent and free of guile, to be entrusted with such information. She would, Zander believed, be incapable of keeping such a secret from a man so sly as Smithson.

For her part, Beth wondered how Smithson had given himself away, how much the man at her side guessed. *Perhaps* that fraction of an instant of stillness had meant nothing . . . too bad she didn't believe it. Zander was too quick. Somehow she must defuse his suspicions. Assuming what was believed about Smithson was true, it would be dangerous for Zander to get in the middle of the duel to be played out in the next few weeks.

Beth sighed softly, wondering again how her mission could have gone so wrong so quickly. Perhaps Suu-Van was correct? The lovable old grumbler had said this mission was

jinxed and predicted in his pessimistic way that Beth's promising career as a trouble shooter would end here.

Her embryonic emotional entanglement with Zander
made that a very real possibility. Because of it, Zander was
dangerous to her continued health and welfare in an entirely
different way from anything Smithson might do! And Smithson was believed to be dangerous. Very dangerous. Given
her rapidly developing attraction for Zander, she didn't want
him involved. For that matter, even without those very personal emotions, he mustn't be involved! Best they keep to
surface things!

She turned to Smithson. "Clothes? Money? A briefing?"

"We have four days before reaching London. Lord
Hawksbeck must be briefed and details of your mission told,
but I must see to my ship. At fourteen-hundred hours we
begin." Smithson bowed stiffly and stalked out just as the
two seamen reentered. The men cleared away the breakfast
and left. Suddenly it was very quiet in the cabin.

For reasons Beth didn't wish to probe, it seemed smaller.
She turned slightly and found Zander's burning gaze on her.
As in a dream she saw him reach for her. Still in a dream,
she leaned toward him, longing to feel his hands, his lips . . .

And woke up.

"No. Zander, you must not."

"Why?"

Beth tried for humor. "I've been metamorphosed into
your cousin. Would you treat a cousin like . . . like . . ."
She couldn't do it. Humor was the last thing she felt.

"A lover?" he asked.

"I had something less proper in mind." What word was
commonly used in this time? "A whore, maybe?"

Zander folded his arms and leaned back. "You pull no
punches, do you? As you must know, if you know anything
of my time and place, I could never behave badly toward a
relative. It would not be the behavior of a gentleman and"—a

touch of cynicism colored his tone—"I *try* to maintain the reputation of a gentleman."

"Then you must not treat *me* so."

Softly, seductively, Zander said, "But you are *not* a relative, are you? And you too wish it, the feel of my hands on you, my lips. . . ."

"What I wish is irrelevant," she interrupted with pointed sharpness, even as she regretted the necessity. "I won't, *can't*, pretend I'm not strongly tempted, so you must help me, Zander." She raised wide open, innocent-appearing eyes to meet his gaze. "I must not indulge in an affair with you."

"Affair? Business? But that is exactly what we *are* to do . . . ah, you mean an *affaire*," he said, correcting her pronunciation by giving the word a French intonation.

She nodded and, just to be certain he understood, put it in plain words. "I must not take you as a lover. It would not do."

"Instead of my cousin—a plan to which I've not agreed— you might travel as my mistress."

"There's a difference between a whore and a mistress?"

"A *great* difference," he said, surprise obvious. "A whore is, well, something far *less* than a mistress. Less than a doxy, even. Perhaps a trifle better than a draggletail?"

"So many words for a prostitute!"

"So many differing kinds of prostitutes! But back to our situation, I believe it would suit best if you were my mistress."

"Best for *you* perhaps! But do be serious," said Beth more crossly than his suggestion deserved. Maybe his words made her angry simply *because* they tempted her! "You know better than I that that's the last thing I can do. I couldn't enter the house to which I must have access if I were so foolish. I'd be allowed nowhere near it, and rightly so," she added, thinking of the young girls who lived there.

Zander's chin lifted. "Well, you cannot be my cousin."

"Don't be stubborn. You've no choice but to cooperate."

"Happily!" he said with a sudden grin. "But you *cannot be my cousin,* Miss Ralston, because it is widely known I *have* no female cousin."

"Not even a distant one?"

"No."

"An exceedingly uncompromising no! Think back a few generations. Surely there's a minor branch of the family tree on which I might be hung."

"Not a single twig," he insisted, then amended, "At least, there's no distant relation who, under any circumstance, would have a thing to do with my father or myself."

"Are you such terrible men?" she asked, curious.

"Our more stodgy relatives don't understand why we've not, long ago, been cast kicking and screaming straight into hell. We *gamble,* Miss Ralston. That we do so in moderation is no justification. We drink and again moderation is no excuse. As I'm certain you've guessed, we occasionally have a mistress in keeping. In other words, those relatives are canting chapel types; there's no acknowlededgment on either side of the other's existence!"

"Hmm. So much for your father's kin. But, your mother's?"

Zander's face lit. "You, my dear, are a genius. My mother is French, you understand, and you might very well be a relative from the continent. So"—he cocked his head and eyed her—"perhaps I found you languishing, a governess in the Lisbon household of some obscure diplomat from an even more obscure principality. I've rescued you and must immediately place you under the chaperonage of a respectable female. My mother, by preference.

"She," he continued when Beth would have objected, "as well as my father whose sense of duty keeps him involved in the government even when there are other things he'd rather do"—he blinked, sorting out what he'd meant to say—"They will have returned to London. Assuming my youngest sister was successful in her urgings that she be brought out this autumn, Juno, too, will be there. But, if we are to do that"—he frowned—"our situation here and now raises a difficulty. To remain respectable in my company you must have a female traveling companion. At the very least, a maid." Zander quirked a brow, his eyes twinkling. "I assume you've had training in dissimulation, Miss Ralston. *You* tell *me* why you have not."

His mischievous expression encouraged Beth and, buoyed by his light manner, she added detail to the design of her imaginary history, suggesting, "Perhaps we met when you first came to Portugal. Perhaps you were kind to a distant relative. Perhaps my position, which was never good, deteriorated, becoming impossible. When I heard you were again in Lisbon I begged your protection." She lifted her hands and shrugged a Frenchified shrug. "What could you do but bring me away with you?"

"I would, of course, but *first* I'd find you a maid." He crossed his arms. "It would be ungentlemanly to do otherwise."

"It is essential that there be another woman if I'm to be considered respectable, is that it? Do you suppose Smithson has a female on board?" She rather doubted it, but added, "If so, she could pretend to be my maid and then be homesick and wish to return to Portugal?"

"But *would* the Fox have a woman on board?" asked Zander rhetorically, not merely doubting, but quite certain there were none. "Very unlikely, but he could conjure one up in your magical way, could he not?"

"This jaunt to save two relatively minor works of art would go far over budget if my superiors were to send me a temporary maid—which is what you suggest, is it not? Whether they'd do so, I've no more notion than a kitten."

"A kitten! That's it! You remind me of a perky little kitten just discovering the world!"

Just discovering the world! Beth stared at her demurely folded hands. With luck, Smithson also believed this her first operation. Actually, several year's experience were behind her, all of it in ETH-arm, the ethics branch of ART, which was a small but efficient para-military unit. More than once her innocent appearance had proven an asset. Villains seemed to think such a naive-looking chit would be too idealistic to suspect an ARTist of subverting rules designed for their protection. The Fox would discover differently, but, she hoped, far too late to do anything other than submit to arrest.

"What goes on in your mind, Kitten?"

"Nothing. Nothing at all. Please don't call me Kitten. I dislike nicknames. Besides"—she stared at him—"I was taught informality is all wrong in this time." She noted his displeasure and, wishing a return of his lighter mood, offered, "Perhaps it would be all right, when we're private as we are now, for you to call me Beth?"

"Beth. Elizabeth, then? I like that. It's my sister Juno's middle name. You see? You two have something in common already. I hope you and she will become friends . . . Cousin Elizabeth."

"Unfortunately Elizabeth is *not* a name I may claim," she said on a dry note. "My name is Beth. Simply Beth."

"Now why"—Zander eyed her—"do I find that difficult to believe?"

She cast him a questioning look.

"It's my considered opinion, dear lady, that you'll never be *simply* anything!"

Three

While Zander and Beth elaborated on Beth's false history, his sister, Lady Juno Knightly, leaned back on her chaise lounge, scheming and, as much as she could, ignoring her governess, who was seated in a nearby straight backed chair.

"Do turn your mind to choosing styles suitable to your station and age," said Miss Wilder, pointing to the lady's magazine open on Juno's lap.

Lady Juno hid a grimace. She'd learned more in five minutes listening to her mother discuss her new wardrobe with their modiste than this method had ever taught her. In a mood to tease, she pointed at the most sophisticated offering.

"That will not do," Miss Wilder scolded. "One must hide faults of figure. Only the plainest and demurest of dress will do. As I've explained to you repeatedly, it will be necessary to compensate for your monstrous height by convincing potential suitors you are a woman of impeccable character. If you *can,* which I much doubt, given the unbecoming levity you are unable to control."

Juno sighed. If only Miss Wilder had a modicum of humor herself perhaps it would be easier to accept such criticism with grace. If *Maman,* for instance, were to accuse her of being too full of herself, Lady Fairmont would do it in only a slightly different tone, accompanying her criticism with a smile and a wry shake of her head. Very likely it wouldn't set up her back. *And Maman would not have re-*

ferred to defects in my form! thought Juno. She wished her brother were home so she'd have someone to whom she could complain.

"If only Zander returns for my party! Please, Miss Wilder," she coaxed, "say you think he'll come."

"Hmm," said Miss Wilder warily, "one may hope, of course, that Lord Hawksbeck returns in time to be present at your come-out ball."

"It will be outside of enough if Zander *doesn't* arrive in time." Juno slid a glance toward her mentor. "I wish him to lead me out, you see," she teased.

"Your father has that honor," replied the governess repressively.

"If Zander is here my father will heave a huge sigh of relief and delegate him to dance with me which, of course, I'd prefer. You know Father dislikes wasting energy on the dance floor"—Reprehensibly, Lady Juno giggled, the chuckle explained when she went on in a falsely deep voice—*"prancing and twirling and leaping and making an exhibition of m'self."*

Even Miss Wilder had difficulty restraining a smile when her young lady brought forward her talent for mimicry, which was very nearly as good as her brother's from whom she'd learned the offensive trick. "You must *not* say such things of your father," she scolded. "It is not respectable."

"It's silly he may say such things of himself, while I may not repeat them. And it's stupid pretending things are not what they are. I'll enjoy my first dance far more with Zander. Not only does he *like* to dance, but he's so tall I won't resemble a giant and"— Juno lifted her shoulders in imitation of her French mother—"everything will be ever so much better if Zander's home." A scratch at the door caught Juno's attention. "Enter," she called.

A new maid, perhaps twelve or thirteen years old, opened the door and began to speak. Then, recalling recent training, she bobbed a curtsy and began again. "I bin toll to say that a gennelman has come to see her ladyship—indeed he has. He's been put in the little room, he has—the sewing room, I mean—the one to the back of the house?"

Nodding, Juno stifled a smile which the solemn-faced little maid would not appreciate. Obviously the child felt important at being allowed to deliver the message. "Did Shipper say whom it was who has come?" But few of Juno's acquaintances would be put in the sewing room! "Was it Rupert Porthson perhaps?" she guessed.

"That be it, ma'am—I mean your ladyship—hmm. *M'lady,* that is."

"Thank you Bessie. That will be all."

"But what do I tell Mr. Shipper, ma'am—your ladysh . . er, m'lady?"

"Lady Juno said that will be all," said Miss Wilder repressively.

The child's chin tilted. "But, he said, he did, that—"

"You may tell Shipper I'll be down directly, thank you," interposed Juno before her mentor could insert still another lecture.

"You are," said Miss Wilder coldly and almost before the door was closed, "far too lenient with your inferiors. Remember your station or they will take advantage."

"Perhaps I'd keep a trifle more distance if you did not keep so much of one," said Juno, the impertinence slipping out before she thought to control her tongue. Quickly, she rose to her feet and moved toward the door.

Insulted, Miss Wilder's voice was nearly lost to a tightness in her throat. "You are not to go down without changing your gown!"

"It is only Rupert!" said Juno as she closed the door behind her.

Juno ran down the hall in a way which would have called forth two more lectures. Not only did she lift her skirts so as to move more quickly than a young woman about to be presented ought to do, but she fled toward the servant's stairs which, according to Miss Wilder, a lady should never use. It was, however, the quickest route to the sewing room.

At her entry Rupert looked up from where he rolled dice against the polished surface of a small Chippendale pie-crust table, the ruffled edge keeping them from falling to the floor. He scooped up the ivories and pocketed them. "Well, mad-cap? What new insanity do you require of me that you send me such an impertinent message? At the very least, it'd've been polite to have said hello, since we've not seen each other for several weeks."

Juno ignored this gibe and got to the meat of his complaint. "Why do you think I require something of you?"

"Cut line, Queeny. I know you're up to something, so what is it?"

Juno lowered her nose to a more normal altitude and eyed him for a moment. She noted his impatience and, rushing her fences, said. "Escort me to Mr. Sam's library. Tomorrow morning. Early."

"A library? Not me. Tell the witch to accompany you."

"That's the last person I want," said Juno bitterly.

"Aha! You *are* up to something."

"Not a thing," she said with an airy flick of her fingers. "I merely wish to take my time." Juno strolled toward the window where Rupert joined her, his red hair redder than ever in the sunlight. She eyed him sideways. "It's possible, of course, I might wish to take out something of which she'd disapprove."

"Another whopper! Come on, Queeny. Tell ol' Rupe what you're up to and I'll think about it. But if you don't stop pitching it rum I'll ask Shipper for my hat and be off—which I should do anyway. I'm late joining friends for a spot of practice at Manton's Shooting Gallery."

Juno tapped her foot. "If you must have it, I've remembered Zander once mentioned that Anthony Richmond, Lord Belmont, patronizes that particular library. It is imperative I speak with him."

"Belmont! An assignation of sorts, is it? You've windmills in your head, my friend, if you think Tony would be interested in a long meg like yourself. Besides, Tony won't be in the way of setting up his nursery any time soon. He's having too much fun with bachelor fair."

Anthony was into the muslin company? Perhaps kept a mistress? Oh dear. Juno's chin lifted to a stubborn angle well known to her friends. "If it's true, as Maman insists, that Zander think of *his* nursery, then it's also true Lord Belmont should think of his. Why not settle on *me* when he comes to it?"

"Because you're a hell-born cat with more hair than wit and not at all in Belmont's style, which ain't a great strapping girl such as yourself but the tiny sort we call a Pocket Venus. You ain't small." Rupert backed up and eyed her statuesque length; his eyes lingered on her features, "You ain't a Venus, either," he said, cuttingly, "although"—he seemed surprised—"you look amazingly well for all o'that, Queeny."

Juno choked back the hurt his tactless words gave her. "However that may be, I'd be an excellent mother for his children and that's all he'll think of when he comes to choose a wife. And of his bride's dowry, of course, but, in my case, *that's* of a size to appeal even if *I* am not."

"Don't put your nose in the air like that to me, m'girl, not if you wish my escort tomorrow."

"You'll take me then?"

"I'll take you, you silly chit, for the pleasure of seeing you come up against something—or should I say someone?—you cannot order as you please!" He caught her arms as she would have thrown them around his neck and held her off. "None of that. You'll ruin m'neckcloth and it took far too much effort to achieve this effect." Juno eyed her friend's cravat rather doubtfully. "And don't," added Rupert testily, "say what you're thinking, or," he added when she'd have said her piece anyway, "I'll change my mind about tomorrow."

But, even without the words, she'd gotten back at him for his thoughtless remarks about her face and form! Juno laughed, a deep purring chortle which always caught people by surprise. Somehow it fit her, which was also a surprise to them. "I'll be good, Rupe," she promised with a falsely demure demeanor. "Truly I will."

"Hah! I don't believe it. I must go now because once we're done at Manton's we're off to Gentleman Jackson's," Rupert said with a newly acquired insouciance.

"It sounds just lovely," Juno responded, but added strictures to the effect he was to be careful he not end up with a black eye because if he did she'd be embarrassed to have his escort on the morrow.

Then, cheerfully, she waved him on his way.

Zander watched Beth with narrowed eyes. One leg was curled beneath her on the window seat, her arm on the ledge under the leaded panes of glass and her eyes trained on the moon-lit and faintly phosphorescent waves. She was nothing like the women he'd known, this adventurer from the future, neither those of his own class whom he met only in the most formal of circumstances, nor those of a far different sort with whom he'd had decidedly *informal* relationships.

This woman, required to sleep in his cabin by the rascally captain, remained calm under circumstances which would have had even his sisters in hysterics and swooning right and left. On the other hand, although she took the enforced intimacy of place in stride, she'd not allow the slightest intimacy of touch—as would the other sort of woman with whom he'd had experience and *they'd* have allowed him much more than a touch!

What would his mother think of Beth, he wondered, not that it mattered. In public she'd accept his story of Beth's background even if she didn't believe it. But, knowing Lady Fairmont—his far too perceptive mother—it was likely that, in private, she'd pounce on every lie and twist him into knots if he tried to deny they were falsehoods.

And his sister? Zander hoped Juno was to have her come-out. She was younger than Beth, but she'd be a natural mentor where society's rules were concerned. Beth could follow his sister's lead when unsure and that would relieve some of the pressure she must feel—however self-contained she appeared.

Beth turned. She tipped her head when she discovered Zander staring at her. "Is something wrong?" she asked.

"Right or wrong has nothing to do with it. I was just wishing I understood you."

"Understanding comes with time." He didn't reply and she turned back to stare at the waves.

Time, wondered Zander, for what? To fall in love as he feared was happening? Because what else could fascination plus tenderness plus desire plus a need to protect add up to? And then? When he'd had time to become totally enthralled? Then she'd disappear from his life.

From his very time.

Zander jerked up from his slouching position against the pillows on the bunk. He pulled his knees up and hugged them tight against the pain in his gut.

Beth would be gone. Not only would he need to deal with his emotions, there'd be other problems as well! After he'd told everyone Beth was a recently discovered cousin come to live with them, she'd disappear. So how would he explain that? What could he say? He hoped the problem wouldn't occur to Beth. It would be his own particular difficulty, one he'd face when she'd left him. Face alone.

How very much alone he'd be . . .

The next day arrived and so did Rupert—finally—when Juno had all but given him up. As they drove to the library, she scolded him about his belated appearance, then drew him out of the sullens by adding a compliment on his new vest of wide blue stripes. "It's all the crack," she assured him.

"Well, it is, but *you* shouldn't say so," he said, not *quite* ready to forgive her for yesterday's disparagement of his cravat.

"Why not? Oh. Because it's cant language and young ladies are not to use such words? *Zander* would think it a joke."

"Perhaps Lord Belmont would *not,*" said Rupert, giving her a sly look.

Would he not? wondered Juno. "It's so difficult to remember such things. Why must women be so . . . *restricted?*"

"Because they are female," said her oldest friend with what Juno considered a prime example of male illogic.

She'd have argued if they'd not just then arrived. After entering Mr. Sam's premises Juno glanced around and smiled broadly. *How lucky I am!* she thought. Standing by the reading table, flipping through a copy of the Morning Post, was the very man she sought.

"Lord Belmont!" she said. "Perhaps you could . . ." The man turned and Juno stared, her eyes widening. "You aren't Lord Belmont," she stated, an accusing note to be discerned in her tone.

One supercilious eyebrow arched in just the way Belmont's might, but, unlike his lordship, he bent a cold, off-putting set of features toward her. "Am I not?" The man's lip lifted slightly in a refined sneer.

"No you aren't and it isn't nice to pretend. You're astonishingly like him, but you're missing . . . something." Juno put a finger against her lips. "I don't quite know what it is, but, definitely, you lack it."

"You are impertinent. I'll not stay to bandy words with a great awkward chit with neither looks nor sense." The man bowed to just the degree which made it an insult and, maneuvering around Juno as if fearing contamination, stalked toward the door.

The door closed behind the stranger and Juno, hands on hips, asked, "What do you make of that, Rupe? Who was he?"

"What I make of it is that you're too hot to hand by half! I *tried* to stop you. I *thought* that was Belmont's cousin, but would you wait while I made sure? Oh no. Now you've gone and done it for sure."

"But who was he?" repeated Juno.

"I just said." Rupert growled in exasperation, but elaborated on his former statement. "Belmont's late father and his uncle married twins. Their respective sons are not only of an age, but very like in countenance. Richard, the one you accosted, resents Belmont for holding the title and does what he can to make life difficult for him. And he won't have fond feelings for *you,* telling him he ain't up to snuff the way Belmont is—however true it might be."

"Is that what I did? It just seemed to me he wasn't quite— I truly don't know. Something . . ."

"You said that," accused Rupe. "Either say what you mean or talk of something else—or better yet, don't talk at all since you'll only put your foot in it."

"Perhaps, you'd prefer to explain why you're looking for *me,*" suggested a familiar, faintly amused, voice. The owner of the voice peered around the end of nearby set of shelves. "Oh, pardon me!" He moved quickly, reaching for Juno's arm to steady her. "I didn't mean to startle you. Are you all right, my dear?"

Juno scowled slightly. "I'm fine and I wasn't startled. I mean, I was, but I wasn't frightened, if you thought perhaps I was. I *mean,*" she said firmly, feeling her ears heat up at her infelicitous flow of words, "good day to you, Lord Belmont, and have you perhaps," she continued politely, "had a recent word from my brother?"

Lord Belmont tipped his head, studying with approval the

young thing who had given his pesky cousin such a rattling good set down . . . but who *was* the chit? His eyes narrowed slightly.

A quick grin revealed a dimple in Juno's cheek. "You don't remember me," she said with pretended chagrin. "How very distressing that is!"

"But I do! You had very much the look of your brother just then. What is it you wished to know?"

"Have you received news of Zander?" repeated Juno patiently. "Will he return in time for my ball?"

"I've heard nothing." Belmont spread his hands at her deep sigh. "How devastated I am that I must answer so!"

"It is difficult, having a brother like Zander. He cannot be *depended* on." The tone of Juno's complaint made it clear that she didn't really blame her brother for the fault and, as she'd meant him to do, Belmont smiled.

"Perhaps," he said, "I should inform the secretary of war of that fact. Bathurst thinks otherwise, you know. It'll set consternation through the halls of power, this news of yours."

Lady Juno pretended shock. *"Lord Bathurst* may rely on him. Zander wouldn't let down the *minister!* It is only sisters who are put off and to whom promises are made only to be broken, so what"—she looked up at him and blinked innocently—"can one do with such a one, Lord Belmont?" She gazed at him with a languishing look, better suited to a more petite maiden, but, since she consciously exaggerated it just a very little bit, the expression became satire.

Well amused, Lord Belmont asked, "What would you have him do?" Too bad she was such a Valkyrie. Except for her height and that too expressive face, the chit was strangely attractive—or perhaps *because* of the expressions which flitted across her features, sometimes too quickly to read?

"If I tell you what it is I wish, will you promise you'll not make it the latest *on-dit?"*

Belmont blinked, wondering what trouble the child had fallen into. But if his friend's sister needed help, then he was obligated to do what he could, was he not? Straightening his shoulders, he took his courage in hand. "I'll not tell your secrets if you wish to confide in me," he said gently.

"It isn't much of a secret, exactly—only that I want him to lead me out at my presentation ball. That's not so *very* bad of me, is it? Even if it is usually a father's prerogative? Perhaps it wouldn't be so very awful if you forget and make it a story for dining out?"

Belmont blinked. Was that all? "But surely it *is* usual for a girl's father . . ."

"My father finds dancing much too fatiguing and detests taking the floor. Father says we girls are far too energetic and wear him out and will we please go away and find ourselves husbands so that he may be left in peace. It is too too demeaning for words, having a father such as ours." She covered a pretty yawn with the tips of her fingers.

Belmont's eyes twinkled at her pretense to tonnish boredom. "If you took him at his word, I believe he'd not like that either."

"Oh, that he *loves* us goes without saying. Will you attend my ball, Lord Belmont?"

Juno's eyes widened in a pretense of innocence which Rupert knew and distrusted. Rupert wondered if he were obligated by gentlemanly codes of honor to warn Belmont he was being had.

While Rupert cogitated his conflicting loyalties, his lordship said, "I believe I've returned a positive response to your mother's invitation."

"Good. Then you'll dance with me," said Juno as if it were a settled thing. "I've so feared," she confided quickly before he could take umbrage at her assumption, "that I'd have no partners who were not inches shorter than myself. It is terrible, this having grown to be the tallest of my sisters. *They* were thought to tower above their friends but *I'm* still taller. You've no notion how cruel it is to have grown to such height as *mine!*"

Belmont looked at her with a certain amount of sympathy. Vaguely he remembered visits to her home, the Aerie, when he and Zander were younger. There had been a gaggle of females, he recalled, and this, the youngest, had been something of a pest . . . or so it had seemed at the time.

Now he discovered an emotion akin to nostalgia, a softness where this particular chit was concerned, that he'd never felt for a daughter of the ton. He would, he decided, be kind to her for Zander's sake and not fear she'd entrap him into marriage because very obviously she was too naive—too *young* perhaps. Beyond that, she'd never appeal to him in *that way,* so he was in no danger of trapping himself. He'd be, he decided, quite safe with Juno.

"I cannot lead you out for your first dance," he said, "as, perhaps, your brother may do if he arrives in time, but do you think you might save the second for me and then, perhaps, the supper dance as well if that is not too forward a request?"

"How wonderful." Lady Juno's features lit up with such joy they were transformed. "Thank you so much. Now my ball will be a success."

Belmont's amusement grew, but, with it, the teeniest fragment of a worry that perhaps he wasn't quite so safe as he'd thought. The chit was oddly attractive when she glowed like that! He swallowed hard, clearing his throat. "How do you know your ball will be a success merely because I've asked you to dance?"

"When it's seen you are willing to lead me out a second time, then those who thought me nothing but a bell tower ringing out the common hours will be certain they are mistaken and take me up. They will follow your lead, my lord."

"Ah! If I'm to put my reputation on the line," he teased, "you mustn't let me down. It will be your duty, Lady Juno, to amuse those other gentlemen or they'll think me a flat and never again look to me for a lead." Juno's husky chortle of appreciation turned eyes but Lord Belmont didn't notice. He knew a sudden urge to discover the secret of calling forth that particularly intriguing sound. "Will your mother allow you to drive in the park with me before the day of the ball? I might," he suggested, "if we see them there, introduce you to friends who are also of a proper height."

Her chuckle was softer this time but just as tantalizing. "I may not answer for my mother's indulgence, my lord, but we are at home Tuesday afternoons and perhaps you might ask her yourself? I'd find it exceedingly kind in you if you were to do so," she added, sudden shyness overcoming her.

That too Belmont found curiously appealing. His smile was uncharacteristically soft as he looked down at her. "Until Tuesday, Lady Juno." He bowed, preparing to leave.

"How wonderful. Until Tuesday," she repeated and watched him go.

A few moments later Rupert poked her. "Will you stop staring in that silly way?" When she didn't respond he poked her again. "You are drawing attention!" he hissed.

"Hmm? I am? Oh. Well, I suppose we may go now."

"Hadn't you better take out a book?" he asked, exasperated. "The witch will think it very odd of you to come home without, when that was the reason for our coming."

Juno felt her ears heat. She quickly chose a favorite, *Sense and Sensibility,* which she'd first read when it was published two years previously, and a Gothic romance of what she hoped would be the more lurid sort. "Now I'm ready, Rupert," she said contritely.

Rupert made quick work of returning her home. "You get down yourself, Queeny, so I don't have to leave my horses again . . ." Juno obeyed with agility. "And don't forget your books!"

Tossing Rupert a saucy look, Juno reached for the volumes. She immediately forgot him, however. As she entered the house she was already dreaming about driving in the park with Anthony, Lord Belmont.

. . . with Tony.

If she were lucky . . . ?

Four

Their ship had arrived in the Port of London on a night tide, but now the sun was high overhead. Beth, still dressed in her sarong, played with lenses built into the captain's window. There were half a dozen hidden among the leaded panes, hinged at different angles so that their ability to magnify could be trained in every direction. She'd stared, amazed, up the Pool of London as far as London Bridge, watching men work amid a clamoring chaos of sounds and sights and movement. She'd known London was an exceedingly busy mercantile city, but the sheer number of ships was unbelievable.

Of more immediate interest, however, was the wharf to which they'd moored an hour previously. The object of her curiosity was the most handsome man she'd ever seen, not that he had *half* Zander's attraction. A handsome face, by itself, would not have held her attention, but the man showed distinct signs of tension ill-hidden by a nonchalance which rang false.

Perhaps, thought Beth, *it's nerves. Ah. The Fox approaches. Now, if only the glass were equipped with an "ear" so I could hear . . . Heavens! Is Foxy so dangerous as all that? Mr. Handsome virtually cowers!*

The conversation was one-sided, Smithson doing nearly all the talking while the gentleman sputtered and gobbled and did everything but grovel. Finally he grabbed for one of the tails to his coat and scrabbled in a pocket hidden there. He pulled forth a small packet and thrust it at the captain.

"What has you frowning so?" asked Zander, entering just then and making Beth jump.

She turned, gesturing. "Of all the strange things," she said, thinking fast, "I wonder if our captain functions as a pawnshop or maybe a fence? Is that the correct term?"

"A receiver of stolen goods? I'd believe most anything of our captain."

Beth moved so Zander could view the wharf. For an instant his whole form went rigid with some unexplained emotion.

"Well?" asked Beth, drawing his attention. *"Did* our foxy captain hand over money?" Beth looked again, just in time to see the cowardly stranger disappear up a narrow alley between two warehouses.

"I saw very little," said Zander slowly, "but I agree it's more than a trifle smoky. You might think to tell those to whom you owe loyalty what you observed," said Zander, his tone too casual. He watched Beth frown, nibble on a finger and feared he'd not fooled her one bit.

Beth was biting more than a finger. She was biting back words as well. Zander didn't know the paintings, her supposed target, were no more than an excuse and he shouldn't be told that proving the captain's perfidy was her real mission so he couldn't know just how important what they'd seen might be.

On the other hand, the coward had been well dressed. Perhaps he was someone she'd meet among Zander's acquaintances? Perhaps his dealings with Smithson could be probed? She hoped so, because, if she were to live with Zander's family, it was going to be exceedingly difficult to keep an eye on Smithson himself!

The longer she was here, the more she believed a male ETH-arm agent should have been assigned the job. The fact an analysis of the captain's character had indicated a man, any man, would arouse Foxy's suspicions while, given his emotional blindness concerning them, a woman would not, hadn't taken into account a woman's problems with the culture. How, if she were wrapped in cotton wool and kept close to home, was she to collect proof of the captain's illegal activities? Completing this mission might prove not just difficult, but impossible!

Zander broke into her thoughts. "I'd not, if I were you, approach the captain about what you saw." There was considerably more bite in his tone then when he'd suggested she pass on word to her superiors.

Beth sighed. If it came to it, she'd tell Zander the whole and, together, they'd plan a means of upsetting Smithson's operation—which was not only illegal and unethical, but dangerous to the future. That, however, could wait. With Zander staring at her in such a way, she must say something.

"Have you solved the difficulty of my female companion?" she asked, peering once again through the lens.

The captain appeared all innocence. Or perhaps one should say he seemed perfectly normal? He yelled and screamed at his crew, waved his arms and stomped up and down as boxes and bales were unladen and carried into a warehouse opening onto the wharf.

Beth wondered about that warehouse. It appeared as ramshackle as others facing the river, but she doubted if it were. One of her first objectives—oops, surely not contemporary usage? Her first target? That didn't sound much better. Whatever the terminology, she must, as soon as possible, get into that warehouse and discover what it hid.

"What?" she asked when Zander laid a hand on her shoulder.

"You weren't listening."

Very true! she thought. "I'm . . . nervous," she suggested. "I fear our plan won't work. I'm not trained well enough to take a place in your home as your mother's guest!"

Zander's hand pressed gently, encouragingly. "Our practice will see you through. We've been over my mother's family tree until you know it backward," he soothed, "and we've the story to account for your background. You've been found, my young cousin, and we'll care for you. It was," he added, his eyes twinkling, "very bad of you not to come immediately to your cousin, my mother, when you found yourself an orphan."

"But I wasn't in England," she said, forcing herself to join in his pretense. "How could I have done so?"

"And," he asked, with pretended gravity, "you could not write?"

"My father was not one to puff off his great relations. I forgot I had such until your name was mentioned in my hearing," she responded to the cue.

Zander dropped his bantering tone, his brows drawing together slightly. "It's a thin story, but I believe it'll serve.

"I could also say that, in my pride, I'd not have made contact even now if it were not that my situation in Herr Whoever's home was becoming more and more uncomfortable."

Zander looked at her questioningly.

"As Frau Somebody grew more awkward," Beth elaborated on her new idea, "approaching her lying-in, you know, he became more attentive to myself, which I could not like."

Zander cocked his head, thinking about this addition to their tale. "Yes, that makes sense. But, rather than *you* telling this part of your story, it's something at which I'll hint and only for my mother's ears. Not something you told me, you see, but Lisbon gossip which I pass on to her for what it's worth. You'll merely insist you disliked approaching me for help and that you don't wish to be a burden. You desire that my mother find you another position, which, of course, she'll not do."

"Your mentioning your mother reminds me. I asked if you'd discovered a solution to the problem of my companion-chaperon and then didn't attend your answer. Have you done so?"

"Very soon now. Another ship, larger but slower, which left Portugal a day or two before us, came up the Thames on the same tide. The customs men will finish with her passengers within the hour. I saw women lounging at the rails. None of them is the sort with whom you would willingly associate, of course, but I'll hire one from amongst them who will ride with us so far as Hanover Square. Once there, she'll show herself at the carriage window while you thank her prettily, which Shipper will note and talk about. Then our new friend will be carried on to her destination—even if that's John o'Groats or Land's End. *Preferably* one or the other, actually! I'd not care to run into the *lady* here in London at some future date."

"Shipper?"

"Our butler." He went on to tell her other servant's names.

She memorized them and then suggested, "You'd best go and hire my companion."

"Will you be all right while I'm gone? I don't like to think of you unprotected from that woman-hating cohort of yours."

"He has yet to provide me with the necessary wardrobe and"—she frowned—"what do you call it? A portmanteau?" He nodded. "Perhaps that business can be attended to before you return and we may leave this place—which will please me."

She looked around the low ceilinged room. It had been truly malicious of the captain to make her sleep in Zander's cabin. It had been embarrassing since Zander had his own notions about a woman who would agree to such a thing. When she would not sleep *with* him and insisted on making herself a bed on the window seat, his continual teasing touches and verbal seduction had tried her determination to the limit! It would have been less embarrassing if she were not so drawn to the man, so aroused by his lightest touch, his voice . . .

Beth shrugged. At least she'd discovered he wasn't the sort who sulked when thwarted, which, when one thought about it, only made him more appealing!

"Now what goes through that overly active intelligence you hide behind that beautifully naive exterior?" asked Zander.

"What? Only what I said. That I'll be glad to leave here."

"What a bouncer," said Zander, but let the fib pass. "You *will* be all right while I'm away?"

"I'll be fine." Beth watched through a lens as Zander approached the captain and said a few words to the scowling man. He moved on, disappearing between the warehouses while Captain Smithson had a word with his first mate whose most distinguishing characteristic was a sheaf of papers which he was never without. Perhaps, Beth thought, even in his sleep.

The captain stalked into the cabin, his scowl deepening. "Women. That they exist is on the part of the deity a mistake."

"Men. That they cannot be civil even when unprovoked is failing number one thousand seven."

It seemed impossible that his visage could darken still more, but it did. "You will be still."

"You will finish your duty to me and provide me with a wardrobe and portmanteau. Since I'm supposed to have escaped an importunate employer, I was very likely unable to bring much away, but it must be my best, however worn that is."

"I'm not a novice that you must teach me! In any case, it is done. You will find everything in the middle section under the windows."

"How interesting. I wonder why you didn't think to tell me in time that I might familiarize myself with the style of apparel and how it is worn. I wonder what response that bit of pettiness will receive when my report is read."

"You will say nothing! You will *not*. I demand it."

"You are not my ultimate superior. My obedience is to Suu-Van. You would have me disobey *him?*"

The Fox looked as if he wished to say more, most of it to her and Suu-Van's detriment. Wisely, he decided against it. "The things are there. You have time now to try the clothing of a Portuguese duenna."

For the second time in their acquaintance Captain Smithson found something amusing. He actually laughed, a high unpracticed "he-he-he." The malevolence underlying his pleasure gave Beth a presentiment she'd not care for the clothing.

She didn't. It was a rusty black, the material cheap and the style plain. That last didn't bother her. She'd never liked frills, something she feared would be in fashion in 1813 London. What did bother her was the feel—and, after a time, bites.

Fleas! Scratching, Beth hoped the villain had not included lice among the livestock with which he'd gifted her.

By the time Zander returned she'd discovered the second dress was worse than the first. "I see a new wardrobe will be of the first importance!" he said, laughing. "Luckily, there is nothing Maman likes better than shopping, so she'll be delighted. Especially if my sister is as uncooperative in that regard as she used to be."

"Didn't you say Lady Juno wished to be presented?"

"Yes. And you are correct in what you *don't* say. If it is necessary for the completion of a goal on which *she* is determined, then Juno will do as she must—even to the penance of standing still for long periods while new gowns are fitted. Have you all you need?"

"I hope so, although I haven't a notion what some of it is. This for instance." She held up a long strip of cloth. "If it matched anything, I'd think it a sash, but it doesn't."

Controlling laughter with difficulty, Zander explained how a woman wrapped the soft material, called a zona, around her breasts, tucking in the end. His chuckles couldn't be contained when she flushed a deep red.

Ignoring her blush Beth admitted that, under a light corset, she was wearing only a chemise. "Should I correct that omission?"

"It won't be noticed under that ridiculous gown. Perhaps we should forget the story suggesting your master showed interest in you! If you wore that monstrosity, I cannot see how he guessed you were attractive."

"Likely it was unnecessary that I be attractive. Merely that I was there, presumably available."

"All too probable," said Zander abruptly and then, lightening his tone, added, "Perhaps there's something from my sister's adolescence stored in my father's town house which may be adapted for you. It would spoil everyone's appetite were you to sit down to dinner tonight in *that.*" He strapped up her box and set it beside his own trunk and boxes. "Are we ready?" he asked.

"Those will be sent on?"

"Yes. Put on that bonnet, ugly as it is, and the cloak of course. The widowed Mrs. Williams awaits our pleasure in a post chaise which will carry her on to Wales where she has family. She's happy to accommodate us since she need not pay out her meager blunt—that is, pay from her slender funds—the cost of a public conveyance to reach them. Now, my girl, get into character. Remember, you were a governess, a brow-beaten creature with no more spirit than a mouse."

"I'll be tired," she contradicted. "Perhaps I've been seasick."

"Far better you try for a subservient manner."

"But Zander, I *cannot* pretend to be a down-trodden miss. I'm not the sort for whom spiritless behavior comes at all naturally."

"You are being difficult, Beth." He eyed her. "Perhaps,

if you keep in mind that you don't know the details of living in my society, you'll feel less cocksure! You'd do well to watch and listen. But you'll learn quickly. Already, you sound more as if you'd always lived in this time—your use of words and your intonation. Any mistakes of that sort will be explained by the belief you've lived all over Europe, traveling with your father."

A chill ran up Beth's back at the thought of the very silly mistakes one could make through ignorance. "Suddenly I feel properly subdued," she said, her tone dry as dust.

"Zander! Zander has come home!" Juno turned from the window to look across her mother's salon at the two seated, talking, on a small sofa. "He has come in a carriage and there is a woman with him who is saying goodbye to another who is inside." Her face glowed with happiness. "I must see him. *At once.*" She left the room in an unladylike rush. "Zander!"

At the bottom of the stairs, Zander braced himself for his sister's usual exuberant welcome. It didn't come. Instead she trod gracefully down the steps and curtsied prettily, her eyes twinkling at his astonishment.

"So, Juno," he scolded. "You've become too much the lady to welcome me as a brother should be welcomed?" A brow arched. "Is that how it will be from now on?"

Juno rushed into his embrace and hugged him, looking up with laughing countenance. "Is that better?"

"Much." Zander held his hand out to Beth, urging her forward. "Now you will give welcome to our cousin, Mademoiselle Elizabeth Thevenard, who has come to live with us. You may call her Beth."

Beth blushed at Juno's frank stare. "Lady Juno?" Her curtsy was nowhere near so graceful as Juno's when greeting Zander.

"Our cousin? But how?" Juno laughed. "No, I don't mean *how,* precisely, but if we're related, why have we not met?"

"Juno, your tongue will have you in a bumble broth if you don't await explanations! I found our cousin in Lisbon where she was duenna to two impossible chits whose sole purpose in life was to torment her. I could not leave her in such a situation, so have brought her to our mother. She was Cousin Henri's daughter."

"Ah!" Juno's eyes lit in understanding. "A *French* cousin. Come along up, both of you. Maman is in the blue salon." She glanced at her brother and away. "You'll be pleased, I think, at who else is there."

Beth noted with interest the younger girl's hint of shy reserve. She hoped Zander approved of the man they'd find visiting with Lady Fairmont who would *not,* she hoped, see through Zander's machinations. She trailed brother and sister into the salon, their tall forms hiding the seated woman and the man standing near her, as, if she'd but thought, the siblings hid her presence from them.

The woman rose in a dainty cloud of fine wool batiste. Her voice was softly melodious as she went into Zander's embrace. "You've come home, my son. I am glad." After a moment she stepped away. "See who visits us," she said on a tinkling laugh.

Zander moved away in order to clasp his friend's hand.

Beth stared. The man on the wharf was *here?* But, how changed! She eyed the man and decided that, although there was a resemblance, it was not the same person. This man was not only less cold of feature, he betrayed none of the nervousness so obvious in the one who cowered before Smithson. And the features were less . . . blurred? Better defined? Who, then, was the man on the wharf? *Would* he help her run Smithson to earth? Beth hid a smile. Whether he would or no, she'd have far more luck using *that* one than *this* man!

"Anthony," Zander was saying, his voice warm. "How

good to see you. I'd thought to look you up this evening,
but this is far better. You may drive me to the horse guards
where I must go immediately and, on our way, you may tell
me all the latest *on-dits.*"

Juno folded her arms. "Lord Belmont has come to drive
me in the park, Zander."

One of Zander's brows curved upward. "Taking up with
my wayward sister, Tony?"

"Merely indulging her need to meet gentlemen of a tallish
habit well before the evening of her formal presentation.
She doesn't wish to look down on all her partners, you see!"
Lord Belmont sent a kindly look toward Juno, making her
scowl. "My child, you understand that I must postpone our
drive until tomorrow? Then," he added, in a coaxing manner,
"with Zander accompanying us, you'll meet far more potential partners than I alone could introduce."

Juno pouted at the offered sop, but her mood lightened.
"I couldn't go now in any case, because of Mademoiselle
Thevenard. Come, cousin. I apologize that we seem to have
forgotten you in the excitement of having Zander home."
Very prettily Juno made the introduction to her mother.

Graciously Lady Fairmont welcomed her unknown cousin
then said, "My Cousin Henri's daughter . . . I see. But you
must be *exhausted* after such a terrible journey! Juno, take
our cousin up to the rose chamber next yours, I think,
and"—her gaze rested on her guest's dreadful gown—"you
must send down my maid in . . . shall we say fifteen minutes?" Juno led her new cousin from the room and, once
the door closed behind the girls, her ladyship's brows rose.
"Well, Zander? Just what games do you play with me now?
Hmmm?"

Zander tugged at his cravat, but quickly dropped his hand
when he saw his mother observe the nervous movement.
"Games, Maman?"

"Cousin Henri's child, indeed! Oh, no need to pucker up,
Anthony. I count you as quite a member of the family. We've

no secrets from *you,* I believe," she said with just a touch
of acid. "Yes, Zander"—she returned to the attack—
"games. Henri never married and I do not believe he left a
convenient by-blow whom you would dare—"

"Maman, spare my blushes!"

Zander's expression of mock outrage brought forth the
countess's tinkly laugh which blended nicely with Anthony's
deeper chuckle.

"Besides," continued Zander, "I did not refer to Henri
Antoine, but to Henri Emile."

"Ah. I see. Henri Emile."

Silence filled the room. Enough time passed Zander began to hope that just perhaps maybe . . . but, it wasn't to
be.

Lady Fairmont once again attacked. "I demand the truth!
I cannot be a party to sponsoring an unknown chit onto an
unsuspecting ton."

"Why not?" asked Zander with a certain insouciance his
closer friends would have observed with fear and trembling.

His mother, too, was aware he was up to deviltry. *"Alexander!"*

He sighed. "Mother, may we speak of this later and in
private?"

"Secrets?" Her brows arched. *"From Anthony, you have
secrets?"*

"I fear so."

Zander avoided his friend's eyes and his friend, equally
careful to look elsewhere, picked a piece of lint from his
sleeve.

"In that case we'll speak later and in privacy. I apologize,
my son."

"It is unnecessary. Tony, if, despite my rudeness, you're
still willing to drive me, I must depart at once."

"More willing than ever, of course!" Anthony winked at
the countess. "How else am I to pry from you your secrets?"

Anthony bowed low to the delightful woman with whom

he'd enjoyed the lightest of flirtations while awaiting Lady Juno's appearance in the salon. He followed Zander down the stairs and out the door. They were waiting on the front steps for Anthony's rig to be brought round when Zander cleared his throat.

"Yes, my friend?" asked Anthony. "I'm to learn your secrets after all?"

"No. Tony, it is not permitted that I explain. You understand?" It had occurred to Zander that, for those who would not believe Beth his cousin, he might contrive to suggest she was a government agent! "I meant to hunt you up this evening for quite another reason. While we were waiting at the docks after custom inspection, I saw your cousin Richard make a trade with a character I don't trust an inch. It's my belief Richard sold something from your collection of miniatures."

Anthony swore softly. "If that scoundrel has once again laid his sticky fingers on my possessions, then it's time I cease being so tolerant!" He scowled and hit the side of his boot with his cane. *"Now* I understand why he lay in wait for me at Sam's a day or so ago where I took care he didn't find me! For a moment, however, Juno mistook him for myself." Tony chuckled. "My dear cousin left very quickly when, in her forthright manner, but without meaning to, she insulted him rather badly. *Such* a set down! I'm so glad I observed it!" His cane whacked his boot again. "But what you saw . . . He needed the ready immediately, I suppose, and when he failed to put the touch to me, he sold something. Blast him!"

"You go too fast, Tony. Until you check, you cannot *know* that what I saw him sell was from your collection."

"It's happened before. He excuses himself, if you will believe it, by saying that since our mothers were twins, then we are more than cousins and should *both* be Lord Belmont and *that we own everything jointly.* What's worse, I think he *believes* it."

"He's always been a trifle loose in the haft," said Zander casually, only to straighten from where he lounged against the door frame. He whistled softly. "Ah, Tony, what a pair!" Zander watched appreciatively as, barely able to control them, a groom rounded the corner from the stables in the mews leading high-stepping chestnut colored horses. "By God, it's not fair! I leave London for a month and my friends are free to snap up the best stock in the country. Have you raced them?"

Anthony allowed the talk to cover the racing news before he turned it back to the woman in Lady Fairmont's salon who had, for a moment and for reasons beyond his comprehension, looked at him with loathing. "Who is she, Zander? Really?"

Zander, who wasn't surprised when his friend probed, chuckled. *"Really,* Tony, do you expect *me* to give away such secrets?" He sobered. "Anthony, it's not unlikely she's in danger. If you love me at all, you'll accept that the young lady is a French cousin."

Anthony cast him a quick glance. "Not Cousin Henri Antoine's offspring, but Cousin Henri Emile's?"

"Exactly."

Anthony cast him another quick glance. "Security's at stake?"

"Yes," said Zander, gravely. It was not a lie, the security of *her* time and organization were definitely at stake. "Believe me, Anthony, if I could tell anyone, I'd trust you. But I'm bound . . ."

"That's all right. I'm mum."

Zander lay a hand on his friend's arm. "I've no doubt."

Anthony immediately changed the subject to that of Brummel's break with the Regent. ". . . You hadn't heard? I thought that occurred before you left for the Peninsula. *Well . . . !"*

Such gossip passed the time until they reached the Horse Guards where Zander, after making arrangements to meet his friend later, said goodbye.

Five

Beth exclaimed at her room which would, she thought, provide a surprising degree of comfort. The narrow tent bed was well supplied with feather beds, as Lady Juno proved to her satisfaction by bouncing on them. A chaise lounge had a low table beside it and a patent oil lamp hung above on a chain by which it could be raised and lowered. Along one wall was a good sized armoire, a long mirror set into one door and beside it a dressing table. "This is lovely."

"It is cramped and uncomfortable," contradicted Lady Juno, "as are all bedrooms here in town. I'd stay at the Aerie, Papa's country estate, you know, except that I must be properly presented to society." Juno sighed. "It is a bore when one might be riding or fishing, assuming one can escape one's dragon. Mine is a terrible witch who would, if she could, never allow me to do anything interesting. Did you have a nasty governess?"

"My life has been a trifle different, I believe," said Beth carefully, wondering at the unknown face which flashed ever so briefly before her mind's eye. She forgot it in making the necessary effort not to laugh at Juno's look of commiseration.

"Ah, yes," said the girl politely. "I believe life is *quite* different on the Continent." She obviously believed it must also be quite horrible, being unEnglish and therefore inferior. She eyed her new cousin. "The first thing we must do is burn that dress," she said and asked in her blunt way, "Have you nothing better?"

"In Lisbon I myself was a dragon," said Beth apologetically as if that explained all. "I pray your mother may find for me a new position here in England."

"You cannot wish that. Besides, Zander said we'd care for you now."

Playing the character assigned her, Beth shook her head. "I cannot allow your family to support me. I must make my own way."

"Bah! It's your family, too." Juno brightened. "I've a solution. If you *must* have a position, you can be *my* companion. There's no way you'd be such a shrew as my Miss Wilder!" She rose impulsively. "I'll go and ask Maman. At once."

A knock forestalled her exit. Juno opened the door to reveal a huge armload of multicolored material. A straight-backed, bird-thin creature poked her long nosed face from behind the dresses she carried and peered into the room. Entering, she laid the clothing on the bed, then surveyed Beth with a critical eye.

"Wonderful," said Juno, clapping her hands. "I see why Maman wished Higgens sent to her. This is my mother's dresser, Cousin Elizabeth. Maman says she works miracles. She'll soon have you properly outfitted, will you not, Higgens? What have you brought us?"

"Some of her ladyship's things." The maid's voice was surprisingly gruff, coming from such a tiny woman. "No, please don't argue as I see you are about to do," she said, speaking to Beth in the same brusque way. "Her ladyship often buys pale colors which don't suit her. I've done my best for fifteen years, but I cannot convince her ladyship they are a disaster with her complexion. Ah, but, *you,* miss! *You* they'll suit right down to the ground."

". . . suit to a cow's thumb," murmured Juno wickedly.

"Enough of your impertinence, Lady Juno. You know you

shouldn't say such things." Higgens sorted through the pile. "Now, M'zelle, if you'll remove that"—she grimaced— "that *gown,* we'll see what must be done to make you fit to be seen by dinnertime."

"Let me help with the hooks," said Juno, scurrying behind Beth. There was a faint gasp as the top few gave way. "Oh my, you've dispensed with your zona. How I wish I might do likewise!"

"Perhaps if you were forced to wear such heavy cloth in such a hot climate as Mademoiselle Elizabeth comes from, then you might dare do so, Miss Juno," scolded the dresser, but added, apologetically, "I think, however, that with this silk, you'd best put one on." The woman handed Beth a strip of soft material and a chemise of the same quality. She gestured toward a chinoiserie screen, its muted orange red the only bright spot in the room.

When Juno would have followed, the dresser held her back, much to Beth's relief. Beth hoped she put on the zona correctly before donning the finely embroidered chemise which fell well over her hips—a fact she appreciated when it became clear nothing in the way of tights were forthcoming! The corset, handed over next, was, unlike the long girdles Beth had seen in museums, no more than a waist-cincher combined with boned material which lifted the bosom a trifle. The dress and matching under-dress were beautiful but too large at the bust and too long. Higgens insisted it would be no problem whatsoever to fix and helped Beth into a warm wrapper—also too long. The dresser then suggested Beth compose herself until time to dress for dinner at which time Higgens herself would oversee the dressing of her hair.

"Would it be possible," asked Beth a trifle diffidently, "to have a bath before dressing? On board ship, you see, it was difficult . . ." She trailed off, wondering if she'd made an inappropriate suggestion.

"Certainly," said Higgens, promptly. "I'll see hot water is brought up in good time."

Beth hoped it was approval she detected in the woman's response. Her inadequate preparation for this era *had* included the fact that cleanliness was *not* considered next to godliness. But Zander had been careful about personal cleanliness and she'd not noticed a heavy scent in the salon which, according to her indoctrination, was often used in an attempt to cover body odor. Nor did Lady Juno offend the nose!

"You do not really wish to sleep, do you?" asked Juno, peering through a door Beth had not previously noticed. "Oh, dear, did I startle you? I'm sadly skitter-witted, or so you'll be told. *I* think it is merely I'm a trifle thoughtless. This door connects with my room as I should have told you. Do you object to company?" she finished on a hopeful note.

"Not at all," said Beth.

"Good. I've not had a woman friend for ever so long. And, excepting my sisters, never one quite so tall as you. Although shorter than I, you are tall enough you would, I think, understand how awful it is to tower over everyone. Perhaps you'll become my confidant?"

"I don't know that you should tell me your secrets," said Beth hesitantly. "I might feel obligated to inform your mother, you see."

Juno eyed her. "I think I may trust you. You look a right one . . . but if you find you *must* inform on me, then perhaps you'll tell Zander? Zander will discuss things with me before going to my parents, you see?"

"I think I could promise that." Beth tried to hide her amusement, but obviously didn't succeed.

"Ah. You, too, feel me a child. It's so tiring, this forever having to convince the world I'm a grown up lady now. I'm *almost* eighteen!"

Juno sighed gustily . . . but Beth noticed her eyes twinkled.

"What did you think of Lord Belmont?" Juno then asked before Beth could respond. "I've been in love with Anthony since I was a very little girl," she said dreamily. "He's Zander's friend and I used to run after them and tease them to take me with them on their adventures." She sighed again, this time for real.

"And did they take you?" asked Beth.

"Oh yes. Well. Sometimes." Juno lay back on the bed. "He's so handsome it's almost enough just to look at him, but he's *nice* with it. He's offered to introduce me to tall men so I'll not feel awkward dancing at my presentation ball," she said softly. With the mercurial swiftness one didn't expect of such a large girl, Juno's mood shifted again. She chuckled, her eyes alight with laughter. "With luck, I'll not tread a single measure with a man to whom I must bend my neck." She raised her eyes to the ceiling as if pleading with Higher Authority.

"When is your ball?"

"A bit over two weeks, now. My father came up to London for talks with the prime minister. Papa is a Tory, you see, and deep in political doings although I think he's really happiest at home shut up in his library with his books. Zander is a Tory too, mostly, but I think he has a few Whiggish sympathies."

"I believe your brother said you have sisters?"

"Three. Cassandra, Hera, and Minerva." Juno grinned. "Our father, you see, is a classicist. My sisters are married and Hera will soon have her second child. If she's sensible, Maman says, it will be a boy this time! Maman is a famous political hostess and holds entertainments with the oddest guest lists. She plays Tories off against Whigs and watches the fireworks. I can't wait until I'm allowed to dine with such company!"

Beth chuckled at the relish with which Juno anticipated her introduction into her parent's life. "Will your Lord Belmont be among the Tories or the Whigs?" she asked and then, mentally, kicked herself for bringing up the topic just when Juno seemed to have forgotten it. She suspected the chit could easily become a bore on the subject of Lord Belmont!

"Anthony is not political, I fear."

"Perhaps you should look about you for someone who is. It sounds like you might follow in your mother's footsteps, but that would be impossible if you entangle yourself with a man who is not interested in such things."

"One might teach him . . ."

"Lady Juno, may I give you a bit of kindly meant advice?" Beth interrupted.

Juno rolled her eyes. "If you must."

"It is only this: Never ever think you may change a man's character. It can't be done. If you cannot love the man exactly as he is, warts and all as they say, then you should wonder if you love the real man or are in love with a dream you've hung about the man like a cloak."

Juno eyed her new friend. "I don't think I like the fact that that made a great deal of sense."

"One never likes to hear a truth which makes trouble for one."

"And you think loving Tony may make trouble for me?"

"Lady Juno, I already like you very much. I do not wish to see you come a cropper—is that correct? Be very careful that you know the man through and through before you cede him your heart. To find out too late, *that* would be a great tragedy."

"Yes, I see how that might be," said Juno, nodding wisely, "but I've known Anthony forever and do know him. But it was good advice," she added generously, "and I'm glad you've come to us, Cousin."

"I think I'm glad too," said Beth softly, thinking of Zander. Her heart would likely be in pieces before this adventure ended, but that she might never have known him? It wasn't to be thought of! Ah, how had she become so deeply involved so quickly . . . ?

Beth listened idly to Juno prattle on about her introduction to society—until one fatal revelation. Considering Juno's confidences as to the state of her heart, Beth wasn't at all surprised at the younger girl's reason for wanting her come-out as soon as possible, but she wished, desperately, that reason had remained unknown: It was a blow to discover that the stately countess had decided it time her only son wed. Juno reasoned that, since he was the same age, Tony must also!

Beth knew Zander must marry, of course. Someday. But she'd pushed the knowledge to the back of her mind, assuming she'd have long departed this age before Zander's nuptials came to pass. That she'd known him only a few days was irrelevant to the fact it would already be painful to watch Zander court a proper young woman, propose to her, wed her.

Beth hadn't spent more than a moment with the countess. She and Juno had been shooed from the salon in such short order she'd wondered if her ladyship had already unmasked her and would demand she be shown the door—not that that might not be a blessing so far as her mission was concerned! But, however short the time, she'd seen enough to believe the countess was rarely crossed once she made up her mind.

And Lady Fairmont had decided her son was to wed. It was inevitable, then, that Zander wed and Beth's heart would break. *Oh, Suu-Van, you old prophet of doom!* she thought, remembering his grumbles that this operation was jinxed. *Why did you not warn me this fracas would be, for me, a gig from hell?*

"Cousin Elizabeth?"

"Hmm?" Beth blinked away her preoccupation. "Sorry. My mind was elsewhere. And do, please, call me Beth."

"Cousin Beth. I like it. And you must call me Juno. I so dislike everyone calling me Lady Juno. Zander and I dislike formality and are happier in the country, which makes us quite strange to the rest of our family. My sisters are only content with dinner parties and balls and a myriad other entertainments to fill the hours. They always regret when the season ends each year. Cassandra and Minerva will be at my ball, of course, but Hera, as I said, is increasing and her husband will not allow her to come. She is very angry. Ah, I could stay in the country forever if it weren't that I feared Tony would wed another!"

"But didn't you say you wished to join the guests your mother invites to her political dinners? Surely you cannot do that except in town."

"Hmm . . . Perhaps when I've more experience I'll like town life as well?" Juno frowned slightly. "I believe Tony spends such of his time in London so I'd better like it, had I not? Life is so difficult sometimes! Since I wish to wed Tony, I must give up my hope to live forever in the country. One must make compromises, I see." The girl thought about that, her chin tucked into her hand. "You are right that one should know the man to whom one gives one's silly heart. I *do* know how kind and gentle and wonderful Tony is, but, although that is important, I forgot there are other things, such as like interests and goals."

"Your Tony has visited your country home, has he not? Is he content when there or always wishing to be elsewhere? Perhaps he's not such a town creature as you think?"

Juno brightened.

But talking about Lord Belmont reminded Beth of the man she'd seen conferring with the captain. Such a noodle *he'd* been! Beth wondered if Zander would introduce her to the fellow . . . Ah! He'd wonder *why* she wished to meet the man . . . and she couldn't explain. Beth sighed.

"You weren't listening," pouted Juno. "I was telling you what an excellent shot Anthony is and how he taught me to cast a line. I'm sure he must like the country at least a little. Or perhaps he once did, but has forgotten? It was some time

ago when he taught me to fish . . ." Juno's voice faded out
and her eyes lost focus.

Beth, leaving Juno to a sudden reverie, closed her eyes.
Later a knock woke her and she discovered, assuming the
clock on her mantel didn't lie, that the day was mostly gone.
She'd fallen asleep and Juno had left her to it! "Come in,"
she called.

A neat young woman named Susie explained that she'd
been assigned as mam'zelle's abigail as well as to maid Lady
Juno. Footmen trooped in, carrying a hip-bath and cans of
water. The maid had the screen moved to protect Beth's mod-
esty or protect her from drafts or perhaps both. Fluffy towels
were hung on a rack near the newly repaired fire and a ball
of soap smelling of violets lay in a dish on a low table near
the tub. Perhaps it wouldn't be so very bad to have a maid?
Beth decided she'd no choice and might as well accept the
situation gracefully!

All too soon she was ready to put her ability to play-act
to the test. Her feet felt extremely cold at the very idea, she
was glad for the delay when Juno knocked and peered in.
The girl's eyes rounded with surprise as she walked all the
way around Beth.

"My," said Juno, "how very lovely you look with your
hair done up like that and everything prime about you."
After a guilty glance toward Higgens who had snorted, Juno
amended that. "Of course I *meant* to say, everything beautiful and just as it should be."

Beth chuckled. "Did you mean that? Well, thank you for
the compliment, but you really must not toss me too much
from the cream pot. I might become puffed up in my own
esteem," she added, using some of the slang she'd learned
for this mission. "I don't think I'd like that. It sounds so
uncomfortable."

Juno's infectious laugh, coming from the room Zander
knew was his protegée's, stopped him in his tracks. He debated whether he might, with propriety, knock and had re-

luctantly decided he couldn't, when Higgens opened the door. She curtsied, a choppy movement characteristic of the woman.

"Ah. Higgens," he said. "How are you?"

The bird-like little woman developed two spots of color on her pale cheeks. "How like you to ask, my lord. Thank you, I'm very well now the weather's dry again." She curtsied a second time and moved away toward his mother's room.

Juno came to the door. "Zander, wait. May we go down with you?" She went on before he could respond. "Look at Cousin Beth." She backed away, opening the door wide. "Isn't she lovely?"

Beth had been an exotic creature on board ship, dressed in her strange garment. There she'd been a entity one might dream about and tease—and hope to seduce. Then, in her crow incarnation, dressed in the rough black provided by the captain, he'd actually forgotten, in the pressure of settling her with his family, that she was attractive. Now, dressed as a proper young woman of his time and place, he found her special in still another way. She'd become *real* somehow, part of his life as she'd not truly been before.

Zander entered the room as if drawn. Facing her from a pace away he lifted her fingers, his eyes never leaving hers. His gaze burned her as his lips brushed her knuckles. He straightened slowly. The silence in the room lengthened, deepened.

"Well, Zander?" said his mother, her voice icy. "Do you bring our new cousin downstairs or have you lost the use of your limbs?"

Beth flushed. She felt the heat flowing up her bosom and throat, far too much of which was revealed, she thought, by the low neckline of her gown. She turned away abruptly, her back straight and her head high.

Zander growled softly with displeasure, but then, forcing a soothing note, he said, "I see you've solved the problem of Mademoiselle's wardrobe. Thank you for being so prompt, Maman. With your usual good taste, you've made a miracle, I think. I freely admit to being awe struck by the change made by a decently designed dress."

Fashion was Lady Fairmont's passion. Zander hoped that introducing it into the conversation would intrigue his mother and she'd not become impossible—as she was capable of doing when given what she thought reason. He must take care he not again reveal the surge of warmth Beth roused, an emotion involving desire, yes, but something more, something he wished to explore, something he feared might take a lifetime to fully understand.

"This gown becomes her immensely," he added.

Lady Fairmont stepped into the room. "Gown? Ah yes. I see Higgens has . . ." Suddenly her ladyship's eyes narrowed and her skin lost color. She moved to the wardrobe and flung wide the doors. Inside hung several more gowns. She turned, her eyes worried pools. "Mademoiselle," she said, her voice urgent, "please tell me Higgens did *not* give you a pale green gown with an over-gown of ecru lace. She cannot have been so foo . . ." Sudden rosy color was a match to Beth's of some moments earlier. "What I *meant* to say is that I've a new gown which arrived only the day before yesterday and she and I had words over it. I fear Higgens, in her enthusiasm to dress you properly, might have included it among the gowns she offered to alter for you. You'll reassure me, I hope, that it was not among those you tried on . . . ?"

"There was no pale green with lace. I couldn't accept something so grand in any case and a lace overskirt in particular would be entirely inappropriate to my age," she said, quoting something Higgens had told Juno. "Besides, I hope you may soon find me a position and I feel guilty Higgens has gone to so much needless work. A gown for daytime and one for evening, surely that would be adequate for my needs?" she asked diffidently.

Lady Fairmont, who never stayed angry for long, threw up her hands. "One day dress and one for evening? Tell me she jests, Zander. You cannot have suggested we'd be so ungenerous to our new cousin as to leave her practically naked!"

"Maman!" scolded Zander, "You will embarrass Cousin Elizabeth."

Zander's tone reminded Lady Fairmont of the fear which filled her as she glanced into the room and saw Zander so mesmerized by his young friend—whoever the chit might be.

Zander, seeing another mercurial change in his mother and fearing another embarrassing interval, held out his arm to her. "Shall we go below?" he asked. "I'll tell you my news and you'll be the very first to know what Wellington said in his private letter to Bathurst. You'll be surprised, Maman, to hear he's cautiously hopeful the Peninsular war may be drawing to an end!"

"Zander!" exclaimed Lady Fairmont, hugging her son's arm and forgetting her fears concerning her unwanted guest. "Can that possibly be true? After all these many years? One has begun to believe the war will go on forever without end. But Napoleon! Surely he'll not allow Wellington to cross the Pyrenees, to actually set foot in France?" Her voice lowered as if she spoke a great secret. "He *cannot* allow it, Zander. It would bring the war, finally, onto French soil!"

"I can give no details. The report to be released for publication is, however, more positive than ever before. Wellington, as you know, is *not* one to exaggerate his position." With a comical look, he added, "Quite the contrary, in fact."

"*Quite* the contrary." Suddenly her ladyship turned and stared at her supposed cousin. "But you! You will be a supporter of Napoleon and will be devastated to hear this news?"

"No, my lady. I'm no supporter of the Corsican Ogre. Although he's a military genius, he's a usurper, a maniac who will be satisfied with nothing less than that the whole world bow down to him," said Beth.

"He'll find himself satisfied with *much* less," said Zander, dryly, "once he's forced to abdicate."

Beth bit her tongue. She wanted to tell Zander that Napoleon would escape the island of Elba over which he'd be given dominion and would, once again, turn Europe on its head during what would become known as the Hundred Days. Knowing what would happen, yet unable to speak of it, was frustrating.

Zander was nothing if not observant. His eyes narrowed. "You disagree, Mademoiselle?"

"No. How could I?" she said, making full use of the innocence of expression which was, according to Suu-Van, her prime asset. She saw that she was not alone in frustration. *Zander* couldn't say he was certain she'd disagree quite easily, if she were not restrained by training that taught she was not to reveal the future. Beth lowered her eyes demurely, giving her innocence of feature every aid.

"No reasonable person could disagree," scolded Lady Fairmont, inadvertently coming to Beth's rescue. "Do come along now. We'll not be before your father if we don't descend immediately. You know how he dislikes it if *he* must wait for *us.* Come along now, Juno, Mademoiselle . . ."

Beth bit off a sigh and, as Juno obviously wished it, she walked down the stairs arm in arm with her, all the while wondering what other near disasters might occur this evening.

Actual disaster *must* he avoided. She wondered if Zander knew how near they'd been in the instant his mother saw them together, that utterly bemused expression on his face. It occurred to Beth to wonder what her own features had revealed! Undoubtedly, her face had been equally enlightening. She felt her skin once again warming. Why had she allowed Captain Smithson to convince Zander to—what was that expression?—*bear lead* her, which led to this predicament.

Juno gently pinched Beth's arm. "He's in love with you, isn't he?"

"I don't know what you mean . . ."

"Do you not? It's the feeling *you* have for him!" crowed the younger girl. "I never thought to see it. *Zander.* Besotted as any footman for a maid!"

The footman stationed in the hall couldn't help but overhear. His ears flaming, he opened the salon doors.

"Nonsense!" Beth gave the young man a commiserating look even as she answered Juno. "It's silly to think such a thing of your brother!"

Beth didn't convince Juno of course, but, if she could make no stronger denials, then Juno could do no more teasing. Not when they'd just joined the rest of the family. It was, for the moment, a stand-off.

Six

"When may we talk?" whispered Beth the next day. Zander's mother's attention was temporarily taken up with catechizing Juno on the proper behavior of a girl when driven in the park at the popular hour of five. Beth suspected she should listen, but had decided it was more important to have a word with Zander.

"What about?"

"There are things I must know."

"Concerning your life here in Hanover Square?"

She cast him a look that held more of loathing than love. He chuckled. They glanced toward his mother, neither wishing to draw her attention. Lady Fairmont wanted answers. The preceding evening she'd turned a natural talent for contriving searching questions onto her guest and been quite obviously exasperated when her son interfered!

"Not concerning your life here, then," he added softly when they were assured Lady Fairmont was preoccupied with Juno. "Then it must have to do with your assignment. That is far in the future so surely of no concern at the moment?"

Overnight Beth had designed a way to get on with accomplishing her true mission in Zander's time without actually revealing it. "I'm concerned," she said, carefully, "by what I saw on the dock. If Smithson is breaking rules, I must determine how far he's strayed from the path. The dangers resulting from interference in the past are real, Zander."

Her mouth tightened. "I *must* assure myself Smithson isn't playing with fire!"

Zander recalled his feeling the captain was up to something, a sense the man had no particular concern for the future but only for himself. What, for instance, if he were acquiring art works of this period and intended, eventually, to carry them into the future where he might sell them and become rich? But he couldn't see how something so unimportant as that would change Beth's future.

He'd some understanding of Beth's fears concerning their becoming involved, the hurt when she'd, far too soon, be gone from his life. He'd an excellent grasp of her peril if Smithson suspected she was a danger to him. But there was that further danger of which he'd no true understanding, the fact that Smithson's behavior, now, could affect Beth's future.

He considered that last problem as he stared down into the oval of Beth's face. It occurred to him he'd never know if her future were affected, if she *personally* were affected. A heaviness settled in his chest.

"What is it you wish?" he asked, accepting he must help her with whatever she must do.

"I must explore that storehouse."

"An obvious hiding place. I'll have it searched. My agent will find a hidey-hole, if such exists."

Exasperated, Beth turned to the window. It was just as she'd feared. "Just how am I to tell your agent what to avoid? Our sly fox may have incorporated gimmicks"—she saw Zander silently mouth the word *gimmicks* "—into his caches which are impossible, for someone of your time who hasn't the necessary but illegal testing devices, to detect. He may have security doohickeys unknown yet. Since I can't explain, even to you, Zander, I myself must go." She caught and held his gaze. "Will you help me or must I find a way to do it alone?"

A muscle jerked in his jaw. "You cannot go."

"Why may I not?"

"It is far too dangerous to contemplate. Forgetting those complications only you understand, that area of London is evil. The worst sort of men and women live there, creatures who would as soon kill as smile. Come to that, they might well smile *as* they kill! I cannot allow you to enter that part of London."

Beth's eyes flashed. "You cannot *what?*" Unfortunately, her voice rose, drawing Lady Fairmont's attention. "By Michael's Glove," muttered Beth softly, wondering if she'd ever learn to control her tongue.

"Zander?" Lady Fairmont rose to her feet and the heavy amber silk of her afternoon gown swished softly around her limbs as she approached. "You have upset our guest? I demand to know what you've said to rouse such heat. It is unlike you to be less than a gentleman, Zander. Apologize at once."

"Maman . . ."

"Please, Lady Fairmont," inserted Beth. "I beg your forgiveness. It is I who have done the unforgivable. Please don't blame your son for my inability to control my tongue. If you must scold, scold me. I am far more at fault than he."

"But not altogether at fault," said Lady Fairmont, her eyes narrowing. "If you were, you'd take *full* blame for this contretemps, would you not?"

Beth wondered how her ladyship knew; she saw approval in her ladyship's gaze. The approval was, of course, tempered by the reserve that underlined the fact Lady Fairmont had not accepted the tale of Beth's relationship to the family.

Beth sighed. It seemed she was doing a lot of sighing these days. "I find your son somewhat over-protective, my lady. I've fended for myself for a long time now. He must not interfere in what I feel is right."

Lady Fairmont cocked her head. "Ah. I see—"

Beth hoped very much her reluctant hostess did *not* see.

"—you argue that a position must be found for you."

Good. Lady Fairmont hadn't guessed.

"Exactly, Maman. I told her I could not permit her to go again into service. She must accept our hospitality. We will introduce her to the ton at Juno's ball. That's the proper thing, is it not?"

"What is there to object to in that? Mademoiselle, I will find you a husband while I look about me for one for Juno. No, no, do not color up. You are, perhaps, a trifle near to being on the shelf, an ape-leader, as we in England say of spinsters, and you've no dowry, of course, except what my husband settles on you." Lady Fairmont wrapped her chin in one hand, supporting that arm's elbow in her other hand. "Now let me think," she mused. "Would you object to a widower? I believe Sir Connaught is seeking a mother for his boys. Already having heirs, I doubt he'd demand much of you, my dear. I mean"—her voice dropped to an intimate level—"those duties a wife owes a husband. I believe you understand me? So, so long as you kept his house and nursery in order you could have a very good life and . . ."

"Maman, I hear Shipper," interrupted Zander, "I believe Tony has arrived. Do tell Juno to retie her bonnet and straighten her sash."

Lady Fairmont whirled, her gaze going critically over her daughter's costume. "Juno, how, in two minutes, can you ruin an hour's effort? Run up this instant and have a new sash tied for you and, when you return, do so without clattering down the stairs!" She turned back. "You've forgotten your parasol, mademoiselle," she added, abruptly. "Please find it."

Obediently, Beth, too, left the room. "Now, Zander," she heard as the door closed. She wondered what her ladyship was saying. She feared the worst. Actually, the worst was that she'd settled nothing with Zander. Finding occasions in the carefully chaperoned climate of a London town house for private conversation was difficult. She hoped Zander had a notion how to solve it.

Anthony, driving a double phaeton, took Lady Juno up beside him. They were a merry group, thanks to Juno who refused to adopt the prescribed bored manner and modest demeanor thought proper to a tonnish lady. Her comments concerning the sights they saw and the people they met kept them all in nearly constant laughter. Even Beth momentarily forgot her concerns.

Zander did not. As they neared the Serpentine in Hyde Park he blandly suggested they walk a bit so the girls could see the fall gardens which were different from the springtime beds.

Anthony, after a glance at his friend, pulled up, leaving the phaeton in charge of his groom who had stood up behind. The two couples strolled, greeting acquaintances and, occasionally, stopping to talk to a friend. When Juno and Tony fell into a discussion of imminent entertainments with Lady Chamberton and her daughter, Zander excused himself and Beth. They strolled some dozen yards further, far enough they'd not be over-heard.

"You fear," he said with no preamble, "that Smithson may make use of inventions which are unknown this time. Doohickeys you called them?"

Beth suppressed a grin. "Also gizmos or gidgets," she added, solemnly.

He pulled lightly at his nose, a habit when he was thinking. "I cannot like it that you'd be in danger, Beth."

"You forget I'm not one of your pampered young ladies. I merely resemble them when dressed in this fashion! I've had training in self-defense which would lay *you* flat on your back." His astounded look made her chuckle. "We can test that, if you wish. All we'd need is privacy for the experiment."

"It's impossible a slim little thing like yourself could prevent someone my size and with my strength from hurting you if I were wishful of doing so."

"I speak truth, Zander. There are martial arts which do

not involve the use of greater strength. One uses the enemy's attack against itself. I see," she added, "that you don't understand and would still forbid me to search that warehouse. Zander, if I *can* best you, will you help me?"

"When and how would you make this experiment?"

"Perhaps a drive into the country? A glade somewhere where we may be private? Or perhaps you know of a good sized room that you might have the use of for a brief interval?" When he looked as if he'd deny her the opportunity, she added, "If you *dare.*"

A muscle jumping in his jaw, Zander studied her expression which challenged him to find a way for her to prove herself. After a moment, he said, "My father has an estate up the Thames just beyond Chelsea. There's a little used carriage house. The loft is, I believe, empty. We'll go there."

"Zander, I fear Smithson may up sail and disappear if I don't move soon, so *when?*"

"As soon as I may arrange it without"—his exasperation was obvious—"rubbing my mother's sensibilities the wrong way! I don't understand what bee she's taken into her bonnet, but it's obvious one buzzes around it."

"Your mother wants you suitably married." She trapped his gaze with her own. "I'm not suitable, Zander."

His eyes flashed. "She insults you. You are—"

"Shhh. She cannot know my situation and we may not tell her. She fears you are infatuated to the point you'll do something foolish. Actually, *any* infatuation, even one involving dishonorable intentions, is a danger to her plans. Juno tells me she wishes you wed *and setting up your nursery.*"

Her emphasis got through to him. He thought about it. "Oh."

"That's all you have to say?"

"What do you wish me to say?"

"I don't know," she answered in a very small voice.

They were silent. Beth stared at the path, poking holes in

the gravel with the tip of her parasol. Zander stared into the trees where summer-heavy growth looked tired and dusty, ready for autumn and the end of their season.

"We'd best rejoin Lady Juno," said Beth.

After a moment Zander forced away depressing thoughts and agreed. "Yes, I suppose we'd better." He glanced toward his sister whose laughter-filled face was radiant as she looked into Anthony's grinning countenance. He took a second, longer, look. "Why, Juno is very nearly beautiful, is she not?"

"She's most attractive. It isn't so much that she's a beauty, but that her love of life, that special *joie-de-vie*, draws one. She glows with it."

"Whatever it is and before I saw it, I'd not thought her old enough to be presented. Now, why"—Zander looked offended—"she's become a woman and forgot to tell me of it!"

"You resent it?"

"Is that so strange? My baby sister? The pest? The nuisance? The dearest of my sisters!" A mock horrified expression underlined his teasing words. "I certainly *don't* approve of her growing up this way."

"Growing up and marrying."

"Marrying . . ." His eyes narrowed.

"Be very careful she isn't forced to wed where she doesn't wish it."

"You needn't worry on that head. I'll see she weds the right man when the time comes, but"—a faintly bewildered look crossed his face—"*surely* that won't be for a year or so."

"Zander, why do you think she insisted she be brought out *now* instead of waiting for the spring season which, I'm told, is more usual?"

He looked grim. "If it's true she thinks herself ready to wed, I must assume she has someone in mind. *Not,* I hope, that ass, Rupert Porthson."

"She's never mentioned the name."

"No, but that wouldn't be surprising, would it? It's un-likely she'd tell you her deepest secrets when she's just met you."

Which didn't stop her for a moment, thought Beth. "I wouldn't tell, in any case, if she'd told me secrets. It wouldn't be honorable."

"You will if you believe she's about to ruin her life, surely!"

Beth bit her lip. "Yes, of course in that case I'd do so."

"Even if it meant revealing secrets?"

Beth nodded.

"Good. I thought you a sensible woman—and it *wouldn't* be dishonorable. It'd be far less honorable to allow her, given her inexperience, to do something terrible when you might prevent it." He stared at her, daring her to disagree.

"We're in full agreement, Zander, but Juno just looked this way. I think she wishes to move on," said Beth, and changed the subject as she started back up the path. "I've enjoyed seeing the ton in all its glory. The variety of car-riages is amazing to one such as myself who has seen only a few still kept in museums." She grinned up at him. "I am *not* amused, however, by the smell. Your horses are beautiful, but they aren't house-broken!"

"My father visited Versailles before the Terror and even the *humans* weren't trained!" Zander said that with a dry tone and a sly look. When Beth didn't respond, he stopped their progress and added, "House-broken, I mean."

It was not, she suspected, a subject he'd raise with a fe-male of his own time. "I suppose bathrooms weren't readily available," she said prosaically, thwarting his mischief.

"Neither bathing facilities, nor adequate means for the relief of very basic human needs," he said, inadvertently pointing out that cleanliness had nothing to do with sanitary necessities which, in Beth's future, were combined into one room, "Father swore his own home would never stink so.

He had a patented water closet installed when our town house was built. It's been replaced as invention has improved that first, less than adequate, model. Before we can put in a bathing room, we must enlarge the cistern . . ." He looked at her, startled. "You amaze me, Beth. We discuss, as if we were two men, a subject which should have you swooning with embarrassment or bored to tears. I find it most refreshing."

"You remind me how easily I may give myself away." She glanced ahead. "Who is that officer? Lord Belmont seems rather irritated. Is it because the other man would be an unsuitable *parti* for your sister? Is that the word?"

Zander looked up, grinned, and urged her forward. "Unsuitable, no. Unlikely, *yes!* Porthson! When did you return to England? Oh! Allow me to introduce Mademoiselle Thevenard, a long lost cousin, who is staying with us. Beth? This is Captain Merrivelle Porthson, a neighbor and old friend."

The officer made polite noises to Beth before grasping Zander's lapel. "I've a bone to pick with you, my friend! I arrived in Lisbon only to discover you'd absconded, hours earlier, with the only speedy transport available! How dare you deprive the *real* military that way! You must have known I followed in your footsteps! I did, you know, very nearly literally! Even so I might have caught you up if my last mount hadn't thrown a splint just hours out of Lisbon. Could I find a new mount?" he asked in disgust. "Only the worst slug I've ever crossed. I *refuse* to call it a horse."

Zander grinned. "You managed, did you not? So. What's the news?"

His friend sobered. "We've come as close as *that* to doing the trick." He held his finger and thumb about half an inch apart. "I'll return as soon as maybe so as to be in at the end! But that won't be for some days. Perhaps a week or two. So," he asked with assumed arrogance, "what notions

have you for my entertainment?" He waited, as if for en-
lightenment.

"Will you be here for my ball, Merry?" asked Juno.

"Your ball? Can you possibly be old enough for a come-
out ball?" he asked. He looked Juno up and down and
grinned when she blushed. "Maybe you are. If I'm still in
London you couldn't keep me from it. Will you save me the
supper dance? Just in case?"

"I'll be happy to save you a dance, Merry, but the supper
dance has been claimed." Juno was obviously pleased she
could say so.

"Cancel it. You can't possibly have supper with anyone
but me," he teased. Juno shook her head. "So, who is the
favored one? Name him and I'll call him out."

"A duel!" said Anthony. "What fun! *I'm* to have the
honor, old friend." He studied his nails in an insouciant fashion. "You wish to duel me for it?"

The captain pretended to cower. "Lady Juno! I withdraw
my offer! Now if you'd been so unwise as to promise it to
my brother, which I freely admit I assumed, I could intimi-
date him into releasing you to me. But Anthony, here! No,
no. I'm not so foolish as to meet *him* across the green! I'll
return to Spain where I've only to face French guns. A far
safer proposition, I assure you!"

Everyone laughed and soon after Juno's party returned to
Belmont's phaeton. They continued their drive, but stopped
often to talk to men on horseback who demanded conversation with Zander about the war and, more or less inciden-
tally, introductions to the women. Lady Juno's glow didn't
fade until they'd left the park by way of the Stanhope gate.
And then it was Anthony's innocent question that caused it.

"Well, minx?" he asked, "Did you meet enough tall men
so that you'll have a choice of husband? I wouldn't have
Porthson, by the way. He's too much a rattle and not at all
suitable. Not in the least the sort of man I'd trust you to."

After a moment's hesitation, Juno asked, "What sort *would* do?"

"What sort? He must, of course, have a strong hand to keep you in line," teased Lord Belmont. "He must be tall since you feel awkward with a shorter man." He frowned. "What else, Zander, must we demand in a husband for our minx?"

"Someone like you," said Zander promptly. "The man would need a sense of humor, for instance, to put up with her fits and starts." Juno glared at him. He blinked, turned to look at Beth and discovered she'd turned her head to stare at the passing houses. He looked back to Juno, found her blushing slightly and looking at her hands which were neatly folded over her parasol. Then he took a look at his friend. "Don't you agree, Tony?"

"Someone like me? Perhaps. But Lady Juno prefers country living, does she not? She needs someone who will let her hunt."

"You hunt," said Juno so quietly it almost passed everyone by.

After a moment's thoughtful silence which included a sideways look at Juno, Anthony agreed. "Yes. Occasionally. With the Quorn." Gently, he added, "Women don't ride with the Quorn, Queeny."

Although she was silent Zander kept them from what might have been an awkward silence by asking Tony how the upcoming hunting season looked to be shaping. Anthony told tales of the Cubbing which he'd attended some weeks earlier.

"The pups are shaping well, then," said Zander. "I wonder if I'll be home for it this year. That would be a change, would it not? Do you suppose I've lost my facility with a regular rasper or a five barred gate?"

Anthony chuckled. "I suspect you've kept your hand in, riding rough in the Peninsula. Tell us!"

Zander looked amused. He filled in the rest of the way

home with a tale of riding cross country with some officers behind one of Wellington's irregular mountain guides. ". . . A born rascal. He'd rather steal you blind than take honest pay for honest work, even when he *enjoyed* the work. He led us by the worst possible route—just to test us, he admitted, when we accused him of it. He was a character," Zander finished, with a shake of his head, as they pulled up before the townhouse. "Will you come in, Anthony? I smuggled home a few bottles of the softest sherry you've ever tasted. My father claims his grandfather had a mountain sherry he'll never forget, but agrees this is better than any he's had in years." Before Anthony could respond, he added, "By the way, you talked to Merry longer than I did. When I left, San Sebastián was under siege. Did it fall?"

"Not yet. Merry expects orders for an assault on the walls any day, which is why he's on tenter-hooks to return. You could ask him for more news yourself, if you'd care to join us. I'm going with him to visit friends who were invalided home on the last hospital ship."

"Let's have the sherry in my room while I change. Very likely"—Zander was suddenly grim—"I, too, have friends among those sent home."

Juno brightened when Zander invited Anthony in but, as he went on, the glow faded, turning to determination. "Maman will wish to see Anthony," she objected. "Perhaps he'd join us in the salon while you change?"

The innocent expression which came naturally to Beth was patently false on Juno's face. Her brother took one look and opened his mouth to question her. Beth, knowing how embarrassed Juno would be, especially with Anthony already imbued with suspicion roused by the girl's question about hunting, pretended to twist her ankle. "Oh-h-h . . ."

Zander turned instantly and found her holding to the side of the carriage, her other hand reaching toward her leg which she'd lifted slightly. "What is it?" he asked.

"I very foolishly put my heel into that crack. Give me a

moment and I'll be fine." But when she took a step toward the house she pretended pain and cast a rueful glance at Zander. "I think I must lean on you, Cousin. Your arm, please?"

Instead, Zander scooped her up, smiling at her startled yip. "We'll take no chances. Ah, there you are, Shipper," he said to the hovering butler. "Kindly ask Mrs. Ambleside to come to Mademoiselle's room prepared to deal with a sprain. It may be nothing more than a twinge which rest will put right, but we must be certain."

"I'd better go," said Tony, feeling in the way.

"Please don't," said Juno, forestalling his exit by putting a hand on his arm. "Do come in and pay your respects to Maman. We might ask Shipper to locate that sherry Zander promised you . . ."

Juno pleaded silently with such big eyes Anthony found it impossible to deny her. Beth, noticing, closed *her* eyes, wondering if she should have a word with her new friend on the subject of scaring off one's prey by being too obvious. But then Zander added his casual invitation to his sister's and Anthony and Juno followed Zander, Beth in his arms, up the stairs. Those two went only so far as the salon while Zander climbed to the next floor. Instead of Mrs. Ambleside, Higgens followed them into Beth's room. She shooed Zander out and closed the door firmly.

"My ankle isn't hurt," said Beth once Zander was gone. The dresser's eyes narrowed. "I see."

"No you don't. Zander was about to embarrass Lady Juno. It was the only thing I could think to do to deter him from saying something in front of Lord Belmont which would put his sister to the blush."

Higgens nodded. "I *see.*" Awkwardly, she knelt in front of Beth. She put her hand behind a slim ankle and lifted. "How badly do you think it was hurt?" she asked, her face lacking expression. Beth giggled. "Perhaps wrapping it lightly and walking with a cane tonight and again tomorrow . . . ?"

"That should deal with the problem," said Beth, equally sober.

"Then tomorrow evening we'll see how you go on . . ."

The two women looked at each other gravely. But neither could restrain their sense of the ridiculous for long and, very softly, hands clasped over their mouths, guest and servant struggled to suppress laughter.

Beth suspected it was highly irregular in this particular time to have secrets with the servants but she didn't let it bother her!

Seven

Two days of low level irritation and major frustration passed with the slowness of treacle—a sweetener Beth found used in the kitchen. She'd gone in looking for Juno's cat and seen the cook, the tin held high, a wide stream of thick golden syrup oozing over the rim. Yes, time flows just like treacle, she thought, looking out the salon window at the rain which hadn't stopped since the night after her pretend accident. She traced the path of a rain drop, that of another . . . and another . . .

Behind her Juno practiced on the most beautiful piano Beth had ever seen. Purchased only a year earlier, the music box sat on six fat legs and had six octaves of keys. The sound was, to Beth's ears, a trifle high, nearer in tone to her grandmother's harpsichord on which she'd practiced when a child than to the pianos of the future with which she was familiar. Beth froze . . .

Harpsichord? Grandmother? Had she truly had a memory from her childhood? But she never remembered! Never . . .

At the salon door Beth looked over her shoulder, half panicked. Zander entered and she turned fully, rejecting the thought, which *couldn't possibly* be a memory. She leaned against the wide molding of the window frame, half hidden in heavy satin drapery and filled her eyes with Zander, making real memories of his commanding form, his face, the beautifully groomed hair. She fed hungrily on the sight, hoping for something to help her through the long hours, the days and years, when she'd never again catch a glimpse of him.

"Juno?" said Zander. "Where's our cousin?"

"She was here," responded Juno and missed a note. She said a word she shouldn't have known.

Zander, glancing around, ignored the oath and Beth stepped away from the wall. "I'm still here," she said and was chagrined to hear a plaintive note in her voice.

"You say that," said Zander, the sound of a laugh ill-hidden, "as if you fear you might never go anywhere ever again! We've just had word from Dovecot Manor that the new roof is leaking. My father wants me to have a look at it. Will you drive out with me?"

Juno turned on the piano bench. "May we? It is awful in town when one cannot go shopping or visiting and no one comes . . ." She tipped her head, studying her brother's expression. "You're scowling. Why?"

"I didn't invite *you,* Queeny."

"But it's raining. You'd can't go all that distance in a closed carriage," objected Juno. "All alone with Cousin Beth and no chaperon? Even I'm not so stupid I'd do such a thing."

"I'd thought to ask Higgens to chaperon," said Zander. "Her cousin works in the manor's dairy."

"Hmm. I don't *think* Higgens takes bribes . . ." Juno's dimple showed. "Surely she wouldn't visit with this cousin, leaving the two of you to your own devices!"

"And if she did? Do you think I'm not to be trusted? I resent the implication I'm a rake. Worse! An *unprincipled* rake! One who'd seduce his own cousin, given the first opportunity to do so."

"Miss Wilder told me—"

Juno spoke in a prim tone totally unlike anything Beth had ever heard from her.

"—men are *not* to be trusted."

Beth concluded Juno was teasing her brother.

"She suggested your *brother* is untrustworthy?"

Zander obviously didn't know whether to laugh or give into anger, an anger worsened, Beth guessed, by the fact he was tempted to behave in just such an unprincipled fashion as Juno implied.

It would be easy to stop Juno's teasing, thought Beth. All she need do is invite the girl to join them. But if she *did,* she and Zander wouldn't have the privacy in which to test her skill against his strength and she needed to win his help checking Smithson's warehouse. Of course Zander didn't expect her to win or he'd never have made the bargain! Poor Zander. He *was* in for a shock.

"Juno," said Zander, "will you do me the great favor of finding an excuse to remain home? I've no intention of seducing Beth, as you so childishly suggest, but we must discuss a few things in absolute privacy."

"Well, why didn't you say so? I'll always agree to help the course of true love."

"Love has nothing to do with it, you minx." He waited. "Well? Have you an excuse? It must be good if Maman is to accept it."

"Truth convinced *me.* Perhaps it would convince Maman, too," said Juno thoughtfully, a trace of color in her cheeks. "I've hopes, you see, that Anthony will drop by this afternoon. If he does, I'd not care to be absent."

"Anthony?"

Juno's blush deepened. "Lord Belmont, I mean."

Zander moved closer. "You can't possibly be so foolish as to set your cap for Tony."

Juno eyed him resentfully. "Why not?"

"Why not?" Zander ruined his valet's fine work on his hair. "Juno, if I can say nothing else to your credit, I can say you're no fool. *You know perfectly well why not."*

"But I don't," she said, stubbornness in the curve of her mouth and the tension in her shoulders. "He must marry.

Eventually. I know he doesn't dislike me. In fact, I think he's rather fond of me. So why not me?"

"The relevant word is *eventually.*"

"Maman says it's time *you* wed and he's the same age, is he not? If you must wed, then so must Anthony."

"I've no intention of walking into parson's mousetrap anytime in the immediate future."

"Maybe *you* have no such intention," said Juno with a grin, "but Maman does. What do you give for your chances?"

"A wager? You'll lose, minx. I very often give into our mother's whims, just as we all do. But I've never done if it's something of importance to me."

Beth stepped forward. "I think you've gotten far from the origins of this conversation," she said quietly. Beth agreed with Juno and feared Lady Fairmont would manage her son with Zander unaware he'd been manipulated. She was not looking forward to watching the process. "Juno, didn't your friend Rupert say he might drop by this afternoon?"

"So he did. I'll tell Maman I can't go because I asked Rupe to visit. I can hardly put him off so late as this. If I pretend I wish it were otherwise, she'll believe it!"

So it was arranged and soon, a large reticule in her lap, Beth stared as Zander pointed out houses in which people she'd met lived. It wasn't long, however, before they passed the toll gate at Hyde Park corner.

"We'll keep to this road until west of Kensington and then turn south. It's a longish way on such a miserable day, but that roof must be checked and it's best done while it rains so I can get a notion how bad it is. I thought you might enjoy the change," said Zander, rather formally and, obviously, for Higgens' benefit.

"I was bored to tears. If you'd suggested we merely go around the block a few times I'd have jumped at the notion . . . !" She trailed off when Higgens frowned slightly. Had she said something out of the way?

"Around the square, do you mean?" asked Zander, half curious and half helping her over the problem with Higgens.

Beth nodded. Once again she'd used a word from the future. It was so difficult, using this period's language when she didn't always know what was proper. Perhaps she'd better be still. During her self-imposed silence she thought over Zander's argument with Juno. "Zander," she asked abruptly, "would you object if Juno *were* to marry Lord Belmont?"

"Anthony? Why should I object? But where did Juno get the notion she and Anthony would ever walk into parson's mousetrap together? She must know he isn't the marrying kind. Not for years yet. By then Juno will have married and have several children in her nursery."

"She seems very attached to him," said Beth carefully.

"If anything, she's merely infatuated," said Zander with a touch of scorn.

"She *claims* she's loved him since she was a child."

"All the more reason to convince her to look at other men. One doesn't chose one's own true love while still in the school room!"

"You've never heard of childhood sweethearts marrying?"

"But this isn't that, is it? Anthony has never looked at Juno with an amorous thought in his head!" After a moment, and apologetically, he added, "Beth, if nothing else, my sister isn't the sort to catch his eye. That way."

For Higgens' benefit, Beth hoped she blushed at this too frank speech, but she feared she hadn't. "She told me her friend Rupert described the women Belmont takes an interest in but it didn't change her mind and I suggested she should look about her for a man interested in politics since she enjoys your mother's political-hostess style of entertaining. Nothing swerves her."

"My sister is not a fool, so why . . ." Higgens cleared her throat. "You've something to say?" Zander asked the maid politely.

"I shouldn't be so forward, of course," said the maid gruffly, "but you can't know Lady Juno has loved Lord Belmont for years. She's made no secret of that among those at The Aerie who love her. She's said she'd marry Lord Belmont or not at all."

"Oh, Lord, and she's stubborn enough to do it, too."

"Marry him?" asked Beth.

"No. *Refuse* to marry anyone else! Does Maman know?"

After the throat clearing and permission-asking glance to Zander, Higgens said, "I think not."

"Should I inform Maman, then?" he asked her.

Higgens muttered that she'd no opinion on that.

"Perhaps not. At least not just yet," suggested Beth. "Lord Belmont has paid Juno more attention than one might expect. Perhaps she isn't so far out in her plans as one would think."

"She has air in her bone-box," said Zander scornfully. Higgens tut-tutted softly at the use of cant words and he apologized to Beth before dropping into a brown study.

Beth contented herself with watching the passing scenery which here, in the rain-washed country, appeared much like an Impressionist painting, a school of art which would not be invented for decades. Or perhaps it was more like the contemporary artist, Constable, who often captured a dream-like and idealistic version of such rural scenes!

When they arrived Beth looked at Dovecot Manor and wondered if it were already known as a Cottage Ornè or if that term would be applied to the style by later generations. Its thatched roof and leaded windows delighted her and she was charmed by the intimacy and comfort of the smallish rooms. Mrs. Wharton took Beth over the house and blushed rosily at Beth's compliments. Of course they ignored the buckets catching drips in two of the bedrooms!

The rain turned to a drizzle as Beth waited in a parlor and then to a mere mist. She asked Wharton to inform Zander she'd be outside, exploring, knowing he'd understand she gone to find the carriage house.

It too was thatched, but the thatch looked much older. She wondered if the leaks would, therefore, be worse. Shrugging, she made her way up a narrow ladder nailed to the wall which led to the loft Zander said would do for their combat. She walked across the plank floor, bouncing now and again. It was solid. There wasn't a chance Zander would go through it when she trounced him. She looked up, frowned. This thatch *was* older, surely. Why was it dry and the house thatch not?

Shrugging the thought aside as irrelevant, Beth pulled the golden sarong out of her reticule. Quickly undressing she wrapped the large square in a different fashion from the style she'd worn aboard ship. This wrap left her arms and legs free, ready for action. She did warm-ups, glad she'd exercised every night and morning. Not that there was space in her room for a real work-out, but at least she didn't feel as if muscles and tendons had shrunk and tightened. When she heard Zander enter below, she stopped stretching, turned, and stood with legs slightly spread. Fists on hips, she waited.

Zander came up the ladder, his head rising above the floor boards. He rushed the next few steps and straightened, staring at her. "Beth Ralston, put on some clothes!"

"If I ruin that gown what do I wear home? I'll change when we've finished."

"Finished! I'll finish you. How dare you stand there like a shilling whore and show no shame? A Convent Garden *doxy* would feel dishonor to reveal her limbs as you are doing!" He advanced, eyes hot and hands moist. "Or did you make a fool of me, my dear Beth? Was I bamboozled into believing you a decent woman? I should have known— given that rag you wear by preference!"

He circled and she moved easily to face him.

"Well?" he shouted. "Have you no defense? You'd best speak quickly, m'love, because, if you can't convince me otherwise, I'm about to do what I've wanted to do since I watched you appear on board Smithson's ship. Witch . . . Harlot . . . Hussy . . . *Slut* . . ." On the last word, he lunged.

Beth looked down to where Zander lay blinking up at her. She was too well trained to get in reach of his hands and, once she'd assured herself he wasn't hurt, she backed farther away. He climbed to his feet, shaking his head.

"Convinced?" she asked.

He snarled and approached again. Again he found himself lying on the floor. This time he didn't stay there too surprised to move, but was instantly up and at her. The result was the same. And still again. He rose more warily this time, approached more slowly . . .

"What will it take?" she asked as he landed heavily.

He stared up at her. "What the devil do you do to me?"

"It's a form of self defense developed in the far east."

"Which tells me nothing. What did you *do?*"

"If you promise to relax and allow me to show you, I'll do so. But if you still mean to satisfy your insulting and base urges, you may go to the devil."

He grinned. "I think you've dampened any, er, *insulting* urges I might have had. So"—he got to his feet—"what do I do?"

"Come at me slowly. I won't actually throw you but will show you the hold I take and the movement which results in the throw."

He came at her, his arm extended. She grasped it in two places, turned into him, leaned over . . . and discovered herself held around the waist by his other arm. She straightened, her back against his chest. "This is the way you keep your word?" she asked.

"I gave you no promise and I deserve one kiss," he murmured into her ear, his breath warm, tickling . . . He rubbed against the sarong. "Beth . . . ?"

"By Pete Seegar's guitar!"

"I truly didn't mean for this to happen, but, Beth, I don't think I can survive without tasting those lovely lips . . ."

"And Happy Harpy's electric fiddle."

"You aren't cooperating, Beth . . . my love . . . ?"

"Sorry, Zander." Beth sighed, shifted her weight, and did something which had him, once again, staring at the roof.

Except he wasn't. His eyes were closed and one arm lay at an odd angle. He groaned.

"Zander!" Suspicious, she approached slowly. "Zander?"

She was, she discovered, right to be suspicious. She'd just knelt on one knee when the arm she'd feared hurt snaked out and enclosed her in a hug from which there'd be no escape. She pressed her hands against his chest, stared into his twinkling eyes. "You're a true bastard, are you not?"

"Beth! You insult my mother!"

"Why, Zander? I thought we agreed this was folly."

He quoted lines from Goldsmith:

> "When lovely woman stoops to folly,
> And finds too late that men betray,
> What charm can soothe her melancholy,
> What art can wash her guilt away?"

"I may have difficulty with the melancholy bit, but I don't feel guilt. You're the guilty one. We had an agreement, Zander." He didn't let her go. "This *is* folly, Zander, and you know it!"

He nibbled on her bare shoulder. "According to Horace, you should *mix a little folly with your wisdom; a little nonsense is pleasant now and then.* Just a little nonsense, Beth?"

"Our agreement!"

"What agreement?" he muttered, his fingers moving into her hair, doing astonishing things to her scalp just behind her ear.

She gritted her teeth. "If I could prove to you I was able to defend myself, you'd help me find a way to search for Smithson's cache."

His teeth, scraping lightly against her skin, did incredible things to her equilibrium. A moan escaped her. His hands, the one in her hair and the other on her hip, played their own role in seducing her to folly.

"But you see?" he whispered. "I've won after all."

"I'd not be tempted by friendship to get close to an enemy so don't use that as an excuse for this . . . this . . ."

"Seduction?"

Both hands shifted to the back of her head, pulling her mouth down to his. His lips brushed back and forth against hers. "Kiss me, Beth. Please. I'm dying with the need to taste you." His mouth covered hers, increasing the pressure slowly but not painfully. His tongue touched her mouth, followed the line of her closed lips.

"Beth?" he asked quietly. "One kiss?"

She gave in to the hot urges forming whirlpools of sensation within her. Collapsing against him, her hands slipped up his chest, around his neck and, relaxing, her mouth opened to his persistent quest . . . Shortly, she found he'd turned them so that she lay on her side and he leaned over her, one hand resting on her waist, the other arm a pillow for her head.

"You're amazing, Beth," he said in a husky voice that creamed around her and stole throughout her mind and soul. "I want more. Much much more."

"Folly indeed," she whispered.

"Still no guilt?"

"No. Just deep melancholy that we may never have more than this." She touched his cheek, cupped her hand to his face and drew it back to hers. "Just this. No more."

This kiss was quite as explosive as the first and when it ended Zander rolled away. "Why no more?" he asked, his arm covering his eyes as if he were in pain. "Beth, we were made for each other. You must know that as surely as I do. Stay with me. Marry me and raise a family . . ." He opened one eye and looked at her. "Someday you'd be Countess of Fairmont, you know."

"As if *that* would bribe me to your bed! Zander, I've a duty. You would never ask one of Wellington's officers to run from his responsibilities. You know you would not," she answered the point. "Well, I'm an officer in our little army. You may think the rescue of art from certain destruction an odd calling and you may think it unimportant compared to defeating Napoleon, but it's important to me and to those to whom I'm responsible." She waited. "Zander?" she asked when he didn't respond.

"Women are not soldiers. They don't bear the responsibility of which you speak. They are to be cared for, cosseted—they are the mothers of our children, dammit! That's far more responsibility than any man ever has, although," he added on a sardonic note, "we don't often admit it. But folly—Beth, continuing to work for ART is folly, not the love we bear each other."

"You're very sure I love you."

"Very sure." There was no hesitation and no question.

For a moment she closed her eyes. "How can you know my feelings?" she asked on a breath of sound, wondering how he could be so very sure when she herself, in heart and mind, was not.

He lifted the arm over his eyes, looked at her, and grinned. "I may not have known you long, love, but I know you'd not have kissed me in that particularly passionate way if you felt no love for me!" He ran a finger from her wrist to the sensitive inner side of her elbow. "Don't tell me differently!"

"It is different for a man, is it not? You need not love me just to kiss me so."

"I need love you to propose marriage. Which I've done. Or didn't you notice?" A touch of hurt colored his words.

"I noticed," she admitted, "but ignored it. You can't mean it."

"But I do. You heard Juno. Maman says it's time I marry. According to Maman, at least, Maman knows best. So I'll submit. I'll marry *you*."

Beth rolled away and, in turn, covered her face. "Don't tease so."

"Who's jesting? You must, I suppose, finish your work here," he said, "and rescue those paintings and also, I suppose, find evidence if you can of Smithson's game. So we'll do that. Together. But then you'll resign from ART and we'll wed and we'll live happily ever after. Come here." He reached toward her.

"We'd better return to the house, Zander," she said in something of a rush. "I fear we've been gone too long as it is."

"What is it, Beth?" He paused and then, his voice tight, asked, "Perhaps that you won't give up the far future to live only in mine? I can see that that might be a far greater sacrifice than any I could make for you."

"It isn't that, Zander. I'd do that in a minute. But you've forgotten the main problem."

"I don't see any problem."

"You're just being stubborn because you *do* know it. I *am* from the future and I don't belong here. You'll want children. *I* want children, but we couldn't have them. My children, here, in the past, would be an anomaly. They might alter the course of history, affect the future so it's far different from what we know it to be now." For a long moment they were silent. She clutched her stomach. "It hurts, Zander. It hurts to even think of what we might have together and know it's impossible."

Zander sat up, his arms loosely twined around his bent knees. He stared at her, stubbornly, silently, demanding she change her mind. She didn't. He sighed, looked away.

"God, it truly hurts . . . Zander?"

"It hurts me too, Beth."

After another moment's silence she repeated, "We'd better go."

He grinned a lopsided sort of smile. "But not like *that*, Beth, love."

She blushed. "No. Of course not like this. You go down and I'll follow in a moment."

He leaned over and wiped his thumb along her cheek. "Just a smudge of dust, love. No! *Please,*" he begged, jerking his hand away, "don't cry! Beth, I can't bear it if you cry." He rose to his knees and leaned toward her, not daring to touch her, knowing that, if he did, he'd not stop with touching.

Beth struggled to contain her tears. "Go down, Zander. You may have to play lady's maid since I mightn't reach all the hooks, but I'm sure you've enough experience for that." She scowled, pretending to chide him, and knew it wasn't entirely pretense.

Again he touched her cheek with the tip of one finger. "Only with *ridding* a woman of her clothes, Beth. I've never helped one dress." He said it with a self-deriding grimace. She smiled as he'd meant her to do. It was a weak smile but a smile nevertheless; the tears were stemmed—for the moment at least.

Zander went down the ladder and leaned against the wall. Stuffing his hands into his pockets, he crossed one leg over the other at the ankle, his head bowed, staring at the pounded dirt floor.

Why had he done it? he wondered. Not that that wasn't obvious. He'd been carried away by the feel of her, by her kisses, so tentative at first, but soon as enthusiastic as his own. But why had he'd confessed love for a woman so far out of his ken she must be laughing at him. She hadn't agreed, exactly, when he'd said she loved him. Perhaps all she felt was a kindly meant affection, a facade of love. A woman from the far future could not truly love someone from her past—a man so *ignorant* in comparison to herself, his life circumscribed by the limitations of his era. He groaned. What a fool he was.

When he heard Beth approach the ladder, he pulled away from the wall and looked up. She stared down at him, her expression as solemn as his own. "Well?" he asked, wondering if she'd tell him it was all a terrible mistake, that only the passion of the moment had carried her away, that he must never touch her again . . .

"It has occurred to me," she said, "that coming *up* a ladder is a far different thing than going *down* it."

He blinked. That was it? *That* was all that occupied her mind? Had their kisses, his protestation of love, his proposal, meant no more to her than that? "You can't get down?"

"If you'd ever been forced to wear a narrow skirt over a tight petticoat you might have a jot of understanding for my problem. As it is, you're exceedingly uncaring. I don't believe this is the same man who just promised eternal love. By the Life of Lena Horne, Zander, was that no more than the heat of the moment? The hope your words would get me into your bed? Turn your back! I'll manage the best I can and hope I don't tear anything."

Zander's brows rose. "You think I might not love you?" He chuckled. The chuckles turned to full throated laughter, the release from his lack of faith in her so freeing he had to hold his sides.

"I don't see the least humor in this situation. Why should I trust facile words when your libido's involved? Men have always used words to fool women."

"Don't be cross love. Please," he coaxed and added, "And when did you learn Latin?"

She reddened. "In the future it isn't Latin, any more . . ." That sounded strange and she worked out why. "I mean *libido* has been taken into every day English. Forget I said it. But I don't see why I *shouldn't* be cross. I truly didn't think you'd *laugh* at me. I know I'm not very experienced, but was my participation in our kisses so very bad?"

He climbed the ladder in about two jumps. Sliding his hands up and down the fabric covering her arms, he wished he were touching skin as he'd done earlier. "Sweetheart, there was nothing laughable about the kisses we shared. I hope we share many more. I laughed because, as I waited for you, I wondered if you could really love me or if it were only the heat of the moment or *worse,* a *kindness* on your part for the poor fool from the past who has had the temerity to lose his heart to you."

"Oh Zander." She lay her forehead against his chest and he wrapped her in a tender embrace. For a long moment they stood there. "I've heard people in love are often foolish," she muttered.

"Let's be different. From now on we'll trust each other and we won't dream up complications where there are none."

"We must talk to each other," she agreed, "ask questions, when we're confused or angry or don't understand."

"Exactly. And now I think about it, I know a way of getting you down that ladder."

"You do?"

"Hmm. But first a kiss." The kiss was all one should be. Tender yet passionate; demanding and, simultaneously, promising; loving. They stared at each other.

"That will have to last a very long time," he said softly.

"It seems hard a man and woman may not be alone together whenever they wish."

"And if we were, how soon would we cease to be satisfied with kisses?"

She glanced up only long enough to be sure it was amusement she'd heard in his tone, then ducked her head again. She knew her cheeks glowed with embarrassment. "Perhaps you're right."

"I'm know I am."

"Well, it's likely you'd know more about all that than I do," she said a trifle peevishly.

Something of which he knew more than she? Zander tipped his head. So, there was much she knew he could never know. He *was* ignorant. But that didn't mean there weren't some areas in which he had more knowledge, more experience. Besides, she knew next to nothing of his era. She needed him for that if nothing else. Perhaps there was not *quite* such inequality between them as he'd feared.

"Zander?"

"I can't know more about love than you, my dear," he said softly, "for the simple reason I've never before experienced it."

"But we weren't exactly referring to *love,* were we?"

"I'd love to carry on this discussion forever," he equivocated, "but Mrs. Wharton will send someone looking for us if we don't return. She's preparing a meal for us! Let me look at you." He turned her, unfastened a hook which was done up wrong. He put it and others right, raked the ends of his fingers lightly over her hair, tucking ends into the simple knot she'd worn that day. Then he turned her. "You'll do, I think."

"Now you."

He turned and Beth put a hand on his hip, stopping him. She brushed his back lightly, then firmly. "I can't get the dust out." She whacked him. "Zander, perhaps you'd better take off your coat so we can beat properly."

"Does it show badly?"

"Your valet, at least, can't fail to notice. Oh dear, a seam is coming apart!"

"Merrit will fuss and stew, but he'll not question me and it would be beneath him to speak of it to others. Come here and I'll let you down to the floor below."

"What do you mean?"

"I'll grasp your wrists, like this, and simply lower you."

So simple, she thought, as her feet touched the floor below.

Eight

Beth stared at the golden square of material laid flat on her bedroom floor which acted as a receiver for goods and information from the future. Sending was the problem. Communicating with Suu-Van was exceedingly difficult with no more power than the limited capacity built into the threads—unless, of course, she were so trite as to write a silly letter, cramping her handwriting into the smallest possible space! But it was a rule with her: Beth was never trite . . .

She looked idly around the room, her gaze settling on a long black thread left over from some mending earlier that day. With it she outlined a cat's face with a mask over the eyes. Would Suu-Van understand? For a moment Beth wondered if she'd gone too far. But Suu-Van liked cryptograms. Surely he'd enjoy this one.

Next she contorted herself into the pretzel shape required to place her toes and her fingers on just the right spots on the sarong. It was an awkward position, but necessary to complete the circuits which activated the micromachinery and the limited energy resources built into the material. She held the position, then, thankfully, uncurled, rising to her feet. The black cat face had disappeared.

Briefly, an oddly high whine that hurt the teeth surrounded her. It stopped and in the center of the gold material lay a neat pile of black clothes, an encoded letter on mono-thin paper centered on top:

You are a lucky child that I know the twentieth century so well, my chuck. Here are your cat burglar clothes with the built-in devices you'll need. About time you contacted us. I'd begun to wonder if our devil had shown claws and scratched you from our lists before ever you'd found our proof. Have you met The Man? Is he beautiful? Take care, child, for it would sorrow me to lose you to The Eternal.
Suu-Van

Beth frowned as she reread the note from her mentor. Of course she'd met their devil. He was the contact point in this era. And Suu-Van knew that. So what did he mean by the man? And beautiful? The foxy captain with his adam's apple and overly long, thin nose could never by any stretch of the imagination be considered beautiful. Who would Suu-Van think beautiful?

A deep red flooded up from somewhere near Beth's waist. Could Suu-Van know she'd meet Zander? Did he have fore-knowledge she'd find a man here whom she could love?

But of course he could; likely, he knew the outcome of this whole caper! Twice, to Beth's knowledge, he'd sent agents into the past, knowing they'd not return. Had he done that to her? If so, surely his wording would be different. In fact, he'd not have mentioned the possibility of her death, would he, if it were an actual probability? Beth suffered further confusion: Her message had been set to return only hours after she'd left the twenty-third century—so why did Suu-Van feel it long coming?

And just what did he know about Zander—assuming Zander was The Man? Did that mean . . . ? But how could one assume . . . ? Beth shivered. This operation was complicated beyond belief. It was bad enough she was falling in love with Zander. It would be impossible if Suu-Van looked over her shoulder as she did so!

Voices roused her from her jumble of thoughts and, hurriedly, she bundled up the sarong, the clothes and letter inside. She stuffed them into her armoire. Surely Juno and her mother were back too soon! Hadn't they meant to call on three of Lady Fairmont's friends? Beth had remained home ostensibly because she had a headache, so she'd better repose herself on her chaise longue before Juno looked in.

The younger girl, opening the door and seeing that Beth was reading rather than sleeping, stepped in. "How are you?" she asked.

"Much better. Should you be home so soon?"

"Now Maman has a headache. Perhaps it is catching?" Juno's eyes twinkled. "I believe her particular headache is named Zander," she said softly, looking toward the door as if she feared her voice might carry beyond it to her mother's ears.

"Tell me," suggested Beth, her head beginning to hurt for real.

"You know Maman insisted he accompany us today?"

Beth nodded. It was one reason she'd decided to remain at home—the chance of contacting Suu-Van, the other, of course.

"He went. Reluctantly, I think. Almost as if he knew what Maman had in mind. When we left the Cheswicks, he told me to get into the carriage and drew Maman aside. Soon she joined me but he strode off down the street and Maman had the headache. So we came home."

"So?"

Juno giggled. She lowered her voice. "You know very well what happened." Beth pretended to be uncertain. "Maman was match making, silly, and Zander wasn't having anything to do with it!"

Beth's head cleared instantly. "I can't believe your mother would be so blatant as to set up his back!"

"Maman wasn't obvious, but Miss Cheswick *was*. She'd been primed by her mother that Zander's visit was important. She made a fool of herself," said Juno with more than a trace of scorn. "Maman meant to introduce Zander to two other young ladies as well, but she's writing notes that the introductions must be postponed."

"Did she tell you all this?"

Juno spoke thoughtfully. "I think she said more than she intended. When she got into the carriage she was upset and needed to talk and I was there. I don't know *exactly* what Zander said, but he couldn't have been very polite which is strange. Zander is always polite."

"No wonder your poor mother is upset. Is there something we should do?"

"Stay out of the way!" Juno laughed again. "You don't know what it's like when Maman is thwarted! She can become a veritable storm, a—a—what do you call those great winds they have in the Islands?"

"A cyclone? Typhoon? . . . Hurricane?"

"That's it. A Hurricane. You know so much," said Juno admiringly. "I don't know how you can."

"I've lived longer and studied and talked to people—"

"You've not had an easy life, have you?" asked Juno gently and Beth wondered why admitting to an education and variety in life led the girl to say such a thing. "Well, that life is over. We'll see you are never again at the beck and call of some thoughtless mistress or need suffer embarrassment from a master!"

"Embarrassment?" asked Beth cautiously.

"It is whispered you escaped from persecution by your last master—that you escaped in the nick of time!"

"Who is talking?"

"The servants, of course. My Miss Wilder told me, a dire warning, you see, of what happens if one is forced to earn one's living. I'd guess Higgens told Miss Wilder and Higgens had it from Maman who must have had it from Zander since I don't suppose you told her the tale . . . Well?"

"Juno . . . Are you asking if the story is true?"

"*Did* you have a man pursuing you and insisting he have

his way with you?" Juno's eyes were about to pop from her head from curiosity.

Beth laughed. She took another look at Juno and doubled over, laughing harder.

Juno pouted. "It is a terribly serious subject. Why do you laugh?"

"Mostly your expression. You looked so hopeful—as if waiting for a high treat!"

Juno flushed. "Did I? I'm sorry, but I'm curious. No one will tell me what happens when a man has his way with a woman and I want to know. I thought perhaps you would tell me."

"Since the gentleman did *not* have his way, I don't think I can." It was only half a lie. No gentleman had "had his way" with her, but her education had been embarrassingly thorough! "I ran away and your brother brought me here. However, I'm much too distant a connection to hang on your father's sleeve as I'm doing. I feel badly about that, Juno. I really should find a position . . ."

Juno shook her head so firmly a lock of hair fell down. She pinned it more or less into place as she said, "No. It must not be. You are too nice, too much my friend. We will present you and you will take and, by the end of the season someone will have fallen madly in love with you and will ask you to marry him and you'll be safe forever and ever." Juno beamed at her idealistic view of Beth's future.

"What if I don't fall in love as well?"

Juno's expression of ecstasy faded. "But that isn't important. Is it?"

"I think it is. Perhaps I'm a strange creature, but I'd rather be a duenna again than marry just any man so that I needn't do so!"

"Don't say that where Maman can hear you. She'd be shocked."

"I'm certain she would." Beth sighed, thinking of her reserved and very correct hostess. "I'm very certain she'd not be backward in saying so, either . . ."

"You mean because she'd like you out of the house," said Juno, nodding. "You mustn't let Maman upset you. She's not at all hard-hearted and won't force you to marry someone you truly cannot like. I don't understand why she's cold toward you, because it's not usually her way."

Beth gave Juno a straight look. *"Don't* you understand it?"

Juno flushed. "Well, I think it may have something to do with Zander's interest in you. For some reason she doesn't feel you a suitable bride for him. I don't understand *that* either, because you'd suit to a cow's thumb!"

"What a very strange expression!"

"Isn't it wonderful?" Juno giggled. "I learned it from one of our maids at The Aerie and have known it forever and ever so long. Now I've used it a couple of times I don't suppose I'll do so again, so don't I'll worry I'll blurt it out in company. Beth, has your headache come back? You look a bit strained around the eyes."

"I fear it has. Perhaps I should try to sleep a little."

"Shall I get you a powder? And perhaps a tray here rather than dressing for dinner?"

"I shouldn't like to make extra work for the servants. I'll dress." She glanced away and added, "After I rest." Would Juno take the hint?

She did. "I'll leave you, if you're quite certain I can do nothing?"

"Nothing."

Juno went through the connecting door and closed it softly. Beth went to it and put her ear near the crack. She heard Juno's hall door open and close indicating the young woman had gone downstairs. Beth went immediately to her armoire and took out the bundle she had hidden in such a rush. Where was she to put it?

Servants made life difficult. The maid she shared with

Juno had the right to get into any of her drawers. Under the mattress would never do. She'd come in one day when two maids were turning it. Beth hugged the bundle to her, spinning slowly, surveying the room. Her eye was caught by the window seat. Would it, like those on Smithson's ship, open?

She lifted gently. The lid squawked. And cobwebs! If there were cobwebs, then no one had looked in it for many a long year and was unlikely to do so anytime soon. Beth dumped her cat-burglar clothes into the storage space and, avoiding the squeak as well she could, eased the top down. The next time she was certain to be alone she must rub candle wax on the hinges as she'd seen a footman do to the library door only a day previously.

But now she was ready for the warehouse. It needed only a few minutes alone with Zander to decide when they'd go!

Her chance came that evening when she went down early to dinner and found Zander in the salon where the family gathered. "Have we a moment, do you think?" she asked.

He glanced toward the door which the footman, quite properly, had not completely closed. "Probably no more than that," he said softly. "Why?"

"We must decide when to take our little jaunt to the wharf."

"I rather hoped you'd think better of it."

Beth glared. "I've no choice. It must be late. The later the better."

"Not this week."

"Are you procrastinating?"

"No. My calendar's full. I'll see about next week."

"He may empty his stash, taking it to the ship. We must go soon."

"Yesss."

"Zander, I'll go alone if I must. You know that, don't you?"

He scowled. "You must not."

"Then *soon.*"

"Perhaps"—he hesitated—"Sunday night?"

"No *perhaps* about it." Beth glared until he nodded. "I'll meet you at the end of the mews."

"You'll do no such thing." He'd forgotten to keep his voice soft and glanced again toward the doors. "I'll escort you from the house."

"Zander, I must leave in a fashion no one knows I'm gone, so don't argue. I'll meet you beyond the mews!"

His scowl deepened but before he could respond the door opened. He turned and found his mother staring at him.

"Are you arguing?" she asked, with an interested look.

"As a matter of fact we are. Women are skitter-witted. Even the best of them. *You* among them, as I discovered just today!"

Lady Fairmont blushed. "Zander . . ."

"No! We've pulled that crow. I apologize that I raised the point again."

Beth suspected Zander wasn't at all sorry. He'd distracted Lady Fairmont from questioning the cause of their disagreement, but left the lady with the good feeling that her son and Beth had argued.

"Zander," his mother said urgently, "you must understand I make my plans for your good. You *must* admit you've reached an age when it is important to think of such things."

"Mother, I have said all that need be said on the subject. I'll not discuss it further. If you persist in doing so, I'll find rooms and move out. I'll not be harassed or pressured or tricked into a marriage of convenience merely because you've decided it's time."

The conversation ended on that abrupt note when Juno and her father entered. Beth had only briefly met Zander's father. Lord Fairmont had been out most evenings and now she studied him as they were re-introduced and realized that that was exactly how Zander would look as he aged.

Lord Fairmont had the same tall well built frame, although his lordship had added a few unneeded pounds.

There was the same wild, carefully controlled hair, although his had silvered at the temples. And the same strong features which lost nothing by the addition of a few lines. Lord Fairmont greeted Beth warmly but then, his mind obviously elsewhere, seemed to forget her, just as absently guiding his wife into the dinner which Shipper announced just then.

Once Lord Fairmont had eased his hunger he looked around the table. "Well now," he said. "What have you planned for your evening?"

Lady Fairmont looked up from her plate. "What?" she asked.

"I merely wondered what you've planned for your evening, my dear," repeated his lordship a trifle testily.

"Lady Grossington's card party, I think. Once Juno is launched, I'll have no time for simple pleasures. And you, my lord?"

"Hurumph. Be meeting with the prime minister as usual. Trouble, trouble. Always trouble. How about you, Alexander? Liverpool asked about you the other day." He eyed his son, a speculative gleam in his eye. "The earl would like to meet with you. I think he has work for you . . ."

"I've arranged to meet friends at Whites, Father. Perhaps another time."

"Hurumph." For a moment it looked as if Lord Fairmont might argue the point. Finally he nodded. "Keep you to that, son. About time we drew you in. Need younger men in the party and you'll soon come to your senses about those Whiggish notions you once held."

"Only a very few Whig notions! I certainly can't go along with their policy that Napoleon be allowed his way!"

"Yes, but now and again you've spouted all that nonsense about Catholic emancipation and other reform nonsense. You'll get over it, though," added his lordship complacently, nodding once before turning to look through his quizzing glass at the tray of desserts a footman held for his inspection.

Tactfully Zander held his tongue although Beth felt he

boiled inside at his father's comfortable assumption. What remained of the meal passed with desultory conversation and no more potential for controversy. Beth was glad. She didn't like it when her host family was at loggerheads. It wasn't comfortable. Especially when she herself was the cause of some part of it.

The days passed slowly. She continued to go down to dinner early, but didn't find Zander alone until Sunday evening.

"What time?" he asked.

"About two?"

"Half an hour to reach the wharf . . . We must start back no later than four to arrive before the servants begin their work."

"That should allow time."

His glower deepened. "You still insist you meet me out back?"

"Yes."

Leaning against the mantelpiece, he stared into the small fire which had been laid to take off the evening chill. Again his mother walked in to find a strained air between them and, relaxing as she rarely did in Beth's presence, she joined their guest on a sofa near the fire to study the length of embroidery Beth had begun.

Lady Fairmont actually seemed pleased with Beth. "You had your last fitting for your ball gown yesterday," said her ladyship. "How did you like it, Cousin Elizabeth?"

Zander looked up at his mother's friendly tone. He glanced from her to Beth and back to the fire.

Beth stifled a sigh and answered that she thought the dress far too expensive a gift. "I feel guilty accepting so much."

"We'll find you a husband quite easily, I think. Far more easily than for our Juno. She'll be a choosy one, I fear." Lady Fairmont sighed. "Children are such a worry," she said, her gaze flitting toward Zander.

"Cousin Juno will make many friends, I think," said Beth.

"She's one who enjoys the company of others and doesn't fear to let them know it."

"Perhaps to too great a degree," said her ladyship, on a rueful note. "My daughter is like a puppy. Too friendly, her tail wagging at the least sign of interest, and yap yap yap when anyone is willing to speak with her. I wish she were more like you, Mademoiselle."

"Perhaps it is merely that I am older."

"It is also that Mademoiselle," inserted Zander, "was forced to take responsibility for herself, to find work to keep body and soul together. It cannot have been easy for her and her experiences in life would mature anyone, is that not so, Maman?"

"It is terrible it was necessary," commiserated Lady Fairmont, "but it is also true, what Zander says, that necessity matured you. I'd not wish such a life for my Juno, even if it *were* to result in greater confidence and a more seasoned presentation of herself."

"One could not wish such a life on anyone," agreed Beth. "I don't think you should worry about Juno, my lady. Her company manners are perfect. It is only among friends she reveals that wonderfully joyful side."

"Joyful." Lady Fairmont stared at Beth, blinking thoughtfully. "What a strange word to use and yet so apt. How odd that a stranger should see so clearly."

"Perhaps it is *because* I'm a stranger. I see what is *now* without all the expectations and memories collected over the years which must make it more difficult to see things as they've become."

"Things? Or people?" Lady Fairmont looked at her son who stared into the fire. "Zander, for instance. How do you see my son, Miss Thevenard?"

"Lord Hawksbeck is, I think, his own man," said Beth carefully. "He has put behind him his disappointment that his father forbade him to join the army and has found a place for himself which satisfies his need to be *doing*. He will, I think, make his own decisions, but will do so tactfully, without harming his relationship with you and his father."

Lady Fairmont smiled. "You are thinking, are you not, of the political discussion at the table the other night. I know Zander has *not* given up all reform notions as his father fondly, but blindly, wishes! I heard my son discussing them with Lady Melbourne—a fervent Whig, you know—just the other evening."

Beth cast a quick glance toward Zander and then back to her hands. It had not occurred to her he attended social affairs. She had, for reasons which now seemed odd, assumed he spent his evenings at his club or other male gathering places. She forced her fingers to relax. She'd no right to object!

But parties. Parties where he'd meet the women his mother wished him to meet? Carefully Beth forced her fingers to relax all over again. Luckily Juno arrived just then forcing her to turn her mind from jealousy for the unknown women Zander met at the entertainments he honored with his presence!

Juno joined Beth in her room once the other members of the family left for their various evening appointments. "It will be much better once my presentation at the Queen's drawing room is done and our ball over. Then we may go out every evening and meet people and see our friends. And dance!" Her eyes glowed. "Haven't you enjoyed our dancing lessons, Beth? I like them much better than visits to the modiste where we must stand still and *even then* get poked by pins!"

"But, Juno, the reason you are poked is that you *don't* stand still."

"I *try*," said Juno, pouting, "but it is difficult." Her mood shifted in the mercurial way it had. "I asked Zander to drive us in the park tomorrow. You'll come, will you not?"

"Tomorrow?" Beth wondered if she'd be too exhausted after this evening's adventure. Could she convince Juno she was tired and meant to go to sleep early? In an effort to do just that, Beth yawned widely.

Juno followed suit and asked, "What else would you do? Maman's planned nothing for us at the time of the promenade."

"Oh, late afternoon. I wasn't thinking, Juno."

"You are the funniest one. But I keep forgetting you didn't grow up here. You don't just *know* how things are done. I do because I've come to London during the season the last few years even if I couldn't do much. Just children's parties and dancing parties where we'd practice and an occasional picnic organized for us younger ones. Of course Miss Wilder took me to exhibits and the Tower and other Places of Interest." Beth heard the capital letters on the last words. "At least," added Juno, "they were *supposed* to be of interest, but mostly they were not."

Beth again pretended to yawn.

Juno did as well, her jaw cracking. "Heavens, I'm sleepy early."

"It must be the heavy gray day we've had," said Beth in a soothing voice. "I find weather like this often makes me tired."

"Maybe so." This time Juno yawned and Beth followed suit. "Oh dear. I guess I'll make an early night of it if you don't mind?"

"Not at all. I'll do the same. Tomorrow is another long day."

"More fittings. For me, at least. This time my presentation gown, and the hair dresser is to come and Maman said I must help decide about the decorations for the ball. Oh dear me yes. A busy day. But we'll have the drive in the park to look forward to." Again her eyes sparkled. "Perhaps, if I'm lucky, I'll meet some new people."

"Don't you think you've met quite enough?"

"Oh, never enough! I *like* people," said Juno, echoing much what Beth had told Lady Fairmont earlier that evening.

"The longer I'm in London—especially now I may look forward to dinners and balls—the more I think I'll enjoy it!" Juno looked sideways at Beth. "You may stop worrying I'll not fit into Tony's preferred way of life, may you not?"

Beth stifled another pretended yawn and grinned. "You, Juno Knightly, are a minx."

"So I am," responded the younger girl in a purring, self-satisfied way.

Beth laughed. "Go on with you or I'll fall asleep just as I am, all dressed up for dinner!"

Juno grimaced, but obediently left Beth to herself. Some minutes later Beth lay on top of her covers, composed her mind, and began the self hypnosis which would relax her into a deep sleep. She also set her mental alarm clock to wake her shortly before two A.M.

Nine

When Beth awoke she was rested and felt ready for anything. She pulled on the all-black, tightly fitting, one-piece outfit Suu-Van had sent her. She fitted the hood over her head, bundling her hair into it, and pulled flaps forward, sticking them against her cheeks, before clipping ties tight around her throat. Next she pulled on gloves which hid the micro equipment she'd use when testing for traps set by Smithson. Finally, she wound a long black hank of specially designed rope in a neat coil around her middle.

Ready, Beth went to her window. Long ago she'd checked out a route down the side of the house. Within minutes she dropped the last few feet to the ground. One long silent moment to see she'd not been heard, and, reassured, she set off for the wall at the back of the property. Beth scaled it more for the practice than necessity. The gate was, after all, unlocked, left that way by Zander. She could have slipped out easily enough.

Luckily, she *had* climbed! From the top, she saw a man lounging against the bricks. She lay atop the wall, waiting for the idler to leave. He didn't. Perhaps five minutes passed when, finally, the man pulled a watch from his fob pocket and tipped it to catch the light from a lamp set into the carriage house wall.

Beth realized it was Zander and cursed softly. The stupid man couldn't obey a simple order! Immediately she realized how foolish the thought was. Zander had no idea he was *supposed* to obey her. In fact, with his nineteenth century mind, it was quite the reverse. He expected her to obey him! Beth slipped down the wall to land in deep shadow at Zander's side.

"I didn't know it was you," she whispered. "I've been waiting for a stranger to leave so I could join you in the carriage as planned."

Zander recovered from his surprise almost instantly, but his voice was irritable when he said, "Quiet. Come along now." He pushed her ahead of him. Suddenly his hand tightened on her shoulder. He ran his other hand over her body. Grasping her shoulders, he shook her. "How dare you come out dressed like that?" he hissed. "Or should I say *undressed* like that!"

"You expect me to climb and do whatever else must be done dressed as I was at dinner?" she asked in an icy tone. "These are working clothes. They incorporate instruments I must have. We're late. Let's move."

"What if someone sees you?"

"No one will see me. Open the door to the carriage. Then step forward to give orders to your driver. It's my guess even *you* won't see me."

He didn't. When he hesitantly entered the carriage a few moments later, he was startled by Beth's touch. "You did it," he whispered.

It was her turn to silence him.

Finally the carriage slowed to a crawl. Zander opened the door and dropped to the ground. He turned and held a hand up for Beth who, allowing his aid, jumped down as well. They ducked into a deep shadow and the coach carried on down the narrow street without actually coming to a complete stop.

"Good thinking," she said. "When does he return?"

"Four o'clock the first time. If I don't get in he's to drive by at fifteen minute intervals until I do."

"I presume he thinks you're doing something for the war

department?" Beth saw a flash of white teeth as Zander grinned.

"How'd you guess?" he asked.

"You had to tell him something. Where's Smithson's warehouse?"

"The next but one."

She studied the street, looked back to the building before which they stood. "I'll go up this one."

"Go *up?*"

"To the roof."

"Now wait a minute. I think you've some explaining to do."

She huffed. What she *had* was a *job* to do! But Zander, his hand around her wrist, waited. "It'll be easier to get into Smithson's property from higher up. The ground level is not only more likely to be booby trapped but may have a live watchman on duty."

"How the devil do you think you'll climb this wall?"

"We *could* break in and go up the stairs, but I'd rather scale the outside." Beth scanned the building and found plenty of handholds for an experienced climber. Zander, however, was unlikely to let her go alone. She unwrapped her rope and, making a noose, tossed it toward a brace jutting out from just above the roof. It took a second toss, but then, holding the rope she walked up the side of the building until she'd reached her perch.

"Coming?" she called softly.

Zander, gritting his teeth, followed. "Now what?" he asked once he'd reached her side.

"Now I work my way across the roof," Beth said. "Can do?"

"Cando? I don't know that word."

"Two words. *Can you* do it?" she explained, separating the words.

"I can do anything you can do."

Beth clasped his arm. "Zander, don't get your self respect

tied up in trying to match the things I do. I trained for years for this sort of thing. If you must know, I wondered if you'd make it up that rope. But I don't think less of you that you've not had my schooling. No one in eighteen-thirteen has, except maybe Smithson. And it's likely he had no more than a short course."

Zander was silent for a moment, his hand covering hers. "You are very right to scold me. And you are also right I should not be jealous of that training of which you speak. But, Beth, I can't help it! I guess I haven't been really happy since that day your tricks so easily overcame my strength!"

"I don't know what I can do," she said helplessly.

"Someday you can teach me how you did it."

"If we have the opportunity I'll teach you—even though I shouldn't."

"Good. Now, on with you and we'll see if I can follow. No. Wait a moment. I need to rid myself of these boots. The bottoms are slippery."

He pulled them off and Beth gave him one of a bunch of cords threaded through eyelets in a leg of her outfit. "Your socks—stockings, I mean—will be black with soot."

"It can't be helped." He tied the boots together and slung them like saddlebags over his shoulder. "Now," he said, straightening carefully.

Beth undid her rope and, coiling it as she went, moved up; he scrambled up beside her. She stood balanced on the roof tree and studied her next move. A moment later she began working her way toward the adjoining building, Zander a little behind her. They crossed the next, slightly higher, roof as well. Creeping to the edge, they peered across a narrow alley at the building which belonged to Smithson.

"Now what?" he asked.

"That window. I'll check it out."

"How the devil do you mean to do that? Fly?" He gave her a quick look. *"Can* you fly?"

"No." She chuckled softly. Some things even her training

hadn't managed to overcome. Gravity was one! "I haven't the equipment for that in this era, so first I must figure out how to attach this rope somewhere."

"And then?"

"Then I'll lower myself to that level and use my equipment to see if there are any gadgets—"

"More of those machines?" he hissed.

"Something which would warn Smithson when someone is breaking in."

He nodded. "A bell, you mean."

Beth didn't, but she wasn't about to try to explain advanced electronics. She looked around. The roof was bare of projections. She lay down and peered under the broad eaves. Along the roof tree was another pulley brace. She wished the thing was on top of the roof instead of under it. She'd have to do quite a wriggle to get down to it without falling!

"What are you doing now?" asked Zander.

"Shush." Beth had to concentrate and didn't need an argument. A few tense minutes later she was in place.

Zander leaned as far over the edge as he dared. "How the devil are you going to get back up here?"

"I don't know that I will."

Beth fixed the rope and, moments later, swung freely at the proper level. Her instruments read negative and she changed the direction of the movement until it angled toward the other building. A few seconds later she'd caught the sill to the window through which she meant to gain entry.

"Beth, how am *I* supposed to get over there?" hissed Zander.

This was it. The moment when Zander faced the fact he wasn't needed—*and far worse*—wasn't wanted!

"You aren't," she said. "Go back to that brace we climbed to first. Wait there. I'll meet you there . . . Bye." As she disappeared through the window, the rope, released from the brace under the eaves, followed her in.

So did a long softly spoken string of oaths not meant—in this century—for a woman's ears.

Zander fumed. He'd returned to the original pulley brace with no difficulty but, once there, couldn't find a comfortable position on the six inch wide beam. He shifted, waiting out the interminable minutes. That Beth had gone into danger leaving him behind had him cursing under his breath again and yet again. Twice he pulled out his watch only to discover time had grown baby feet and crept forward at such a slow pace it drove him nearly mad. Was this how mothers and wives felt when their men were in danger?

He should break into the ground floor! Very likely she was mistaken in her belief that Smithson used inventions from the future. She'd explained why, if such were found and the principles discovered too soon in history, it was dangerous to Smithson's own future and surely the man wouldn't want that?

Then Zander remembered the captain's arrogance, his self-satisfaction and his willingness to kill simply to rid himself of an immediate problem. The man was an arrogant fool and very likely Beth had the right of it no matter how much Zander wished it otherwise. If he were to do as he wished, he might put her into the very danger from which he wished to save her.

But, Lord! Why didn't she come? He looked along the roof, thought of returning to peer over the edge at Smithson's warehouse, thought better of it, and grumbled softly to himself about women who didn't know their place and refused to accept help as a proper woman would. He was still grumbling when a soft hiss from ground level caught his attention.

"Come down quickly," whispered Beth. "I hear the carriage."

Zander caught the rope, slipped the noose over the end of the brace and walked his way to ground level. The rope slipped to the ground almost before he'd found his feet and he wondered how she managed that trick. They stood well back in the shadows on either side, leapt into the carriage as it passed, and were on their way home.

"Well?" asked Zander politely.

"Three secret caches."

Zander started, then relaxed again against the padded squabs of the seat. "I didn't truly believe you'd find anything. What was hidden?"

She sighed. "As I feared, he's had time to empty them. I'd guess he transferred everything to that damn ship of his. He'll leave port and store extra energy slowly over months and months so that he may send them forward to whenever he leaves!"

"He won't leave any time soon," said Zander.

He didn't manage to rid his words of all smugness and, as a result felt his ears heat. He was acting like a boy longing for the approval of his first female interest and was glad the dark hid the fact that his skin must be glowing bright red.

"Why not?" she asked. "All he need do is load up a cargo and go."

Coping with embarrassment, Zander nearly missed Beth's query. "It's simple." He stared at where his fingernails would be if he could see them. "I bribed various port authorities to find reasons to keep him from sailing. He can be tied up for weeks."

Turning toward him, Beth touched his arm. "That was well thought of. Thank you!"

Before she could remove her hand Zander covered it with his own. A wry laugh nearly escaped, as her compliment roused in him another feeling common to the boy experiencing his first infatuation and he was relieved she couldn't see how happy her approval made him. Instead of revealing that happiness, he growled, "I suppose you must now search the ship?"

"Yes. I don't know how, but I'll think of something."

"We'll think of something." Zander picked up Beth's hand and played with her fingers. "Beth, promise you'll do nothing on your own."

"No," she said gently. "I promise I'll try to keep you informed of my plans, but if Smithson is illegally forwarding art from this era he must be caught as soon as possible and made redundant."

"You would kill him?"

"No. A very long time ago the south seas were beautifully empty. A *very* long time ago. Male offenders are put on one island, females another. It is prison, of course—but idyllic."

"They've no means of escaping to more populated parts of the world?"

Beth chuckled softly. "The world in general is not a hospitable place. The prisoners are aware they are better off staying where they are!"

"I'd be tempted to try to find the woman's island!"

"Impossible. It's not in the same century."

"You can't mean there was a time when there were no other humans in the world?"

"Yes there was."

"But . . ." Zander was silent. He sighed, accepting. "That's cruel, is it not, that they cannot even have the comfort of sex?"

"Given how large our organization is there are very few criminals, but those know the penalty. Unfortunately, like most serious criminals, they tend to believe they'll not be caught. Smithson certainly thinks he's immune to discovery!"

"Smithson will be sent to this past of which you speak?"

"If I find the necessary proof, yes."

"But *how* will you catch him? He'll not be taken captive without a struggle. You'll be in serious danger."

"By Sita's Sitar, Zander, when will you accept that I've no choice!"

"Are you swearing? Should you use such language?"

"You'd make a saint swear!" Beth fumed silently and then, resigned, she explained. "You'll not cease arguing until I reveal the *sole* reason I was sent to your time. Zander, it has *nothing* to do with two mediocre paintings hanging somewhere in Kent. I'm here to entrap Smithson and nothing more. We've done all we can, analyzing energy drains and discovering art where it shouldn't be. We *know* he's responsible, but we must, by our laws, actually *prove* Smithson is doing this evil thing."

"Could you not transfer him to your time and give him a job where he'd do no more damage?"

"Men of his stamp do damage wherever they are. I must have proof."

The carriage pulled up in the mews. Zander had a few words with his driver, thanking him for a job well done. When he'd finished Beth had vanished. Since he'd been standing by the gate, he assumed she'd once again gone over the wall. He found her in a tiny gazebo.

"I feared you'd let yourself into the house by whatever means you used to let yourself out," he said when he'd joined her.

"We'd not finished. What you must understand, Zander, is that I'm a professional. In four years I've caught three other traitors. The temptation is, evidently, greater than I can understand or perhaps the tests do not uncover, as they should, weaknesses which lead people into temptation. Suu-Van, my supervisor, thinks we may have to work out new methods of training or find new ways of recruiting agents."

"Since you've gone after other desperate men and survived, that means I shouldn't worry?" He grabbed her arms above the elbows and shook her lightly. "You are nonsensical. How can I help but worry when you pit yourself against men such as Smithson?"

"Two men and one woman. Of the three, the woman was the most dangerous! Zander, I know what I'm doing. I'll do nothing foolish."

"I cannot stand by and tamely watch you do . . . whatever you must do."

"No more could I if you went into danger. I must plan my next move carefully. I think it's likely," she said, eying him sideways, "I'll need your aid, so I doubt I'll do anything of which you're unaware."

"I suppose I must be satisfied with that."

"It's the best I can offer, Zander."

He pulled her against his chest, held her close, his hand running over the cap covering her head and neck. "You feel odd. I've never touched such material. It's not silk, I think, but what else can it be?"

"It's silk, but a specially spun fiber which hides equipment which should *not* be in this time. Equipment, Zander, which I use reluctantly. Inventions of the future should stay there!" She snuggled close. "We shouldn't be here like this."

"No." His fingers found her chin, tipped her face up. "No, we shouldn't." He stared down into her eyes. "Beth?"

She tipped her head a trifle farther and he lowered his. Their lips met, touching lightly. Beth brought her arm around him and his hands moved up her back, trailed down her spine. The kiss deepened. They broke it, held each other close, for the moment satisfied they were in each other's arms.

Later, when Zander roused himself from his preoccupation, he discovered he could actually see her. "Beth! Love . . . !" She moved sleepily in his arms. "Beth," he said urgently, "you must get to your room. Immediately."

"Hmm?" She looked at him, looked around, blinked sleepily. "I went to sleep!" She slipped from his embrace and stretched. Opening her eyes she glanced at him, found his skin a darker color than expected and glanced down her slim form at which he stared. She giggled. "Exceedingly unladylike attire, is it not, my lord?"

"Exceedingly," he said, his voice dry as dust. "Also enticing and intriguing and rather becoming in a way I'd have thought impossible if someone merely described it. You've a lovely form, my dear," he said suggestively.

"Thank you, my lord," she said on a prim note, but her eyes laughed. "I must go. Thank you for your help, Zander." With that she disappeared.

As hard as he tried Zander didn't catch a glimpse of her until she leaned out her window and waved to him, blowing him an impudent kiss. Zander looked at the lightening sky. He heard the first rumble of morning traffic on the street beyond the house, the first sleepy voices as servants began their day. He looked at his evening clothes and sighed. Their condition would send his valet into the boughs for sure.

He sighed a second time. He'd rather liked the coat and doubted he'd be able to wear it ever again!

Zander let himself out into the mews. He strolled to a hotel where he took a room. Just as he was about to drift into sleep Zander wondered if Beth might order him up a costume like her own. At least he'd not ruin another suit of clothes if he were dressed in that totally improper fashion! He chuckled softly, envisioning himself in those closely fitting black hose and long sleeved shirt which came tight and high around the neck. He added the black hood and, just for the mystery of it, a narrow mask.

The chuckle turned to a laugh which awakened a testy soul in the next room. At least, that would explain the pounding on the wall above his head! With a soft apology, Zander snuggled under the covers and, this time, allowed himself to drift off to sleep.

Ten

Zander came to take Juno and herself to the park just when Beth wondered if she could manage another moment of proper civility to Lady Fairmont who had kept her daughter and guest busy the whole of the day. Brother and sister were quite as silent as Beth while they drove to the park where Juno immediately perked up and began to look about herself.

Zander steadied his team among the throng driving along the Row. When he could, he said, "Beth, you're exceptionally quiet which is unlike you, I think. Are you tired?"

"I didn't sleep well last night," she admitted, her eyes twinkling. "And you?"

"My slumber was somewhat disrupted as well," he said, solemnly. "Perhaps the full moon disturbed you?" he suggested, a teasing note in his voice. "Do you find it often interferes with your rest?"

"There was no moon last night," said Juno, interrupting. "It's far more likely excitement is Beth's problem."

Beth and Zander exchanged a wry glance. Juno had no notion how close to the mark she was!

"I *know*," the younger girl continued. "I wake up and remember the most delicious dreams . . ." A particularly dreamy expression crossed her face as she recalled one of her better dreams.

Zander was reminded his sister thought herself in love with his friend. "He won't have you, you know."

"What?" Shock jerked up Juno's head. "What do you mean?"

"Anthony. He's not on the look-out for a bride. You'll make me an uncle twice over before Anthony decides it's time to wed."

"I've no notion of what you speak," said his sister, well up on her high horse, but Beth noticed how Juno's skin paled. "Such nonsense," she added.

"Is it? I hope so. I love you, Juno. I'd not like to find you in the briars because you foolishly set your heart on the unobtainable."

Juno bit her lip and Beth quickly asked if Juno and her mother had decided between the potted rose trees and the ferns for decorating the musicians' dais. Juno's look thanked Beth for offering a way out of a discussion she'd no wish to continue. Instead, she launched a long recital of exactly how she and her mother had decided to use both.

When the party again reached Fairmont House, Juno traipsed up steps and in the front door. Zander held Beth back, guiding her across the street to the small park in the middle of the square. "I did that badly, did I not?" he asked, his tone rueful.

"I fear you did. By suggesting Juno may never achieve the dearest wish of her heart, you've very likely dropped a long way in her esteem!" Beth gave him a pitying look.

"How do I retrieve myself?"

"Get her her heart's desire!" Beth drew in a deep breath and plunged on. "I think you'll find, if you observe him, that Lord Belmont is far more smitten than he's willing to admit. It's in his eyes, Zander, when he looks at her and in the affectionate amusement he obviously feels and his care for her comfort when he takes her driving and, most of all, it's revealed by his irritation when another man spends more than a polite moment talking to her and . . ." She raised her eyebrows when Zander held up his hand. "Yes?"

"You've convinced me. Now explain how I'm to convince Anthony."

"Assuming you should."

"What does that mean?"

"Assuming he has none of the characteristics of the man we saw with Smithson the day we arrived in London? They are related, you said."

"Tony is *nothing* like his cousin. I sometimes think Richard has become a trifle mad due to his obsession that he, not Tony, should have inherited. Then too, he games and is often in financial hot water. Because he's a gamester, he's rarely found in respectable places which is why you've not seen him. Tony isn't crazed and doesn't game to excess . . . !" Zander's grin faded. "Beth, if there's the slightest chance of bringing Tony up to scratch, I'd like nothing better. So what do I do? I don't wish to put my foot in it as I did in the park!"

"I'll think about it . . . Will you, hmm, be in for dinner?" She gave him a sideways look from the corner of her eye.

His brow quirked. Politely, he asked, "Is there a reason I should *not?*"

"Your mother will toss me into the street if she discovers I've warned you, but I don't think her tricks fair! She's invited the Chambertons and the Grossinghams. You know better than I that each family has a pretty daughter of marriageable age."

Zander adopted an obviously false look of chagrin. "I don't understand how I could have forgotten something so important, but I've recalled a long standing invitation I cannot break. I'm to dine this evening with Merry and Anthony. We go on to . . . hmm, the opera, I think."

"Why do I feel you should instantly remind your friends of the engagement since, very likely, they, too, have forgotten?"

"Hmm. There's no time to waste."

"None at all, since it's already time we go up to change."

Beth made a move away from him, but Zander put out his hand and touched her arm, stopping her. "Yes?" she asked, looking up at him.

"Beth, you do feel comfortable here, do you not? In eighteen-hundred and thirteen, I mean?"

A look of surprise crossed her face. "It's odd, Zander. I've never had so little difficulty adapting to a new environment. I feel very much at home." She glanced at him. "But I've had so much help from you and your family it isn't surprising."

"Is there perhaps another explanation? Is it possible you *belong* in this era?" he asked diffidently. "You said you've no memory of a time before you were rescued. . . ."

"I had to have been born sometime." Beth drew in a deep breath and set aside the tempting notion. The odds were, after all, very much against it. Her voice held a warning when she said, "It's unlikely, Zander. Don't waste energy making up scenarios in which I can stay here because, in some sense, I belong here."

She turned on her heel and crossed the street, entering the house and going straight up to her room. Then, despite the good advice she'd given Zander, she dreamed wonderful daydreams about how this *was* her birth era. She even allowed a speculation or two about whether Suu-Van would let her transfer from ETH-arm to Art's Anchor division so she could take over Smithson's position here as anchor . . .

The notion was so very tempting. Taking over as anchor would make it possible for her to remain, make marrying Zander something more than an utter impossibility and, unlikely as it seemed, allow them to live happily ever after.

It *was* an impossible dream but Beth continued to dream it right up until the abigail entered followed by footmen carrying cans of water at which point she roused herself. The gown Susie laid out for her was much more elaborate than she'd expected and, tentatively, she asked if it were appropriate to wear such a lovely creation for a small dinner such as was planned for that evening.

"Lady Fairmont had Miss Higgens tell me which gown, Mademoiselle. Did no one warn you you are to go on to the opera after dinner?"

The door to Juno's room burst open. "Isn't it wonderful, Beth? We're to be allowed to visit the opera!"

Beth, thinking of Zander, grimaced. His mother might not be completely thwarted after all! "I hope your father has a large box," she said. "With all of us, the Chambertons and the Grossinghams and all, we'll need it."

"I don't suppose the men will go—except Zander. Maman means to talk him into escorting us. So it'll be you and me and Maman and four guests. That's seven—eight if Zander accompanies us. It's quite a comfortable number, actually."

Juno was wrong. The numbers were uncomfortable from the moment Lady Fairmont realized her son had escaped her net. Only her closest friends would have known she was upset but, unfortunately, both Lady Chamberton and Lady Grossingham were such friends. "I'll not pretend," Beth heard Lady Fairmont say. "I deliberately *forgot* to tell Zander. I knew he'd make an excuse to be elsewhere if I did." She frowned. "I cannot understand why he's not here."

Beth crossed to where Juno talked to Lady Emma Chamberton and Miss Rose Grossingham. She'd met them during morning visits and didn't think highly of either. Lady Emma had finished her third season and approached a desperate age. She tended to be far too obvious in her pursuit of Zander. Miss Rose, on the other hand, had all the faults of the confirmed bluestocking. It was, thought Beth, too bad that in this particular age a woman with intellectual ambitions invariably came equipped with a chip on her shoulder as well.

Although Beth had more sympathy for Miss Rose's problems than she did for Lady Emma's, sympathy alone wasn't enough to induce liking. She didn't blame Zander for running. *It's just too bad,* thought Beth, *that this evening his running and his mother's plans are likely to put them on a collision course!*

The collision occurred at the second interval. Zander, Merry, and Anthony strolled the foyer looking for friends and acquaintances, totally innocent and unexpecting. Zander suffered a mild shock when his mother left the Fairmont box followed by the two young women he'd hoped to avoid.

"Ah. There you are, Zander. A sudden decision, I presume?" said Lady Fairmont, acid dripping. "Your valet was of the opinion you'd no particular plans for this evening."

"Mother?"

Lady Fairmont bit her lip as Zander used the English form of the word.

He turned to the others and bowed. "Ladies Chamberton and Grossingham? Lady Emma and Miss Rose? Good evening to you." He turned back to his mother. *"My* valet, you say?" asked Zander, his voice as chilling in its way as one of Gunther's ices. "Obviously, *not* my valet. Not if he speaks of my plans. I'll have to see about a new one, will I not?" His gaze met and held his mother's. "One who understands his loyalty is to *me?"* he finished silkily.

Lady Fairmont paled. "Zander . . ."

"Good evening, ladies." He bowed again. "I hope you enjoy the music." He turned on his heel and walked off.

Anthony, talking idly to Miss Rose about the latest news from the Peninsula, was caught off guard, but he deftly excused himself and went after his friend. Captain Porthson wasn't so lucky. Lady Emma, her fingers on his arm, on the old theory of a bird in hand as compared to two in the bush, had Merry trapped between two of the pedestals bearing statues which lined the foyer wall.

Lady Fairmont recovered and seeing only the captain available moved in on Lady Emma, told the girl her mother wished to speak to her, and then, herself, kept her prey trapped. "I was unaware my son had plans for this evening, Captain."

"What? Plans. Well . . ." Merry tugged at the high collar of his uniform.

Beth took pity on him. "Lord Hawksbeck mentioned while we were driving that he expected the opera to be particularly good this evening," she said.

Lady Fairmont turned her ill-temper on Beth. "You knew I expected him to dine in——"

"No, my lady," said Beth firmly, "I did not. I knew guests were expected, of course, but I did *not* know you expected your son."

"You're not stupid," hissed Lady Fairmont. "You must have known——"

Beth, feeling no guilt that she'd warned Zander, shook her head. "To my knowledge you've never desired his company that you've not made a point of informing him of it."

Two spots of color appeared on Lady Fairmont's cheeks. "Well, as to that . . ." She sighed. For a moment she looked into some blank distance. Finally she glanced to where the captain still stood at attention, tiny beads of sweat dotting his forehead. Suddenly she laughed. "Merry, you may take word to my son that I've been made to understand it's my own fault he didn't appear at my dinner table this evening. Good night, Captain." She nodded regally, collected the eyes of her guests and swept back into the Fairmont box.

Beth, as she was about to follow, heard Merry Porthson's low voiced but intense comment, "Mademoiselle, I owe you one!"

"Why does he owe you?" hissed Juno.

"I suppose he thinks I saved him a scold. Your mother has not been pleased with your brother this evening, don't you agree?"

Juno merely chortled in answer in that enticing way she had and led Beth into their box. It was much later when Juno remembered that Anthony had come nowhere near her even though he might have done so easily enough during the interval. If he'd wished to.

Could Zander be correct when he said she could not win him? That night Juno's dreams were not so pleasant as usual.

Eleven

Two days later Zander was busy at his desk in the sitting room of his suite when Shipper knocked and entered the room. His nose well up in the air, the butler announced, "A *person* has called to see you, my lord. A Captain Smithson. He claims to be acquainted with you?"

"Smithson? Here?" Zander sat back in his chair and fingered his pen. "Now, what can the Fox have in mind? You say he asked for *me?*"

"Yes, my lord." The nose lowered by half a notch. "I've put him in the porter's room, my lord."

"Don't think very highly of my guest, do you, Shipper? I suppose I must join him there rather than you bringing him here? It wouldn't do, would it, to have him traipsing about the house if you've that low an opinion of him!"

The butler bowed himself out, not bothering to respond to a question to which the answer was, he felt, quite obvious.

Zander spent another full minute wondering what the captain wanted. The solution, of course, was to ask, but it would never do to go down in shirtsleeves and slippers. After all, one must uphold Shipper's sense of dignity! He spent all of twenty minutes dressing appropriately for a morning call from someone of the captain's status—as defined by Shipper.

Zander softly opened the door to the small porter's room and was unsurprised to discover Smithson pacing the floor. The captain wasn't the sort who cared to be kept waiting.

"You wished to see me?" asked Zander.

Smithson turned on his heel. "Yes. I must see you."

"Well, you see me. Now what?"

Smithson nearly growled. "You will have my ship released."

How, wondered Zander, *did Smithson learn I've meddled in his business?*

The man's next words suggested he had not. "I've tried bribes. Many bribes. I've tried blackmail. Papers filled out. Papers and more papers. Office after office." Smithson pulled at his thinning hair. "I try everything and nothing goes down."

Zander arched a brow. "Goes down?"

"Nothing happens," Smithson corrected himself. "But you!" He pointed one bony finger. "You see a lord here, a lord there, and my boat will be released." The sly creature actually looked hopeful. *"Yes?"*

"Why am I making no sense of this conversation?" asked Zander mildly, elated by the success of his own careful bribery.

Smithson glared. He calmed himself and plastered a travesty of a smile across his face. "It is simple. My ship is laden. I must sail. I cannot get permission. You"—he pointed—"will get it."

"Let me see if I understand." Zander went to one of the straight backed chairs and pulled it away from the wall. He seated himself and, careful not to stretch the material at his knee, crossed his legs. "You've put on cargo for your next voyage but cannot get the papers necessary for leaving port." He stared at Smithson. "Is that it?"

The captain nodded. "I must go."

"What, exactly, can I do?"

Again that false smile. "You know people. You see people. You get me permission."

"But I don't know such people," objected Zander.

"You get introductions," said Smithson.

"You don't understand how our government works.

Someone cannot just *say* you may go. The laws must be obeyed."

Smithson gave him a pitying look. "It's not so. Nowhere is it so."

"In this country it *is* so," insisted Zander. "Besides, I don't understand your problem. Fill out the proper forms and be done with it."

"I do so! Inspectors crawl all over my boat. I pay fees. I pay fines. It goes on and on." Smithson raised his fists in the air and shook them. "I *must sail.*"

Zander uncrossed his legs and recrossed them the other way. "So. You're being harassed."

"Yes! Harassed."

"Sounds to me as if you stepped on someone's toes. If that's the case, there's nothing I can do." Zander rose to his feet and moved toward the door. "Once the person—or *persons*—you insulted no longer feel aggrieved, they themselves will see you are allowed to go." He shrugged.

"Wait!" Smithson gritted his teeth. "It necessary is. I must go. You must see the proper personages."

"Impossible." Zander waved a languid hand. "If it is truly a question of harassment by underlings among the port authority, then direct orders from some vague figure far above them will not help. Those responsible for your problem will simply find new ways to evade the order and continue playing their game until satisfied with their revenge."

Smithson growled. He paced from side to side, then turned to stare, baffled, at Zander. "You are impossible."

"I suppose you feel that way, but perhaps you've little understanding of this age? Of the way things work here in England?"

"Bah. All bureaucracy, anytime, anywhere, is venal!"

Zander pretended innocence. "But you said you'd tried bribes and they'd done no good."

Again Smithson gave Zander that baffled look. Zander stared right back, his expression blandly inquiring.

"You will not help."

"I *cannot* help. But then," he added thoughtfully, "if you *will* have it, it's also true I've no particular reason to wish to help." Zander grinned, but it wasn't a particularly pleasant expression. Compared to the fox's travesty of a smile it was downright wolfish! "If you were in my place," he asked, softly, "would *you* help *me?"*

"No!" Smithson growled. "No," he spit out. "I'd not. Never."

"Then where did you get the ridiculous notion I might help you?"

"I must go!"

"Why?"

"I have business," mumbled Smithson evasively and would not meet Zander's eyes. "I have schedules."

"How sad. I fear your schedules must be altered, must they not?"

Smithson glared. "I will go."

"If you mean you'll sail regardless, you'd best keep a sharp watch for the river patrol. You'll get taken up for— well, I've no notion for what, but if you haven't the proper papers, they'll make life more difficult for you than it is already, think you not?"

Again Smithson glared. "You will not help?"

"I *will not help, "* repeated Zander.

Smithson turned on his heel and left. Zander stretched and yawned before he too entered the hall just as Shipper closed the door behind the captain. Beth, half way downstairs, watched, a speculative look in her eye.

"Good morning, cousin," said Zander as Shipper returned to his pantry at the back of the house.

She responded equally politely and added, "Was that Captain Smithson?"

"Hmm?" Zander pulled his eyes away from the slim lines of her body and forced himself to meet her eyes. A faint redness crept above his cravat. "Yes," he said, his words unexceptional while a different, if silent, communication passed between them. "It seems the captain can't get permission to sail. The poor man believes it's harassment and, poor deluded fellow, felt I might know who would cut the knots tying him up in port. Unfortunately," finished Zander on a pious note, "I know of no one who might help him."

"I'm sure you deeply regret that you cannot come to his aid," she said, her features quite as austere as his. She went on in a far more serious vein, "Zander, did he say *why* he's in such a hurry?"

"It seems he has a schedule and is very anxious he keep to it. Beth," he added softly, after a glance around the hall to see that it was empty, "do you think your superiors might introduce a common seaman onto that ship and let *him* get the proof you need?"

She came closer and she too spoke softly. "You didn't truly look at his crew did you?"

"It was a crew." Zander shrugged his indifference, his eyes again traveling down the simple lines of her rose colored morning gown, lingering here, there . . .

He roused a warmth that made it difficult for Beth to go on. Slightly cross, she said, "Each and every sailor had features similar to our foxy captain. I'd guess they're all related."

Zander tore his eyes from her figure and met her gaze. He sighed. "So my notion won't work because the fox will hire only relatives. Your proof must be found another way?"

"Yes." She turned away from a strong temptation to reach out and touch him, draw him close. To avoid doing so, she clasped her hands behind her back. "Which means I *must* search that ship."

"Beth, he'll never leave that vessel unguarded. Even if he doesn't fear someone such as yourself, there's a great deal of petty thievery to say nothing of outright piracy up and down the river. He must protect himself and his ship against villains worse, in some ways, than he himself! Human wharf rats are as common as the four legged variety in that area of London."

"I don't expect it to be unguarded," said Beth in the tone of one explaining something to a simpleton. "What I hope is that it will have only a few men on board."

Now Zander had a baffled look. "You cannot truly wish to face the danger involved when searching his ship."

"What has what I wish to do with this? I have my duty, Zander. I cannot say, *oh dear, it might be a trifle dangerous so I guess I won't do it . . .*" She eyed him, watched his cheeks darken as blood flowed into his face. "Zander, will you do something for me?"

"If I can," he said, caution in every syllable. He eyed her warily.

She grinned. "Merely hire retired sailors to squander time near where Smithson has moored. Have them observe the comings and goings. I want to know how many men have shore leave and when and how many remain on board ship at any given time. You see? Once I know that I can decide when it would be best to make my attempt."

"You'll not be dissuaded?"

"No."

He sighed. "I didn't think you would. It'll take a couple of weeks, or even more, to get a reasonably good notion of the routine."

Beth frowned. "There's no danger of Smithson sailing?"

This time Zander's grin was spontaneous and infectious. "He won't leave England anytime in the foreseeable future!"

"You seem very certain, Zander."

He shrugged. "Every bribe he offers, I double. The men working the dock haven't seen so much money in all their lives!"

"But," objected Beth, "this is terrible. You must give me an accounting so you may be reimbursed!"

"Beth," he said, and it was his turn to adopt the patient

tone of a tutor to a slightly slow student, "it may be a fortune to men on the docks, but it's a mere trifle, not worth thinking about." When she'd have objected he covered her mouth with his fingers. She subsided. "What are your plans for today?" he asked conversationally as a footman came through the green baize door at the back of the hall.

"I've library books to return. Juno wishes to visit Ackermann's rooms."

"When did Juno acquire the current rage for collecting prints."

"So far as I know she has not. She wishes to view an exhibit of porcelain imported from the mysterious East, or so Ackermann's advertisement claimed."

"You don't believe that taradiddle, do you? Oh, not that Ackermann's claim is false, because he's an honorable dealer, but, that Juno wishes to view it?" Zander's brows rose when she refused to be goaded. "Well, if you *do,* you *won't* when I tell you Anthony has an appointment to preview prints Rudolf Ackermann will, tomorrow, offer the public for the first time. What I want to know is how my devious sister learned of Anthony's visit!"

Beth chuckled. "Perhaps not only your valet tells tales, but another man's man as well?"

About to give in to the urge to touch the delicate gold of her cheek a second time, Zander held back. "Surely Juno can't have subverted Pouncenbye to her needs! I'd thought to steal him from Tony to replace my Merrit, but I won't if he has no greater sense of loyalty!"

"You shouldn't be so quick to condemn Merrit. Your mother used Higgens. He let the information slip during an otherwise innocent chat about the dress proper to various functions and the proper care of a wardrobe."

"Now, how did you discover that interesting tidbit? Because, somehow, you did, did you not?"

"I don't know if you'll approve . . ."

"Try me."

Beth sighed. "I like Higgens. Quite simply, I asked her. Since she must keep her position with your mother as best she can, she did as ordered. All you need do is make clear that such information will not be forthcoming in future."

"Thank you. I'll do that." Still again he wanted to touch her, feel that wonderfully golden, warm-looking skin . . . "Frankly, I wasn't looking forward to breaking in a new valet when Merrit, for the most part, suits me very well."

"Now you won't have to, will you?" With difficulty Beth turned from his yearning look. "Juno? Ready so soon? I'll just get my pelisse and hat and join you in a moment."

Zander, realizing they'd been interrupted, again, decided the hall was no place in which to indulge in a trifle of dalliance. "If you'll wait, I'll go too," said Zander. "Well, Juno?" he asked when his sister pouted, "Would you like to ride in style behind my new team of matched grays?"

Interest lightened her expression. "The grays? I didn't think they were broken to town use."

"It's true we'll be taking a chance," he said, tongue in cheek and a twinkle in his eyes. Not realizing he was bamming her a worried look crossed Juno's face. "But you *will* take us up?"

"I'll take you up."

Suddenly Juno remembered her reason for the outing. She shook her head. "No. I fear Beth would feel unsafe. She's not so comfortable with horses as we are. I suppose it must be because she was raised on the continent where they don't have such wonderful horses . . . ?"

"Very likely," said Zander, dryly. "However that may be, you shouldn't insult her courage." He glanced up the stairs. "Here she is. We'll ask her."

Juno waited until Beth reached the hall. She shook her head very slightly no as she said, "Zander's offered to drive us about behind his new team. I personally don't believe they're trained well enough for busy streets. Their skittishness is likely to make you uncomfortable."

"Sounds lovely," said Beth blandly. "Have you ordered up the carriage, Zander?"

"It only awaited your approval. While the team is brought around, I'll just change my coat and get into boots. You may wait in the little salon," he added over his shoulder, already part way up the stairs.

"Oh, we may, may we? And what if we don't care to wait there?" asked Juno, but he was well beyond hearing long before she'd finished speaking. She sighed and stalked down the hall. "Brothers. They can be the very devil, can they not?"

Beth chuckled. "Don't let Miss Wilder hear you say such a thing!"

"But Miss Wilder is carefully tucked away in her room reading a French novel. She can't possibly hear me."

"A French novel?" Beth had a vague notion that, given this time's values, such books were considered rather risqué. "Surely your mother doesn't approve that you read such things."

"*I* don't read them. Oh," Juno admitted, "I tried one once, but it was a bore. Too much of the French was beyond me, you see. I pretend I don't know of Miss Wilder's passion for them. *She* believes it a great secret and feels deliciously guilty whenever she manages to acquire one. But I think however much guilt she endured, she'd not forego the reading of them!"

Zander returned and the carriage was announced almost on his heels. The stop at the library took little time since Beth merely returned her books. They continued on to Ackermann's, Juno's excitement growing to the point she actually bounced, once, on her seat.

Beth placed a restraining hand on her knee. A warning look had Juno adopting a pose of unutterable boredom. "That's almost as bad," whispered Beth, a chuckle barely repressed. Juno just grinned in response.

The rooms were thin of customers. Only a few collectors

studied prints, helpful clerks pointing out details. Juno
strolled slowly, her eyes darting here and there, but, before
she caught sight of her quarry, she found herself in a back
room, Beth's hand firmly on her arm, and no choice but to
study the porcelain, her ostensible reason for coming. Juno
couldn't refrain from regularly glancing back toward the
main room, however, and Beth wondered if her friend would
remember a thing they'd come to see.

Zander disappeared to find his friend and suggest that the
four of them adjourn to Gunther's for ices. Later, when the
enlarged party started off, Beth found herself alone in the
curricle with Zander, Juno tucked securely up beside Anthony in his phaeton.

"How did you manage that?" asked Beth once Zander
maneuvered his still inexperienced team through a particularly narrow passage between a brewer's dray and a furniture
mover's fourgon.

"Manage not to hit anything?"

"Idiot. Manage to leave Juno alone with Anthony."

Zander grinned. "Easy. I told him I wished to be alone
with you. He was quite agreeable to helping true love along
its way."

"True love."

"I make a joke of it because it's so important, Beth."

She sighed. "I know. But we mustn't build castles in the
air. I don't belong here."

"You don't know that."

"No. I don't, do I?" She remembered the odd feeling
she'd had recently when standing to have a hem pinned. It
had seemed a familiar but detested necessity which she'd
suffered many times before. *Surely,* she thought, *familiarity
was only because Juno had complained so much about fittings, complained she hated being poked by pins, hated
standing still for hours at a time . . .*

"Beth, can't you ask your superior if there's any possibility we have a life together?"

"Suu-Van will only tell me I must remember my past on my own. Until I do he isn't likely to admit I belong here or anywhere else for that matter." Beth heard a trifle more bitterness in her voice than she felt proper, given she owed her very life to Suu-Van.

"Have you felt so much at home in any of the other periods in which you've worked?"

"You know I have not. But we explained that. Living with your family and having the help you've all given me . . ."

Zander sighed, shrugged away a stiffening in his shoulders and nodded. "All right. Beth, will you do something for me?"

"If I can."

"Try to remember?" He turned a grin her way, but it was a trifle lopsided.

"If you only knew how hard I've tried! But I'll try again. I've more need now than ever before to discover the truth. Is that Gunther's?" she asked, sighting the pineapples denoting the confectioner's premises.

"Yes." He pulled up. "Here. I'll help you down so you may join Juno in Tony's rig. He and I'll get the treat. Ices are all right, are they not?"

Beth thought the day a trifle cool for a cold sweet, but, no one else seemed to agree. Besides, oddly enough, since she'd never tasted Gunther's most famous offering, her mouth watered at the thought of it. It was almost as if she *had,* at some time in the past, been offered the same thing in the same way . . . ? Was she remembering? Or did she merely wish to remember and, because of that, her mind played these tricks?

She turned to a blissful Juno and heard, in far greater detail than she wished, every word which had passed between her *soi-disant* cousin and Zander's friend. She was glad when the men returned from the other side of the green with four small glass dishes mounded with the most delicious of pineapple flavored ice.

For half an instant it seemed a different young man stood grinning at her, a blond head where Zander's was dark, a longer, more oval, face where the present one was square chinned, broad of brow . . .

Then the vision faded and again Beth couldn't decide if it were truly a memory, or only wishful-thinking. Whatever it was, it was disconcerting and she was glad she and Juno were driven back to Fairmont House where she could be alone in her room. But once alone, she discovered her thoughts merely scuttled round and round in circles, which was no better!

Was there truly a possibility this was the era of her birth?

Early the next morning Juno bounced into Beth's room, waking her. "Beth, Maman says we're traveling north soon after our ball! Old friends mean to hold their daughter's come-out ball at their family home and Maman insists we must support their decision. We'll be at least two days on the road getting to Friar's Place—"

Beth felt her head spin and touched her forehead with one hand.

"What is it?" asked Juno, alarmed. "Are you ill?"

"Just . . . just a trifle dizzy. Friar's Place?"

A fairy tale of a building with wings stretching away on each side, the whole set on rising ground in the hazy distance in rolling park land. . . .

"Dizzy," she repeated.

"Oh dear. I shouldn't have awakened you so abruptly," said Juno, contritely. "You go back to sleep, Beth. Our ball is a day after tomorrow and you can't be ill for *that.*"

Beth didn't hear her. Surely, she thought, she'd never seen such a building—not even in a print or in some forgotten painting in an ART supported museum. *Was* it possible she was actually beginning to remember? But she'd had years in which to remember and no hint of her past had ever worked through the barriers in her mind. Surely this was imagination, her mind playing games with her, a game which teased her by suggesting what she *wished* true *was* true. Surely it was only that she wanted for her life to go on with Zander, here in his lifetime.

Ah, but she *mustn't* allow herself to hope!

"Beth?" Juno's voice interrupted her whirling thoughts. "Are you worse? Should I have Higgens in?"

"Higgens? Oh no. That's not necessary." Beth pulled herself together. "Sorry, Juno. I'm fine . . ."

. . . *Fine until the moment comes I must leave you and your family. And Zander,* she thought. *Oh yes. Most particularly Zander!*

Twelve

Later that afternoon Juno stood carefully poised in the middle of Beth's bedroom. She dipped. "I can't do it," she wailed when, for the third time, she was unable to rise. She'd been practicing the deep curtsies assiduously all week. "Why can't I do it? I did it just fine this morning! What will I do? Tomorrow I'm to be presented to the queen and I can't curtsy! Beth, what will I do?"

"What you'd better do is rest your legs."

Juno, momentarily unable to raise herself, plopped onto the floor. "Don't let Miss Wilder hear you use that word," she hissed. *"Limbs,* Beth. A table has legs. A lady has limbs."

"Whatever you call them, rest them."

Scrambling up, Juno tilted her huge hoop and managed to seat herself more or less gracefully on Beth's chaise. "I hate this thing. How could anyone wear such cages day in and day out?"

"Once you've put the gown over it you'll forget the problems and wallow in compliments on how beautiful you look." Beth hoped the lie would soothe her young friend. Juno's gown followed the prevailing fashion of high waist and low cut bodice. Beth privately thought that, over the hoop-extended skirt, Juno looked very much like a large hand bell with a short handle! "Your presentation gown," she added, "is magnificent."

That *was* true. Satin flounces were trimmed with pale

gold fringe and white silk roses, these details repeated more daintily around the over-skirt and again, in a still more delicate version, at the neckline, a jeweled aigrette would hold white plumes above a golden diadem nestled in Juno's hair.

Yes, the gown was magnificent. Unfortunately, in it, Juno looked a veritable giant.

"What did you say? *Wallow?* Pigs wallow." Juno giggled. "Sometimes you are so funny. I hope you don't mind it when I laugh. I cannot help it."

Beth smiled. "I don't mind."

Juno rose to her feet and poised herself for another curtsy.

"No!" When Juno threw her a questioning look Beth said, "You must rest yourself. You've practiced so much you've very nearly worn your *limbs* to the knees. You'll curtsy beautifully if the muscles aren't so exhausted they can't function."

"I don't feel the least tired."

"I'll make you a bet."

"A bet! Yes." Juno rubbed her hands together. "Tell me."

"That last time you tried to curtsy," said Beth, holding Juno's gaze, "I'll bet you your new zephyr scarf against the coral necklace your mother gave me that your legs trembled."

Juno went into the other room and returned to toss the scarf on Beth's lap, "How did you know?" Again she maneuvered her hoops so she could sit, managing it with a grace Beth envied.

"I just knew," said Beth evasively. "Are plans complete for your ball? Was it decided that Zander will lead you out?"

Juno lay back on the chaise, her hoop-extended petticoats flying up to reveal the blue garters tying up her stockings. She ignored her skirts, staring dreamily at the ceiling. "Zander will lead me out for the first set and Tony, bless him, has asked for the second. After that I'm promised to Captain Porthson and then Rupert and I forget Tony's friend's nam' and then a friend of Zander's and *then* it will be the supper dance and Tony has *that*."

Beth smiled. "And after supper?"

Juno waved a limp hand. "It doesn't matter. I'll have had my two dances with Tony and the rest is of no consequence whatsoever." She sat up, pushing her hoops into a more decorous position. "Who leads *you* out?" she asked, having just thought of it. "Oh Beth! Perhaps I should *make* my father do his duty so that Zander is free to partner you."

"I believe Zander arranged for your eldest sister's husband to have that honor. Your brother requested the second dance and the supper dance."

"And after supper?" asked Juno slyly.

"After supper? I don't believe enough men have asked for a dance to fill that part of the evening," Beth responded, refusing to allow Juno to see that, for her too, anything beyond the supper dance was irrelevant.

"That's a bouncer," said Juno.

"A fib? Perhaps I exaggerate, but I don't remember names and, actually, I'm not convinced that *anyone* asked except to be polite. After asking *you* to dance, they could hardly avoid asking me, but I never supposed they seriously meant I was to save them a dance."

"It would be exceedingly impolite to ask and not mean it."

"Then perhaps I'll not be a wallflower after all."

"You?" Juno chortled that lovely low laugh. "No fear! The men will flock about you, relieved you are not such a bean pole as I. I'm far more likely to suffer the fate of the oddities on the marriage mart and *not take*."

"Does it worry you, Juno?"

Juno shrugged. "There's only one man about whom I'm concerned. Tony blows hot and then cold. *It's most discon-*

do you mean?"

day he is exceedingly concerned for my comfort

and watches that no one approaches me who should not and does his best to make me laugh. The next he ignores me. It would drive a saint to perdition, Beth and I'm . . ."

Beth spoke along with Juno: *"No saint.* I know. But who is?"

Juno giggled at Beth's raised eyebrows and jesting tone. Beth's brows returned to normal and Juno, sobering, her eyes unfocused and her mouth drooping, drifted in a pout unusual to the effervescent girl.

"Juno," soothed Beth, "you knew when you began your campaign that no thought of marriage had crossed Lord Belmont's mind. Now, once or twice, it may have done so, but you mustn't push too hard or you'll frighten him away. Just a steady, but subtle pressure, maybe?"

"Is that a hint you think me too obvious?"

"Sometimes," said Beth gently and Juno seem to fade. When Beth saw how unhappy she'd made the girl, she added, "There's hope. He bristles, you know, when you banter with someone he thinks might actually be a suitor."

"Does he?" Juno brightened. "Perhaps I should *try* to make him jealous."

Beth immediately wished she'd not given Juno the encouragement of her observation. "That rarely works. A man not yet on the hook is more likely to shrug and think you unworthy of his attentions." Beth smiled at Juno. "Just be yourself. He likes you and that's half the battle. He may not have admitted yet that it's more than liking, and, I warn you, it's possible he never will, but I think you've been going the right way to work."

"But it's taking so long!" wailed Juno. Her shoulders rose and fell on a sigh. "I guess I thought I had only to come to town and present myself to him, a young lady ready for marriage, and he'd know immediately it was *meant.* It never occurred to me I'd have so much worry and sometimes even the fear he'll never realize he loves me. Beth, I get so discouraged I wish I'd never heard Maman telling Papa that

Zander must marry. If I'd not, I'd be at home escaping Miss Wilder's gimlet-eye and happy to sneak out with a gun."

Beth gave the younger girl a curious look. "When you first spoke about Lord Belmont I thought his love was the last thing to concern you, that you only intended that he ask for your hand."

"I thought it would be enough. To be his wife. I thought I'd not care if he had other interests, because I'd know he must come back to me." Juno frowned. "How could I have been so stupid, Beth?"

"Young, perhaps, rather than stupid? Besides, that Miss Wilder of yours filled your head with the notion that tonnish marriages are *not* love matches and that you, in particular, could not expect such. That was particularly foolish of her, was it not? Give me a reason why, just because you're tall, you shouldn't know love?" asked Beth rhetorically. "There are tall men in society, are there not? Many will discover it's far more comfortable dancing with someone their own size. They'll also like it that they needn't bend down to hear you speak. Nor"——Her eyes twinkled——"will they have to put you on a stool in order to kiss you. I'd like to be a mouse in the corner when *that* occurs to an overly tall gentleman!"

Juno blushed rosily, her face softening into a dreamy look. "I can't imagine anyone kissing me but Tony."

Beth didn't admit that, in her dreams, only Zander would do, but she thought it.

Next morning, at a very early hour, Beth woke to the sound of many feet tramping back and forth in the hall. Lying in bed she heard heavy steps cross and recross Juno's room. Finally a door closed; gradually silence fell. She had just dozed off again when Juno's voice, expressing shock followed by displeasure, woke her. Beth rose and found her robe. She knocked once at the connecting door and went through.

"It is too bad of you, Susie," Juno scolded their maid. "Now I'll have red eyes and will look terrible."

The maid stood near where Juno knelt, bent over a basin, her hair sopping wet. The girl wrung her hands, tears in her eyes. She sent a look toward Beth which begged for help.

"What is it, Juno?" asked Beth. "What has happened?"

"This silly girl has gotten soap in my eyes! You can't imagine how they sting."

"Who's silly?" asked Beth, smiling at the maid. "In my opinion, *you* were, Juno Knightly! How could you have been so stupid as to open your eyes? We'll rinse them as soon as the soap is gone from your hair and by the time you leave, they'll be fine." She nodded to the maid to finish Juno's hair. "Need I warn you to close them so you get no more soap in them?" Beth teased.

Beth carefully rinsed Juno's stinging eyes. When they felt better Juno apologized to the maid. The long process of drying her hair began, Juno seated on a stool before her fire and the maid brushing and brushing, while her mistress muttered and mumbled, convinced she'd not possibly be ready in time to leave for St. James Palace and her presentation to Queen Charlotte.

Later Beth stood in the doorway at the front of the house and tried not to laugh as, with her mother's and butler's help, Juno attempted to get into the Fairmont coach. The poor girl had to worry not only about her wide hoops but also the tall plumes decorating her head dress. The fact she was so tall herself didn't help. She truly fit her pet name of Queeny.

"Someday you'll have to worry about that," whispered Zander from just behind her. Beth glanced over her shoulder. "When we're wed and Maman takes you for your presentation," he explained.

"Zander . . ."

"Shh. I refuse to give up my dreams until all hope is gone. Until *you* are gone."

Beth ignored him. She had to ignore him. Besides, the lump in her throat would allow no words, either of warning or of false encouragement.

"There," he said when Juno and Lady Fairmont were properly settled and Shipper stood away from the door to the coach. "They're off." When the coach left the square Zander said, "Now they've gone, we may leave as well."

He took Beth's pelisse from Higgens and she slipped into it without thinking. Then, taking her bonnet from the maid, he tied the bow under Beth's chin. He handed her her parasol and reticule which she accepted equally without thought. Then he took her elbow and urged her down the steps. His curricle, the matched grays led by a young groom, turned the corner from the mews and arrived just as they descended to the pavement.

"Excellent timing," he said.

"Easy," said the boy impertinently. "I just waited out of sight until I heard Coachy's whip snap and then waited a bit more and here we am."

"Here you am indeed." He flipped the lad a coin which was deftly caught.

Zander helped Beth into the curricle. It wasn't one of the dangerously unstable high perch designs, but the swan neck seat was higher than Beth liked and seemed to suspend her directly over the road. She clutched at the edge, her hand hidden under her skirt.

"Let 'em go," Zander told the groom.

"Where are we going?" Beth asked once Zander's pair were moving well.

"It occurred to me recently that that beautiful golden glow I love so much is fading. Then my father asked that I check a property in Sussex which lies a couple of hours from town. So I schemed to kidnap you and would have even if it were *not* so warm and sunny." He grinned. "It took very careful planning, I'll have you know."

"And Higgen's help?" His grin widened but gave no other answer. Instead he said, "Now we're away from Mayfair and anyone who might recognize us, you may put away that parasol and let the sun restore your color."

"I don't dare," she said, half joking, but half horrified at the thought of tan lines. "My face would tan, but what of the rest of me? I don't think that would look so good!"

"The *rest* of you?" Zander took his eyes from his horses to look at Beth. He started at her face and made a quick tour on down toward her toes. *"All* of you?"

Beth blushed. Nevertheless she spoke firmly. "All of me."

"What sort of society is it that allows a woman to bare her whole body to the sun?" A muscle jumped in his clenched jaw.

"What sort of society is it," she mimicked his tone, "where a woman's reputation may be lost by merely riding out into the country, alone for a few hours, with a man?"

Zander felt heat in neck and face. "It's an open carriage," he said a trifle defensively. "There's a trust-worthy house-keeper at Beechwood Place."

"Nevertheless . . ."

"All right," he said crossly. He drew in a deep breath and added, "Every society has oddities, *but . . .*" He paused.

"I *fear* I can read your mind, Zander. And very nasty thoughts they are!"

After a moment he grinned at her. "Not nasty. It's merely that I'm thinking that once we wed I must make a place—a very private place—where we may lie in the sun, together, in any state we wish!" He leered at her, but with a humorous touch which disarmed her. "Well"—the leer faded into a smile and his voice softened—"maybe the thoughts *have* become a trifle nasty, when I think of all I'd do with you in that very private place, except *nasty* isn't the proper word."

"Zander, don't make plans!" Beth spoke more sharply than she might have done, irritated that she too could imagine the things they'd do. They weren't at all nasty!

"I can't help myself." The smile faded away as well. He cast her a hesitant glance then stared between his horses down the road ahead. "Beth, please tell me you were alone when you bared your beautiful skin to the sun."

"You wish me to lie to you? I've told you it's a more open society, a freer age, less hypocritical. Men and women sea bathe in the nude, Zander. They lie on beaches side by side. An occasional couple may touch in an intimate way—but for deeper intimacy they retire to privacy."

"For lovemaking."

"Yes. To make love."

Again he glanced at her, this time with a frown. Again he looked down the road, a certain tension revealed in his voice. "My naked body on board the captain's ship was nothing new to you."

"No."

"But mine should have been the first to rouse in you those feelings I wish to explore with you!"

"It is."

Startled, he jerked the reins and was forced to take several minutes from their conversation to sooth and settle his pair. "Beth," he said, once he'd done so, "sometimes you are unbelievable. How can you not have been excited by all that male flesh?"

"You don't see how I could have viewed nude male bodies and not feel what I feel when I think of yours? Does every woman you see arouse such feelings in you?"

"I do not see them naked."

"You have imagination. You can think of them undressed. Can just any woman, undressed, make you feel lust?"

He shrugged. "I suppose it depends on whether I'm in the mood or not."

"Ah." In a dry voice, she added, "All cats are black in the dark."

"Hmm? What have cats to do with anything?"

"An expression from an era I've studied intensively. It means it makes no difference what woman you have if you are in the mood to have a woman."

"Don't sound as if such a notion caused hurt! One feels

an itch, one scratches an itch." In a faintly patronizing tone, he added, "It means nothing emotionally."

"I see." If possible, her tone was dryer still. "Then if we *were* allowed to wed, which is something we must not permit ourselves to believe for an instant, but if it *were* allowed and then you were sent off as you were to the Peninsula and I were to remain at home and feel that itch while you were gone, it would not matter if I satisfied it with some convenient male?"

Zander audibly gritted his teeth. "It's not the same for a woman!"

"It's exactly the same for a woman."

He sent her a frustrated look. "Are you saying you'd demand the right to take lovers—or alternately, require fidelity from a spouse?"

"Would not you? Require fidelity?"

"Beth, I tell you it is not the same. Women must guard their husband's honor and bear only his children."

"Ah. But if it were impossible for her to become pregnant unless she wished it?"

"What!"

"There are ways of preventing pregnancy, Zander."

His grim expression deepened. "Yes. There are ways. Even now there are ways! They are not used by decent women."

"Nonsense."

"It's not!"

Beth didn't respond.

"What can you possibly mean?" he probed.

"You've only to look around you. Within your privileged class woman don't stop having relations with their husbands—or someone else—after they've born a mere two to four children, but they *often* stop having children!"

"I don't understand."

"More likely, you don't wish to understand. The women living in poverty bear one child after another for the whole of their lives—which are thereby drastically shortened. The rich do not. It's my contention that the rich know how to prevent conception whereas the poor do not. That's all."

"Not all women of my class are so barren . . ."

"Some have a child every year, yes. Far more do not." She gave him a challenging look. "Why do you think that is?"

"Something different in the diet . . . perhaps?"

Beth chuckled. "You don't believe that."

"No, it is far more likely they *do* cease to welcome their husbands to their beds. I *know* a couple where that's the case. The man makes no secret of the fact he's a mistress in keeping where he may take his ease."

"I accept that to be true for the occasional pair, but in all cases? Your own mother bore only five children and I know she and your father. . . ."

"You'll not mention my mother in such a context! She's a decent woman."

"Of course your mother is a decent woman. *You* insist contraception is indecent. *I* do not!"

"Nor will I have a wife who takes lovers," he said, seemingly changing the subject.

"If I were your wife you'd have no need to worry. But, likewise, I'll not marry a man who keeps a mistress. I'll not even marry where he'll *take-his-ease* with an occasional random woman because his wife, me, is unavailable."

"You're unreasonable."

"No," she said sadly. "I'm merely a creature of my time as you are of yours."

"Where do I get the notion you'd expect me to adapt to your values rather than you to mine?"

Beth sighed and clutched one hand tightly over the other. "Does it matter?" she asked, bitterness not far from the surface. "Since we'll have no need to answer such questions?"

"It matters." Zander paused. Finally he chuckled. "What's worse, I argue merely because of pride and stubbornness.

You'd have no need to worry that I'd stray from your bed, Beth."

She turned a querying look his way.

Red surged up his neck and into his face. "Must I explain, my love?"

She nodded a firm sharp dip of her head.

He sighed. "I went to one of the more reputable houses. I thought it would be less painful to be in your presence if I relieved the frustrations eating at me—"

Beth felt her jaws tightened, her teeth clench painfully.

"—for all the good it did me," he finished ruefully.

"I don't understand," whispered Beth.

"None of the women were you, Beth, I came away unsatisfied."

The tension drained away. "Will you think me terribly selfish if I say I'm glad?"

"I don't know that selfishness has anything to do with it." He turned a grin her way. "Possessiveness maybe? We're a pair of fools, Beth. Why do we argue when we agree? Except about the contraceptives, perhaps . . ." He looked at her, drew in a deep breath. "Beth, we'll discuss it again when I've had time to think about it. Whatever decision we come to about *that,* we'll agree to be a totally unfashionable couple and live in each other pockets, shocking the ton and perhaps finding ourself ostracized for such unusual behavior!"

"If we marry . . ."

"I refuse to lose hope," said Zander. "I prefer to think positively."

"While I must remain rooted in reality and remember the possibility is so far from reasonable as to be non-existent," Beth reminded him.

"Today let us pretend we're married, that we'll always be together."

Her brows arched. "I assume you do not mean to find a bedroom in the country house toward which we travel and take that pretense to its logical conclusion?" she asked.

"I certainly would if you would, but I know you will not. No, merely a stolen kiss or, perhaps, I might be allowed to feel you in my arms again? My hands allowed to touch you as they've done before?"

Beth had a seductive vision of the two of them in some private spot enjoying the sun, his hands free to roam, hers as well. "Zander . . ."

"I know." He allowed a sigh to escape him. "We must be very careful, must we not?"

"I begin to wonder if I want to be careful," she mumbled.

"What?"

She didn't respond.

"Beth?"

Beth felt her complexion darken. "Nothing. Please don't regard it."

But, even as she spoke, Beth vowed that, when her mission ended, she'd take a holiday and seduce this man she loved so much. She and he *would* find that private place in the sun and she'd make dreams, memories, which must last for all the years to come. Already, at the mere thought of leaving Zander, her heart ached and a faint sense of desperation imbued her very soul.

"You've gone off inside your head, Beth."

"Hmm? Never mind. Is it much further?"

"We're barely half way, my love."

"One thing I'll never like about this era is how long it takes to get from here to there! Do you remember telling me you believe steam engines will become a major mode of transportation?" He nodded. "Let me assure you such inventions are much improved. This little jaunt? In such a vehicle, it might take all of twenty minutes—assuming traffic weren't too heavy."

Automatically slowing his team, Zander turned, stared at her. "Twenty minutes? Impossible. I do not believe you! I *cannot* believe you! It is nearly fifteen miles!"

"Perhaps you understand, now, why I find traveling behind horses unreasonable and uncomfortable?"

Having again broken the rule forbidding her to tell Zander about future inventions, Beth ignored it. She told more tales of how life would change although she chose carefully telling Zander about things so far beyond anything he'd imagined as to verge on the order of fairy tales.

"Maybe," said Zander hesitantly, as they pulled into Beechwood's drive, "with some help from you I'll be allowed to see these marvels for myself?"

"I don't know." Beth was thoughtful as she continued. "You're the sort of man ART needs. Perhaps when Smithson is sent to his lonely paradise you might be taught to replace him as Anchor . . ."

Beth relaxed. Perhaps she'd have plenty of time to seduce Zander.

Not that he'd take much seducing!

Thirteen

Zander and Beth returned to London to find the house in an uproar. Miss Wilder had fallen gravely ill while everyone was out and the servants had not known how to cope.

"It is just like her," said Juno unjustly.

Beth remonstrated.

"Oh well then! I know she cannot help herself, but it is so very inconvenient. I visited her . . . Beth"—Juno's eyes widened—"one side of her face droops like melted candle wax!"

The poor woman has had a stroke, thought Beth and feared her arrival had brought on the condition. Miss Wilder hadn't concealed her dislike of the addition of a stranger to the family, even though she believed Beth a relative. Beth suspected Miss Wilder feared for her position, that it would be lost to her even sooner than expected!

In fact, from something Beth had overheard Miss Wilder tell another governess-cum-companion, the woman had hoped to be kept on until Juno married. *". . . some distant time in the future, if at all."* Miss Wilder had gloated. *"Such a bean pole as Lady Juno is, so outspoken, so apt to forget all which has been taught her of ladylike behavior. What man would have her?"* she'd finished smugly.

"Has your mother told her she'll be kept here and nursed?"

"I don't have the least notion what Maman has or has not said to her. Finding her ill ruined all the excitement of my presentation and she has very likely ruined my ball as well. It is too bad of her!"

"How can she possibly ruin your ball?"

"Is it not obvious? Very likely she'll die just to spite me," said Juno with unusual acid. "It will be necessary to cancel my ball."

"Miss Wilder is not about to die."

Juno stared at Beth, wide-eyed, painfully hopeful. "Are you certain?"

"Quite certain. Assuming, of course, she doesn't suffer overly much from the fear she'll be put into the street just as she is—which might very well bring on another attack!"

"Maman would never do such a thing. And if that will make her well, I'll ask Maman her plans and tell Miss Wilder myself."

Juno rushed from the salon and Beth was about to go to her room when Zander entered. "Such a to-do," he said.

"Is she very bad?"

"The doctor doubts she'll recover completely. I've discussed it with my father and he agrees she be given a pension and a cottage on one of our estates."

"She mustn't live alone, Zander, when her health is so precarious. Perhaps your mother knows of someone?"

"I can, if you please, think of a candidate all by myself, a distant cousin who has battened on my father for years. She and Miss Wilder deal well with each other. I'll just go mention *that* to Father as well."

Zander, too, left the salon and again Beth was about to follow when the door opened for a third time. This time, Lady Fairmont entered, a deep frown creasing her brow "Ah, there you are, Mademoiselle."

"May I be of help? Poor Juno fears her ball will be ruined and we cannot have that!"

Lady Fairmont frowned at Beth's levity. "I fear someone must sit with Miss Wilder. I hope I may impose on you to do so?"

Properly sobered, Beth replied, "I'll be happy to help."

"I'm very sorry to ask it of you, but she becomes exceeding upset when left with only a servant. Given the behavior on the part of my servants when the emergency arose, I cannot find it in my heart to blame her," added the countess, revealing where Juno had learned the use of acid.

"Perhaps once she knows she's to receive a pension and a cottage she'll be less . . . demanding of your attention."

"Is she to be pensioned off?"

"Zander just told me Lord Fairmont decided it would be best."

"Doubtless Zander had a finger in *that* pie. But you may be correct. Juno insists she fears she'll be put out in the street on her own. However that may be, I'd appreciate it if you'll sit with her from directly after dinner until I return from Lord Castlereigh's."

"You mean to sit up with her during the night?"

"Someone must." Lady Fairmont shrugged.

"It should be me, I think. I may go to bed now and sleep so I'll not sleep tonight. But you"—Beth shook her head—"it is important *you* be in good form for Beth's ball tomorrow. If I must leave the dancing early no one will care, but you, as hostess, must stay, however tired you become."

Lady Fairmont stared at Beth for a long moment. "I try very hard to dislike you, Miss Whomever-you-may-be, but you make it very difficult for me to do so."

"Should I apologize?" Beth chuckled. "It's difficult to decide what to do with me, is it not? I appreciate that you've allowed me to be part of your family. Sitting with Miss Wilder may make up a trifle for your sacrifice."

Lady Fairmont nodded regally. "If you are to take night duty, then you'd best rest now. I'll see you're awakened in time to dress for dinner." Once again Beth started across the salon for the hall door. "Mademoiselle, your duty to Miss Wilder will not be for long. We soon leave London for a bit. Our friends have pinched pennies ever since a major fire destroyed one wing of their home and much of value to them. They mean to bring out their next daughter in the country. She is, I believe, to marry a neighbor's boy . . ." Lady Fairmont paused. "Are you all right?"

"All right?" Beth blinked, blinked again. Finally she brought her hostess back into focus "Yes. Of course I am. Why should I not be?"

This time when she moved toward the door Beth was allowed to escape. *All right?* she wondered as she climbed the stairs. Was she? That sudden sharp hurting flash of . . . memory? . . . when Lady Fairmont mentioned fire was excessively frightening and far different from her usual amorphous fear of fire. There'd been a brief but vivid vision of a long narrow room or wide corridor. Heavy frames in a row along the inside wall. Dark paneling, deeply coved ceiling, a polished floor. Gothic windows, one after another, framed in gray stone and marching down the outer wall . . .

The vision had been so real, and so had the roaring flames sweeping toward her to engulf her, to swirl around her, to play with the hem of her nightgown and the ends of long hair flying behind her as she ran and screamed . . . and screamed . . . and screamed.

Had it been that way? Was that what Suu-Van had seen? Had it really happened or was her imagination again playing tricks on her? Beth went to her bed but couldn't relax. Instead, her mind reviewed each and every "vision" she'd had since arriving in 1813.

Was it merely that she wanted desperately for this to be her birth time—or was it, by some totally unlikely chance, *truly* so? Beth stared at the window seat in which the sarong, with its secret power source, lay hidden. Dared she contact Suu-Van?

Beth sighed. Settling the mystery of her past was not an emergency on which she should waste the limited energy. Eventually, face to face, she'd ask Suu-Van questions, discover what was real and what was imagination or, worse, no more than wishful thinking. She'd lived ten years with no past. She'd survive however long it took to settle Smithson's hash.

But, by Riddle's git-fiddle, she'd have it out with Suu-Van as soon as possible! And she'd discover if there were the slightest chance her love for Zander would not be wasted . . . But this wouldn't do. She had a long night ahead of her with a patient who required a great deal of patience. She must rest. Beth composed herself, going through a series of tension relaxing exercises— and was forced to repeat them when once was not effective. Finally she slept.

Her long night's vigil ended when Juno relieved her. Again Beth slept, her body refreshing itself. After a light lunch she returned to the sickroom, meaning to send the younger girl off to a well-deserved rest of her own.

"Beth, I've been reading in French from this book. Miss Wilder seems to like it even if I cannot pronounce all the words correctly. I'm certain she'd appreciate it if you, who must speak French beautifully, continued the story?"

Before Beth could panic at the thought of attempting to read aloud in a language in which she'd had no training, Zander's welcome voice intruded.

"It's been years since I practiced my French," he said. "I'd enjoy the opportunity to do so." He took the book from his sister's hand, read the title, and looked up. "You've been reading *this?*" he asked sternly.

"I don't understand the half of it and you must not agitate poor Miss Wilder. Look at her."

"I shall not inform my mother of your taste in literature, Miss Wilder, but I cannot allow innocents such as Beth or Juno to read such nonsense. I'll finish it for you. Juno, take Beth off and do whatever it is girls do to prepare for a ball. Miss Wilder and I will get along quite well without you, will we not, Miss Wilder?"

Miss Wilder looked as if she were not at all sure!

* * *

Their festive evening started with dinner for forty friends and relatives. Juno, seated at her father's right in the place of honor, was partnered on her other side by a slim young man with guinea gold hair. Unhappy, Juno's eyes flitted, often, toward Lord Belmont who sat beside a sophisticated widow of questionable virtue.

Anthony, she thought, was too well entertained.

Juno could not stop fidgeting until she recalled that Tony was her partner for both the second and the supper dance. Feeling much more the thing, she asked the young man a question. It must have been the right question because her dinner partner glowed and spoke so volubly he waved away every dish in the second course while he went on and on about . . . something.

Beth's dinner partners were, on one side, a friend of Lord Fairmont interested in nothing but political questions and, on the other, a Knightly cousin still at Cambridge and destined for the church. The meal seemed interminable.

It might have been less boring if she could have seen Zander from where she sat, but she couldn't. Lady Fairmont had taken great care with the seating arrangements. Her ladyship spent hours arranging and rearranging her table before she was satisfied. Except, Lady Fairmont did not *look* satisfied.

Beth remembered that Zander had disappeared from the salon just before Shipper announced dinner. Only moments before the butler entered, he'd returned, a cat-eating-cream expression twitching the corners of his mouth. Beth had a sneaking suspicion the two young women chosen to sit, one on either side of him, had had their place cards moved! But would Zander have had the nerve to disarrange his mother's carefully planned table? Beth decided he very well might—especially if he perceived that his mother was match making.

Which, of course, she *was*.

Then, dinner over, Beth stood in the receiving line beside Juno, smile a plastered on her face. Surreptitiously she rubbed her gloved hand against her thigh, clenched it and released the tension. She wished she had Lady Fairmont's ease of manner and that the hundreds of introductions weren't one huge blur of names and faces. She glanced at Juno. Juno looked as glazed as she felt. Why did the ton put their daughters through this nonsense? Finally the influx of guests slowed to a trickle.

"My lord," said Lady Fairmont to her husband, "take Juno and our cousin into the ballroom. I'll remain here a trifle longer."

Lord Fairmont, a twinkle in his usually serious eyes, offered an arm to each young woman. Properly coached, his lordship paused inside the double doors at the top of shallow steps leading down to the ballroom floor. When eyes turned their way he murmured, "Armed for battle, my dears?"

Juno giggled. Beth smiled. Both girls relaxed.

"Now," continued a jovial Lord Fairmont, speaking for the girls' ears alone, "let us try very hard not to trip over our feet while going down the stairs. Do you see? My son and son-in-law await you. I suggest you pay no attention to anyone else, just to reaching your partners in a suitably upright position. Ready? Heads up now. One two three . . ."

Zander took his sister's hand by the fingertips, raised it and, his other hand on his hip, led her to the center of the dance floor. Beth followed, her hand similarly held by her partner. They turned and faced each other. The men bowed. The girls curtsied. Somehow they got through the complications of the dance without missing a step. The music ended with a flourish and again they bowed and curtsied.

"Well," said Juno. "I'm glad *that's* over. Beth, I'll never thank you half enough for coming into our family. I'd have had to do that *alone* if you were not here!"

By this time they'd reached the edge of the floor where Juno's father stood. He beamed from one to the other. "I'm honored to introduce two such lovely young women to the ton—ah." It seemed impossible, but his lordship's smile broadened. "Here's Anthony. Do you wish a dance with one of my beauties, Anthony?"

Beth thought Lord Belmont gave her a quick curious glance as if it had never occurred to him to think her a beauty. She bit her lip to suppress a grin, but then Zander offered his arm and suddenly nothing else was important.

Beth's eyes were often trapped by his as they danced. Once she found herself blushing for no reason at all. Dancing, when with Zander, was more than an enjoyable form of exercise. It was awareness as hands joined. It was an accelerated heartbeat when he smiled. It was moving as one with the music. It was *almost* as good as being alone with him . . . Beth was certain, as it ended, that this dance took only half the time of the first. But then, any dance with Zander would be over too soon.

Later that evening, Beth smiled at a glowing Juno. The girl had danced one dance after another and never once had Beth seen her with a man too short for the embarrassingly tall young woman. Tony and Zander had done their work well, decided Beth.

After Juno complained about her problem, Beth had observed tonnish men. Far too many were an inch or more shorter than Juno. An inch wasn't bad—or so Beth had tried to convince the younger girl, but, tonight, Juno had sworn to have nothing to do with any man who couldn't, at the very least, look her straight in the eyes. So far she was successful in that vow.

Zander claimed his supper dance. It too was too soon over. Afterwards, they promenaded around the room with other couples until the crowd thinned. Then Zander opened a pair of French doors leading from an alcove onto a small balcony. They moved beyond the light to the balustrade.

"How did you do it?" she asked him.

"Do what?"

"Find so many partners of an appropriate height for Juno?"

"I had very little to do with it. Tony may have called in a favor or two, but I'd guess many like the fact she's tall—at least for the dancing."

"I told her that might be the case." She glanced up at him, away.

"When your eyes sparkle like that, you've been up to mischief. Just what else did you tell her?"

"Only that they'd enjoy dancing with someone their own size—and still more, kissing someone they neither had to break their backs to find nor pick up to reach!"

"You didn't!" exclaimed Zander, both outraged and amused. "Juno has enough notions in her head without adding to them. Maman would turn you out for suggesting such a thing."

"You know there's only one man she wishes would kiss her," said Beth on a dry note. "She'll not turn into a flirt, or worse, because I teased her a little."

"Do you suppose I'd prefer kissing a taller woman?" He asked the question blandly and it took Beth a moment to realize he referred to someone other than her reasonably tall self. "I should perhaps test it . . . ?" His voice trailed off, looking at her from the corners of his eyes.

Beth turned, leaned against the railing, her heart beating far too hard and fast. "You'll do no such thing, Lord Hawksbeck!"

He grinned. "You rise to the bait so nicely, Mademoiselle Thevenard! You took it hook and bait, did you not?"

"*Some* things, my lord, are too serious to joke about."

He sobered. "Are you seriously angry with me, Beth?"

Beth looked away, clutched at the chill stone. "I don't know. I didn't realize how insecure I am."

"Insecure?"

"Why else would I feel as if the chandelier fell on me when you suggest you'd kiss someone else? And yet I *know* nothing can come of our love. I *know* I must leave when

I've completed my mission. I *know* you must marry another, that you'll get yourself an heir. I *know* all that and yet . . ."

"And yet you love me. I love you too, Beth. There must be a way. A man may adopt an heir, you know. Given time, I'll be able to accept that you use your contraceptives, that we have no children of our own. If we agreed to that, then could you stay?"

"I don't know. Possibly." She bit her lip. "I will discuss it with Suu-Van."

"When?"

She risked a glance his way at the emotion in his question, looked away from the tension in his face where every bone was stark against tight skin. "When I return. It's against common sense to waste what little energy I have available. It is not like the equipment built into Smithson's ship which can gather energy from the sun and store it until needed."

"From the sun?"

"Again I've said something I shouldn't. Ignore it, Zander."

"Very well." He too stared over the moonlit garden.

Somewhere late-blooming roses scented the air. Beth thought she'd never again smell that aroma that she didn't think of this night, of the tension growing between them. Could they be together? Forever? If she had herself sterilized so she couldn't interfere with Time even if she wished? Or would that in itself be interference? Did Zander, someday, have a child or grandchild or great-great-great grandchild important in the furtherance of history? Beth groaned softly.

"What is it, love?"

"Nothing. We'd better go into supper or your mother will come looking for us. I don't think I could face Lady Fairmont just now."

In the dining room they discovered Tony and Juno had saved seats for them. "Where have you been?" asked Juno. Tony attempted to shush her. "It is just Zander. He'll not mind if I ask indiscreet questions."

"But Mademoiselle Thevenard might," said Tony reprovingly.

"Beth will not eat me."

"Beth ripped out her hem during that last dance," said Zander, "and was forced to fix it, so you see, Juno, there's no reason for anyone to eat anyone, is there?"

"Only a hem?" asked Juno, disappointed. "I imagined such wonderful scenes in which Zander took Beth into his arms and passionately kissed her!"

"I assure you that however much I might have liked kissing Beth, I did not," said Zander bitingly. And truthfully, of course. "Beth, what may I get for you?"

"Anything." She looked at Juno's generously loaded plate. "Far less, please, than Lord Belmont got Juno!"

"I noticed Juno didn't eat her dinner," said Lord Belmont. "If she isn't hungry she should be!" He glanced around for one of the servants refilling wineglasses. None were near their table. "I'll get us more wine, Juno. Be right back . . ."

"Quickly," demanded Beth. "Who sat beside Zander at dinner?"

Juno's eyes twinkled. *"Not* the suitable young ladies Maman planned to see seated there! Lady Sefton was on one side and the Dowager Duchess of Ware on his other. Maman was livid!" She chuckled, that wonderful laugh enveloping them and drawing eyes.

"It will be war between them if she's not careful," said Beth softly.

"He's in love with you," responded Juno. "Why cannot Maman see that?"

"Perhaps," said Beth carefully, "she feels I'm an unsuitable mate for him, Juno."

"Her own cousin? Nonsense."

But I'm not a cousin, thought Beth. *No relation at all.* And Lady Fairmont knows it. Just then Zander set her plate before her. She glanced up, smiled. But the smile must not have been all it should have been.

"What is it, Beth?"

"Nothing." He frowned at her. Beth looked away, adding, "Nothing new, that is."

He nodded, accepting that she could not feel entirely joyful when their future was so very much in doubt. Tony returned followed by a footman bearing wine and champagne. Tony's light-hearted mood matched Juno's and the two soon had Zander and Beth laughing and teasing in return.

But, even as she chuckled at one of Tony's sallies, Beth felt weighted down by the cold dark heavy center she seemed destined to carry forever. However much they hoped, it was unreasonable to think she and Zander might have any future at all.

At least anything more than an interlude.

Fourteen

After supper, Beth spent some moments in the woman's retiring room and then retraced her steps to rejoin the revelers, only to wish she'd *not* returned. Peering from one of the alcoves, she pulled off a slipper and rubbed her instep. Why had she not gone directly to her room? No one would have noticed. No one been the wiser. Very likely, no one would have cared!

Nearly hidden by the draperies Beth noticed a boorish military man with whom she'd danced earlier. He'd warned her he'd find her later and now he neared her hiding place. Beth backed farther behind the curtain and touched cool panes of glass. She remembered Zander had opened doors in another alcove to let them onto a balcony. Without thinking, her hands searched for and grasped slim metal handles.

She pressed down, made an opening wide enough to slip through, and closed the doors behind her. Beth's silk clad feet met rough gravel; she moved restlessly, stepped on a sharp piece of grit and yelped softly—then was worried that she'd been heard. But no one disturbed her where she breathed deeply of chill night air. Rather than the night blooming roses, it now smelled of drifts of coal smoke which tickled the inside of her nostrils. But that didn't matter. She was free!

Beth stripped a ribbon from the loops just under her bosom. She pulled up her skirts and slipped the ribbon between her legs—*limbs,* she corrected herself, grinning—and pulled it up, front and back, tying it at her shoulder. Her skirts tidily out of the way, she searched out a route up the wall.

Once she reached the parapet surrounding the ballroom roof she balanced on it, did a simple routine she'd learned for the exercise horse when taking gymnastics, and then, chuckling at such nonsense, ran along the stone work to the main part of the house. There she worked her way along the wall to her window, carefully testing hand and toe holds as she went, fearing the brick might crumble at her weight. Clambering over the sill onto the window seat, Beth heaved a sigh of relief. She released the ribbon and allowed her skirts to drop back to where they belonged.

"It's about time you came," growled the captain's disembodied voice from the direction of her bed.

Beth stiffened, peered into the dark room. "What do you want?"

"I'm your superior. I need your help. I give the orders."

"I was sent to rescue those pictures in Kent. I don't see how I'm to help you."

"That lordling you've englamoured. You will use him."

"I've . . . englamoured? . . . him?" Beth chuckled.

"He'll do your bidding."

"I doubt it."

"He will!" The bed creaked as the captain got up. He moved toward her, a darker shadow against the shadows which were her room. Reaching her, he grasped her chin in a hurting pinch. "He must. Hear me?"

"I hear," she said between barely moving lips.

"If he does not, then I'll destroy him," hissed Smithson.

Beth blinked. It'd never occurred to her that villains actually hissed!

When she didn't respond, he added, "You wouldn't like that, I think."

"I don't like the thought of anyone being destroyed, now or whenever!"

"Pretty thought, yours, but impracticable," said the captain. "You tell him to get my ship released."

Beth jerked her chin free. "He told me you asked that of him. He wondered what you thought he *could* do. If there was nothing he could do then, why do you think he might do something now?"

"Bah! He can arrange it."

"Isn't that wishful thinking? Zander's not active in politics. He isn't a military man. He takes no part in the City's business. How is it you believe he can help you?"

Inwardly, Beth cringed at the growl of pure frustration coming from Captain Smithson's throat, but she stood slim and straight, allowing no fear to show.

"I must go. I must *go*," wailed the captain. He shook his fists at the heavens. "Will no man me help *sail?*"

"Then you believe me that Zander cannot?"

"He has said it." The captain seemed subdued and somehow diminished. "You have said it. I suppose I must believe it."

"You'll not harm him for what is not his fault?" Beth held her breath.

"No."

"Hadn't you better go? Guests will be leaving and you mustn't be seen."

"Bah! I'll not be seen."

Beth heard the faintest of whirs. Slowly the captain drifted up until his feet were above the window sill. He drifted out the window, dropping toward the ground. Beth leaned out. "That's forbidden in this century!"

"Bah!"

Zander stood on the tiny balcony on which Beth had stood some minutes earlier. He held her slippers between his fingers as, worried, he searched the darkened gardens for a hint of movement, a clue to where his Beth had disappeared.

Finally he was rewarded, but instead of feeling happy he'd caught sight of his errant love, he gasped at the indistinct image of a figure floating inches above the path. At the fence the figure rose gently until its head was silhouetted above the brick-work, obviously checking no one was beyond. Then, an awkward twist of the body and the floater dropped out of sight.

Beth was gone. Somewhere . . .

Zander, already irritated she'd slipped away from a ball held partly in her honor, was furious she'd left the house secretly, using the ball as cover. But, most of all, there was a growing terror she'd be caught down along the docks, exposed for a woman, used as brutal men use women, killed. And there was nothing he could do.

He could not disappear. *He* must pretend nothing concerned him. *He* must dance with the young guests, speak politely to their chaperons, check occasionally that all was well in the card rooms, do—thanks to his equally errant father—all those multitudinous things a host did at a ton party of importance. Somehow, he must pretend there was nothing on his mind but the happiness of the Fairmont guests.

So he danced, chatted, took a hand of cards, went for lemonade for a shy newcomer to the social scene, and all the while, irritating him by its irrelevancy, he knew a great curiosity to see, at first hand, how Beth had managed this most recent trick! She'd told him inventions existed in the future which would amaze him, but she'd also said she couldn't fly here and now. She'd lied!

"Where's Beth?" asked Juno, clutching his sleeve in the early hours of the morning when the company had thinned somewhat.

"She went to bed," said Zander shortly. He thought of the supple slippers he'd folded and put in a hidden pocket. "She said her feet hurt."

"Poor Beth." Juno chuckled. "Poor me, too. I'm walking

on the stubs left when mine wore out completely! Oh! It's a marvelous ball," she said, smiling at the same shy girl for whom Zander had fetched lemonade. "There can never, ever, have been a come-out ball to match it."

"Tell our mother, not me."

"But I've seen you, Zander!" Juno poked him. "You've worked as hard as anyone to make my ball a success. In fact, I think Father rather high-handedly left you to it and disappeared into the library ages ago."

"So he did." Zander's scowl frightened off a young would-be Corinthian who had searched all evening for the courage to ask Zander if he'd give him an introduction to Gentleman Jackson's Number 13 Bond Street boxing establishment, the pinnacle, just then, of the young man's ambitions.

"Zander? Why do you frown?"

"It's too bad of our father. I'd assumed I might disappear after supper when many of my friends left." His eyes clouded with a vision of Beth floating along that path—and his need to follow her. "When Father told me what a good job I was doing and that I must be a good boy and keep it up since he had business with the Prime Minister I'd no choice but to stay."

Juno's enticing chuckle even warmed her brother's spirits. "Poor Zander," she pretended to commiserate. She looked around and her eyes lit on Tony, who was once again speaking to the youngish widow, his dinner partner, and very obviously enjoying the conversation. Enjoying it far more than Juno could bring herself to appreciate! She sighed. "Maman is too old-fashioned for words."

"No waltzes?" For a moment his gloom lightened and Zander actually grinned at his sister.

"No waltzes. It is too bad of her."

"Juno, that you've been allowed to *learn* the waltz should be more than enough. You well know it isn't danced in society. Would you cause a scandal?"

"If it's waltzed on the continent, then why is it not allowed here?"

"With whom would you dare to dance it?"

Juno promptly responded, "With *you,* the dearest of my brothers." She laughed her contagious laugh.

"Your *only* brother," he said, dryly. But he relaxed and grinned at her. *Perhaps* Juno hadn't had Tony in mind when thinking of the scandalous waltz, but he'd better say something more. "You put all thought of the waltz from your mind, Juno. You'd be sent home to the Aerie in disgrace if you were to do something so outrageous."

"I know. I'm not stupid. But . . ."

"Juno . . ."

"Oh well. One can dream." She pouted.

"Yes," Zander agreed, "one can dream." He turned his attention to a woman with three girls all very much of an age who approached just then. "Lady Jepperson? You are leaving? You've had a good time, I hope?" He smiled at her daughters who nodded as one, like puppets on a single string. The guests moved on and Zander growled, "Do you think this will ever end?"

Juno laughed, her eyes twinkling up at him before she smiled at her next partner, Sir Terrence, who waited nearby. "I hope not!" she called over her shoulder as he led her out. Her laugh effervesced. "Oh, I hope not!"

Zander, seeing that all was well, gave into the urge which had ridden him for what seemed hours and, slipping away, he climbed a set of servant's stairs two at a time. He paced down the carpet covered hall to Beth's room where, glancing both ways, he opened her door and stepped in. He stopped.

A lamp turned very low threw a rosy glow across the bed. "Beth!"

"Hmm?" She raised her head from her pillows. "Zander?" She rubbed her eyes and yawned. "What is it?" she asked. "Is something wrong?"

His weight pressed down the side of her bed. "When did you return?"

"Return?" She yawned, blinking away sleep. "I've not been anywhere."

"Don't lie. I saw you go."

Pulling the covers up, Beth hugged her knees. "I told that idiot—"

Zander grasped her already sore chin in just the place Captain Smithson had pinched. "What idiot?" he demanded. "An assignation, Beth?"

She pushed his hand away and worked her jaw, gently rubbing it. She hoped there'd be no bruises. "Nothing of the sort," she said tartly, not being one who woke from a sound sleep in a cheery mood. "The idiot was our precious captain. He hoped to blackmail me into convincing you to get his ship released." She yawned again.

"And where did you see the captain?"

"Here." She gestured.

"He came to your room and you let him in?" Zander demanded.

"No I did *not*. I found him here when I left the ball."

"Why *did* you leave the ball?"

"Zander, what is this?" asked Beth. "Why are you putting me through the third degree?"

"The what?" he asked politely.

Beth groaned. "I did it again. By Elvis' blue suede shoes! Zander, I'm half asleep. Can't you grill me tomorrow?"

"Grill you? Put you over hot coals and cook you?"

Beth closed her eyes tightly. "Zander, should you be here?"

"No."

"Then why are you?"

"Because I was worried about you." He reached toward her, drew back. "I had to see if you'd returned."

"But I've not been anywhere."

Zander finally got it straight. "Then what I saw must have been the captain. What made him float like that?"

Her eyes snapped open. "I *told* him he'd be seen!"

"What you told *me* was that it's not allowed to have such things." She had not lied. She'd not been in danger. Those facts finally smothered Zander's rampaging emotions. "Didn't you tell me that?"

"His use of such devices is just one more indication he's the villain my superior thinks him, is it not?"

"Couldn't you convict him for possession of such things in a time they don't belong and be done with this?"

"It's a crime, to be sure, but not so great as stealing from now and selling it where it doesn't belong. That must be stopped."

"But if you cannot prove he's done the latter?"

"I must."

"Why?" When she was silent, Zander reached for a curl and wound it around his finger. "Why must *you* prove his villainy?"

"Need I say it?" He nodded, once, his mouth a grim line. "It is my work, the thing I do, my *duty,* Zander."

His belligerency collapsed. "Yes." He tugged very gently at the curl and she leaned into him. "Yes." He sighed. "Your duty." Zander's free hand cradled the back of her head, his fingers rubbing gently against her scalp. They found her ear, her earlobe . . . "Have you any notion," he asked, "how much I fear for your safety when you speak of doing your duty? That man would kill and think no more of it than of snuffing a candle."

"Another reason he must be banished."

Zander pushed her a trifle away, tipped her face up, and stared down into the lamp-lit oval. "I cannot bear to think of losing you."

"Please, Zander," she pleaded. "This . . . thing between us . . . it is impossible. You know it is."

"No. It was fated that we meet and fall in love."

Zander lifted Beth's chin, touched her lips with his own, the kiss deepening when she didn't pull away. He put his arms fully around her, let his mouth touch hers in another way, kissed her ear, her cheek . . . and, tasting salt, looked at her.

"You're crying," he accused.

"Do you think it's easy for me, knowing that when I've finished here we're likely to be parted forever?" She remembered her thought that Zander might be made Anchor in the captain's place. "Perhaps not *quite* immediately—not if you are trained to the work here."

"We would be together?"

Beth remembered the intensity of the training and giggled. "For all the good it may do us! You've no notion how hard you'll work."

"Even if I can do no more than hold you while I sleep, it will be more than we have now."

The low light was enough to reveal the glow of her blush. "Zander . . . !"

He kissed her again, this kiss nearly violent in its intensity, in its demand.

"Zander," she insisted, when she could speak, "You must go."

"Yes. I'll be missed."

"We'll talk tomorrow."

"Yes. And the next day and everyday you continue as our beloved Cousin Beth." He lay her back against her pillows. "I love you."

"I love you too, Zander," she said softly. "But it's not enough. Not when time separates us, one from the other."

"No. When centuries separate lives, then love alone can never be enough." He stared, pensively. "But perhaps centuries do not separate us." Again he played with a smooth pale golden tress. "You've admitted to a feeling of belonging . . ."

Beth's jaw firmed. "I must not allow wishful thinking to confuse me."

"No"—he paused—"assuming it is wishful thinking . . ."

"Zander, out of all the eras available, it's inconceivable to me that I come from this particular year or even this decade. Go. Before I cry in earnest. I don't want you to see me cry." She tried for a smile which didn't come off. "I'm not a pretty sight when I cry, Zander."

He swallowed, his own eyes flickering damply in the glow of the lamp. "Good night Beth."

"Good night," she whispered and turned her face away.

The next day everyone from the scullery maids right on up to Lord Fairmont himself was exhausted. The latter took himself to his library and the snores emanating from behind closed doors told how *he* spent *his* day. The knife boy and everyone else—including Lady Fairmont—worked to return Fairmont House to its usual pristine state. Then bouquets began arriving. Juno danced around the front hall reading first one note and then another.

"Isn't it delightful, Beth?" she asked, when another delivery proved to be from Tony. That note disappeared down the front of her gown after a quick reading made her cheeks glow. She arranged those flowers herself and took them to her room, returning in time to greet the first of the morning callers coming to thank the Fairmonts for a delightful party.

Juno participated in the banter and laughter with only an occasional glance toward the doors through which she hoped Tony would enter. Beth, sitting quietly with her embroidery—she'd been astonished to discover she was adept at the art—smiled and nodded, but rarely added to the conversation filling the salon with a subdued but constant noise.

It was quite late when Zander and Tony arrived. Zander went to his mother and, leaning down, whispered in her ear.

Her ladyship looked startled, glanced to where Tony bowed over Juno's hand, and nodded. Once. She beckoned Beth to her side.

"Yes, my lady?" asked Beth. "Is there something I may do?"

"Zander tells me Tony means to ask Juno to ride in the park. He thought you and he might go as chaperons. Please retrieve shawls and bonnets for the two of you."

Beth said goodbye to the women clustered around Lady Fairmont and, soon, was helped into Lord Belmont's open carriage where she settled her skirts to give Juno room. The men sat facing them, their backs to the horses. When the driver set the team in motion Zander reached for Beth's parasol, opened it for her, and handed it back.

He grinned. "A lady must be careful of the sun, must she not?" The reference to her penchant for sun-bathing and his desire to join her in that occupation had her suppressing a smile at his audacity!

Carefully sober of feature, she replied, "Very careful, my lord."

Juno reminded the others they'd soon be leaving London for the country. "I can't decide," she added, "whether I'll enjoy it or whether I'll regret leaving town at just this time. What do you do, Tony? Do you attend the Anwicks' party?"

Beth froze.

"I'd not come to a decision yet," said Anthony.

"I hope you'll go," said Zander, lazily. "Poor Steve will wish all his friends to rally round on this particular occasion. He cannot be very happy about it, can he?"

"Lord no!" said Tony and then apologized for his language. "Not if his sister is to be permitted to wed into a mere squire's family. That *on-dit* took some believing! At least, I believe there's no money there?"

"None of which I'm aware," responded Zander. "Stephen has some reason, I think, to feel a trifle resentful."

Stephen. Beth mouthed the name silently.

"He has reason if his father's still obsessed with restoring the destroyed wing of the house!" agreed Tony.

"But," objected Juno, "you'd not have his sister forfeit her long time love just for a *building,* would you?"

"It seems a little hard on Stephen that he alone sacrifice himself to that self-same building, does it not?"

"Zander, that's nonsense. Who, after all, will inherit? It is not his *sisters* who will live there once they've married, or even if they do *not.* Once Stephen brings home a wife they'd move to the dower house, would they not? So why must Agnes wed to satisfy her father's passion for restoration?"

"Agnes?" asked Beth so softly only Zander heard her.

He glanced her way, his look sharpening when he discovered she stared right through him. As he watched, she silently mouthed the names. *Stephen, Agnes . . . Anwicks?* Then Beth seemed to return from a very great distance. He watched her smile at some wry thing Tony suggested and heard his sister's delightful chuckle.

Putting aside his questions concerning Beth, Zander looked at Juno—and decided he must warn his sister so that she not stare at Tony with her heart in her eyes that way! It was not done. Besides, very likely such behavior on her part would scare Tony off and he'd run from her as far as he could go!

"I don't believe," said Beth, the teasing twinkle Zander liked back in her eyes, "that I've thanked the three of you for rescuing me from a miserable death." When they looked her way, she dramatically added, "I was dying of boredom and you saved me. Thank you!"

"Boredom?" Juno's look sharpened. "Were you not enjoying our visitors? But you must have done! At least three men came expressly to see *you.*"

"If they did, they cannot have been very interesting, can they?"

Juno giggled. "Not even Sir Woostering?"

Beth looked doubtful. "Was that," she asked, "the willowy boy who insisted on reading his very bad poetry?"

Juno laughed outright. "Yes. He compared you to a marigold! Was that not—hmmm—inventive of him?"

"Juno," scolded Zander, "you shouldn't laugh when, very likely, he stayed up the remainder of the night writing his poem. Not but what he should have thought of something better than a marigold!" Zander eyed his love. "The soft yellow of a duckling's fluff? Or perhaps the gold of an angel's halo? Or maybe," he suggested, "the delicacy of a sun warmed golden plum?"

"Not that last!" objected Juno, looking at her brother askance. "Surely that's a trifle suggestive!"

"Do you think so?" he asked a speculative look in his eye. "Do *you* think so, Beth?"

"I think the whole is nonsense," she said, her cheeks glowing with embarrassment. "An angel's halo, indeed!"

"Hmm," said Zander, "So, are you no angel?"

"Of course she is," interjected Juno. "How *dare* you even hint that our Cousin Beth might be other than she should be?"

Zander's lips twitched and his twinkling eyes met Beth's. She turned away, fighting her own nervous desire to giggle. Cousin Beth indeed! She was not at all what she *should* be! She stared at nursemaids watching over a gaggle of children while she got feelings of mild hysteria under control.

"Well Beth?" Zander drew her gaze. "*Are* you all you appear?"

Choking back a laugh, Beth said, "Zander, you've carried a bad joke too far!"

"She scolds me!" He pretended anxiety. "Juno, is *that* the behavior of an angel?"

"It is if you deserve it!" said his sister.

"But do I? I've had no answer . . ." He felt about Beth's head and ears. "Hmm. I *feel* no halo, but tell me, is it the sort of thing one feels?"

Even Beth could no longer resist his clowning. The banter became general and several people strolling in the park commented on the lively quartet so obviously enjoying each other's company.

Fifteen

A few days later Juno noticed that Tony particularly disliked it when she spoke with Sir Terrence Forthright. Juno, from the moment she saw Tony's aversion to the baronet, decided he was just such a one as she wished to know better.

Sir Terrence, a self contained young man, was only a hair's breadth shorter than Juno. He was personable and had a decent fortune which, although Juno's dowry was a trifle more than he should expect from a bride, was well enough he'd not be labeled a fortune hunter. But Sir Terrence was surprised when his polite interest roused one of the jewels of the ton to favor him! When Juno maneuvered him into asking her to drive her in the park, he went away bemused, but returned at the proper hour, driving a borrowed equipage with a neat black gelding between the shafts.

"I didn't bring my own carriage to London," he explained.

"That's quite all right, Sir Terrence. You needn't apologize for a trifling lack of dash."

He gave her a startled look, met a sideways look coming his way and relaxed. "Why do I have this odd feeling I'm being used?" he asked, his tone bland.

"Used?" Juno turned a nice shade of pink. "Well," she admitted when he merely nodded, "perhaps it's because you *are?* Do you mind? Terribly? We may return at once to the house and I'll find another means to my end."

He smiled a quick flashing smile which disappeared, leaving him his usual sober self. "Instead, why don't you tell me what is in your mind?" He glanced at her when she didn't respond and discovered she was biting her lip. "I have," he added in an off-hand manner, "six younger sisters." When that didn't result in a confession, he chuckled. "I suspect, I've guessed," he said, giving her another sideways look, "but I'd like it confirmed, please."

"My problem is simply that I can't play the sort of games which come so naturally to many of my acquaintances," Juno complained.

"Do you truly wish to play a game?" he asked, sympathetically.

"No! It's no game to me, but life and death." He raised his brows and Juno giggled. "Well, perhaps not *that,* but it *is* my *whole life.*"

"Lord Belmont?" he asked with sympathy and added, "I'll not tell, of course. You chose me because you believe you may trust me, and you can."

"Am I so very obvious?" asked Juno, tacitly admitting his guess was correct.

"Only to me. You see, I suffer a like complaint. The woman I love wants nothing to do with love. She's a widow now, after a hateful marriage into which her father forced her when she was too young to object. I cannot blame her for enjoying her freedom, I suppose, but I've loved her for years. I'd hoped that, when she found herself free to do so, she'd turn to me."

"She hasn't?"

For a moment Juno's new friend was silent, "In an odd way I suppose she has. She frequently asks my advice on money matters and when, on occasion, she finds herself in the sort of difficulties in which a lovely young lovely widow *can* find herself—well, she comes to me for rescue. You might say she depends on my continued friendship when an ill wind blows, but wants no interference when skies are blue."

"I'm sorry."

He chuckled again. "I'm a patient man, Lady Juno. When she discovers how shallow are the pleasures she now enjoys she'll give them up and, when that happens, she'll turn to me. She's not a frivolous woman by nature. Her present behavior is only a reaction to the years of . . . the years when . . ."

"When her husband treated her badly," finished Juno.

"Exactly," he agreed, relieved to have been extricated from the necessity of describing *how* his love had been treated—which was, after all, no story for a girl just out! "So." he said after a brief moment, "we are two cooing doves, you and I, both pining for our loves."

"How true! For my part, I've known Tony forever and have loved him almost as long. I fear he sees me as Zander's young pest of a sister and hasn't noticed that I've grown up."

"And have become Zander's elderly pest of a sister?" teased Terrence, chuckling.

"Do you suppose that is the problem?" She turned a painfully direct look his way. "That he can see me as nothing but a pest?"

"I don't know how any man could look at you, Lady Juno, and see anything but a very lovely, intelligent, and delightful young woman."

Juno face warmed again. "Thank you for those kind words." She ducked a quick look his way before her chuckle surrounded the carriage in a cloud of good feeling. "Do you mind," she asked, "if I quote you?"

"Pest!" He grinned, but followed that with a shrug. "If you think it'll do you any good then you may quote me. Ah. There goes my lady," he added and dipped the end of his whip to where a very dashing curricle swept past the end of the drive along which they moved.

"My goodness," said Juno, her eyes rounding. *"That* is your love?"

Sir Terrence threw back his head, laughing. "You, Lady

Juno, have listened to all the nastiest of *on-dits,* have you not? Confess it now! You think her wild and lost to all decent behavior."

"Yes."

His chuckle was a trifle forced when he realized that was the full extent of her response. "I'll not suggest you meet my lady, not so long as her reputation is so badly tarnished, but please believe her current wildness is an aberration. When she comes to her senses I'll introduce you and you'll discover she's truly a sweet woman much in need of love."

"Then why will she not accept yours?"

"She will. Eventually." The last was said with grim determination, but Sir Terrence's features smoothed out as the dashing widow and her escort appeared around a bend. He tipped his hat to his lady, then, instantly, turned to Juno and listened as she described the widow's shocked expression.

Juno had no need to exaggerate one whit and, when they'd passed the other couple, she twisted around only to discover the widow looking over her shoulder, a frown marring an alabaster brow. Juno nodded and turned back to Sir Terrence.

They went on another few yards in silence. Then Juno, in a plaintive tone, asked, "Why do I feel *I've* just been used?"

Sir Terrence cast Juno a startled look. "Now where"—he pretended affront—"could you have come by such a silly notion?" He grinned. "We are even, my lady, are we not?"

"We are. I think we should make a pact and agree to allow ourselves to be *used* whenever the other deems it necessary, do not you?"

"Ah! I'm a trifle more cautious than you, Lady Juno, or perhaps it is merely that I'm older and wiser? I've seen misunderstandings ruin all for a couple who quite obviously *should* be together. I'll not allow you to use me if I think it will interfere in the success of my courtship and you, my dear, should feel the same."

Juno gave thought to that. "But you agree we may be friends?"

"I'd like to be your friend," he said gently.

"Good." Juno drew in a deep breath. "Do you, too, go into the country to the Anwicks?"

"I believe we'll be there."

About to suggest that she begin *using him* there, Juno realized what he'd said. "You mean the both of you? You *and* your widow?"

"I mean me and my widow."

"Then I will hope to see you there, Sir Terrence. I wish to go home now, please. We go to the Lievens tonight. The patroness, you know? Maman told me I must look my best and behave in my most proper manner so I'll get vouchers to Almack's next spring." Juno sighed. "It's such nonsense. *Of course* I'll be given vouchers. Do you know how very special that is *supposed* to be to one such as I?" Juno turned a wide-eyed look his way, her pretense at innocence rousing another chuckle from her escort.

"I've heard," he said with a straight face, "that a young woman will do most anything to achieve the sacred vouchers to Almack's. And some of the stories indicate that I don't exaggerate when I say *anything!"*

"Perhaps that's why I don't value them," said Juno. "It will be unnecessary to strive in any way to attain them. My family's status alone is sufficient. As I told Rupert Porthson not long ago, I suspect I might tie my garter in public and still be given vouchers!"

Sir Terrence, after a moment's shock, shouted with laughter, startling his horse and those of several nearby riders. Chaos reigned as several animals kicked up their heels or tried to unseat their riders. When Sir Terrence had driven away from those who'd been most discommoded, he scolded, "I begin to see why Belmont thinks you still a pest! How dare you make such an outrageous remark to me?"

"I suppose I didn't think."

But Juno felt a trifle smug. Tony had been among the horsemen whose mounts were unsettled and he'd shafted an angry look her way which promised retribution. Perhaps, unusual as it would be for him, he'd be at the Lievens tonight? It was, she thought, the only place he'd get her to himself long enough to ring a peal over her.

Zander had plans of his own for that evening which had nothing to do with the Russian ambassador's ball. He'd invited several old friends, all married, to Vauxhall Gardens and meant Beth to go with himself as escort.

"I think it a very bad idea," said Beth.

"It's an excellent notion," responded Zander, something close to a dare in his tone.

"What would your mother say if she discovered I'd gone, with you as my escort, to a pleasure garden?"

"Since we'll be well chaperoned there's nothing she *can* say," he said flippantly, a comment which didn't ring true.

"She'll say it anyway," insisted Beth, a comment which did! "The thing I cannot predict is just whom she'll say it *to.*"

Zander chuckled. "I'll protect you."

Beth eyed him. "You don't deny she'll be angry."

Zander fiddled with the tassel that ended the cord tying back the drapes. "She'll be angry," he agreed.

"She doesn't like it that you pay me so much attention."

"I'll tell her it's necessary for our work."

Beth bit her lip. "If that were true, I'd not object, but I sometimes feel as if you do all you can to *delay* my work."

"The captain cannot leave port. Men watch the comings and goings from his ship as you've asked. There's no hurry, Beth."

"I fear he'll become suspicious and destroy the evidence."

"I doubt it. He's far too arrogant. A man such as he never

believes he'll be caught and punished. Punishment is for lesser men!"

Since Beth agreed she was forced to drop that argument. "I cannot put it off forever, Zander."

"One would think," he said thoughtfully, "that you actually *wished* to leave me." He eyed her. "Which you *will* do once you've the proof you need." Still Beth said nothing. "So perhaps I *have* stalled a trifle in finding time to escort you to search his ship . . ."

"Zander, I don't *need* your escort. What I *need* is the information I asked you to gather."

His lips compressed. "It's in the way of being collected. A pattern may be emerging but I can't yet be certain." She said nothing. "Beth, give it until after our visit to the Anwicks."

"I've offered to stay with Miss Wilder, see to her continued progress."

"You'll go."

Beth swung around, found Zander glaring at her. "I do not *wish* to go." Which, although she could not for the life of her explain why, was nothing more nor less than the plain unvarnished truth.

"You must go or put a slight on my parents. They'll be thought monsters that they deny you such a simple treat."

Beth chuckled. "You, my lord, are a complete hand!"

"Yes I am, am I not?" His anger faded, his gaze gentle, soft, and loving. "Beth, you'll come to the Anwicks and when we return my information should be complete. We may then plan a raid on Smithson's ship. I promise."

"You do understand it must be done? That I cannot forget it, letting one day slide endlessly into another"—Beth bit her lip, her eyes dropping from his, rising to meet his gravely—"however much I wish it otherwise?"

"If you did not have that sense of responsibility, I'd not love you half so well. I know that. But that makes our situation no easier to accept. So . . ." He again twiddled with the drape tie. "You'll come this evening?"

"Mademoiselle will go where, Zander?" asked his mother who entered the salon at that inopportune moment. "She has told me she doesn't believe she should accompany us to the Lievens' which is where we go and, because of that decision, I sent her regrets. She cannot come with us, Zander."

"Us, Maman? *I* do not go to the Lievens'!"

Lady Fairmont's spine, which had been as straight as a poker, seemed to stiffen still more. "You'll escort your sister and myself."

"I think not."

Beth slipped from the room muttering excuses which neither heard. Their voices rose, loud behind the closed doors. She looked around. Feeling guilt, as any eavesdropper should, she pressed her ear to the crack.

"I've told you to stop throwing half-feathered birds in my path, Maman! They are each and every one a dead bore! I'll choose my own wife."

"That . . . that tart!"

"If you refer to our guest you are wrong. She is not what you say and I'll thank you to cease to even think such insults!"

"You'll not marry such a one."

"I would in an instant if she'd have me."

Beth heard an almost inaudible gasp. "Zander . . ."

"She has far more important reservations to such a match than you could ever have, Maman," said her son, his voice hard to distinguish since it was softer now, the harshness gone.

"I don't understand how that can be, but I must thank her."

In the short silence which followed Beth imagined mother and son embracing.

"I don't know," said Zander almost too softly for Beth to

hear, "just how long it'll be before I recover, my dear, but I wish you'll not push insipid little girls my way until I've done so."

Was there, wondered Beth, just a touch of the famous Knightly humor in his voice? She pushed away from the door and walked toward the stairs to the next floor. Zander *would* recover. For his sake, she must believe he'd do so. But would she . . . ? she wondered, as she entered her room. Beth couldn't fully convince herself she would.

Perversely, perhaps, she decided she'd go with Zander to Vauxhall Gardens. She'd collect memories; more memories couldn't possibly make it more painful when she must leave this time. Leave him. She bit back a sob, controlled herself and scribbled a note to Zander.

Beth took it to his room and gave it into the hands of his valet, making no secret of having sent a message. To do so would only make it chaff for gossip, whereas handing it over openly might make her behavior so unsuspicious no one would bother to think anything of it. Or so she hoped. She returned to her room and searched her wardrobe for just the right gown for their evening together. It was surprisingly difficult to choose!

Later that evening Lady Fairmont hurried Juno out to their carriage without a glance at her son. Zander followed her with his eyes.

"I'm the cause of dissension," said Beth. "I don't like it, Zander."

"Mother sulks when she cannot have her way. It's unpleasant which is the reason we mostly give into her whims, but this is far too important. I cannot allow her to choose my wife. The reason for her pettish behavior is that she's finally accepted it."

"How can you say so? If she had, she'd not have gone off in a huff."

Zander chuckled. "You are far off in that bit of logic, Beth. It is because she *has* given in that she is, as you say, in a huff! If she were still plotting, she'd be smooth as honey. Shall we go?"

He held a hooded cloak for her and handed her a fancy mask-on-a-stick which, thought Beth, must have a name, but what it was she didn't know. She sat beside Zander in a coach across from a couple she'd only just met and idly twirled the silly bit of feather trimmed nonsense between her fingers.

The gentleman, a former officer who had lost an arm, told a very long, very funny, but ultimately upsetting tale of losing the commissariat during the retreat to winter quarters the preceding winter. "We ate acorns since there was nothing else," he finished as they pulled up to the land gate entrance to the gardens. "It was, I believe, the longest three days of my life!"

"Especially since you were wounded and, while taking care of others, didn't care for yourself as you should," scolded his wife.

"Ah well, I paid for that lack of attention, did I not?" There was a rueful note in his tone as he lifted the stub of his arm.

Zander led them toward the rotunda where an orchestra tuned up for the evening's dancing. "Will you waltz with me?" he asked Beth softly. "Even if it is considered scandalous?"

"Yes." She refused to be coy or hesitant about something she wanted as much as he did.

The evening with the other couples was more enjoyable than most Beth had experienced since arriving in 1813. The women were all near her own age. All had seen something of the world, having followed their military husbands to the Peninsula.

It was very nearly time for the fireworks display when one of the women admitted a desire to see the famous Dark Walk. "Surely it cannot be dangerous if we all go together," she finished. "Beth, would you not like to go? Very few women of good reputation ever do so, so you'd have tales to tell your grandchildren!"

"Is that what you want? A tale to tell your grandchildren?" asked her husband.

"I merely wish to visit a place I know I should *not* wish to see," she said and giggled. "Do say you, too, would like to go," she urged her friends.

"I see no difficulty if we stay together," said another. Her eyes twinkled. "I'll freely admit I've been curious."

"You may see things you'll find embarrassing," warned her husband.

"A kiss here or there? Or rustling and giggles off to the side? Would that embarrass any of us overly much?"

"Mademoiselle should be protected from such things."

"Miss Thevenard?" asked the first woman, her voice suddenly hesitant. "Would you be terribly embarrassed?"

"I doubt it," said Beth with spirit, but then looked at Zander. "I'll do whatever you decide," she added more demurely.

"We'll come since it should be pretty well deserted," he said, "but if I feel there's too much, hmm, *activity* going on, despite the fireworks display which most everyone attends, we'll leave."

The women lifted the hoods of the cloaks over their heads and found their masks. The men tied on masks and resettled their hats.

Soon they strolled toward the famous Dark Walk, the talkative woman telling Beth stories about it which, as a foreigner, she'd likely not have heard.

". . . So you see why mothers warn their girls of it!" They approached the bowered opening and she teased her husband, asking. "Is that it?"

"You very well know it is. This is a nonsensical thing we do," he added on a sigh. "Shall we get on with it and get it over?"

Zander held Beth back until the others had started down

the dark path which wound around on itself in such a way that each couple was soon out of sight of the others. Beth heard giggles and rustlings to say nothing of shrieks—some of which did *not* sound motivated by pleasure—from somewhere ahead.

"I've seen enough," she said when they'd gone only a short way.

Zander called to his friends that they'd meet at the gate when the fireworks display ended, assuming they'd not found each other sooner. He put his arm around Beth's waist and started back. They were where the path turned most sharply on itself when Zander stopped, his hand covering Beth's mouth. His action brought him a glare, but he was too busy listening to notice. Then Beth, too, heard a well known voice!

"You've been ordered not to contact me!"

"I had to. You don't understand. . . ."

"I do understand," taunted the captain. "You need money."

"You can sneer! My cousin is as wealthy as that Greek fellow, but will he give me a decent allowance? No. So what is left, but that I get my share any way I can. You know I only bring the best," wheedled Richard Richmond.

"That is true. So. What have you brought?" asked Captain Smithson.

"Two more of those miniatures. They're small, valuable, and easy to transport."

TransPort! Beth instantly thought of the machine which made time travel possible, but then she realized that, however many other laws the captain broke, it was unlikely the Richmond heir knew Smithson's real identity.

"Let me see," ordered Smithson. A flare of light glowed through the leafy branches of the bower in which the two men hid. "Hmm. Very nice."

"I know the value of things," said Richard, offended. "I only bring you good things."

"But only when you need money! And you want money."
Smithson was briefly silent. "So . . . there's a *painting* I
want," he added softly.

"No!"

Beth heard what sounded like a mixture of horror and
fear in Richmond's voice.

"I won't do that," he said. "Not again!"

"If you expect to continue living, you'll obey."

"I'll kill *you!*"

"You won't kill the golden goose." Smithson's evil
chuckle sounded. "No. So, it's an order, hear me? You'll get
me the painting."

Beth heard a deep sigh.

"I'll try," mumbled Richard. "But," he added more
loudly, "I have need now for the dibs to be in tune. Pay
me."

"You give no orders," said Smithson. His tone sent shiv-
ers up Beth's spine.

"But I tell you I must have money!"

Beth heard the clink of coins.

"Damn you," wailed Richard. "It's not enough. The miniatures will reap you a monkey at least. Just the jeweled
frames are worth that."

"But you don't know what danger *I'm* in," said Smithson
soothingly. "I'm lucky to get half that."

"I don't believe you."

"It matters not. What I give, you take."

"Give those back." There was a brief scuffle, an 'oof,'
and, after a moment's heavy breathing, Richmond's voice
insisting, "Give them to me!"

Smithson was again silent. "Perhaps a bit more," he finally said and more clinks sounded. "That's enough. You'll
receive your orders in the usual way. You will obey. Now I
go. You wait, then go your way."

Even after the second set of steps dragged themselves off
toward the well lit main paths Zander didn't move, didn't

remove his hand from Beth's mouth. She opened her lips and licked his palm. Zander looked down at her, seemed to come back from some far place of reverie.

Very slowly he lifted his hand—and even more slowly he lowered his mouth to take its place. The kiss was all Beth could ever have asked of one. Wild and sweet and hot and wanting, demanding . . . yet gentle and tender and . . . no longer there.

"I shouldn't have done that," he whispered. "I swore I'd not do it again until I had the right to do so."

"That I acquiesce is not permission enough?"

"I want you to marry me, Beth. You know that."

Beth sighed. "Shall we go?"

"You'll not argue?" he asked with a touch of wry amusement.

She raised eyes glistening with longing to meet his. "We've made all the arguments, Zander."

"In my not so humble opinion it's likely we'll have a few more—since neither of us is the submissive sort!"

A loud bang and a spray of colored light appeared in the sky, partially obscured by the leafy branches overhead.

"But not now," said Beth.

It was Zander's turn to sigh. "No. Not now. Come, my love. Let us behave ourselves and join the crowd watching the fireworks."

"Zander." He paused and looked down at her. "Zander, I will *like* seeing them," she said. When he looked skeptical she added, "I never have."

So there was something more he'd done which she had not. Zander shook with silent laughter at the ridiculousness of it. "What a deprived life you've led, my love. Come along, then! We must not permit such deprivation a moment longer."

Even though she insisted the Vauxhall fireworks were nothing to the very *special* fireworks Zander's kisses produced within her, Beth stood at his side, awestruck.

She also insisted they stay to the very end!

Sixteen

"The Anwicks are very old friends, Beth," said Juno, grasping the strap as the carriage wheels slid into a rut.

Zander, who had entered their carriage at the last stop, added, "Steve is nearly as close a friend as Tony, although, since his sister died, I've seen less of him."

"She was very little older than I," added Juno, sobered by the thought.

Juno and Zander were doing their best to distract Beth from mild travel sickness, something she'd never before experienced.

"I truly wish I'd thought of a reason to stay in London," muttered Beth, turning a scowl to the window.

Beth didn't know why she was so anxious about this visit, but she couldn't deny, to herself at least, that she was. Perhaps what Zander called travel sickness wasn't that at all but this other thing, whatever it might be. She noticed that they drove along side a fence made of fancy brick-work and her nerves set up a new clamor.

"Are we there?" she asked.

"Almost, Are you very tired?" Zander's voice was solicitous.

"Perhaps a trifle." But, it wasn't that . . .

"Surely you knew what it would be like. You told me," said Juno on a vaguely accusatory note, "that you traveled a great deal with your father."

"Yes, but it has been some time now," said Beth, inventing an answer. "One forgets how bone shaking it is."

Juno's astonishment was clear in blinking eyes and open mouth. "But, Beth, this carriage is *very* well sprung!"

"Juno, I don't disparage the carriage, but my bones, which, perhaps, have traveled so much they dislike the mere notion of travel!"

Juno grinned. "Think if we were with Maman and Higgens! I'm glad Maman decided an extra carriage would make us all more comfortable."

Zander threw his sister a teasing grin. "She merely thought *she* herself would be more comfortable without your incessant chatter and well known inability to sit still!"

"Do you think so?" Juno grinned a slightly wicked grin. "If that's her reasoning, I'll take care she never learns I'm capable of sitting as still as stone—when I wish it. Isn't it nice we've gotten so far ahead of the others?" She didn't await an answer, adding, "And isn't it lovely Miss Wilder is ill and could not come?"

"It is never lovely that someone is ill," scolded Beth. She spoiled it with a chuckle. "If you mean it's more pleasant that we need not *enjoy* her company, then that's another thing entirely."

Juno glanced through the window as the carriage slowed. "Ah. The gates! Soon you may rest those weary bones," She waved at the gatekeeper.

"Do you remember Agnes, Juno?" asked Zander. "There are so many girls I cannot keep them straight. Stephen himself pretends he can't. He says they blur together into *a blob of foolish femininity.* Another expression he's used is *a mass of giggling girlhood.*"

"Zander! How awful."

"I merely quote my friend," said Zander, pretending innocence. "It's not *my* opinion—although it *might* be," he added, thoughtfully, "if I had to deal with the lot of them. The eldest girl, the one who died, was the only one I knew.

She'd trail along with Steve and me, especially when we went fishing. Do you fish?" he asked Beth.

Beth closed her eyes. Behind her eyelids a picture formed of a grassy bank, slowly moving waters, the dripping fronds of an ancient willow . . . Such visions had happened more often recently, instant picture responses to the odd comment or question. She never knew what would set one off. Worse, she had no idea if they meant anything or if it was merely her mind playing tricks for no better reason than that she wanted to stay with Zander.

"I don't know, do I?" she said after a moment. She shivered.

"You truly don't feel at all the thing, do you?" asked Juno, speaking softly and laying a gentle hand on Beth's arm.

Beth squeezed her eyes shut, wishing to be alone to think of this latest image which might or might not be returning memory. "I'll be fine once I've rested," she said when she realized Juno awaited an answer.

"Yes. Of course." Juno straightened. "Ah! There's the house. I do wish I'd asked Jonsey to stop just here. See Beth?"

Beth obediently leaned to look out Juno's window, but the coachman had not slowed and the view was slipping beyond sight. She caught only the merest glimpse of an oddly unbalanced building. "What an odd structure," she said.

"Once it was the most beautiful house for several hundred miles," said Zander. "The fire which destroyed the west wing destroyed the proportions, giving it an awkward look. Stephen says it will be his duty to marry an heiress rich enough to restore it. It's not a prospect which pleases him."

"Which very likely explains *my* invitation," said Juno, nodding wisely.

Zander chuckled. "*You* are safe, little sister. You are nowhere nearly rich enough to do what must be done."

"Am I not?" For an instant Juno wondered if her fortune was enough to draw Anthony into her net. "I thought my dowry exceptional."

"As dowries go it is more than adequate. It is not, however, a nabob's fortune, which will be needed here."

Zander's response relieved his sister's mind and she asked, "It will take so much as that to restore that wing?"

"To do it properly, by which I mean recreating the original design with the same materials and techniques." Zander touched his love's knee. "We've arrived, Beth. You'll soon be able to rest and recover your spirits." The carriage pulled to a stop. "Welcome to Friar's Place."

Zander dropped down to the ground. Thwarting the groom, he lowered the steps himself, helped his sister down and then looked up, ready to help Beth. He frowned at the oddly blank expression with which she stared at the facade of the building. When she ignored his hand and jumped down in a rather hoydenish manner, even, perhaps, a *childish* manner, his confusion grew. He and Juno followed Beth up the many steps toward double doors.

The doors swung open moments before the trio reached the top. Several footmen stepped around them and ran down to unload baggage. Beth appeared oblivious not only to them but to the plump butler standing aside to allow their party entrance to the grand hall. She stared across the polished floor to the twin staircases curving up in a double arc to a landing where the steps split and curved away in opposite directions. Above, rising up another floor, was a second, identical, staircase. The odd design resulted in an unexpectedly high ceiling which was painted in the Italian style, each floor surrounded by a balcony.

Beth started forward, broke into a little run and started up the stairs, turning at the first landing toward the east.

"Elizabeth," hissed Juno as Zander took a few steps forward.

Beth stopped a bit up from the landing, faintly awkward,

but she didn't turn. "You spoke to me?" she asked, her voice pitched a trifle higher than normal.

Zander heard the butler mutter, " *'Lizbet!*" in a shocked tone.

"Where do you think you're going?" called Juno.

"To join Swiftie, of course. Mama will be exceedingly unhappy if I'm late. She . . ."

Beth turned as she spoke and her eyes lit on Zander. She stared for a moment. Then, an odd expression crossing her face, she sank to her knees and rolled bonelessly down to the landing. When Zander reached her, Beth was unconscious. He ignored Juno's strident request that he instantly explain what had happened.

The butler joined them, white as his shirt, and stared, a fearful look, at the unconscious woman. "Why, she's no young thing!" He was obviously astounded to find a mature woman where he'd thought to see a child verging on womanhood.

"No she's not. Standish—it is Standish, is it not?" Zander asked the butler who nodded, "Direct me to Mademoiselle Thevenard's room."

"I thought it Lady 'Lizbet come back," muttered the man, then seemed to a recollect himself and flushed as red as he'd been pale before. "I'll fetch Mrs. Woods, my lord. I've no notion where the daft woman's taken herself off to," he scolded. "Should be here, she should."

Standish started down the steps to find the housekeeper but stopped when Zander said, "Standish, a word with you." They both moved down to the hall floor. "Standish, what happened here"—he caught and held the butler's arm—"I'd not discuss it with anyone if I were you."

"No, my lord," agreed the butler, making a mental reservation that the agreement excluded Mrs. Woods.

"Mademoiselle," said Zander, suggestively, "is particularly sensitive to . . . to . . ."

Standish's eyes widened. He mouthed the word "ghosts" and trembled, casting a fearful glance around the hall.

"Whatever," finished Zander. "If, for a moment, a presence seemed to, hmm, invade her, it won't happen again"—he hoped—"and it would be unkind to frighten the maids or the women guests with talk, would it not?"

Standish imagined the panic among the maids if it were revealed a ghost had taken up residence at the Friar's—and such a ghost! Two maids would quit without notice, another who would succumb to one bout of hysterics after another and the others would be useless for anything but gossip *and all that with a houseful of guests, more coming, a ball and meals to cater—no!*

It would be best, Standish decided, if he didn't even trust Mrs. Woods! She'd let something slip to her friend, her ladyship's dresser, who would be bound to tell his lordship's valet. Word would spread. Standish cast another fearful look around the hall and took himself off at slightly more than his usual dignified pace to find Mrs. Woods.

Beth, recovering long before she was carried up to her room, fumed and fretted and very nearly lost patience before she was left alone. Immediately, she slid off of her high bed and picked up her reticule from the stool before her dressing table. She slipped a hand inside and into a fold of the golden material tucked into the bottom of it. Dared she waste power so frivolously?

Yes! She did. She *had* to know!

An Adam's style writing table stood before the window. Gripping the bag tightly, Beth stalked toward it. She never let go the strings of her reticule while she wrote on a tiny bit of paper no larger than her thumbnail: " *'Lizbet Anwick. Friar's Place. Respond."*

After folding the paper she shook the gold material into a square. Setting her bare feet on their spots, she dropped the paper into the center and set one hand to its position. She was about to contort herself in order to touch the fourth point, closing the circuit, when it occurred to her someone might walk in.

Beth locked the door, completed the connection, and held the awkward position for what seemed five minutes but was more likely five seconds before the bit of paper disappeared and, thankfully, she unwound from the pretzel shape required of the operator. She stretched.

A small, nearly transparent, info-sheet appeared instants later. For a long moment Beth stared at the mono-thin note which would, she hoped, explain her history. She picked it up, laying it aside. Staring at it, she folded the gold material and returned it to her reticule. Then she unlocked the door and, picking up Suu-Van's response to her abrupt demand, hurried back to bed.

As she twisted the message right side up a knock sounded at the door. Using a word she'd never before allowed to cross her lips, Beth stuffed Suu-Van's memo beneath her pillow. "Enter."

Lady Fairmont, who had just learned the tale of Beth's odd behavior from a worried Juno, opened the door. Juno, on her mother's heels, crowded in before Lady Fairmont was fairly through it.

"Really Juno, if you cannot behave like a lady, then I shall have you removed from the guest floor and retired to the nursery with others who have yet to learn to act appropriately in company!" was her mother's acid comment.

"I'm sorry, Maman, but Beth—"

"Beth apologizes for acting in a way unsuited to someone who *has* learned how to go on in company," said Beth dryly. She smiled a wry smile. "I cannot explain what happened and will not attempt it." And how true *that* was: She neither understood it nor would she explain it if she did!

"Zander suggests you were possessed by the ghost of Lady 'Lizbet Anwick who died some years ago. It seems unlikely."

"All I can tell you is that I started up the stairs to see an unknown woman whose name I spoke." Actually, she now remembered her beloved Swiftie, but could hardly admit to that knowledge either. "I seemed, at the time, to know exactly where I was going."

"I remember! You mentioned Swiftie. She's the governess, is she not?"

"Miss Swift is indeed the Anwick governess," said Juno's mother. "It was she whom you wished to reach?"

"What happened is rather vague," said Beth apologetically, wondering what sort of rumors were circulating. Possession by a ghost indeed!

"You seem none worse for your experience," said her ladyship with something less than her usual assurance.

"An hour's rest will set me up. I'm sure it was no more than an instant's aberration."

"It was exceedingly frightening!" insisted Juno.

"Perhaps for you who observed it. For me? I felt perfectly normal until I fainted. I never faint!"

"Don't sound so outraged," laughed Juno, reassured by Beth's normalcy. "Anyone would faint if a ghost came into them and then departed—which is what Zander says happened."

"Don't be absurd," said Beth. "There are no such things as ghosts."

"So I've always believed," said Lady Fairmont slowly. "Juno, you will tell *no one* what happened," she continued sternly. "Zander assures me the butler may be trusted for the simple reason that panic among the maids at this particular time would be a disaster. We'll say to anyone who hears that something out of the way occurred that Beth was overcome by travel-sickness and collapsed. Juno? Do you understand me?"

"Yes Maman." Juno tipped her nose very slightly into the air. "I know better than to start rumors about my *friends*."

"Beth?"

"I've no wish to sound as if I were a fool. I'm unlikely

to claim a ghost took possession of me, if only for a moment!"

"Good. I'll expect you to be up and dressed for dinner. Juno, leave your cousin be now. Zander said the journey tired her excessively. Even if nothing had occurred downstairs, she needs rest." Lady Fairmont took a last lingering look at Beth before removing herself and her daughter from the room.

The door closed behind them and Beth retrieved Suu-Van's response.

"So. You discover your lost past, hmmm?" The excessively tiny print was hard to read—to say nothing of the fact Suu-Van had put the whole into code which must be deciphered from memory. *"I saved you from the fire which destroyed the west wing of Friar's Place in 1810. If you had lived on in your birthtime you would at this moment be eighteen years of age. I think you have met The Man? Hmmm?"*

The man? Had she met the man. No! That isn't what Suu-Van asked: Had she met *The Man*. A grin crept slowly over Beth's face. *The Man?* Zander? Surely Suu-Van wouldn't give ridiculous hints about a relationship if a future between herself and Zander were impossible? Surely he was giving her permission to dream?

Even if that future must be as Zander's mistress rather than his wife, would that not be better than to lose him altogether? At least in this era such a role would not be unusual and, after all, *someone* must take over once Smithson was unmasked. Why not herself?

Beth read the message once more before destroying it. She smiled as she crawled into her bed. When she fell asleep she was still smiling.

Elsewhere, Zander in tow, Lady Fairmont followed directions to the room where what remained of the Anwick family portraits hung. She'd a grim look to her which kept Zander silent, but he wondered what went on in his mother's all too brilliant mind.

"I'm disappointed," said Lady Fairmont, looking around the temporary gallery. "So very little was saved?"

"I doubt if *anything* was saved. Steve told me the whole of the west wing was an inferno within minutes of the fire's discovery."

"Then where did they acquire this admittedly inadequate collection?" His mother turned slowly, hands on hips.

"I would suppose the Friars is very like the Aerie, would not you? If we lost only the picture gallery, there'd still be portraits of you and my father in the main library and his father's full-length study in the Great Salon and *his* grandfather's whole family hanging on the first stairwell landing and I can't remember who on the second and Great Aunt Ethylene hidden away in the Blue Bedroom and . . ." He shrugged. "I've no notion how many ancestors we might collect if we made a thorough search."

"You've made your point," said his mother dryly. She moved forward to look at the first family grouping. There were three such portraits altogether and she studied each, her arm firmly through her son's. Willy-nilly, he moved as she did and, not stupid, grew more and more upset by what he saw.

"Now, Zander," said his mother, seating herself on a backless bench in the middle of the room, "Without questioning the whys and wherefores, I acceded to your demand that I house an unknown young woman. I allowed her to be known as a member of my family. Now, I must have the truth. To foist upon the ton an Anwick family by-blow is outside of enough! I'll not be party to it." Lady Fairmont's glare deepened to the point frown lines appeared.

"If I swear, on my honor, that she's not a by-blow, will that do?"

"I've the evidence of my eyes," said his mother with an acid note her family knew well. "If I've recognized the connection—finally—you must believe others will as well. Especially when we set her beside the family!"

Zander sat farther along the padded bench. "I admit it's a coil."

"The truth, Zander."

"You wouldn't believe it."

"Try me."

Zander cogitated. He could find no story she'd accept and could see no way around obedience. "Will you agree to pretend it's merely a fanciful tale I tell and promise you'll never repeat it?"

Lady Fairmont eyed him. After a moment, when the stubborn woman had met and been blocked by her resolute son's determination, she nodded.

Zander drew in a deep breath and blew it out again. "It began," he said, "on the Bay of Biscay on the journey from Lisbon . . ."

Making it sound a fairy tale made up for children, Zander told his mother something of what had happened and a bit more of Beth's history as she'd told it to him. Lady Fairmont moved not a muscle during the time it took Zander to begin at the beginning and go on to the end.

". . . So, Maman," he finished, "you see why it's not an acceptable truth and *certainly* not one which may be passed about to explain Beth's existence. We must make up some other tale if we're to put off the ton which you believe will connect Beth to the Anwicks merely because of some random resemblance." He shrugged.

" 'Lizbet . . ."

"I thought of that when Beth fainted. It would solve so many problems, would it not? But you forget that, if 'Lizbet lived, she'd be no more than eighteen."

"I thought I insisted you were to have the very best education available, my son," said his mother, suddenly relaxed and much amused.

"If you suggest I'm incapable of adding and subtracting . . ."

"Ah! But add and subtract from what?" An eyebrow arched quizzically.

"From what . . . ?" Zander blinked. He stood and paced the room. After a moment he swore softly, then more loudly. "Bedammed to all the blasted limitations within which I must live!" he finished and, remembering his mother's presence, apologized.

"You've made the deduction?"

"I've made the deduction."

"You too believe it is likely she's the Anwick's daughter, 'Lizbet?"

"It's all too possible, is it not? There is even the name. 'Lizbet, Elizabeth, *Beth*. Three years ago in our time someone from the future rescued Beth from the fire. She's lived a full decade in their time and matured into the lovely woman she is today and then, for some reason, she's been returned to our time just three years after she was presumed to have died!"

"Zander, my son." Lady Fairmont beckoned. He approached and she caught his hand. "You are very much in love with her, are you not?"

"We discussed this before." He spoke coldly with bitterness, then forced stiff shoulders to relax.

"I was relieved when you told me Beth herself was against a marriage between you, because . . ." She bit her lip, staring up at him. "Zander, do you truly not understand?" He shook his head. "I feared a misalliance, my son."

"And now?"

"Now?" Her brows arched. "Why, it would be no misalliance. Not the eldest Anwick daughter!"

"She can never be acknowledged as an Anwick offspring!"

Lady Fairmont cast him a disgusted look. "I care no more than you what is said of us, but I care a great deal what *I* know. Your Beth was always acceptable to me in every way but the one. Now we know her birth is unexceptional, why"—she shrugged—"what problem do you have?"

"Several," said Zander, promptly. "We are faced, still, with the problem that she *looks* like an Anwick. Beyond that there is the inescapable difficulty she's only here temporarily. Maman"—he turned a white strained face her way— "she'll return to the future where I cannot follow. We'll be separated as surely as if one of us were dead." If possible he grew still more gray in face and voice. "In fact, Maman, in the future which she inhabits, I *will* be dead. Centuries dead." His whole body showed how completely hopeless he felt.

His mother clasped his hand. "Might she not refuse to go?"

"She bears an officer's rank in her organization and has as strong a sense of responsibility as any officer the Marquis of Wellington has under him in the Peninsula. You do not know—"

"No," interrupted her ladyship, "and it is not necessary that I know. She'll be unhappy you've revealed so much as you have."

"No more than an unbelievable story, Maman." His mouth twitched in a travesty of a smile. "A tale with which to entertain the nursery!"

"Hmm." She patted the hand she still held. "Whatever happens between the two of you, we must explain her likeness to the Anwicks." Thinking deeply, she pursed her lips in the delightful manner which always intrigued her offspring. "I wonder if my cousin and his wife did not stay with us in eighty-eight at a rather monstrous house party your father and I held to celebrate"—She waved a hand in an arrogantly dismissive fashion—"something. I don't remember just what. I wonder," she added, "if perhaps we did not also have *Albert* Anwick as a house-guest . . ."

For a moment Zander goggled. A sputtering laugh escaped him. "Surely you aren't suggesting . . . No, you *could* not." Her brow arched, queryingly. "You would make use of poor old Albert's penchant for seducing pretty women?"

"Albert and my cousins are dead and won't be hurt." She pouted for a moment. "A murmur in one or two carefully chosen ears, perhaps?"

"You've the best head in the family, Maman!" said Zander admiringly. "I'll see Beth and tell her this new twist to her history."

"No."

Zander, already on his way to the door, stopped and turned, hands on hips. "No?"

"If you are caught coming from your cousin's room, you'd be married willy-nilly. I've no wish for such a scandal, to say nothing of the complications if she disappeared later! Besides, when you wed, it will be properly, with all due pomp and ceremony and, if not at St. George's, Hanover Square, then in our own chapel at the Aerie." She glared at him, the glare turning to a smile. "*I* will talk to Beth."

"*Mother . . .*"

She touched his arm at his use of the English rather than French maternal form. "I'll take great care not to upset your Beth, my dear, but she must be told."

"That I've broken my word and revealed her secret?" His bitterness could not be hidden and he didn't try.

"Zander, Beth is very nearly as intelligent as I," Lady Fairmont scolded. "She'll accept it was necessary. Now. I request your escort to my room as it is more than time we dress for dinner." When they arrived at her door Lady Fairmont spoke softly. "Cease to worry, my son. Beth knows us well. She'll not blame *you.*" Lady Fairmont, who knew herself nearly as well as others knew her, smiled a self-deriding smile.

"How can you accept it so easily?" he asked. "I saw Beth materialize from nothing and, even so, I had difficulty believing my deductions from the clues given me."

"Perhaps I *wish* to believe." Lady Fairmont touched her son's arm. "I want you happy, Zander."

"Perhaps that's impossible . . ."

"Zander, you weren't raised to fall into despair at the prospect of facing your fences. This is merely another fence," she scolded. "A high one to be sure, but just a fence." She told him to go since she was already late and had little time to waste. Half an hour later, having rushed her preparations to a degree which surprised even herself, Lady Fairmont again knocked on Beth's door and was admitted. "Are you ready, Mademoiselle?"

Beth rose from the stool before the dressing table. "I will be when I collect my scarf and reticule . . ."

"Beth, sit down, my dear. We've several things to discuss and very little time. Are you aware," Lady Fairmont continued abruptly, "that you have much the look of the Anwicks? Very *much* their look?"

"I've yet to meet anyone of the family, Lady Fairmont."

"You may believe me when I say the resemblance is excessive. I've discussed the problem with Zander and we believe we've a solution—if you do not object."

"I'm listening," said Beth noncommittally.

"I've imagined a relationship between Albert Anwick, deceased, and your purported French mother, also deceased, during a house party I and my husband gave in eighty-eight. I hope it will not distress your sensibilities that you will be rumored to be a love child accepted, either knowingly or otherwise, by the woman's husband?"

"The woman? My *purported* mother?" asked Beth cautiously.

Lady Fairmont nodded, smiling approval. "I made that slip deliberately. And I was correct to think you'd the sense to catch me out! You see, I could think of no way of leading gracefully to the admission I forced your history from Zander."

"My history?"

"That you did not die in eighteen-ten, but have lived many years in the future?" Her ladyship smiled.

"How did Zander know I've finally remembered. . . . Ah! I suppose he guessed it from what happened at our arrival." Beth sighed. "I think no one has ever broken security the way I've broken it over and over during this operation. Suu-Van will have my head."

"It is surely unnecessary for him to know."

"I do not keep secrets from Suu-Van and could not if I would. He's far too perceptive." Beth eyed Lady Fairmont. "You don't appear particularly upset."

"Actually, I'm relieved. *Exceedingly* relieved. Now you may marry Zander and be happy. I feared a misalliance, you see, which I would not have tolerated, but now I need not." Lady Fairmont beamed.

"Marriage to Zander is the dearest wish of my heart, my lady, but I can see no way to achieve this devoutly-to-be-wished conclusion. Did Zander not explain to you the problem of anomalies and how such might change the whole fabric of the future?" When Lady Fairmont shook her head, Beth explained.

"I see," said Lady Fairmont thoughtfully. "Yes, a danger in most cases where such as you, coming from the future, fall in love with such as my son, but it does not apply, surely, since you were born in this era."

"If I'd lived my normal life, I'd be no more than eighteen."

"But at eighteen," objected her ladyship, "you'd be an unexceptionable bride." She thought for a moment. "I see no problem at all that the marriage has been delayed until you are . . . twenty-four?"

"Twenty-five. I fear to hope. And, until my duty is done, nothing may be settled. My lady, hint to no one that Zander and I might wed. The time may come I simply disappear. Then you may tell people my greatest sin is an excessive pride and, unable to accept your charity, I found myself a position with a diplomatic family returning to . . . Turkey?

Persia? Somewhere where no one is likely to check on the truth of the story!"

"I refuse to entertain the notion all will not come right for you and my son." When Beth made no response, merely lowering her head and staring at her clasped hands, Lady Fairmont continued, "Beth, you've not agreed we may spread our farradiddle of your purported fall from grace."

"Of course," said Beth promptly. "I'll agree to anything so that life not be complicated more than need be for you and yours."

"When will you do whatever it is you must do?"

"I must be in London for that."

"Is that why you offered to remain and care for Miss Wilder?"

Beth nodded. "I'd hoped that with the household gone, except for Lord Fairmont and some part of the staff given leave of absence I might have more freedom." Beth's lips compressed. "This project has taken far longer than projected! I must finish it."

"Of course you must. We'll return to London at the end of next week and you may get on with it, whatever *it* may be?"

"Ten days," said Beth, ignoring the faint hint of a query.

"A short visit, of course, for such a long journey, but Lord Fairmont prefers me in London when he's there." Lady Fairmont eyed Beth. "There's much a proper wife may do for a political man, you know."

"If that's a hint Zander will take his place in the Party"— a wry twist to her mouth, Beth shook her head—"I fear you'll be disappointed."

"In him or in you, my dear?" Her ladyship smiled. "No. Do not answer. Time will tell."

A knock sounded and Juno put her head in the room. "Maman?"

"Come in or stay out, but either way close that door!" scolded Lady Fairmont. "The rooms in these old houses are far too drafty. And one more warning, Juno! Make as little as possible of Beth's exhibition upon arrival. We will go down now since we've no reason to make an interesting entrance. Come, girls . . ."

Despite her wishes, there was no way Lady Fairmont, a striking woman in her own right, could avoid an entrance. *Especially* was it impossible when she had a woman with the ashy blond Anwick hair on one side and her magnificently tall daughter on the other as the three came down the impressive Anwick staircase!

But, from then on and as much as possible, Beth effaced herself. It wasn't difficult to avoid the Anwick family since the women were busy with last minute preparations for the formal dinner and ball while the men kept male guests out of the way. Beth doubted, however, that she'd be so lucky throughout her visit.

On the other hand, she hadn't counted on coming face to face with her brother during the ball! Stephen approached her soon after the late supper. Worse, it was the waltz which Lady Anwick had learned in Germany and loved. Since many refused to have anything to do with the scandalous dance, the floor was practically empty when Stephen pulled Beth from her chair.

"I do not waltz," she hissed.

"I'm very certain you do," he said, his voice grim. He swung her onto the floor and, since Beth could not bring herself to pretend to stumble, she waltzed. "I've heard," he said, sneering slightly, "that I'm to call you cousin."

"It is the *last* thing you should call me," she responded sharply. "Mademoiselle will do." Beth caught Zander's eye. He shook his head, telling her there was nothing he could do.

"Ah yes. Mademoiselle. I think if you did not look quite so much as I imagine my sister might have grown to look, I'd feel less bitter about your existence."

"I hardly think I should apologize for my existence!"

"What right have you to live when my sister died a horrible death?"

"What right has anyone to live? You, for instance." Beth took note of a deep pain he couldn't hide. "Or is that the problem? You live when you feel you, too, should be dead?" She met and held his gaze. *"That* would have made your family happy, would it not? Your death would have balanced the right and wrong of things?" Less sternly she added, "We all have crosses to bear, my lord."

"What would *you* know of pain or loss or hardship? My sister whom you resemble too well is *dead.*"

"My father died in Portugal." Beth had told the story so often she'd begun to believe it! "When I'd sold up our possessions and paid his bills nothing was left. A friend of my father's found me a position as duenna. If my cousin had not arrived in Lisbon when he did, I'd have lost my honor to an importunate employer. Zander rescued me from that. I may not be dead, my lord, but I've known hardship and fear. Don't think that you alone have a right to feel bitter."

Stephen looked over her shoulder, staring into a vision only he could see. "I should have saved her. She called for me. I heard her and I didn't go."

"Were you *allowed* to go?"

He flushed. "I was held down by three footmen and my father, but 'Lizbet couldn't know that. She died, betrayed."

His words recalled another scene to Beth's mind: A panicked teen screaming for the big brother who always saved her from childish horrors. Slightly flushed Beth responded, "She'd surely not be so selfish as to wish you dead as well."

Beth wished she might tell this bitter young man she *did* forgive him! If only she dared to tell him the truth, that his sister hadn't died, that he danced with her at that moment. But she mustn't. Security had been breached to an unconscionable degree already. Nevertheless, he *was* her brother, one she remembered as loved and loving. Surely, she could reach him somehow.

"You've allowed that for which you cannot be held responsible to ruin your life," she said. "That's unfair to those who love you to say nothing of unfair to yourself. No loving sister would wish it."

"You've no notion. You cannot know . . ."

Beth lost her temper. "I know you are wallowing in self-pity and making life miserable for everyone who loves you and only because you are incapable of forgiving yourself for something which could not be helped." She glared at him. "Grow up, Stephen Anwick. Become a man instead of a spoiled brat who will throw a life-long temper tantrum for no very good reason."

Stephen stopped dancing, automatically catching Beth when she stumbled and setting her right. "How dare you?"

"You've called me cousin. Then I take the right of a cousin to tell you a few home truths to your face." She glanced around. "Do we dance or have we finished?"

"You'll agree we've finished. And, even if you do *not* agree, we *have*."

He turned on his heel and left Beth standing in the middle of the floor with everyone's eyes on her. Beth smiled sweetly, curtsied, and walked off the floor in the direction opposite to that taken by Stephen.

Unfortunately, it was also opposite to where Zander stood and where Lady Fairmont and Juno waited anxiously. Zander, seeing he could not get to Beth, followed Stephen.

Seventeen

Stephen stalked through his family's guests looking neither right nor left. Zander, conscious of the rising murmur, left a trail of apologies as he followed. Then, blocked for a moment, he lost sight of his friend. In the anteroom, he caught the eye of a footman.

"Lord Stephen," he demanded. "Which way did he go?"

"Toward West Exit, my lord." The footman leaned nearer and lowered his voice. "That's where he always goes when he has *that* look." His ears turned red at daring to speak so to a guest and he straightened into immobility.

West Exit, Zander recalled, had been designed as a temporary door leading to a narrow, equally temporary, terrace built over part of the foundations to the destroyed wing. Zander found Stephen there, clutching a plain iron railing and staring into the fire-blackened pit.

"Stephen?"

"Go away."

"Not until you explain how you could so insult a young woman under my protection."

"Do you want satisfaction?" sneered Stephen.

"I don't know. Do I?"

"The boot's on the other foot. *She* insulted *me*."

"Hmm. Do you say so?" Zander eyed his friend and wondered how far he dared push. "What did *you* say to make her lose her temper?"

Stephen turned and leaned against the railing. He glared.

The glare faded under Zander's steady look and his gaze dropped to where his toe scraped back and forth against the stone work. "I suppose I deserved it."

"Knowing Beth, I'm damn certain you deserved it—whatever it may be." Zander thought he heard something very near a chuckle, but there was a watery note to it that indicated tears not so very far beneath the surface. "Well?"

"She suggested I grow up and stop acting the spoiled brat throwing a temper tantrum," Stephen admitted sourly. Zander chuckled. After a moment Steve looked up and grinned. It was almost the old grin, the one lost along with Stephen's sister. Stephen reached to either side and grasped the rail. "She told me," he said, "to stop feeling guilty for something I had no way of changing but, if I'd tried, would have added to my family's grief. That she's correct makes it no easier. My dreams . . ." He swung around, staring into the foundations. "God, Zander! Night after night. 'Lizbet screaming my name from within that raging inferno. I haven't had a decent night's sleep in three years!"

"Steve," said Zander softly, "if you could forgive yourself, I think you'd find your sister forgave you long ago." Only after he'd said it did Zander realize how very true that was. Beth, 'Lizbet if one preferred, wasn't the sort to hold a grudge.

Stephen was silent for another long moment. "Standish told me an odd story." He turned back. "I didn't credit it at the time, but . . . I wonder."

Zander made an encouraging noise, even as anger filtered through that the butler had, after all, spread the tale of Beth's unusual entrance to Friar's Place. He wondered how far it had gone.

"Standish insisted your mademoiselle was momentarily possessed of 'Lizbet's ghost. You were there, Zander. Tell me what happened?"

Zander opened his mouth . . .

"And don't fob me off with tales of travel sickness,"

added Stephen, "which is how Standish said you mean to explain it."

. . . and closed it.

It occurred to Zander that the notion his sister's ghost had invaded Beth might be useful, that perhaps the "ghost" wished to communicate with Steve. Zander was willing to lie through his teeth if it would do Stephen good. He drew in a deep breath and let it out slowly. "Beth herself," he said, "doesn't understand it. She's never been here, had never heard of Miss Swift, but upon entering the hall she instantly started up the stairs. When Juno called after her, asking where she was going, Beth said she must find Swiftie. Then she fainted."

"Standish believes 'Lizbet's ghost is haunting us. He came to me because he needed to speak of it to someone." Stephen paused. "I've never before credited the existence of ghosts, but this . . . this is pretty incredible." He met Zander's gaze, his eyes filled with pain. "But, Zander, if it *is* 'Lizbet's ghost . . . why didn't she come to me? Why use your Beth?"

"I don't know. I've only told you what happened. But perhaps your 'Lizbet won't rest until you forgive yourself. How could she rest when you act as if you could never atone for failing her, let alone live with yourself or"—Zander's brows quirked—"allow anyone else to live with you?"

"Et tu, Brute," murmured Stephen.

"If I repeat my cousin's comments, I apologize for boring you. Or perhaps I don't. Very likely, someone should have said them long ago!"

Stephen ignored that provocative remark. "But I *can't* forgive myself."

"For what?" Zander allowed exasperation into his voice. "For not dying along with your sister? What good would that have done?"

"There should have been something, some way . . ."

"You *know* there was not."

"Something . . . !"

"If it *was* your sister's ghost, don't you think you should listen?"

Stephen sighed. He stared over the void which had once been a beautiful part of a much loved home. "My father's urging me to propose to the newest nabob's daughter," he said, seemingly changing the subject.

Zander hesitated only a moment before following his friend's lead. "The newly knighted Sir Robert's girl? She was at school with some of Juno's friends while he was in India. I believe she's unexceptional and not so very hard to look at"—Zander grimaced—"as heiresses go, that is."

"Which means she's plain as a platter." Stephen sighed. "I may as well agree. The next heiress my father finds me might be worse."

Zander spoke before he'd thought. "Perhaps some of what you feel is not guilt, but that you *resent* 'Lizbet's death. After all, if she'd not died she too might have married conveniently and helped fill the coffers . . ."

Stephen turned, glaring. "I've never thought any such thing. Never!"

"Methinks you protest a trifle too loudly, my old friend."

"Dammit, Zander, what sort of unmitigated clod do you think me?"

"A very human one?"

Stephen snorted, half disgust and half chuckle. "All right. I'll admit I've felt resentment—but not toward 'Lizbet! It's worse since Agnes was given permission to marry our neighbor's son, a long standing childhood thing in which my parents will not interfere. *She's* not expected to sacrifice her life to a building, to my father's obsession with returning Friar's Place to its former beauty. He thinks of nothing else."

"Yet he isn't sacrificing Agnes," said Zander softly. "Would he not if he were truly obsessed?"

Stephen looked over where the missing wing would one day rise again. His jaw clenched, a muscle jumping in a rapid tattoo alongside his jaw. "I shouldn't blame him. I too wish to see the Friar's as it was. So. I'll do my duty. But I'll do it primarily so I need listen to no more lectures on what that duty is!"

Zander spoke sharply. "That isn't fair to the woman you'll wed! I mean, if you resent *wedding* her, can you avoid transferring that resentment *to* her? It isn't *her* fault her father's wealth will fill your needs!"

"Blast!" Stephen's lips compressed for a moment. "I'd not thought of the woman who will be my bride, her feelings and her needs. Your cousin has the right of it, does she not? I've become a sulky little boy." He extended his hand to Zander who, without a moment's hesitation, took it. "The first step toward growing up is to make an apology to Mademoiselle Thevenard and"—Stephen grimaced—"as publicly as possible! Shall we go?"

They went to find Beth, but she'd escaped the ball which, in any case, had palled once she'd danced her two dances with Zander. She'd found still less pleasure in it when the whispers began!

As the evening progressed, so did the gossip concerning the contretemps on the dance floor. A very few, aware that, since the fire, Stephen's temper was as wild as one of Whinyate's rockets, suggested it was Stephen's fault, but most blamed the strange woman with the features of the Anwicks. Stephen now had another reason to feel guilt, but, this time, he *could* atone!

The next morning a footman, as ordered, informed Stephen the instant the breakfast room was as full as it would hold—including Beth. He entered, winked at his mother who presided over the coffee and tea urns and rushed to the place where, ignored, Beth sat. Stephen fell to his knees behind her.

"Forgive me," he said in ringing tones. "Forgive me my

gaucherie and boorishness and"—he lowered his voice for her ears alone—"most of all, forgive that I've only just begun to grow up."

Beth turned in her chair slightly and Stephen moved sideways on his knees. He gave her a wry pleading look, his hands clasped in a begging manner. He nodded, several quick hopeful nods, his eyes wide. Beth chuckled.

"How," he asked in dramatic tones, "may I atone for my dunce-like behavior?" At the words he snapped his fingers. "I have it!"

Stephen rose to his feet and beckoned a footman near. The servant nodded twice at the words whispered in his ear, then started toward the door.

"A big one, mind, and don't forget the pins!" called Stephen. "Good morning Mother, everyone?" He grinned. Beth gave him a wary look and his smile grew wider. Once at the sideboard heavy with the morning viands, he said, "How hungry I am. It must be that apologizing gives one an appetite."

Just as Stephen set his heaped plate at an empty place the footman returned and handed him a large sheet of heavy paper. Deftly, Steve twisted it into a cone and pinned it into that form. He plopped it on his head.

Silence had settled over the room at his entry. It continued as the guests followed Stephen's actions. When he began to eat they looked from one to another, confused, no one quite willing to ask questions. After his first few bites Stephen glanced around. "Everyone's so quiet," he said. "Did you all wear yourselves down to nothing, dancing all night?"

"Stephen," scolded his mother, half laughing and half ready to cry, "explain yourself. At once!"

"Explain?" Stephen's eyes turned up, trying to see the top of his head. "You mean the dunce cap? But it's obvious." When a chorus of voices told him it was *not*, he asked, "How can it not be? Having acted the dunce last night on the dance floor, I'll wear proof of it until Mademoiselle

Thevenard decides I've atoned for behaving the ass. Although less than I deserve, she'll not, I'm certain, make it an over-long penance. Zander assures me she has a kind and forgiving heart." He smiled around the table.

His mother stared at him, her confusion giving way to hope. "Stephen, you . . . you . . ."

"Yes, Mother?" His eyes twinkled at her in quite the old way.

"Oh, my son!" Tears streamed unashamedly down her face and she carefully patted them away. "It was terrible losing a daughter but having lost my son in an entirely different way has made it so much *worse.* Welcome home, my boy!" she said softly. They smiled at each other.

Later that morning Beth tracked Stephen down in the billiards room and, publicly, gave him leave to remove the cap.

"Thank Heaven," he breathed. "Have you any notion how difficult it is to play this game while balancing that thing on your head?"

After watching for a few moments, Beth wandered on and came to the hall where Juno was collecting the young people together for a stroll to the stables.

"I hope to talk the head groom into supplying us with mounts. Will you ride with us, Cousin?" asked Juno, her arm through Anthony's.

"You know I don't ride," Beth scolded.

Having brought his own cattle, Tony had been intending to ride when Juno stopped him. He showed no signs of irritation, however, that he'd had to postpone his exercise while Juno organized everyone else. But the moment he noticed Sir Terrence Forthright descending the stairs he suddenly appeared anxious to draw Juno away.

Beth waved the group off and wandered on yet again looking for . . . for Zander, she decided, rueful at the knowledge her morning would be incomplete until she'd talked to him. It was somewhat lowering to think she might actually go into a decline if she must return to the future, leaving her love behind. Suu-Van, she decided, would laugh himself silly at the prospect. Which thought reminded her of her mentor's note.

Could he mean it was permitted that she marry Zander? Did she dare allow herself to think it? Beth decided she did not. At least no more than a tiny breath of hope, but even that was better than the utter desolation which had gone before!

She located Zander in the library surrounded by older men of a political persuasion. Zander, seeing Beth, used her presence to make his excuses. They found cloaks and wandered for an hour in the drab gardens where late fall was edging toward winter. It was not too unpleasant a stroll however—so long as they stayed out of the wind!

Except for the constant return of disconcerting memories, the rest of their visit to Friar's Place passed pleasantly for Beth. As well the usual entertainments at a country house party, Beth found much to amuse her in watching Lord Belmont attempt to carry on a flirtation with Forthright's widow while, at the same time, doing his best to keep Juno away from Sir Terrence. She pointed out the situation to Zander who also found it amusing.

Finally, Beth faced the dreaded carriage ride back to London—it didn't matter how well sprung Juno insisted that carriage might be. She had, she decided, been badly spoiled by her life in the future and must do as she'd told Stephen Anwick to do. She must grow up and accept the limitations of the world as it was.

Especially, she must do so if there was any hope at all she might be allowed to remain here . . . !

London hadn't changed, of course, except to become dirtier, the soot and smoke worsening as the weather did. Then too, the moist air flowing upriver from the estuary combined with cooler nights and resulted in foggy mornings, sometimes *dreadfully* foggy mornings. Beth feared that Captain Smithson might simply slip anchor and slide down river on an outgoing tide with no one the wiser. She *had* to get herself onto that ship.

With that aim in mind, it still took two days to find a moment alone with Zander. "I dare not put it off," she insisted, stalking along the garden path with a stride no well brought up tonnish miss would use. "Why do you not understand that I might lose him altogether?"

"Slow down, Beth. It won't be long now," he added soothingly when she'd done so. "I've some notion as to when it'll be safest." He sighed. "Not that it will ever be truly safe, of course."

"You hope to avoid my going at all." She glared, her eyes accusing him of sabotage.

"I do not like it that you believe you must search his ship. You know that. But I also know you'll do it on your own if I don't make it possible for you."

"So?"

"So what?"

Beth felt her teeth clench to the point of pain. With care she relaxed her jaw, moving it from side to side. "Zander," she said, her voice carefully controlled, "just when do you think I may be allowed to do what you know I must do? When will you give me *permission* to continue my mission which," she went on her voice rising, "might already have been completed if you and I had never met?" She raised clenched fists and shook them. "Why, by Tex Ritter's apple fritter, did you have to be in that cabin when I arrived!"

"What would you have done if I'd not been there?"

"What I may do even yet," she said between gritted teeth. "Disappear into the mass of humanity who live near the river!"

"No, Beth! You'd be dead or sold into the worst form of slavery before your first day was finished!"

"You've no notion the sort of disguise I might adopt.

Would a ragged old crone selling country simples and barely keeping body and soul together be in trouble? Or a widow woman, perhaps, bent and crippled. Or maybe even a *boy,* a—"

"Stop!" he interrupted. "In the first place, you'd not understand the speech which, believe me, is far more than a simple problem in pronunciation. The London underworld has its own language which we call thieves cant. And forget about pretending to be a boy. A pretty boy may suffer the same fate as a pretty woman. There are brothels where . . ." Realizing he spoke of things about which a woman should know nothing Zander clamped his mouth shut.

She admitted her shocking lack of innocence by asking, "Just how do *you* know of such places?"

"How *does* one know such things?" He glared. "Just don't think of going off on your own, whatever the disguise."

Beth rounded on him, her temper hanging by a thread. "Then, my lord, *get me onto that ship.*"

Zander was silent for several paces. Finally, curious, he asked, "Do you hate it so much, living with my family?"

"I do not hate it. You know I do not, but I've work I must do. If you'd not been sent back to London in time for Juno's presentation ball would you have told Wellington"—her voice dropped to a lower register—"sorry sir, can't wait for those dispatches. Must dance at my sister's ball, sir, so you'll have to send them along with someone else . . ." Her eyes widened as a grin spread across his face along with a certain amount of color rising up his neck. "Zander! You didn't!"

The grin widened, his elusive dimple appearing for the first time in many days. "Not in those exact words. But Wellington had messages he wished delivered, so, although he hadn't the whole of it, he let me go. Merry brought the rest not very much later, but in essence I suppose I told Wellington, sorry, can't hang around, old boy. You'll have to—"

"I can't do that," she interrupted, turning away.

He sighed. "No I don't suppose you can, any more than I'd have done it if I'd not known Wellington had information he wanted the Horse Guards to receive as soon as possible." He stalked along the path for half a dozen more paces. "All right. I'd hoped to wait until next week to see if the pattern continued, but I'll arrange it so we make the sortie tomorrow night."

"Why not tonight?"

"Because tonight," he said patiently, "you are promised to Juno and Maman and go to the Fevershams'."

"I'll make an excuse."

"You'll enjoy it." When she looked as if she'd argue, he added sternly, "If you *allow* yourself to do so, you'll enjoy the Fevershams' party."

"I'm not good at enjoying myself when there's work to be done!"

"It'll get done. Trust me. I've got it well in hand."

"That's something else I'm no good at, trusting someone else to do *my* work. All along you've done nothing but thwart me, so how *can* I believe you?"

"I haven't thwarted you. I've merely done what any good general would do. I've gathered facts, Beth, and assessed them. Assuming routine is followed, that ship will *still* have three or four men on board when you, I, and half a dozen river rats board it. I've told the men they may ransack it for what they can find so long as their business covers what you and I do, which is the search *you* must make. That way, if we fail, we'll not have roused Smithson's suspicions and may go back for another try. Will the plan work, do you think?"

Beth listened with her mouth open. "You've done all that without allowing me a share in the planning?"

"Will it do or will it not?"

"I'll think about it."

He chuckled. "Are you annoyed because I've taken such

an active part? That, all by myself I've managed to make adequate plans?"

"Sour grapes?"

"It isn't an expression I know, but rather expressive nevertheless and yes, I wonder if your lack of enthusiasm hasn't something of the sour grape about it!"

Beth stalked on, her hands tightly clasped behind her back. "Perhaps that *is* the problem, Zander. I work alone. I rely on myself. I'm not convinced Smithson did me a favor when he put me into your care, Zander."

"Nonsense. However certain you are of yourself, you have no notion of the hell existing in the stews near the wharves. Believe me. You'd not have awakened from your first sleep. The most vicious and most ugly examples of humanity that ever lived dwell there."

"Not everyone."

"Perhaps not even most, but how could you have known whom to trust?"

"I had an address to which I could go. A seeming country woman."

"Someone else from the future, Beth?"

Beth raised her eyes to the heavens. "Zander, I am not supposed to tell you this!" But she did. "The woman came from somewhere in *my* future."

"She's from *still farther* in the future?" Beth nodded. "Why?"

"Because of Smithson. Or so we believe. She stopped long enough to introduce herself and tell us where she could be found, that's all."

"If she's here because of the captain," said Zander slowly, "why hasn't she done what you were sent to do?"

"It's possible her mission has nothing to do with mine. Perhaps it is merely serendipity she's in your era just when I need a safe house."

"Does she know you've arrived?"

"I don't suppose so. She *must* have another job of work

about which I've no knowledge and in which I'll take no part. But when we knew she was coming for reasons of her own, we were pleased to have the address available for me."

"But if she's from your future, why doesn't she know she isn't needed? Why didn't she know you'd be safe with me?"

Beth glanced his way, then back along the path. "The mission isn't finished, Zander. Perhaps we *will* need her."

Zander thought about that. "You mean something will go wrong and you'll need her help?"

"That, perhaps. Or perhaps something else. Something beyond our ken."

"But . . ."

"Zander, we have to *live* our future. One must not, ever, attempt to discover how one's own life goes."

"Why not?"

"Think about it."

He smiled. "If I knew where I was to die, I'd never go near the spot?"

Beth nodded. "And thereby distort history. Besides, life is boring if one knows too much."

"Is that why one doesn't search one's own . . . what did you once call it? One's life-line?"

"A weak person occasionally succumbs to temptation. Thereafter that person feels like a puppet. Even if they wish to change something, they find it can't be done. Oh, perhaps for the moment, or even a few weeks, but something always happens to pull the person back into the life they will or would have lived. Perhaps it's because there are too many lives for a single everyday sort of person to seriously change anything." She shrugged.

Zander stopped her and frowned down at her. "But would that not imply there can be none of those anomalies you fear?"

"Not at all. Those people have been unimportant historically. What if *Napoleon* died as a child? That would have *major* consequences, would it not? A hypothesis: What if, next week, Wellington were thrown from his horse and killed. Could anyone take his place? Or would the French push the English back still again?"

A horrified expression crossed Zander's face. He grasped her shoulders, shaking her slightly. "Beth! Surely you aren't suggesting . . ."

"No I'm not! I used that example because it does *not* happen. All I'm asking is whether you think history would change if it did."

"In other words, small lives very likely have little effect, but important lives, if changed, might change the whole?"

"That or that *many* small changes can add up and make major changes in the long run. It's all theory, Zander. If— when—you go into the future, you may dip into tapes where theory is argued."

"Tapes?" A frown pulled a vee between his eyes. "Ah! You refer not to ties for gowns, but still another invention. I'll not ask, Beth."

"Do you see how easy it is to make mistakes?"

He grinned. "What I see is that Maman is waving to us from the sewing room window. Shall we go?"

"Do you think there are guests?"

"Very likely."

"Then I'd best take the back stairs and freshen up before coming down. My skirts have picked a great deal of dust and, oh dear, a bit of mud . . .!"

Late that afternoon, as Beth soaked in a bath, she mused over the change in the salon that day. The tension was gone. The ever present, albeit polite, battle between Zander and his mother was over. Lady Fairmont had given up tricking or pressuring or, as she'd once done, ordering Zander to pay attention to the young women accompanying their mothers. More than that, somehow the countess made it clear to all

she was no longer aiding and abetting hopeful young ladies
to a marriage with her son!

Beth smiled wryly. The resulting gossip should be interesting! Lady Fairmont had, too obviously, been trying to
find her son a wife. That she'd ceased to do so would be
noted. Would people say Zander had tossed the handkerchief
to some lucky chit or, alternatively, that he'd convinced his
mother he would not! Most likely, a combination would
make the rounds.

What did not occur to her was that she'd have a place in
the rumors. That evening at the Fevershams' a young lady
of her acquaintance snubbed her. When another snapped out
a particularly waspish comment concerning undeserving to
say nothing of *ancient* cousins, she guessed what was being
said. Waiting her chance, she guided Juno into an alcove.
"You've hung on Lord Belmont's sleeve all evening," she
said, "so you've probably not noticed, but will you discover
something for me?"

"If I can."

"Find out what's being said about . . . well . . ."

Beth found it hard to phrase her request. She tried again.
"It sounds silly, but I think there's gossip about Zander and
myself." She felt a blush rising up from her low neckline.
The fact she was blushing caused her to blush still more.
Fuming, she fanned herself briskly.

"But Beth, everyone seeing the two of you together
speaks of it."

Beth compressed her lips. If only she *knew* it would be
possible to stay with Zander. If only Suu-Van had not allowed his sense of humor freedom and had actually told her,
one way or the other, that she could or could not remain
and marry Zander . . .

"Juno," she said, "the gossip must be stopped."

"I've no wish to stop it, not if it means you'll wed Zander."

"Has it occurred to you there might be reason we *can't?*"

Juno eyed Beth. "I can think of none"—her eyes widened and she gasped—"unless you are wed already!"

Beth reacted automatically, shaking her head, and then wished she'd not done so. It would be an excellent excuse if one were needed. "Not that," she said when Juno's smile returned. "Nevertheless—"

Juno raised a hand. "I can think of no other reason and I'd *like* you for sister. But, if there is a truly good reason you wish the rumors stopped, then it is Maman to whom you should speak. She can halt gossip by merely raising an eyebrow!"

"In that case, Juno, perhaps I should find your mother!"

Beth searched for Lady Fairmont. Her ladyship must stop whatever was being said, because if she did not, and if—a pain shot like a nail through her head—Beth was forced to leave Zander, the gossip might be not just *nasty,* but *dangerous.*

Lady Fairmont was no more interested in halting the gossip than Juno. "There's no problem now I know exactly who you are."

"The problem, Lady Fairmont, is not what I wish or what Zander wants, but what is allowed." She whispered her fear that her disappearance might result in rumors of murder. "What if Zander is brought under suspicion? I couldn't bear to think I'd caused such problems . . ."

"Murder . . ." Lady Fairmont scanned the crowded room. "Yes. There are some who might suggest it. I'll do what I can . . . but Beth . . ."

"Yes?"

"I'll be very disappointed if you leave us and make my son unhappy."

Lady Fairmont's glare of protective motherhood pulled Beth's emotions between tears and laughter.

"Do you think *any* of us will be happy?" she asked. "Certainly not *I.*"

Eighteen

Beth watched her ladyship's first foray into the battle to convince the ton there was nothing of a serious nature between her son and her guest and then retreated to the retiring room set aside for female guests. She found it blissfully empty, so pulled a book from her reticule and sat down to read.

Zander might believe she should enjoy herself but she couldn't. She was preoccupied with the coming adventure when she and Zander would have only a brief time to search Smithson's ship for contraband. Would she, this time, discover Smithson's cache? Of course she would. Perhaps, once she'd found the proof, she'd relax and enjoy parties such as this. But for now, the distraction of a good book . . .

As Beth turned the last page, two women entered. Beth ignored them, returning her book to her reticule and twitching her skirts into place. Then their conversation caught her ear. ". . . Yes, I like that Italian artist very much. The color! And the depth in that plaza scene! Quite amazing, is it not? I don't understand how it is done, do you?"

"I've studied Canaletto's work extensively, Henrietta, and I believe it has to do with the way the lines are angled and that he makes the size of things change as you seem to go into the picture. I've experimented and will show you the results if you'd be interested," the second woman said smugly.

"I'd appreciate that," responded Henrietta with all the humility of a beggar asking alms. That woman, the mousier of the two, trailed the more assured woman from the room, adding, "Was it not good of Lord Feversham to open his gallery this evening? I don't believe I've seen anything so beautiful since we . . ."

A Canaletto? *Here?* Beth decided to explore in the hopes of finding the painting. She asked the way of a convenient footman and, eventually, reached the gallery situated on the top floor. She eyed a series of fog bedewed skylights which, during sunny hours, would give the room ample natural light. Tonight, light was supplied by chandeliers.

Beth seated herself in an alcove across from the Canaletto and lost herself in contemplation of the life and color and the *glow* which seemed to flow from the canvas. Some time later she realized she was not alone. Her first thought was that Lord Belmont had joined her, but almost instantly the man's furtive movements convinced her it was the cousin, Richard, whom she'd last heard, although not seen, at Vauxhall Gardens.

The sweat running down the side of his face suggested imminent skullduggery. Beth waited. While waiting, she debated what *she* should do if he *were,* as she thought, about to steal one or more canvases at Smithson's behest as the conversation that night had indicated would happen.

Should she stay hidden? Allow Richard to leave with his booty? Follow and see where and to whom he delivered it? Or should she apprehend him before he could take the paintings? She glanced at her narrow-skirted gown and sighed. There was no hope of following him when dressed in this fashion.

By Pietro's pink piano, she thought, watching him approach the very painting she'd enjoyed so much. *Bach Beethoven and Brahms!* she added for good measure as he took out a tool which should never have been allowed in his hands. The first swipe of the Exacto Knife slit the canvas near the right side of the frame. Another swipe and the other side was cut.

"What are you doing?" she asked.

The villain jumped, squawked, and jammed a cut finger into his mouth. He swung around and glared.

"Why are you cutting out that painting?" Beth asked, making full use of her seeming naiveté.

Sweat poured down Richard's face. "Because I've bought it. I'm taking it home with me."

"I don't believe you. A footman would remove the painting from the frame. One would never cut it out!"

"You know nothing of such things."

The man stalked toward Beth, the knife held tightly in a shaking hand. Beth suspected he meant to cut her throat. The cynical thought crossed her mind that he'd likely botch the job, given how panicked he was. For the moment she pretended to shrink from him. The instant he was in range, however, she swung up both feet. She kicked the hand holding the knife with one toe as she simultaneously kicked him beneath the chin with the other. The knife flew away and Beth shoved both feet into his mid-section.

Richard fell backwards with a whoosh of exhaled breath. While he recovered, Beth swooped on the knife, dropping it into her reticule. At the same moment the jovial sounds of male voices could be heard on the stairs.

"You'd better run," she suggested politely, when Richard, a trifle wobbly, stood up. "You'll be caught if you don't."

He too heard the masculine laughter and raced toward the far end of the gallery, whisking out the door there just as the men entered the other end.

Faintly, Beth heard the clatter of Richard's feet as he raced down a secondary staircase. She noticed one man look that way, a frown on his face. Beth, pretending fear, pointed at the painting. "He was cutting it. He meant to steal it. Oh, thank goodness you have come!"

Lord Feversham's interest was in the damage to his painting, but the gentleman who had heard the footsteps called to one of his friends to help him chase down the villain. The two soon returned, a rueful look about them. "Lost him, Feversham. Sorry about that."

"Look what he did!" raged the Baron. "He's cut both edges!"

"Must have been the sharpest of steel to have done that so smoothly!" said another man. "He'll have ruined a good razor, is my guess!"

"Just be glad this young woman interrupted him, my lord, or he'd be long gone and the painting, too. Are you all right, Lady . . . er, Miss . . ."

"Mademoiselle Thevenard," she murmured. She put the back of her hand to her brow. "I don't feel at all well," she complained.

The younger of the two who chased after Richard was one of Juno's court and offered to find Lady Fairmont. The other, ignoring her seeming condition, sternly questioned her about the thief's looks, his size and even what he was wearing. "He wasn't so very big, was he," said Beth breathlessly, uncertain why she lied. Tony and Richard were nearly as tall as Zander. "And I don't know how he looked, do I? His face was covered, wasn't it?"

She drooped so the men couldn't see *her* face. *Why,* she berated herself silently, *don't I simply reveal Richard's name?* Perhaps because Lord Belmont wouldn't like it and Belmont was Zander's friend, she decided.

Lady Fairmont arrived, Lord Belmont in tow, and, scolding and cajoling, they led her away. As they went down the stairs to the entrance hall, Beth saw Richard hovering near the door.

She met the would-be villain's eyes. An evil sneer winged her way, his expression changing to fear as he recognized his cousin, then to hatred as he returned his gaze to Beth. He took his hat and cane from a footman who arrived just then and exited.

Beth wondered if she should feel concern. Surely the man was too pusillanimous to attempt murder? But if he did . . . something easily managed in an era when a shove at just the right moment would have one falling under the sharp horror of shod hooves and iron bound wheels. But Richard Richmond was, she believed, a man who was unlikely to murder in cold blood. Once the heat of the moment was gone, he was far more likely to resort to *looks* which should kill! Perhaps the greatest likelihood was that he'd flee.

Lady Fairmont called for their carriage and took the girls away. Seeing how disappointed Juno was, Beth insisted they need not interrupt their evening. Besides, Beth wished to discuss with Lord Belmont, as soon as possible, the fact Richard had descended to outright robbery, not just the self-justified sales of his cousin's birthright!

Unfortunately, Lord Belmont didn't join them in the carriage as Beth had hoped he would. And he had, according to Juno, no intention of attending the ball to which they proceeded—a more accurate explanation of Juno's disappointment, perhaps!

Zander, much to everyone's surprise, *did* attend. He and Beth had the supper dance. Beth decided she'd had quite enough of dancing as soon as she'd had her second dance with Zander and could not have another. She yawned, her jaw cracking, and was glad her fan hid her gaping mouth! In another era she'd not have had something so suitable to hide behind! But the yawn reminded her she'd an excellent excuse for departing the party.

She moved among the guests, pausing to respond to a compliment here, a question there, until she found the countess. "Would it be possible to leave soon?" she asked when certain she'd not interrupt her ladyship's desultory conversation with an elderly lady. "I find I'm more fatigued than I'd have thought possible." For Zander's mother's ears alone, she added, "My experience at the Fevershams' has caught up with me as you thought it might."

"Ah, my dear, you *would* put a brave face on it! Just let me place Juno under the protection of a friend, and I'll take you home."

"I can easily go alone . . ."

"Allow me to know my business, Beth. Besides"—Lady Fairmont's eyes twinkled—"a ball is not my style of party. I'm perfectly happy to be forced to take you home!"

"Sleep well, child," she said somewhat later. "I'm sorry it was necessary that you leave the ball, but these things cannot always be helped."

"I am not a child to pout at trifles, Lady Fairmont."

"No. You're not a child." Lady Fairmont watched her young guest drink the laudanum she insisted Beth take and then, quietly, leaving the light set at a low flame, she left the dimly lit room.

Beth swore softly that she'd been unable to avoid the dose and wondered if the drug would put her to sleep when she needed to send a message to Suu-Van concerning Smithson's giving Richard a disallowed invention. Hoping, in her half drugged state, that she could manage the awkward position required for message sending, Beth pulled the curtains back to reach the window seat and the sarong hidden there.

Lounging against the cushions was Captain Smithson himself!

"What are you doing here?" Adrenalin, flowing into her veins, counteracted some of the drugging effect of the opium.

"You come with me," he growled. "Now."

"At this hour?" Had Richard gone instantly to the captain? Had Smithson put two and two together and come up with three? He couldn't know she'd been sent to unmask him, but he'd know she'd recognize the source of that knife! A touch of panic stole up Beth's spine. With the laudanum in her system she'd be no match for the Fox. "I'll do no such thing."

"You *will*."

"Why should I?" she asked.

"When I give an order, *you* obey."

"And if I do not?"

"I'll see you are very sorry." The shrill ugly laugh Beth detested filled the room and then he looked around, obviously worried he'd been heard.

Trying to make her mind work, Beth yawned a gaping jaw-cracking yawn. "You pick the damnedest times."

"You'll come."

She could find no way out and Beth sighed. "Let me change to something more suitable than a nightgown, then."

When she was ready the man rolled cat-like to his feet and opened the window. At least tonight he wasn't using the floater! Beth followed. If the man had guessed she'd bubbled him, then he'd as happily kill her here in her room as elsewhere and in her current condition she'd have little chance of thwarting him. The more time that passed before he attacked the more the drugging effect of the laudanum would dissipate and the better her chance when he did strike.

Beth put all thought of Zander from her mind, the fear she'd never see him again, her regret they'd had so little time together. She dozed during the carriage ride, hoping more of the drug would wear off. She felt only a trifle better, however, when they transferred to a small boat and were rowed to where Smithson's ship lay to anchor.

She asked no questions. As they approached his ship, she finally realized she irritated Smithson by *not* nagging him for details of why he'd come for her and by *not* making guesses which he could deny! Beth hid a grin as she climbed the rope ladder and, on deck, waited to be told what next. She was motioned toward the captain's cabin . . . and balked. The cabin was too small for proper self-defense.

"Why?" she asked.

"Because I say so."

"Smithson, you don't like me. And it's obvious you enjoy

baiting me, but I'll not move one more foot until you explain what this is about."

Smithson motioned and, slow to react, Beth was lifted from her feet and *carried* toward the cabin. She fought. Twice she connected in a punitive way with one of her silent captors, but they didn't release her. As was inevitable, she was shoved into the cabin, falling to her knees. The door slammed shut behind her. Beth scrambled to her feet, her eyes on the man awaiting her, her cheeks flooding with color. "Suu-Van!"

"Hmm. Such a dramatic entrance." Her superior's brows arched, his mouth pursing. "But why, my dear, are you so disheveled?"

"Our dear friend out there plays games," responded Beth with a trifle more acid than was her habit. "He wouldn't tell me why I was to enter his cabin so I resisted." Beth gestured at her torn gown and bedraggled hair. "This is the result."

"Another count against the man," said Suu-Van, switching to the language known only to those who worked in Eth-arm. Seated in an over-large, armed chair made of oak, the huge man studied his protegee. "You do not look well," he added, continuing in the secret language. "Does this era not agree with you?"

"If I look exhausted, it's because I had little sleep last night, or do I mean the night before? On top of that, tonight I've danced myself to a stand still at a grand ball right after *not* being killed when I thwarted a theft at the soiree we attended elsewhere!"

Suu-Van chuckled, his jowls wobbling and his belly rolling. "You have fallen on your feet I see. I'd thought it might be so, but your lack of progress is worrying."

Beth's eyes narrowed. "I don't suppose you managed to monitor this ship while you've awaited my arrival?"

"Hmm. The ship. No." Suu-Van waved a hand. "This cabin? Yes."

"Good. It'll be a help that I've that much less to check."

"And just when do you think you'll manage that small bit of work?" he asked, with an innocent look she didn't understand.

Beth sighed. "It is difficult."

"I'm sure it is."

Had Suu-Van hidden a grin just then? Surely not.

"When you selected me for this job," she said, slowly, "you forgot to take into calculation the fact that women are not free to move about as they wish. Upper class women, at least. That fact, along with dear Smithson placing me in the care of the son of a peer, has very nearly made this whole project impossible. So," she said with a grin, "you'll be forced to admit my lack of progress is all your fault, will you not?"

"Hmm. So I will."

"Worse, security has been breached. Twice."

"Twice?" he asked sharply.

Very briefly Beth recounted all that had happened since she'd first arrived in this very cabin.

"You've had a difficult time, have you not, my child?"

Beth grimaced. "You always were good at the understatement, Suu-Van. But is that all you have to say to this mess?"

"That is all."

Beth studied him, baffled.

"But you still have a duty to fulfill," he said softly.

"Zander has set it up for tomorrow evening or do I mean *this* evening? He's being excessively cautious about my skin, or so it seems to me. Have a bit more patience, please."

"Hmmmmmm. Patience. It is difficult, this patience. I was never good at it. . . ."

"You're laughing."

He smiled. "No, child. I merely tease a trifle. Our Smithson will return you to your place and I'll give myself some few, hmm, hours? days perhaps? to see what I may see."

"What you may see?" she asked, pouncing on his words.

"I require a small vacation, I believe, before returning to my work. I am curious about this era which I've never visited . . . and there is a woman of whom I've heard. Smithson will escort me, but, fear it not! He'll never know I've contacted that female to whom you were to come."

"I *do* fear Smithson, Suu-Van."

Her mentor's brows climbed his forehead toward his balding skull. "You think you are no match for this sly fox?" he asked.

"In a fair fight I'm more than a match, but he'll not fight fairly, will he? And very soon he'll know I've suspicion if not proof he's responsible for stealing art here. You see, Suu-Van, the theft I interrupted this evening involved an Exacto Knife!"

"An Exat . . . Hmm!" Suu-Van frowned. "I see. Our friend supplied the knife, of course, but he's arrogant and will think you cannot be certain of that, that you might believe a renegade loose in Time. However that may be, I fear he'll not be happy when he learns you know. So. Another reason I will be available in case of need when you search this ship."

"As I said and assuming everything goes as planned, we'll make that search this evening. Suu-Van, I must go."

Suu-Van nodded. "Enjoy yourself while you may, my Beth."

A pang caught at her heart and her eyes went quickly to meet his. *While I may.* "Yes," she said slowly. "I will." *Or I would,* she thought, *if it were not that you've just told me it will end.*

A deeply depressed young woman returned to the Fairmont town house. Bone deep aches slowed her and her skirts obstructed her as she climbed the wall to her window. Beth took one look at the man stretched out on her bed and sighed, flopping down onto the window seat in much the boneless posture in which she'd found Smithson earlier.

"I don't suppose you'd care to tell me where you went this time?"

"Zander, must we have this discussion tonight? I've already done too much with far too much of your mother's laudanum in my system! I don't want to talk. I only want to sleep." She yawned another gaping yawn. "And sleep and sleep and sleep." *And preferably sleep myself out before I must tell you I am ninety-nine percent certain we'll not be allowed to remain together!*

Zander stalked toward her. "I on the other hand am wide awake and exceedingly angry. You've been on that ship, have you not?"

"Yes." Beth yawned.

"Just yes? No explanation? No excuses?"

"No."

He grasped her shoulders and shook her and then, aghast at what he'd done, pulled her into his embrace.

Beth lay her head on his shoulder. It felt so good to lie in his arms.

"Beth, Beth, what am I to do with you?"

"Trust me?" she muttered.

"When you left me behind to worry and fret, to chew my nails down to the quick?"

"Just believe I've a modicum of good sense; try understanding that I'm trained in ways you cannot imagine; and, finally, believe that not everything is under my control."

"So?"

Beth yawned and snuggled into his embrace.

"Beth!"

She raised her head, turned it, and laid it back against his shoulder.

"Beth Anwick Ralston! Answer me."

Beth opened one eye, closed it. "In t'mornin."

"Now."

She shook her head and snuggled closer.

Zander sighed. He carried her to her bed where he sat, holding her on his lap. *"Now,* Beth, I want answers and no more games." She didn't respond. "Do you hear me, Beth? *Beth,"* Zander repeated when all he got was a soft snore, "I insist you explain yourself."

Beth straightened, angry he was angry but too sleepy to spar further with the man she loved. "Suu-Van arrived in Smithson's cabin. Smithson took me to him."

"Damn."

"Yes, and drat and blast and bloody hell. Not that words will do any good. I'm sorry if you worried, Zander, but, believe me, I'd no choice." She yawned.

"I see you did not." He waited for more but again she lay against him, her eyes closing. "Well? Did your Suu-Van have further orders for you?"

"No," she said sleepily. "He just wondered why I took so long on such a simple job."

Zander's arms tightened. "He's not looked into the history books?"

"Do you think there'd be anything in the records to explain my extended stay with you? Someone so insignificant as I?"

"Perhaps not." Again he waited for her to continue. Again she did not. "Beth," he finally asked, "do we go on with tomorrow evening's plans or will he take care of everything?"

"We carry on."

"Then"—he gently transferred her to the bed—"you'd better get some sleep."

"Tha's what I sai'." she muttered.

His soft chuckle warmed her. "Good night, my love."

He bent and kissed her softly before pushing away. At the door he checked no one would see him leave her room. Beth, one eye cracked open, watched until he closed the door behind himself. Then, with a sigh composed as much of despair as of relief, she prepared for bed, hid the torn gown in the window seat and, finally, at long last, allowed herself to slip into a deep restful sleep.

Nineteen

Wrapped in a long dark cloak which hid her black working clothes, Beth waited in deep shadow near where Zander spoke to a little band of raiders. Two boats awaited them, tied to iron rings sunk into the foundation wall of the warehouse. While Zander spoke to the men, she stared down rickety wooden steps to where they bobbed on the out-going tide.

"No more than twenty minutes," he repeated, sternly. "However rich the pickings, you'll not enjoy them if you're dead."

It occurred to Beth to wonder if Smithson were greedy enough to booby-trap his cargo with possibly lethal security measures. Should she warn these men who might inno-cently—well, not *innocently* of course—be hurt? But a con-temporary cargo would be worth next to nothing in comparison to Smithson's real cargo, the art he meant to sell, illegally, in markets he'd reach through the use of the transporter device on his ship.

Beth hadn't looked forward to their night's work since taking the Exacto Knife. If Smithson already knew, there would be new surprises against an incursion onto his ship. If he didn't yet know, he might this very instant be meeting with his stooge. He'd return to his ship knowing she'd come, however much a beginner she was thought to be. In either case, the work would not be easy—although the captain was still likely to underestimate her just as he would any woman.

Beth stared over the vessels waiting clearance to unload

or load cargo, to restock rotten sail and worn rope and whatever else kept a ship in port. Even at this late hour there was more activity than she thought reasonable. One ship, lit by lanterns fore and aft, slipped silently down the channel toward the estuary. Traversing the river directly in front of that ship's bow, a tiny rowboat defied it. On board still another vessel a crew unloaded huge bales, the orders, oddly muffled, echoing hollowly from the wooden walls behind her. And, everywhere, faint streams of mist trailed low over the water or streamed up into arabesques which drifted into nothing or swirled around hulls against which waves slapped in monotonous regularity.

"Ready, Beth?"

"As ready as I'll ever be. Remember, Zander, that my claiming that knife last night will alert Smithson to his danger. This is unlikely to be the routine search we've hoped it would be."

"You've said that. Make up your mind. Either we go, or we wait until he decides nothing will come of Richard's folly and relaxes his guard."

The muscle near Beth's ear rolled into a knot. Did she lead these men to death? Would Zander be killed? But there was the chance Smithson hadn't yet learned of Richard's fumbling, was unprepared for invasion . . .

"Now is best," she said, heading down the steps and settling herself on the forward seat of one of the boats.

At river level the mists appeared far denser than they'd seemed from above. They rowed in near silence among the larger vessels and Beth wondered how the men knew how to find one particular ship among so many. Time ceased to exist. *Now* was an eternal moment in which she traveled forever over the stinking water . . . toward danger.

While Beth worried, Juno stood in a small room near a ballroom, another couple unknowingly acting as chaperones for herself and Anthony. As he berated her, Tony held her arm, assuring she didn't escape him. Not that she'd particularly wanted to, of course.

". . . You're a fool, my girl!"

"A fool," repeated Juno.

"He'll never ask you to wed him."

"I haven't thought he would," muttered Juno, wondering if by any chance in the world it was jealousy driving her love to say such things—or did he truly believe her the fool he called her.

"You are merely flirting then. Is that it?"

"It is not. I never flirt with Sir Terrence!"

"That's what it must look like if he knows you don't expect to wed him. He's only playing with you, girl!"

"He's not playing."

For a moment Tony was silent. "Not? You believe he attempts your seduction, then?"

Juno's mouth dropped open. She blinked rapidly several times.

"Nonsense. *Rupe's* my friend. And," she added when Tony would have made an obviously disparaging remark about Rupert, "so is Sir Terrence." She folded her arms, becoming more than a trifle angry herself.

"I've no wish to disillusion you, Juno," he said in a patronizing tone which set her teeth on edge, "but since you'll not listen to reason I must inform you that Sir Terrence is in the toils of Lady Merrivelle."

"I know."

Tony's eyes widened in shock. "You *know.*"

"Tony," Juno explained with what patience she could, "He and I are friends. He's explained and I understand why she's made a by-word of herself."

"He won't wed you."

"You can think of nothing but that, can you? Must every man with whom I speak have an interest in marrying me?"

"Yes," he responded promptly. "You're in London to find a husband."

"I'm in London to be introduced to the ton," she contradicted and the mulish expression her family knew well settled onto her features. "I'll wed if and only if the man I love asks me to marry him." Juno, fearing she'd said far too much, turned on her heel and walked away.

A few feet into the ballroom she noticed Sir Terrence trying not to stare toward his love who flirted with another man. She hooked her arm in his. "Will you dance with me, Sir Terrence?" asked Juno, glancing back to see Tony scowling at her.

"Hmm? Haven't we had two dances this evening?"

"Oh. I guess we have." Juno sighed.

"Something the matter?"

"Nothing except that Tony just rang a peal over me and my ears still ring!"

Sir Terrence glanced around to see Tony glaring at him. "Your Tony appears upset. With me?" he guessed. "Will he call me out?"

"He asked if he should, but I made him see that for the nonsense it is."

Sir Terrence, casting another glance Tony's way, wondered if she had. "I think he'd not be so stern if he weren't more involved than he knows."

Juno's lips formed a pout. "Then I wish he'd discover it!"

Sir Terrence chuckled. "You, my dear, are a delight." He smiled at her in a kindly way. "I've actually wished my heart were free so that it could find its happiness with yours."

Juno laughed in turn. "You're wonderfully good for a girl's confidence. And, if you'd been watching *your* heart's desire these last few minutes, you'd see she's beginning to discover the direction of *hers*. Her heart's desire, I mean. You'd best soothe her sensibilities or we'll have her doing something foolish, along the lines of cutting off her nose to spite her face!"

"Can't have that!" he said in pretended horror. "It's such a lovely nose!"

Bowing, Sir Terrence took his leave of Juno and, against all usage, crossed the corner of the dance floor in time to steal his love away from her next partner. Juno smiled approval and, thinking she'd like a lemonade, turned to find Tony just behind her. She stepped back and heard a rip as the flounce of her skirt caught under her heel.

Tony heard it, too. His expression a trifle rueful, he said, "I was about to ask you to dance, Juno, but I think, instead, I'd best escort you to the woman's retiring room!"

"And wait for me?" she asked, taking his arm.

"You truly aren't hurt he's gone directly from your side to that woman's?"

"Since I told him he'd better go before she did something stupid that would ruin everything for the two of them, I don't see how you think I'd be concerned for myself."

"Did you tell him that?"

"Hmm. The sense of it anyway. She'd been casting us *such* looks. I feared she think things about Sir Terrence similar to those *you* were thinking."

Tony didn't respond. They threaded their way through the crowd at the door to the ballroom but, once they reached the hall, he stopped her. "If Sir Terrence is not the love you wish to marry, is it Rupert?"

"Rupert!" Juno stamped her foot. "You called me a fool earlier, Anthony Richmond, but it is *you* who are the fool." She stalked off down the hall and into the room where a maid would sew up her flounce.

For a tuppence, she thought, I'd not return to the ball-room . . .

But the further thought, that he might actually ask, again, that they dance, sent her back out into the hall just as quickly as the flounce could be mended. Tony did ask, and it was, for Juno, the best half hour of the evening—even if he didn't refer to her temper tantrum or ask, again, who it was she loved. Or, perhaps because he didn't?

While Juno and Tony danced and Beth and Zander slipped over the dark Thames waters, Suu-Van and a bent old woman watched Smithson meet Richard Richmond in a lane near the Mayor's residence in the City.

"It wasn't my fault," shrieked Richard, staring wildly at the thing in Smithson's hand. "Someone was coming. I *had* to run, I tell you."

"Without the painting. *Fool.* Why am I surrounded by fools?"

Richard opened his mouth to respond but, at the glare directed his way, closed it. Even from where Suu-Van and Li Jian stood, they could see the gentleman with the captain quite literally shake in his shoes.

"You get me that painting."

"How? The Feversham won't entertain again anytime soon."

"You will break in. Climb the walls. Force a window."

"Me? Climb walls? Captain, I'm not trained in circus tricks! *I can't break into Feversham's house."*

"Don't argue. Just get the picture."

"I can't."

"You can. Where is the knife."

"I dropped it, I told you. I don't know"—Smithson growled deep in his throat—"Maybe Mademoiselle picked it up," suggested Richard quickly.

"Mademoi . . . *Thevenard!?"*

"I believe that's the stupid chit's name."

A cone of faintly glowing light showed at the end of the rod in Smithson's hand. The howl of fear, panic, pain, which rose in Richard's throat, was the briefest of sounds, suddenly cut off. He went rigid. An instant later the faint light disappeared and Richard collapsed, bonelessly, to the dirty street, his head hanging between his arms, his hands spread against dirty cobblestones, the fingers white with strain.

"You're a fool," said Smithson indifferently. "Get the picture or suffer. I'll see you suffer *that* until you die."

Suu-Van, at the first hint of the odd light, started forward, but Li Jian caught his arm. Reluctantly, Suu-Van eased back.

Panting, Richard tipped his head up, stared at the man towering over him. "What sort of devil are you?"

"Devil?" Smithson's un-funny laugh chilled them. "Devil!" The cackling laughter rose shrilly. "A devil I am! Yes."

"He's mad," whispered Suu-Van.

"Yes. He must be stopped."

"Why have you"—Suu-Van turned a curious glance Li Jian's way—"done nothing? You, unlike my agent, have had the freedom to act."

"In my time, we too need proof. Opinion is not enough and what we believe is mere opinion."

"His use of that weapon and his earlier use of anti-gravity in this era will have to be sufficient if nothing else is found."

"That will banish him from *travelling* in time, but banishment alone will not stop him recruiting others to do his will. Besides, we've reasons . . ."

When she didn't continue Suu-Van's brows clashed together. "Has he interfered with history?"

"One small dislocation, which, over a few decades, returned to normal. When we discovered that spike, I was sent to see nothing more occurred."

"What do you consider proof?"

"I await it," she said, evading an actual answer.

After a moment Suu-Van asked, "Then you know what will occur?"

"Oh yes. But until it does, he's not guilty, is he?"

"If the thing for which you wait moves history from the rails, then I wonder you do nothing to prevent it."

"What will happen, has happened, has it not? Or will, given where we stand in time."

"And, for you, it will not truly interfere in the future."

"Do not be bitter," she said, and added in a sweetly reasonable tone, "If we *prevent* its happening, who knows what changes might occur."

"You give lessons from our primers for novices. It is well to review the basics for I see now that you cannot interfere."

"Nor may you," she warned.

Suu-Van swallowed hard. "Beth . . ."

"You *know* she is not harmed. You know her future!"

"Ah. Well then . . ."

"Well then, nothing." The seeming old woman bent over her stick and turned to hobble away. "Come. We go now."

Suu-Van saw Smithson striding toward a narrow alley which would lead, eventually, to the river. "He's returning to his ship?"

"Of course. His tool-fool told him of the lost knife, did he not? Told him who took it? He knows your agent, your beloved Beth, will be forced to search his ship, does he not?"

"Ah. At least he still thinks her a novice! He'll expect a mere female Rescue person, not a fully trained ETH-arm agent." Suu-Van hurried after the scurrying woman who looked far too ancient to move so quickly.

But she was not at all ancient, as Suu-Van well remembered. A regal woman, her long hair in multiple braids, the braids interwoven in an intricate fashion on and around her head. Suu-Van would not have admitted it to a soul, but he dreamed of letting down that hair and seeing it flow around Li Jian's slim form . . .

Richard Richmond made his way through the City feeling none of his usual trepidation. He was, instead, listing a hundred ways in which he might slowly and painfully kill Mademoiselle Thevenard. After all, his egotism told him, if it weren't for her, not only would he have had the painting, but he'd not have suffered from that devil's instrument. He still ached. And cold. *Bone deep cold.*

Worst of all, he must make another attempt for that painting. Somehow, he had to get into the Feversham town house, up several flights of stairs, and into a room which, since an attempt had already been made, might be guarded day and night.

It couldn't be done. Sweat rolled down Richard's face. He tugged at his cravat, noticed he'd entered a better street, and waved down a hackney. It couldn't be done and he wasn't about to try.

Twenty minutes later Richard let himself into his cousin's house and went straight to Tony's library where he poured a large glass of brandy. He downed it and poured another which he took to a chair near the small blaze which always burned in the library grate. He settled down to wait. It was his cousin's fault he was in this mess and his cousin could get him out of it . . .

". . . and how you think *I'm* to blame for your greed and dishonesty, I haven't a notion," yelled Tony, running fingers through his hair and glaring down at his nearly dead drunk cousin. "It is *not* my fault."

"Is. *I* should be Lord Belmont. *I* should own all this. Isn't fair." Richard closed his eyes, opened one. "Your fault."

"My very existence, I suppose!"

Richard nodded with the careful solemnity of the intoxicated. He closed his eyes, his head lolling against the high back of the chair.

Tony sighed. "What the devil am I to do with you? I can't turn you over to the magistrate, which is what I should do."

Richard opened one eye, studied his cousin warily for a

moment, then satisfied Tony really would *not* give him up to justice, closed it again.

"On the other hand, I can't allow you to steal me or anyone else blind." Tony glared. "Blast it all, Rich, you didn't used to be such a . . . a . . ."

"Blot on creation?" asked his cousin, slurring the words.

"That'll do," agreed Tony. He frowned. "I can't make a decision instantly. As always, your room is prepared for you. If you would oblige me, you'll not leave it until I give you permission. If you won't stay because I wish it, perhaps you will for the sake of your skin."

Richard struggled to his feet. "My skin?" he asked on a sneer.

"Yes. I'd hate for your devilish captain to get his sights on you before I've decided on an appropriate punishment myself!"

At the thought of the captain, Richard sobered slightly. He shuddered. "I believe," he said carefully, "that I need a rest. I'll sleep in . . . late. Very late." He staggered across the room.

Tony winced when he bumped one of the cases in which the collection of miniatures was displayed, but eventually his cousin made it to the door.

Before exiting, Richard turned, stared blearily across the room. " *'Tis* your fault, you know. All of it . . ."

The door slammed and Tony dropped into the vacated chair. What the *devil* was he to do about his cousin? The admission that he'd actually taken to thieving from collections other than the Belmont holdings made it imperative there be no more delay in coming to some conclusion concerning Richard's future.

The West Indies, perhaps? The family property there? Orders to the factor to keep him close, in essence, under house arrest? An old affection for the Richard who had played with him, gone to school with him, an affection long forgotten, rose up in him. How had his cousin come to this? Was there something he could have done? Should have, done?

And why did one have to face such problems when all one really wanted to think about was the problem of what to do with Lady Juno?

Beth grasped the knotted rope and was, moments later, crouched in the shadow of the rail. Zander followed a trifle less silently and the men, one after another, spread along the deck, their bare feet making no noise. Beth raised her arm. Still in silence the invading party searched for the four men Zander's watchmen reported were still on board.

Beth found the first. She took him out using a pressure trick she wished she'd thought to teach Zander. The next crewman saw his attacker and raised his voice in a ululating screech that brought the other two running. Beth stopped one; the other raced toward her knife in hand, but, twisting agilely, he jumped Zander. He slashed Zander's ribs, drawing blood, before he was stopped by a knockout blow to the chin.

Swearing roundly, furious he'd not avoided the knife, Zander checked his wound. Beth called their raggedy bunch together and, as she spread a healing cream on Zander's cut and slapped on a skin-thin bandage, told them to lock the crewmen into a cabin.

"Then you're free to loot as you please, but you remember, you've little time for it."

"Where are *you* going?" asked Zander, wondering what she'd put on his wound to so instantly take away the pain.

"Smithson's cabin."

"You said your Suu-Van searched that."

"I had a thought . . ." The door was locked. She knelt before it, running her hands over the frame, the surrounding area and the door itself. Her eyes never left the dials revealed by flaps turned back from parts of the gloves.

"What are you doing?"

"Analyzing defenses." She moved to the small port hole that looked out onto the deck and chuckled. "Amazing how blind people can be," she said, satisfied. Taking a wire from a seam along her leg, she slipped it between the window and the frame, wiggled it, swore fluently, but, after a few tense moments, pushed open the window.

"Give me a leg up," she ordered Zander.

"Let me in the moment you're in."

"If what I think's true, *then* I'll let you in. Otherwise, I'll come back out. Watch for our friend," she said, as she disappeared.

It was Zander's turn to swear fluently and rather more imaginatively than Beth had done.

"You'll wake the dead, Zander," she said a few moments later from the open door.

"Did you find it?"

"Yes. Right where I feared it would be."

His brows arched. "Feared?"

"The fool has, by a means I don't understand, built a cache into the TransPort unit itself."

"So?"

"So, if I open it, I may destroy it." She shrugged.

"So . . . ?" he insisted.

She sighed. "So we wait for the captain and we, hmm, *encourage* him to open it."

"I'll tell the men they'd better leave." A short time later he distributed coins as he ordered them off. "We find it necessary to wait here," he told them. "Get yourselves to safety, quickly, and thank you for your aid." The men shrugged, slipped over the side one after another, and disappeared. Zander turned, found himself facing Smithson. "Good evening," he said politely.

"You're a fool."

"I suspect you think the whole word populated by fools," said Zander.

"It is. Where is the woman?"

"In with the cache."

A startled look crossed the captain's face, and, as he glanced toward the cabin door, Zander leapt forward, catching the hand which held what he guessed was a weapon although it looked like nothing he'd ever seen. He held that arm high as he simultaneously caught Smithson's throat with his other hand.

A beam of light danced wildly around the heavens; it burned across a spar, then the mast, leaving dark marks; it flashed across a warehouse window and glass exploded into a thousand pieces. When it touched the Thames, water steamed. Zander concluded the weapon was more than he wished to face. He raised his knee while pulling down hard. The villain's forearm slammed across his thigh and the weapon skittered across the desk to be scooped up by Beth who aimed it at the captain.

"You can release him, Zander. Then come here please."

Zander released the captain who made funny mewing noises in his throat.

"ETH-arm," said Beth, holding up a medallion. Zander wondered where it had been concealed, given the skin tight garments she wore. "You'll not move, Smithson. Not one fraction of an inch. I don't trust you."

Zander backed toward her, keeping an eye on the captain. "That thing," he said. "What is it?"

"Something else which should not exist in this age. Put your hand on mine. Yes. Just like that. Do you feel that sliding bar just where my finger is?"

"Perhaps a quarter inch high?"

"That's it. If he moves so much as an eyelid, you slide it toward you about an inch and sweep the light that appears straight across Smithson's legs. Don't, if you love me at all, touch me with it!"

"You can't do that!" screeched Smithson

"Oh yes I can, Smithson. I'm ETH-arm. Zander, it's likely

he has other power weapons on him. Until I drain the energy he's carrying, he's dangerous as a mad dog. *Any* movement on his part may be lethal. Don't hesitate to cut him off at the knees."

"No!" Sweat beading Smithson's forehead gleamed in the dancing light from the lantern hanging on the end of a spar.

"It's simple, is it not?" asked Zander pretending innocence. "Don't move. Ah! I've got it, Beth, and, unlike you, I've no compunction about using the thing." He smiled the wolfish smile Beth had seen once before. "Not on scum like your captain has proven to be!"

Beth hesitated. "You'll not kill without need."

"Of course not. But if I think he'll harm you, that's need enough. And, since I'm not trained in your ways, I'm very likely to believe most anything a danger, just to be safe. I'd suggest you remain perfectly still, Smithson."

Smithson froze.

Beth circled behind the captain, removing still another wire from another seam in her working clothes. She attached it to a point in her glove, ran her gloved hand over the captain's back, around his sides, down his legs and up between them, around in front and up and over his head where she hovered.

"Inventive of you, Smithson," she said. "This is the first time I've discovered a power source in someone's hat!" She made another attachment, twisted a tiny dial on the back of her glove, and waited. Occasionally, she ran her hand through the whole routine over body and head, retesting.

"That's it. Smithson, you follow me into your cabin. Zander follows you. The three of us will remain well apart at all times, hear me Zander?"

"Clear enough."

"You orders take? From a mere *woman?*"

Zander chuckled. "Beth is not a *mere* woman. She's *my* woman. We take orders from each other. It depends on who has the appropriate knowledge."

"You're a *man*. I'll pay much if you turn the laser on her, the . . . gun, I mean. You'll share my treasure," Smithson coaxed. "There are other women. Many women. You'll be rich, have any woman . . ."

"He's quite the comedian, is he not?" asked Beth.

"If that means he's a jokesmith, then I've never heard anything so funny in my life."

"You're a fool!"

"No, Smithson. You're the fool."

"Bah."

"He's delaying us until his men return, Zander. Let's get this over."

"His men?" Zander chuckled. "You think I'd allow them to interfere?"

"What have you done?" asked Beth, curious.

"I've a dozen good men on the watch for them. I warned them the enemy might know tricks that would make an honest fight impossible, but I doubt Smithson allows anyone but himself a weapon such as this."

"Well done, Zander. So, Smithson," said Beth, "we've all the time in the world. Would you care to continue amusing us with your comic routine? Or would you like, one careful step at a time, to disarm the cache you've hidden in the TransPort equipment?"

"You found it."

"I found it."

"I will not," said the captain, crossing his arms.

"Then perhaps," suggested Zander, "I should simply kill him now."

"No!" howled Smithson, his arms falling to his sides and the sweat again flowing. "He's uncivilized! He's an animal. *Don't trust him!*"

Beth, laughing, doubled over. "This is as good as a play."

"Except that in one sense, he's correct, Beth," said Zander, thoughtfully. "I'll kill him rather than allow him to go free or to take things into the future which belong in my time."

"He's an ETH-arm prisoner, Zander. He must be tried and convicted and sentenced by our laws."

"Nonsense, Beth. I've got the weapon, so he's *my* prisoner. Do you release that cache," he growled, "or do I kill you?"

Smithson looked from one to the other. "I cannot."

"Why not?" asked Beth before Zander could speak. *Would* he kill, she wondered, slightly worried. Surely not.

"Cache is linked to the future," said the captain slyly. "Can't be done here."

"When in the future?"

"I don't know. I find the art. I send."

"I don't believe him," said Zander. He'd been watching the captain while the captain watched Beth. "He's lying, Beth. Not perhaps, about having orders for specific paintings, but he's lying about the cache."

"Not! I lie not."

"You'd lie through your teeth about anything and everything. You lie by preference!" Zander lifted the weapon. "Beth what would happen if I pull this trigger a small way? Just a teeny tiny bit? Would it kill?"

Smithson howled as Beth explained that it wouldn't kill but would be exceedingly painful.

"I'll experiment," said Zander, dreamily. "I may never again have the chance to operate such a . . . a gadget." He allowed the faintest glow to appear in a wide cone from the end of the weapon. Slowly he swept it toward the Captain. "Still think you can't open that cache, Smithson?"

"Can't!" he screeched and cringed away from the approaching beam. "Woman! *Don't let him.*"

"But I'm merely a woman. How can *I* stop him?" asked Beth, deciding that Zander was playing with Smithson, hoping to break him to their will.

A scream tore from the captain's throat only to be cut off

as the beam swept across him. Beth, knowing the effect the light had on a victim's nerves, winced. The scream returned to existence as the captain fell to the deck, writhing, his body cramping.

"An interesting effect," said Zander mildly. Inwardly, he was more than a little appalled by what a touch of the weapon's power did to Smithson's body. When Smithson lay still, panting, the sweat dampening his clothing, Zander raised the weapon again. "Do you think one more dose, Beth?"

"No!" The man panted, shakily rising to his feet. "No. I'll fix it."

"I think not," said Beth slowly.

"Beth," said Zander, a trifle impatiently, "will you make up your mind?"

"He must tell me what to do. If I think it will do no damage *I'll* do it. Zander, can't you see he plots revenge?"

"Hmm. Very likely." Zander gestured with the weapon. "Into the cabin, Smithson. Let's get on with this." Zander paused in the doorway and called Beth to his side. Watching Smithson, he whispered, "You think he'll attempt to kill us all?"

"He *might* prefer death to life in the past although I think him too much a coward."

"That's my thought, too. All right, Beth. Do what you must."

They entered the cabin and while Zander never took his eyes from Smithson, Beth encouraged the man to speak long and volubly about the delicate task of opening the cache.

Outside, on deck, Suu-Van stood near Li Jian, his head cocked toward the listening device she held between them. "Now?" he asked, beginning to feel a dread he couldn't explain.

"Soon," she said.

Twenty

Beth listened carefully as Captain Smithson lectured on the engineering which had added the cache to the intricately designed TransPort equipment. She asked three questions, nodded at the answers, and ordered him to give her line by line instruction for opening the cache.

Zander was irked that he understood not one word. Watching the captain's changing expressions was almost interesting enough to make up for his ignorance elsewhere, however. More than once he wondered if Beth had become so fascinated by whatever it was they discussed she forgot just who it was she discussed it *with!*

Smithson's first three instructions opened up a design area in what Zander discovered wasn't exactly a carpet no matter what it looked to be. As she continued working, Smithson appeared both nervous and elated.

"Careful, Beth," muttered Zander when he saw Smithson, unconsciously, draw back.

She looked up. "Did you say something?"

"I suggest you think about what you're doing."

Smithson, his voice hoarse, interrupted. *"No.* Don't listen to him!"

"Do you see?" asked Zander. "He's tricking you. I've no notion how, but he *wants* you to do what you're doing. I don't like that!"

Beth set down tools so tiny Zander wondered how they'd been crafted. She studied Smithson's features, looked down at her work, looked off into space. Faint lines etched themselves between her brows. Suddenly, what had been faint lines deepened drastically and Beth stared at Smithson.

Horror dripped from her voice. "You wouldn't!"

The captain slumped, becoming a bundle of rags. "Why wouldn't I?" he asked. "What awaits me that I would not?"

"But to blow up half of London, to"—her brows climbed toward her hair—"change the whole of world history! How could you think of doing such a thing?"

"Always I've wished to do it." Smithson shrugged.

"Beth," ordered Zander, "what you're saying frightens you, but surely what you seem to suggest isn't possible! Tell me you exaggerate."

Beth turned slowly, her eyes trailing away from the captain. She felt as if she were composed of brittle plastic rather than muscle, sinew, and nerves.

"Beth?" asked Zander, gently.

"He was directing *my hands* to turn the power stored in this thing into a *bomb*. He wanted to blow up not just this ship, but this whole stretch of river. Depending on just how much power he has stored, that would include not only the warehouses and docks and the East India Company waters, but very likely St. Paul's Cathedral, maybe as far west as Parliament, surely the Tower of London and—"

"Destroy the Tower?" interrupted Zander. *"No."*

"Why that in particular, Zander?"

"Because there's an ancient prophesy that if the Tower falls, then England is finished. I don't say I believe it, but . . ." He shrugged, not saying he *didn't*.

"Believe me, Zander, if that device he was directing me to build had gone off, England, as you know it, would be finished!" Beth set to work, sweat beading her brow, and slowly and carefully she dismantled what she'd put together. "There," she said, at last, exhaustion evident not just in her features, but in the way she held her body and in her voice. "I've put it back the way it was. Trained engineers will have to take this thing apart and find the hidden art." She stared at it a bit longer and looked sharply at Smithson. "Why, when you have the genius to invent this thing, did you not go into research?"

"No money," said Smithson and shrugged.

"Patents . . ."

"Maybe a patent on big idea. If one is given it." This time he didn't even bother to shrug, his posture one of defeat.

"What do we do next?" asked Zander.

"I contact the future."

"Beth, have you had training in building these things?"

"No."

Zander was silent for a moment before asking, "But you know enough you realized what he wanted you to do?"

"Anyone would. His *lecture* made sense. After that, without thinking, I merely followed his directions. If it weren't for you, Zander, not only would *we* be dead, but the whole of History would be distorted in ways I think might never come right again."

The door opened. Zander swung around, swearing, although he didn't take the weapon from Smithson. "Beth . . . !" He relaxed when he saw her smile.

"The cavalry to the rescue!" she said. "The Indians better scurry for cover."

Zander frowned. He looked toward the strange woman and met her smiling eyes. "Did that make sense?"

"Not to me, but I also am from different time. Suu-Van? Will you translate?"

"In the mid-twentieth century there existed a form of entertainment in which the American West's cavalry, at the last possible moment, was depicted as galloping to the rescue of settlers beset by Indians. It has become an expression, nothing more. In real history, it was the settlers, to say nothing of the army, who did the invading, of course."

"I see," said Li Jian. "But the bomb was not completed, so there is nothing to rescue."

"Yes there is," said Beth. "I can't solve the riddle of how Smithson built a cache into the TransPorter. He told me the theory and I thought he was giving me instructions for opening it when Zander warned me he was up to something. When I figured out what I was doing I very nearly"—she glanced at Zander and red flowed up her cheeks—"did something embarrassing!"

Suu-van chuckled while Zander and the woman from the far future looked at each other, again feeling left out and, therefore, drawn together.

"My Beth," said Suu-Van, "I have said you talk too much!"

"Want to know something, Suu-Van?" said Beth pertly, "I actually begin to believe you!"

"You've recovered from your shock, I think?" asked Li Jian when she ceased to chuckle.

When Beth agreed, the woman from the far future asked Beth to explain what she remembered of Smithson's lecture, since Smithson, who should have done it, simply stared at nothing at all and refused to speak.

"I see. I hadn't a notion that particular procedure was known before twenty-one-ninety-six." She tipped her head, eyed Smithson with a new light in her eye. "Well! They were right, then," she muttered. "He is one of them."

Suu-Van and Beth exchanged a look. Beth shrugged.

"If you will assist me, Miss Ralston," added the woman from the far future, "I believe I can retrieve your art without doing damage to the basic function of the TransPorter."

Even with her advanced knowledge, it took Li Jian the better part of an hour before she gently opened a door to a space which couldn't possibly exist—or so Zander insisted, not apologizing for the swear words which slipped one after another from his mouth.

"There is nothing actually impossible, Lord Hawksbeck," said Li Jian using Zander's courtesy title in the formal way she had. "It is merely a question of discovering how to do whatever the mind has conceived may be done. If one can ideate a thing, then that thing exists. There is also a theory that if something is ideated, it then comes into existence if it didn't already exist . . ." She glanced at Smithson but he appeared completely oblivious.

"Ideate?" asked Zander, attempting to follow the explanation.

"If you can dream it up," translated Beth, "it's possible to find a way of doing it, whatever it may be."

Zander nodded. "I see," he said. Not-so-innocently, he asked, "Then, the fact I imagine Beth and myself married makes it possible?" He looked around, smiling. "We merely have to discover how it may be accomplished?"

Everyone laughed but Smithson who, Beth thought, had fallen into some sort of trance.

Zander glanced from one to the other, his smile fading. "You've unmasked Smithson," he said, speaking quickly. "Beth's work is done. If I don't speak now, it's all too possible she'll disappear and be gone from me forever!"

Suu-Van put a hand on Zander's shoulder. "How quickly might you arrange for this hypothetical wedding between yourself and my Beth?"

"Even with a special license it would take two or three days. With Maman taking a hand, it might, with luck, happen inside of a month! Barely."

"And your mother is such a one she'll insist on stirring the pie?"

Zander looked at Beth, found her staring back. They chuckled. "She'll insist," said Zander on a dry note.

"A month. It is my suggestion that when you leave this not-so-hypothetical wedding, you stop at a convenient inn. Beth will at that time and place remember to contact me." Suu-Van chuckled at the sight of Beth's reddening cheeks, his large frame shaking. *Eventually,* she will remember! Your wedding night may well be the longest on record, since it will last something approaching two thousand one hundred and sixty hours!"

"Don't tease," scolded Beth. She took Zander's arm and looked up at him. "He means . . ."

". . . we'll spend the first three months of our marriage in the future where you'll renew that golden look." No one missed the satisfaction he felt at the notion. Then he frowned. "When I may watch over you, that is!"

Again Suu-Van's sides shook with that silent laughter. "I think, my Beth, that you have broken more than the rule saying one such as he not discover our existence, have you not? But that is by the way, since you knew we'd wish to adopt your Zander." He stared at his ward. "When you return to this era you will take the position of Anchor here, will you not?" He smiled when Beth nodded. "Happy, my Beth?"

"Very happy," she said and moved under Zander's arm, snuggling close.

"In that case, it is time my prisoner and I go up through time. Will you trust yourself to our primitive equipment, Li Jian?" Suu-Van asked politely.

"I'll come with you to your time, Suu-Van. Then we'll have a little discussion about just whom it is who has acquired this particular prisoner, will we not?"

Suu-Van chuckled. "Hmm. I think it more likely we'll have an *argument* on the subject!"

"Wait," said Zander, fearing they'd disappear on the instant. "What do we do with Smithson's crew?"

Suu-Van's brow arched. "It occurs to me belatedly to wonder why his crew has not come to their captain's rescue. But wherever they are, need anything be done with them? Can they not simply discover the captain missing?"

"We believe they're related to Smithson that he Trans-Ported them back so he'd have a crew he could trust," explained Beth. "As to where they are, Zander had a shore gang capture them and incarcerate them"—she looked up at Zander—"but I've no notion where."

"A nearby ship. They can be brought here if you wish."

Suu-Van sighed. "If they are from the future, they must be returned there."

"How will you know?" asked Li Jian.

"Hmm?"

"Smithson might have found his ancestors in this time and hired *them,* weaving some tale of magic or even"—with a moue of distaste, the woman from the far future glanced at the captain—"telling them the truth." She looked from one to another. "So. How will you know?"

Suu-Van growled. He had plans for Li Jian and himself and hated each and every delay. "Lord Hawksbeck? Please take me to the prisoners."

Zander passed the weapon to Beth although he didn't think she'd need it. Smithson *had* put himself deeply into a trance, perhaps self-induced catatonia, from which it might be difficult to rouse him. The men left and Li Jian asked if marriage and anchor duty were what Beth wanted.

"I was amazed when Suu-Van so casually released me from ETH-arm, but, yes, I'm glad."

Li Jian smiled. "Not too far into Suu-Van's future the records of past ETH-arm officers are analyzed. It is discovered, not that it was a surprise, that the longer one does that duty, the more likely one will fail."

"You mean die," said Beth, putting the fact bluntly, not softening the truth as Li Jian had done.

"Yes. It is decided ETH-arm officers will undertake only a set number of cases before they transfer to another unit which they choose themselves."

"And have I had that number of cases?"

"No. Assuming you lived under that rule you would have several more before you made such a choice. I merely tell you this, Miss Ralston, so that you need not feel too much guilt that you are transferred from ETH-arm."

Beth laughed. "But I feel no guilt! I'm far too happy I'm to wed my Zander. It is very bad of me and a terrible precedent we set because, even if this is officially my time, I am, to all intents and purposes, dead to it. I worry we may dislocate time and yet I cannot feel it is wrong when we feel so much love for each other."

"It was the merest tic of a clock in Time."

Beth gave the older woman a worried look. "Then we do jog it?"

"You are older than you would have been if the fire had not occurred. You've more poise and are more of a helpmate to your husband than the eighteen-year-old who, without the tic, would have wed him and, at that age, would have had much to learn. Your sophistication helps to move him up in his work, which is diplomatic in nature, more quickly than might have been the case."

Beth stared at the woman, her mouth open. Finally she closed it, opened it again, and again closed it, her mind spinning at the speed of light. Finally she asked, "Are you saying the *real* dislocation was the fire in which I'm thought to have died and not the fact my death didn't happen?"

Li Jian's brows arched on her high smooth brow. "Why yes, I thought that clear."

"No." Beth blinked. "Not at all! I've assumed my survival was the glitch."

"Glitch?" repeated Li Jian brightening. "Glitch . . . , glitch . . . ," she repeated several times as if memorizing it. "I like that. I'll research the word and return it to use in my time—a little hobby, you see. But to explain," she continued, "you would *not* have been saved if it were not meant. I must guess, then, that Suu-Van assumes he broke rules by which *he* is supposed to live. But that particular rule is broken often, is it not? And a reason is discovered for each such rescue, is it not?"

"I've a friend," said Beth slowly, "who discovered a particularly useful variation on some aspect of a theory I never understood. But she was saved from an era only a few decades from the one in which we were living."

Li Jian nodded. "I know the story. If that particular woman had not survived, that particular bit of theory would have gone undiscovered for a century or more, in which case a certain invention would not have been made and several very important decisions by WorldGov could not have been implemented. You see that that woman could not die? She must be saved? Even if the person who saved her didn't know he was serving Time's Will, it was so."

Beth's mind again grappled with thoughts far outside any she'd ever had. "Are you suggesting there is a source of power, an interest in our existence, which guides such things?"

"Who can know?"

"But such twitches in History are . . . No, not that . . ." Beth's eyes went out of focus as she thought through her confusion. "But . . ." Again she stopped, frowned, deciding such could not be the case.

Li Jian chuckled. "I think you'll find, as do we all, that thoughts concerning free will and predestination are difficult. Such problems are not solved even in my time, so do not feel badly *you* cannot find the answer. Ah . . ." she added, as the door opened. "What decision have *you* reached?" she asked Suu-Van.

"That from wherever in time they've come, they cannot be allowed to remain in this one," he said. "They know too much."

"So?"

"So they'll be brought here and we'll TransPort them. Once they are in the future we'll decide what to do with them. Beth, Zander says that if he doesn't get you home immediately, your absence will be discovered and difficulties result."

"What I told him is that the scandal would be so bad it might send us permanently into your future!"

She smiled. "I doubt it could be *that* bad."

His brows rose high over his wide eyes. "With you dressed in that particular fashion? *Worse!*"

"Then we'll go. Suu-Van, I'll send a message to you when we're ready for TransPort. It shouldn't be much more than a month."

"Ah! If only I could be at your wedding to give you away!" he said, a twinkle in his eye.

"And why could you not?" asked Beth.

Suu-Van blinked several times. A broad smile crossed his face. "I would like that. You will think how to explain why I did not come to your rescue when you needed me in Lisbon, but you are capable of such minor prevarication."

"You may be thought a peripatetic godfather with whom, because of your wandering habits, I'd lost contact," said Beth promptly. "I happened to find you again, here in London."

"Godfather. Yes. I will be your godfather." He beamed and Beth hugged him, getting a big bear hug in return. "I will see you at your wedding, Lord Hawksbeck. And now, good night."

Half an hour later Zander let them into the back garden of Fairmont house, "Satisfied, Beth?"

"Very. And you?"

"Yes. We'll talk tomorrow, because what I said about scandal will come true if you don't go in now."

Beth grinned, placed a quick kiss on his cheek, and, moments later disappeared from view. Zander scowled. That disappearing trick, he decided, was another of her little ways he'd learn once they were married!

Beth reached her window in record time, pushed it open, and stood in the opening ready to step down into the window seat. A hand grasped her ankle, held it. For half an instant Beth prepared to defend herself. Juno's voice, grating over her ears, stopped her just in time. "You've been gone all night. You've used my parents' home and misused our trust."

Beth sighed at Juno's bitter tone. Closing the cloak around her, she asked if she might step on into the room before she made explanations, although, at that instant, Beth hadn't a notion what those might be!

"I was so pleased when Zander brought you here," Juno said as she watched Beth step down, then on down to the floor. Backing away, she seated herself on the chaise. "Now I must tell Maman, you know."

"You once requested, that if I ever felt there were something I could not keep to myself, that I talk to Zander first. I said I would. Will you do the same for me?"

Juno hesitated. "Zander . . .?"

"He knows where I've been. He too was involved."

Again Juno hesitated. "I know Zander occasionally does, um, *things* for the War Office. I once overheard him talking with Father."

"Then"—Beth inwardly heaved a sigh of relief—"you know more than you should!"

"You, too?"

"Me, too," said Beth, thankful Juno had found a satisfying explanation all by herself.

"It isn't fair," complained Juno.

Beth blinked. "What isn't fair?"

"Why, that you may have adventures and I may not. Do you know how very bored I am with my life?"

"I thought you were engaged in a life and death struggle with Lord Belmont," said Beth, relaxing a bit more.

Juno pouted, the pout turning to a sigh. "Tony is a fool."

"What has he done now?" Beth clutched the cloak, wrapping it around herself, before sitting down in the window seat.

Juno gave her a spirited review of her evening and Beth managed to refrain from yawning until Juno, dreamy now, came to the dance she and Tony had shared.

"His steps and mine match so perfectly, Beth. You cannot know how wonderful it is to dance like that."

Then Beth yawned. "Perhaps one day I'll discover the wonder of it, but right now, Juno, all I want is to sleep"—she yawned again—"until noon!"

Juno headed toward the connecting door. Her hand on the handle, she paused. "I apologize for the things I said and will let you sleep now. But first"—her teeth flashed white in the dawning morning light—"you'd better get out of those awful leggings and hide them before a maid comes to light your fire! I wonder how you dare!" she finished. The closing door cut off the warming sound of her delightful laugh.

Beth looked down her length and discovered that, as she'd thought, she was covered from neck to toe. She glanced at the window, remembered how Juno had grasped her ankle, how she'd had to step down into the window seat and from there to the floor. She sighed, recalled Juno's advice she change, and, as tired as she'd ever been in her life, she nevertheless got up and prepared herself for bed.

And then she *did* sleep until noon.

Twenty-one

Anthony Richmond, Lord Belmont, tugged at his cravat, stared at the door to the Fairmont town house, started toward it for the second time and then, shaking his head, turned to walk away.

"Cold feet, Tony?" asked Zander, who returned just then from an early morning ride.

Tony grimaced. "I can't do it."

"Do what?"

Anthony's chin set in a stubborn line.

"Come, Tony, out with it. We're old friends, are we not?"

"I'm too old for her."

Zander controlled an urge toward laughter. "Tell you what, Tony. I must change and have breakfast. We'll have it in my sitting room, just the two of us. You can spout all the nonsense you like and I'll not demand you explain a word of it. After all, what are friends for?" He led the way up the steps to the open front door.

Muttering, Tony followed and seated himself in Zander's sitting room, a huge breakfast spread between them. Zander, who'd had no sleep the night before, poured himself a second cup of coffee and asked, "Too old for whom?"

"Thought you weren't going to ask questions."

"I lied."

Tony grinned, but the smile faded. "You know."

"Juno?"

"But I think she needs me, Zander. Or"—Anthony

flushed—"someone like me. Someone a bit mature to temper her high spirits but not hold the reins so tightly she loses all spirit. And *not* some idiot who would use whip and spurs to control her, nor the other sort who would encourage her fits and starts with a tallyho and away we go! I've evaluated the men she seems to like and I'm worried. Zander, you've not been around much lately, so you might not know, but she's involved with Forthright." Tony looked up to find Zander shoveling buttered eggs into his mouth. "Zander," said Tony, his voice touched with acid, "if you are uninterested in the information your sister is headed for trouble, forgive me and I'll leave."

"I'm interested. Sir Terrence, you say. Thought he was enamored of the gay widow, although one doesn't see him chasing her the way most do."

"Try and tell your sister that." Tony looked confused. "But, then, she watches him dance with the widow without a qualm. I don't understand her."

"What does she say?"

"She *says* they are friends." Tony grimaced.

"If that's what Queeny says, then that's it."

"Don't trust him," muttered Tony. "I know for a fact he's proposed to the widow. He must be playing with our Juno, Zander I'm worried to death about the situation."

Zander hid a grin. "So?"

"So *what?*"

"So what do you think to do about it? Especially," he added, "at this hour of the morning!"

"I've been thinking ever since I left the ball last night. Zander, she's the only woman I've ever danced with whose steps truly match mine! I don't have to mince along or . . . or . . . I don't know."

"Very important that your steps match," said Zander with a completely sober expression, but, inside, bubbling chuckles wanted out. Tony gave him a glare, then once more stirred the mess on his plate. Zander added, "You may be confused about what *you* want but I'm totally certain. You might congratulate me."

Tony lay his fork aside. "Congratulate you?"

"I've asked Beth to marry me. She's said yes."

Tony stared. "Mademoiselle Thevenard?"

"Is it so surprising?" asked Zander, uncertain whether he was irritated or chagrined. Or perhaps he'd give into the laughter which surged toward the surface with only the slightest of provocation now he'd been assured Beth would wed him.

"I don't know about surprising . . ." said Tony slowly. "I just didn't know you'd ever given headroom to the notion of marriage."

"I didn't until the notion took up heart-room!" admitted Zander and grinned what he suspected was a decidedly inane looking grin.

Tony's eyes widened. His hand went to his breast, touched his lapel, his cravat, dropped. "Heart room," he repeated softly. He looked up. "Zander, how did it happen?"

"How did what happen, Tony?"

"I've fallen in love with the silly chit!" exclaimed his friend, the oddest combination of horror and elation mixed in voice and expression.

Zander's brows rose. Reluctantly he again decided he didn't dare laugh. Tony wouldn't appreciate his reasons! "You love Juno?" he asked.

"Crazy, isn't it?" Tony slumped back in his chair, his elbow on the arm, and his hand supporting his chin. "Ridiculous, actually. I must be an ancient in her eyes. She used me to set her feet on the right path—you know, introducing her to our friends when you weren't in town to do so. So obviously she thinks of me as just another brother. It's hopeless, Zander."

"She's always admired you excessively," said Zander cautiously.

Frowning, Tony waved that away. "I don't want admiration."

How much dared he say, wondered Zander. It wasn't fair, surely, to reveal his sister's feelings; that was for her to do. Still, he'd better give Tony a nudge so he didn't run like a wounded hare! "I can't speak for my sister's heart, but I've seen her watch for your arrival and relax only when you come. She doesn't watch anything like so anxiously for me, a *brother*."

All he got for his pains was a deeper scowl.

"Talk to Beth," he suggested. "Maybe she'd have advice for you."

Tony brightened momentarily. Then he slumped again. "Advice! Very likely that I take myself off and let Juno get on with finding a proper husband without my forever interfering when she takes up with some here-and-therian or a fortune hunter or some rogue she should never have met!"

"Rogue?"

"Sir Terrence."

Again Zander fought chuckles; Tony was so jealous he'd never admit Sir Terrence was a reasonably decent human being.

Once again Tony waved his free hand. "I keep going in circles, I tell you. I want only the best for her. I want her to be happy. I don't want to tie her up to someone nearly old enough to be her *father*. That *would* be the act of a gentleman, would it not?" he finished sarcastically.

Zander muttered, counting on his fingers. "Old enough to be her father assuming you'd been truly precocious! Blast it, I can think of no one I'd rather have for a brother. Haven't you the guts to at least put it to the touch? You've no notion what she thinks. Only what you *think* she thinks!"

Tony ignored Zander. "Maybe I will talk to Mademoiselle Thevenard."

"But not this morning. She's sleeping in. Come back about one and we'll go for a drive. I must take a look at a rethatching job. They made a bad hand of it the first time and I want to see it was done correctly this time! Since it's an exceptionally mild day, Cook can pack a basket for a winter picnic; maybe we'll do a bit of fishing."

"Fishing? You suggest we go *fishing* when I'm worried sick abo—"

Zander held up a hand, stopping his friend in mid-word. "Think about it. At least if she's fishing, she isn't making up to Sir Terrence, is she?"

"We'll go fishing. One? Then I've time to finish some business with my cousin. I've decided Richard will do very well in the West Indies and the sooner I get him on a ship the better for all of us. See you later."

Not long after Juno wailed, "Fishing? You suggested we go *fishing?*"

"Why not? If he's fishing you'll know where he is, will you not?"

"But, Zander, there's nothing romantic about *fishing*. I don't want Tony reminded of when I was a little girl and insisted he teach me to fish!"

"Tony likes to fish. Reminding him that you do too would be no very bad thing. He might not know it. That you still fish, I mean."

"Well . . ."

"Or you can sit demurely on the blanket with a book until we're ready to eat and then be very ladylike and set out our pick-nick!"

Juno grimaced. "That doesn't sound much like me, does it?"

"No it doesn't. Don't pretend to be so very grown up, Juno, that you can no longer enjoy the simple pleasures."

She sighed. "Should I wake Beth?"

Zander looked at the clock on the mantel. "Wait until noon. Order her a light lunch on a tray and then wake her. She's not like you, Juno," he said with a grin. "It doesn't take her hours to get ready!"

"That reminds me, brother-mine." Juno's eyes narrowed and she checked they were alone before whispering, "The next time you go off on an adventure, as you did last night, I demand you take me, too. It's not fair Beth may have adventures and I may not!"

Zander's brow's snapped together. "How did you . . . !" he roared. Color reddening his ears, he listened. Then, "How do you know?" he asked quietly

"When Maman and I got home last night I went to her room to discuss the ball and found her gone. I waited forever and she actually"—Juno's eyes rounded like an owl's—"came in through her window!"

"I'm amazed you didn't rouse the house when you found she was gone."

"I like Beth. I wanted to warn her I'd tell Maman, but she reminded me I asked her to tattle to you if she ever felt it necessary to tell tales and she asked, please, would I do the same. I know I shouldn't know it, Zander," Juno added earnestly, "but I once heard you talking to Father about work you do for the government. I guessed she'd been helping." Juno sighed. "I won't tell anyone. Not even Tony. *But it isn't fair!*" she finished and stalked off.

Zander shook his head. Life could certainly get complicated, he decided, and hoped that Juno, at least, would never discover the real truth of Beth's odd existence. It was bad enough his mother knew!

The sun slanted from rather low in the sky when the four fishermen reassembled at the abandoned basket and blanket. "Did you catch anything, Beth?" asked Juno. She watched with possessive gaze as Tony set their string in the water and tied the stringer to a convenient root.

"I mostly, er, watched Zander," admitted Beth, not quite truthfully. Fishing hadn't been first in either mind. "Did you two talk?"

Juno sighed. "We came very near to having a right good argument, but I did as you advised and suggested that, for today, we just enjoy the unseasonable weather and the freedom from city manners and relax. Tony agreed," she finished, something of surprise in her tone.

"And did you?"

"Did we what?" asked Juno, staring hungrily at Tony who talked to Zander.

"Did you," asked Beth patiently, "relax and enjoy?"

"Yes. At least I did. He wasn't picking at me or lecturing me or trying to make me see sense about this, that, or the other. It was like old times." Juno sighed. "On the other hand, I doubt I made one bit of headway."

"Headway?"

"Sailing into the wind, I think. A navy friend taught it to me. Beth, what am I to *do?"*

"Do about what? Sir Terrence?" asked Tony belligerently from just behind them.

Beth wondered how he'd gotten there without Juno's realizing he'd approached. Juno twined her fingers together and looked at Beth with desperation in her eyes, before running away along the river path. Beth glanced up to find Tony staring after Juno with a similar look in his own.

"She's running from *you,* you know," said Beth. "She's tired of your misunderstanding everything. One more lecture and she'll be crying."

"But I only talk to her because I lo . . . er . . . like her so much."

"Say what you mean, Lord Belmont," suggested Beth.

"All right. I love her," he responded with a trace of the belligerence that often goes with newly acknowledged affection.

"Why don't you tell *her,* rather than *me?"*

"And make a complete fool of myself?"

"The fool is the man who can't or won't see beyond his nose."

Tony was silent for a long moment. "Mademoiselle—"

"Call me Beth. Zander said you know he and I are to wed and I cannot be formal with the man who is Zander's closest friend."

"Beth, do you . . . are you saying . . . could it be . . ."

Her eyes rolled as she pretended exasperation. "Now I wonder *why* you are Zander's closest friend."

Tony glanced toward where Juno had disappeared beyond a plantation of young oaks which had not lost their coppery colored leaves.

"Go find her," said Beth softly. "Find her and be honest with her."

Tony hesitated only a moment, then he, too, moved off down river.

"Did I do the right thing?" asked Beth without looking up to see if Zander had approached the blanket. She knew he had.

"What did you tell him?"

"To stop lecturing her and to be honest with her."

"If he isn't a complete idiot, perhaps all will be well." Zander settled himself near Beth, lay back, his hands clasped behind his neck. "Of course there's a strong likelihood he's a complete idiot." He grinned at her. "Love can do that to a man, you know."

"And to women. I'm glad we decided to talk out our problems before they festered and wormed their way deeply into our emotions."

"That would be a good rule for when we're wed, too, Beth."

"Agreed." She laid her head into his shoulder. He put an arm around her. Before long both were soundly asleep.

Half an hour later Juno and Tony reappeared hand in hand. Juno glowed. Tony wore the half-stunned, bemused look, of a newly engaged man, but he, too, had a special warmth of expression every time he glanced at his Juno. Which was often. They neared the blanket so involved with each other they were on it before they noticed the sleepers, who had turned and were spooned together.

"Good Heavens," whispered Juno. She cast a speculative eye toward Tony and red spread up her throat and into her cheeks.

"I thought Zander looked tired, but this is outside enough!" Tony nudged his friend's foot, nudged it again when he got no response.

Zander opened one bleary eye. The other popped opened and he looked from his sister to Beth. Very gently he extracted his body and arms from around his love. Very quietly he rolled away and stood up. He reached for Juno's arm and walked her away from the blanket. "You didn't see that." Juno cocked her head. "Besides, last night Beth agreed to marry me."

"I should think *so,* if that's the way you go on!"

"Juno!"

She grinned. "I was wondering, actually, how it would be to sleep with Tony that way."

"Juno!"

His increased volume caught Tony's attention as well as disturbing Beth's rest. She rolled over and yawned.

"Juno Knightly, if you ever say such a thing again I'll turn you over my knee and give you the paddling I obviously should have given you long ago!"

"Tony! Protect me!" called Juno, laughing.

"From Zander?" Tony strolled closer, his equilibrium rapidly returning now he'd proposed and, unbelievably, been accepted. "But who will protect *me* from him?" Juno giggled and Tony chuckled. "Should we tell them?" asked Tony, smiling down at her, "or wait until your father makes it official?"

"I believe you *have* told them," said Juno. She lifted her arms and whirled in a circle. "Isn't the world marvelous?"

Tony caught her wrist just in time to save her from a tumble into the river. "You wouldn't think it half so wonderful if forced to ride home sopping wet. And if you aren't hungry, then you should be. Woman! Feed me."

"Hmm. That's going to be the way of it, is it?" asked Juno, her hands on her hips and her eyes narrowing.

"It *should* be, but I doubt it will be," grinned Tony, holding out his hand. "Come, minx. Let's both of us feed your brother and *his* betrothed."

"Oh! Unfair. You knew before I did!"

"Zander told me this morning when he and I breakfasted together."

Tony and Beth watched Zander lift Beth to her feet, hold her steady for a moment. She dropped her forehead to his shoulder, then stepped forward and snuggled into him. Zander's arms drew her close. It was obvious to those watching those arms were protective and warm and loving.

"I'm so happy for them," said Juno softly.

"I'm still too happy you've accepted my suit to have room to feel anything for them," said Tony equally softly.

"I'd have accepted the moment I arrived in town if you'd only had the sense to ask me," teased Juno. "Haven't you guessed yet that I came up to London for no other reason than to trap you into a proposal?"

Tony's eyes narrowed. "What about your flirtation with Sir Terrence!"

Juno stamped her foot. "I have told you and told you. Sir Terrence and I are *friends*. That means, in case you still do not understand, that we like each other but we do not love each other." She spoke carefully and clearly as if to a child, her chin jutted forward.

Tony glowered. "I don't approve the friendship."

Juno's mouth compressed. "Tony . . ."

"Juno, don't fly up in the boughs! I don't approve and I won't approve, because I cannot believe he doesn't have designs on you. How could any man," he added, quickly when she pursed her lips angrily, "not have designs on you? *I have.*"

Juno's temper subsided. "Believe it, Tony. He has designs on no one but his widow. You see, Tony, we talked, one to the other, about the ones we loved when we could talk freely to no one else."

"The widow is not a woman I wish you to have for a friend, Juno," said Tony quietly.

"Sir Terrence says he hopes that, when she comes to her senses, perhaps I'll come to know and like her. And befriend her. But he too says I'm to have nothing to do with her until that day arrives."

"She may never—"

"Don't say it, Tony. Sir Terrence loves her and is very unhappy."

"We'll hope all will be well for them, then," he said, hoping his Juno would get no more involved then she already was. He turned her back toward the blanket. Beth had unpacked the basket and the four fell on the food as if they'd not eaten in weeks.

"What is it about eating outside?" asked Juno. "I always find food much more appealing at a pick-nick."

No one bothered to respond. When they finished all were sad the day must end. Tony, in particular, didn't look forward to the ordeal of asking Lord Fairmont for Juno's hand—not that he had any reason to believe he'd be refused.

Lord Fairmont had dealt with love-struck young men when his older daughters became engaged. He led Tony through the ordeal with an experienced and gentle hand. Lady Fairmont was another problem entirely. Later that evening when told both her offspring had become betrothed in the last twenty-four hours, she stared, horror struck. She turned the look toward Beth and then on Lord Belmont. "No."

"Maman!" said two voices, one masculine and one feminine.

"No! It will not do. I cannot manage both a wedding and a betrothal at one and the same time. No."

"But what is there to do?" asked Juno, bewildered. "My father has permitted Tony to speak to me and Beth is old enough she doesn't need anyone's permission. How can you say no?"

"You, Juno," said her mother in an uncompromising manner, "will simply have to *wait.*"

"What?" Juno reached for Tony's hand, clutched it. "Wait?"

Lady Fairmont nodded. "Until after I've arranged your brother's ball and wedding. Then we'll see to *your* betrothal ball and make that announcement and *then* plan your wedding. I'm very sorry you must be patient, but your brother insists he and Beth wed on the instant." She scowled. "But whatever he says about immediate weddings, there is no way on earth we can prepare it in less than six weeks. Two months would be far better. A January wedding, perhaps . . ." Lady Fairmont ignored four glowering faces. "Yes, a January wedding for Zander and we'll arrange your betrothal and wedding during next spring's Season, Juno."

"I won't fight Juno's battles, Mother," said Zander, "but I'll not dawdle along until January for all the nonsense women find necessary. Either you arrange a wedding in the chapel at the Aerie on Tuesday, the fourteenth of December, or Beth and I will be married by special license still sooner and go on our marriage trip *without* your blessing."

"The fourteenth of December! But Zander that is less than a month. It is not possible to collect bride clothes and arrange the details for a proper house party by then."

"Beth may acquire all she needs in the way of a wardrobe *after* the wedding. As to a house party, I don't know about Beth, but I'd prefer a very small wedding with only the closest of friends and relatives attending."

"Nonsense. Such an occasion is very useful for cementing political—"

"Mother!"

Lady Fairmont had the grace to blush slightly. "You know it's true. Your father will wish—"

"This is *my* wedding, Mother."

"That's the third time you've said Mother . . . You'll not be moved?"

"I will not."

"Beth?" asked Lady Fairmont, a pleading note not quite hidden.

"I'm very sorry to be disagreeable, Lady Fairmont, but I support Zander's wishes in this. Our wedding is important to *us* and we're not the least interested in putting on a show or using the occasion for political purposes!" A note of distaste for the idea wasn't well concealed.

"But it is such a *waste!*" said Lady Fairmont. She glanced at her son's adamant face. "Oh all right, but, even so, I don't see how it can be arranged by the fourteenth."

"If you recall, we wish a *simple* wedding." Zander, now he'd won his point, relaxed. He chuckled. "Now I come to think of it, Maman, perhaps that's beyond you—something *simple,* I mean. You've never done anything simple, so very likely, you don't know *how.* I fear," he added, tongue in cheek, "you don't understand the meaning of the word!"

Even Lady Fairmont laughed.

Twenty-two

Beth, snuggled against Zander's shoulder, then moaned as the carriage hit another bump. "The one thing, my much beloved husband, which I'll never get used to in this era is the primitive means of travel I must endure for your sake."

"I'll have you know . . ." began Zander a trifle huffily.

". . . that this is a very well sprung carriage. You wait until you've experienced a really well sprung, hmm, *equipage, then* you'll agree."

"Which is something I'll do very soon now." His satisfaction was obvious. He glanced at the top of Beth's head. His bride, he thought. There was satisfaction in that, too. "Not," he added, suggestively, since they'd been married only four hours and twenty minutes, *"instantly,* of course."

Beth chuckled. "No. Definitely not instantly. How much further to this inn of yours?"

Zander cleared his throat. "Hmm . . ."

"Yes?"

"Not exactly an inn," he mumbled.

"Not?"

"Hunting lodge . . ."

Beth squirmed closer, something neither of them would have thought possible. "Even better," she muttered, nuzzling the tender area just below his ear.

One brow arched. "I feared you'd chide me for not following orders."

"There'll be no strangers around . . . I assume?" She pulled away to look at him.

"Servants part of the day, but we'll mostly be alone." More satisfaction. He couldn't hide it and didn't try. His eyes, heavy looking, narrowed as he stared at Beth. *My wife!* he thought. He kissed her, rearranged her so she lay across his lap and kissed her again. Deeply.

Some time later he lay his head back, took a deep breath, looked at her bemused expression, and, when she'd have pulled him back to her, shook his head. "Behave yourself, wife, or we'll embarrass our driver." Reluctantly Zander settled Beth to the side and leaned into his corner. "Talk to me."

"Or else?" she asked, her tongue firmly in her cheek.

Zander grinned. "Or you know what else!" He played with her fingers. "It was a nice wedding, I thought. Well, it was when one ignored Maman's complaints!"

"I ignored them quite easily, so it was a *lovely* wedding . . . Perhaps Suu-Van looked a trifle droll in your style of formal wear, but beyond that, it was perfect."

"Droll, you say?" Zander chuckled. "Your Suu-Van is very nearly as fat as Prinny, is he not?"

"We do not call him fat," scolded Beth. "Merely well upholstered."

Grinning, Zander lifted her hand. He noticed that she tried hard not to a wince at another bump and kissed the palm, closing her fingers over the kiss. "We'll be there soon," he said, a promise in his voice.

Beth cast her mind around for another topic. "Your Merrit seemed most unhappy to be left behind."

"So did your maid. And he was. He claims it took weeks to get me back in proper shape from when I went to Portugal without him, that my clothes were ruined and my hair still isn't shaped properly. He keeps snipping at it," added Zander, aggrieved.

"Very soon now you'll have no use for contemporary

clothing so it'll stay in much the same condition as when he packed it."

"You forget we'll have a marriage trip to complete once we return, but, then, we won't have a great deal of use for clothing here, either! Will we?" Zander smiled broadly when Beth blushed. "Beth, my Beth, how much I love you!"

"I love you, too," she said softly.

"You aren't upset I don't know all those things you've learned? That I'll very likely never know so much as you do?"

"Don't sound so anxious. We'll live *now,* will we not? Then future knowledge will not only be by the way, it'll be dysfunctional."

"Disfunc . . . ?"

"You see? A word I shouldn't use. My excess knowledge slips out and causes problems. It's dysfunctional." When he still frowned, she added, "Zander, I've just proved it, have I not? By saying something I shouldn't? You'll not have that problem."

"But *you'll* know I'm uneducated in your sense, and, by comparison, I'm rather primitive!"

"I didn't fall in love with any of those over-educated sophisticates with whom I studied. Well? Did I?"

"You didn't, did you." Zander eyed her, sighed softly. "I can't help being jealous, I suppose. Of all they know and don't even know they know"—his brows rose and, for an instant, his dimple appeared—"if you know what I mean?"

"Oh, I *know!*" They laughed softly at the silly joke. "Zander," she added, "is it much farther?"

He squeezed her hands. "Maybe five miles. Tired?"

"Yes. Also impatient to be alone with you. With no chaperone!"

"Hussy!" he teased.

"Do you mind?"

"I once told you, in what seems the distant past, that we'd make a by-word of ourselves, that we'd not pretend our emotions were unengaged, that we'd sit in each other's pockets and . . ."

She stopped his flow of words with a kiss which he took to himself and gave back fourfold. Later, when the carriage rocked to a stop, Zander lifted his head, looked around, blinked, and looked back to where Beth, once again, lay across his lap.

"You, my love," he said, "had better do something about that disarray before the coachman opens the . . . Opps!" He grinned. "Too late. You may go, Jonesy," he added to the red-faced man staring, pop-eyed, at his master's new wife who, by any standard, was *not* dressed for company. Of course, neither was the master! "We'll have no need of you until the end of the month. Once you've unloaded you may return to the Aerie where you'll make yourself useful."

"Yes sir," said the coachman, the red deepening. ". . . er, right away, sir," he added averting his eyes. Leaving the door open, he turned away.

Beth hid her equally red complexion against her husband's bare chest. "That, my lord Hawksbeck, must be the most embarrassing moment of my life."

"Good."

"Good?" Beth pushed away and glared at Zander.

"Good. Now, although I hadn't planned it, I think we're even."

"Even?"

"You've been paid, my love, for laying me on my back that time with your totally unfair fighting practices!"

"I," she said, putting herself somewhat to rights, "would say we're more than even. *Your* expertise with ties and hooks suggests there are *far better ways* to place another on her back, think you not?" When Zander didn't answer she looked at him and partially swallowed her laughter. "Zander?" she asked, using every bit of useful innocence her expressive face allowed. "Why are your ears so red?"

"You . . . !" He controlled his embarrassment. "We're

even, did I say? Definitely not. But you wait. When I do have you on your back . . . !" Zander nodded, satisfied. Beth was, he thought, at least as red as he himself must be.

Suddenly he leapt from the carriage and reached for his bride. He carried her in the front door of his lodge. Ignoring two bemused servants, who quickly curtsied as he passed them, he went up the stairs and into his bedroom. Kicking the door shut he spun around in circles, Beth in his arms, then took the next few necessary steps.

Lifting Beth, Zander dropped her on his bed. "And *now,* madam wife . . . !" he began, as he stripped off his shirt.

"Oh, yes," interrupted Beth breathlessly. She reached for him. "Now!"

Dear Reader,

I enjoyed writing A TIMELESS LOVE. Zander and Beth have friends scheduled to TransPort back to ancient Troy in order to return jewels stolen during the Trojan wars. They must hide the treasure trove where Schliemann finds it in 1873. Someday, maybe, I'll find time to write *their* story!

In April 1997 Zebra's *A MOTHER'S LOVE* will include *Darling Daughters* which is my tale of a bereft father who has no notion what to do with his sad-eyed little girls. The neighbor's niece knows however, and makes them smile. That's what she's doing when he first sees her. A bit of a difficulty arises when our heroine's aunt convinces her the gentleman is interested in her only for the sake of his daughters, but the couple weds anyway. For the daughters' sakes? Well . . . not entirely!

My next book, A LADY'S LESSON, appears in September. Two new Winchester students discover each has lost a parent. The one has an over-protective mother, the other a father so busy in London he rarely sees his son. The boys conclude each will be happier with the other's parent! With a great deal of ingenuity (to say nothing of luck) they contrive to exchange homes. Lord Blackthorn is not happy he's forced to leave London to put things right. That is, he's exceedingly annoyed until he meets Frederica. From then on he spends more of his valuable time arranging to court her then he does on politics. Finding free time isn't easy however, but the boys take a hand to help things along. Their plan goes awry, but even that helps get their parents together.

I love to hear from my readers and I respond if you include a self addressed stamped envelope.

Cheerfully,

Jeanne

Jeanne Savery
P.O.Box 1771, Rochester MI 48308